LET THEM WHIMPER

LET THEM WHIMPER

A FULLY JUSTIFIED (IN NO WAY PERSONAL)
ARGUMENT FOR THE ABANDONMENT OF
HUMANKIND

A NOVEL

K. ENTERANTE

Published by Oblivion Press
San Diego, CA

First Edition

Paperback: 979-8-9877338-0-6
Ebook: 979-8-9877338-1-3
Audiobook: 979-8-9877338-2-0

Edited by Intrepid Literary
Cover design by The Book Designers

For Sofia, my heart, who had a hunch.
For my father, who inspired me to write.
For my stepfather, who challenged me to improve.
For my mother, whose courage lets me be me.
To my father and stepfather: I miss and love you both.

TABLE OF CONTENTS

PART I
Cockadoodledoom   1

Interlude I: America Renewed   133

PART II
Eden's End   143

Interlude II: Headlines and Headers or Storms of
the Century   265

PART III
The Fateful Five   275

Interlude III: The Present   435

PART IV
Let Them Whimper   437

Acknowledgments   447
About the Author   449

PART I

COCKADOODLEDOOM

(SEPTEMBER–OCTOBER, TEN "YEARS" BEFORE NOW)

1

THE COMING OF THE BLACK
(COCKADOODLEDOOM)

———

HERE COMES MY DEATH, and fast—but we'll come to that later, at the end, which is now.

———

(I)T WAS COMING, and fast—too fast for local and national and international forecasters alike to pinpoint precisely what it was, much less reach a consensus.

Frazzled meteorologists and weather experts worldwide spent no less than three weeks disputing the freaky splat on the Doppler as it barreled across the Pacific toward the northern California coast. Despite the cryptic absences of red-green couplets and a telltale "hook," the great majority sniffed and waggled their fingers and pegged the raging patterns twitching on-screen for a tornado. Twisters themselves were not terribly uncommon—California had seen hundreds of little guys in the past decade alone—but this one, coloring much of the radar's screen a midnight shade of purple, moved with an exotic, skittish sort of life, and it was big.

One Point Reyes cult of aggrieved farmers kept tabs on the looming arrival of what they judiciously dubbed "Cockadoodledoom" and took to the woods, where for five days and five nights they lit apocalyptic pyres in the dusky dark. On the fifth night, the long night when the towering, twitchy miasma blew in, howling and screeching its way inland, cult members were gathered around the flames, fiscally forsworn farmers singing over the cries of roasting livestock and/or pets, dancing naked under stars they could not see. The forest owls had gone. Every last town up there, Berkshire included, had evacuated almost in full, while those who lingered beheld the beginning of the end of the world up close.

It was nearly five minutes past midnight on a stillborn Sunday in late September when the swirling, titanic anomaly swept through Berkshire. No homes were destroyed; no lives were lost; no harm was done on any level in any conceivable way, though if he ever got the chance, Calvin Taphor might try to tell You otherwise.

It would depend on Your kindness.

———

SEE what I see and be curious. See two young men in a fifth-wheel RV parked on the wooded outskirts of Saw-whet National Park, camped in the hills overlooking the small town of Berkshire below. See these two for who they were: twin brothers, twenty-one years young, the first twin sleeping soundly in his sleeping bag in back of the RV, the second hunched over the first, flushed and sweaty and salivating. The sleeping twin snuggles his favorite toy in the world, a trash lid painted over with Captain America's stars and stripes; the crouching twin grips a meat cleaver—the one he talks to. As one brother snores, the other struggles to act on the hissing whispers he's always catching from the blade, like scissors in his ear.

Be sure to log their names, Calvin and Trent Taphor, the former with Down syndrome, the latter . . . well, You'll see. Soon enough, You'll see what Trent has done—what he's *chosen.*

In time, You'll come to see these twins for who they've become: the harbingers of my doom and Yours. I'd ask You to ask me how we got here, but if You don't mind, I'd rather just show You. I've got maybe five seconds to do this tale justice—to warn You of their humanity.

Give me these five measly seconds; I promise You'll leave here satisfied.

———

By that point—at tale's end—we can talk more about who I am, and why You should take what I say into careful consideration. For now, all You have to do is listen.

———

Trent Taphor, gripping in his calloused, cat-bitten hand the handle of his late mother's trusty, coruscant Dexter Russell—a fine, visually imposing make of cutlery, if he said so himself—brought down his arm with everything he had. Dex did the job like always, the keen edge of the blade connecting with meat, slicing wetly through. Blood slashed the glass of the tiny back window, blending with the black. The rat stalking the ledge above Calvin's head died without its own head to squeak with.

Trent watched Calvin lurch upright, wailing, bonking his head on the protruding corner of the overhanging ledge before wailing some more. Trent pocketed the rat's head for later, made little shush noises to calm his brother, who always tended to see more than he'd ever let on. This grim fact was one Trent had wrestled with ever since Anne Kell spoke up for the first time, in the closet at Crest High, with the stink beetle he'd discovered playing dead behind the door.

"Can it, bud. You'll have the neighbors lighting torches."

Their dad used to joke the same whenever Trent and Calvin got up to a fuss upstairs at their old house in suburban southern California. Calvin kept wailing.

A ferric stench filled the constricted space at the back of the trailer. Trent eyed the gooey blade still in hand and, better late than never, hid Dex behind his back. Calvin's wailing ceased, the transition to hushed resignation light-switch quick. Trent pretended to pick his butt, blindly wiping off the flat of the blade.

"Rat at the window," said Trent. "Just scared it off."

"My head!"

"Does it hurt?"

"It's big!"

"Don't rub it if it hurts."

"Everywhere!" Calvin cried out. "It hurts everything everywhere!"

"Lemme go snag some ice."

Trent went and came back with an ice pack wrapped in a paper towel, having slid Dex between a crusty, congealed stack of plates in the kitchenette's sink.

Calvin held the pack to his forehead, the puffy folds of the wrap obscuring his eyes. Trent took advantage of his twin's temporary sightlessness, reaching up and snatching the fat dead rat by its vermiform tail. He flung it over his shoulder with one swift heave, but, having released his grip on the tail a tad early, the headless vermin sailed high and nailed the ceiling fan in the center of the trailer. It dropped somewhere in the vicinity of the dish-cluttered kitchenette, where it hit the wood floor with a meaty slap Trent hoped only he could hear. He realized he'd been talking throughout, trying to mask the chucking with chatter, and that he'd had his face pressed right up to Calvin's, their foreheads sharing the ice.

Trent received from his sniveling twin a two-handed shove to his chest, sending him way back on his heels and making him backpedal for balance as something sharp bit into the bulge of his Achilles, then it was ass over teakettle, their dad would've said. The ankle-biting culprit turned out to be the sharpened steel edge of a trash lid hammered and repainted to resemble Captain America's weaponized shield—Calvin's "all-time toy" as of October last year.

Trent sat stunned and silent in a sea of Calvin's toys, the dredged-up dross of Saw-whet National Park—Trent's place of work and worship. Supplementing the reimagined, reconstructed shield were dusty, barely-played-with-anymore restorations: Thor's hammer (toilet plunger wrapped in duct tape and tinfoil), Wolverine's claws (sawed-off tent poles), Iron Man's rocket-blaster (heavy duty rubber glove), Green Arrow's bow (aptly shaped log with an industrial fishing line), Batman's utility belt (a plumber's yellow-painted tool belt), etc.

Trent brought his knee to his chin and massaged the area near the split in his heel and then looked up to see Calvin, evidently ripe with rage, worming himself free of the sleeping bag. Calvin grunted and snorted in the back window's filmy pool of moonglow; his shadow on the trailer's curved back wall presented the perverse image of some big bug being born. They each got to their feet around the same time.

"What've you got to say for yourself?"

"Hafta peeeee," said Calvin, clutching himself down there.

"You don't shove. It's rude to shove."

Calvin yowled, a sudden outburst that banged the eardrums, pummeled the brain.

"Say you're sorry and you can go," said Trent.

Calvin spoke in a low muttered tone.

"Can't hear you."

"SORRY!"

"Not good enough," Trent said. "I can tell you're not really sorry."

"I'M SORRY FOR THE *RAT!*"

Trent sucked in some air. "What'd you say?"

"I—AM—SORRY—FOR . . . THAT."

"For *what*, Cal? Tell me right now."

Calvin pantomimed the answer Trent sought after, his grimace contorting the already loopy, lopsided features of his face into something extra ghoulish.

"I'm taking away your shield."

Trent turned and marched, lugging the trash lid, high stepping over toys and toolboxes, kicking aside empty beer bottles and soda cans on his way to the kitchenette. Calvin's response put the helpless shrieks of abused housewives to shame. Eavesdropping campers, had there been any in the area, would've been compelled to dial the park rangers, which would've set Trent's site-issued smartwatch to beeping, hardly a contender with his brother's screams.

Trent dropped the lid to cover the corpse of the headless rat.

"GO AWAY!" Calvin shouted. "DON'T LEAVE ME!"

"I'm not going anywhere."

"DON'T THINK I CAN'T HEAR YOU, YOU! PACKING UP!"

"I'm right here."

"DON'T SHOOT! NOOOOOO! DON'T GO DOWN THE CHUTE!"

"Shoot?"

"I'M NO CHICKEN! HIS VOICE IS FULLA BEES!"

Trent hit the lights and yelled his brother's name.

"COCKADOODLEDOOOOO—MUH!"

Trent blinked against the wash of light and squinted at Calvin, now standing directly over the shield five steps away, clenching the sides of a framed photograph—*the* framed photograph—so tightly his big hairless hands shook. Calvin's knuckles were white and bulbous, his stance hunched and apish. He'd cut the oral antics with the dawning of the light, his face locked in a vapid paralysis of long-ing. Drool puddled at the corners of his pooched lips like foam. The bubble in Calvin's lips grew to the size of a disgorged eyeball.

Trent eyed the framed photograph. "Where'd you get that, Cal?"

He put a hand on Calvin's shoulder, a foot on the trash lid. Calvin snapped his head Trentward without moving the shoulders, making a protective X with his arms as he clutched the frame to his chest. His eyes were round and reticent, yet somehow fearless.

"Remember the monkeys?" said Calvin, popping the bubble. "Soooooo funny."

"Can I see?"

Calvin turned his back on Trent, slumped to his knees, and bowed his head, kneeling on the shield and crushing what lay beneath under his awesome weight. Trent detected the familiar crunch and crackle of brittle bones breaking. The wind outside gusted, rattling the windows, lashing the walls with scree.

"Game time," said Calvin, and then he began to count slowly out loud. On seven, Trent told his brother to get up and give up what he was hiding.

Calvin counted off eight and then nine and then stopped. Trent waited, wishing he'd taken out the rat with stealthier means. There was a hissing noise, like streaming piss, and somewhere outside a faint, rolling rumble like distant thunder. Well aware of the weather report and regionwide evacuation, Trent weeks ago had decided to stand his ground; these days he called the accuracy of any and all forecasts into serious question, what with the volatile nature of Mother Nature's vicious menstrual cycles, and anyways the weather was out of control everywhere, with enough tornados and hurricanes and tsunamis to make Poseidon's head whirl right off his neck. Trent couldn't even picture himself packing.

Saw-whet Park was home, even if it burned.

Turned out the hiss really was piss.

"Dammit, Cal."

"You said a bad word!"

"Go wash your shorts."

Calvin made a show of getting to his feet, using both wrists and the edge of the opposite counter to hoist himself up, refusing to let go of the framed photograph. His knees tottered. His at-one-point royal blue gym shorts dripped on the hardwood. Calvin placed the frame on the counter facedown. Trent had his hand stuffed in the pocket of his chinos, the side of one finger slotted just inside the rigor mortis mouth of a rat that died pre-squeak. The teeth felt sharp.

Trent followed his twin out the door, having to indicate the general direction to the standpipe in the dark woods. Trent didn't offer Calvin the help he didn't ask for, watching his twin stagger off shirtless into the hot and hazy night. There were a million sounds out there, the blended music of nature nocturnal, though when Trent listened for the saw-whets he heard not a hoot. His site-issued smartwatch beeped its midnight beep.

He went inside, disposed of the rat's body back outside, then— back inside again—he wiped down the ledge above Calvin's bed, then the hardwood in the kitchenette. He trashed the now very red rag and stowed the rat's head with the other four heads—for later. He'd run fresh out of surfaces to disinfect and out of minutes to stall and delay the inevitable.

He faced down the facedown picture frame and flipped it over.

———

DON PHILLY WATCHED The Dark from behind a tall, thick tree, hidden from view. They were assembled in a clearing in the deepest part of the woods, feeding the flames, a pyre of roasting cats and calves and pigs and sheep and too many chickens to count. They were singing over the various squeals of their livestock. They'd done this for four nights straight, tonight marking the fifth. "Cockadoodledoom"—the violet and violent-looking splat seen on radars around the world, the thing whose apocalyptic arrival they had spent the entire last year prepping for and practically worshiping— was supposedly due to hit Point Reyes within the hour. At around nine o'clock, however, Don Philly had ingested disgusting amounts of psilocybin—"cow shit that makes you *see*," Lord Cred had said, and now Philly had no idea of the time.

Don Philly of Cocoa Beach, Florida—very much not a bankrupt farmer—had driven across America all the way to Point Reyes on the northern California coast to research and write a novel, because Phillip K. Dick had done the same when he'd wished to be taken seriously as a literary wordslinger. Dick's not-very-much-talked-about artistic insecurities resulted in *Confessions of a Crap Artist*, Philly's all-time favorite novel, the reason he'd hung up his thirty-six-year-old hardhat for the proverbial pen. He'd decided last year he'd research and write about whatever or whomever he encountered on the journey northwest, which more or less was how he found himself sworn into The Dark, a cult of bankrupt farmers awaiting Cockadoodledoom.

Bunch of crazy motherfuckers, The Dark.

The Dark were named in direct opposition to *The Point Reyes Light*, the weekly newspaper published in western Marin County dedicated to rigorous reporting and engaging prose since 1948. It had gained national attention in '79 for its Pulitzer-winning coverage of the Synanon organization, "one of the most dangerous and violent cults America has ever seen," a Santa-Monica-founded drug rehabilitation program turned cultish in the early '60s with the establishment of an alternate society emphasizing the significance of a self-examined life. It went full-fledged cult in the late '60s with the advent of the Game, during which members professed the unvarnished truth about themselves and endured unrestricted verbal criticism from their peers in return, a supposedly therapeutic practice resulting in personal growth and vasectomies and aborted babies and terrifying acts of extreme violence. The Church of Synanon disbanded in '91; Philly didn't deem it at all coincidental The Dark formed around the same time.

Philly peeked around the tree only to see The Dark still naked and dancing and burning their animals for reasons that remained very much unclear. He'd made sure to sequester himself far enough away to escape the heat of the flames, which reminded him too much of his excruciating initiation one year ago to the day, an affair they termed the "Last Roast" for obvious, physically fiery reasons. Philly, now fifty-five years old, had been The Dark's fifty-fifth inductee, and with all he had going on, it was safe to say he hadn't written a word for the novel.

Three side characters, however, *were* making waves in his mind. The first would be Larry Mufasa, based on a man named Gary Mustafa, whom Philly had confronted at a pit stop in Gatlinburg, Tennessee. He'd caught Mustafa stealing a saggy bundle of balloons tied to the roadside diner's sign, and he'd asked Mustafa what that was all about, and the prolix response Philly received was certainly one worth writing about. The other two sides remained shadowy inkblots of untapped imagination, though they crackled fiercely with female energy; he knew he'd name them something symbolically sharp-witted, perhaps even allegorical, like Faith or Hope, or both. All he knew about Faith and Hope was that they knew each other, that their relationship had soured with time. One had betrayed the other in some critical way.

Before writing anything, though, what he needed most was a compelling protagonist.

He turned away from The Dark only to find himself on the phone with his third wife, back home in Florida: Brenda's successor's successor. He couldn't remember calling her.

"Bunch of crazy motherfuckers, Marlo. I'm dead serious."

"Oh, Dee, I'm sure you're just, like, overreacting."

Philly bit his lip and said, "I've got permanent burns all over my body."

"Which, like, you said'll make for one hell of a scene—*ohhh, fuck yeah!*"

"That's if I ever get the chance to actually write the damn thing."

"Oh, *Dee.*"

"Marlo?"

"Yeah, baby. *Right there.* I mean here. I mean I'm right here, Dee."

"What time is it?" said Philly.

"Clock says almost two."

"Why're you still up?" he asked his wife.

"*Fuck me.*"

"I think maybe I oughta come home."

"Sorry, I'm just . . .*fuck* . . . just a lil' tired. *Don't come*—home."

"Do you hear them singing? The squeals? Fire's like fifty feet high." Marlo giggled in Philly's ear. "They made me eat a bunch of magic mushrooms."

"Fuuu*n*. Sounds fun, Dee."

"They think the end of the world's coming."

"*Oh god, I'm coming.*"

"Absolutely not. You're not getting involved in this—I won't allow it."

The loud squeals seemed everywhere. Don Philly had to move another three trees down. There were no stars in the sky. He couldn't remember Marlo's age—late twenties, he ventured, maybe younger. He felt he could throw up any second. It occurred to Philly that he was a sad person. The Dark were still dancing with no clothes on.

"Still there, Marlo?"

". . ."

"They're calling it Cockadoodledoom. This thing that's supposedly coming."

". . ."

"Their cult names all rhyme with *head*. They call *me* Lord Fed."

"What about head?" She sounded like she was eating something, talking with her mouth full: *whatta-bow-heh?*

"You sound like you're eating something. Like you're gurgling."

"It's the reception, I bet. Plus, like, aren't you, like, tripping out?"

"I miss you," he told his third wife, seeing behind closed eyes an image of his first.

". . ."

"Hear that? I said I miss you."

". . ."

"Yoo-hoooo? Brenda?"

". . ."

"Think I lost you," said Philly.

"Love you too, Dee."

"There you are."

"I'm right here."

"You know what, Marlo, I get this feeling all this has been written down."

"You're the one who dropped everything just to go write for a year or whatever."

"Like this whole thing is just some great big setup and I'm stuck smack in the middle of it. Like I have no control over any of this, whatever this is."

"Don't leave, baby."

"Are you saying I should come home?"

"You can't leave—I hid your shoes!"

"You were right, by the way. I should've packed more than one pair of shoes."

"Hey, Dee, what's the moon looking like in California?"

"They took my only pair of shoes, The Dark."

"It looks weird on TV."

"We're to feel the earth with our feet. To feel connected to the earth."

"Jesus, what the hell *is* that?" said Marlo.

"It's just something they believe. You find things to believe in when you're out of money. I should write that down."

"You should probably get out of there, Dee. It doesn't look good, whatever it is."

"Are you even talking to me?"

"Did we ever sign those papers?" Marlo asked. "Regarding your will?"

"Thing is, Marlo, I don't plan on dying any time—oh god, what's *that*?"

"Please tell me we signed those papers."

"Oh god, it's really real! It's happening! Everything Lord Bed ever said!"

"What about the bed?"

"It's . . . it's *huge*. It's huge and it's *loud!* Can you even hear me?"

" . . . "

"It's coming right at us!" Philly screamed.

"You're such an asshole for, like, leaving me here all by myself. When we met during that layover in Georgia and you said you lived in Florida, I didn't picture *this*."

"I can't hear you! So I'll just shout really loud to paint you a picture!"

"I pictured, like, Miami."

"It's like a tornado but blacker and solid and like . . . *alive!* It's all buzzy, too, like static radio, and the trees're going *nuts!* There are a bunch of churning clouds way up above it, and it goes up through the clouds, and the whole thing's flickering or twitching, and, like, there's this unnatural light to it all like nothing I've ever *seen!*"

"I know. I'm seeing it on TV," said Marlo. "You're probably going to die."

"It's in our camp! They're in my *mouth!*"

Don Philly knew there was no way Marlo could have possibly understood him. There were too many . . . *things* in his mouth.

"Hearing you die's making me see we should've divorced long ago," said Marlo.

Don Philly spat and slapped at his hair. The fire in the clearing went out.

"If somehow you survive this, I'm leaving you."

"BRENDAAA!!!"

"Who the fuck's this *Brenda?* Have you been cheating on me, Dee?"

"I LOVE YOUUU!!!"

"This is, like, officially grounds for divorce."

" . . . "

" . . . "

"Are you there, Marlo?"

"I'm here. You're there. So where does that leave us?"

"It's gone. It's moving away. Inland."

"Are you all right, Dee?"

The goopy dots with legs or whatever were out of Philly's mouth and hair. "Still alive. So what were you saying? I wasn't able to hear most of it."

"I wish you were home. *You* . . . stay here with me, baby."

"You know what, Marlo, I gotta go—The Dark's calling for me."

"Fine, then call me in the morning. Or come cockadoodledoo me."

"If you mean wake you up, I don't know if I'll be up before you, but I'll try."

"You. Start your book."

"You're my muse," said Don Philly. "Don't ever forget that."

"What an honor."

"Sometimes you almost remind me of someone I used to know."

"Let me guess," said Marlo. "It's Brenda."

Don Philly, on pure reflex, flung his phone into darkness. It took him forever to find it, with only the moon to help out. Eventually he rejoined The Dark in the clearing where Lord Bed was there to greet him, the sick-sweet spice of char and rot and something esoterically tropical in the air, the earth warm and somehow distant beneath his feet. Don Philly had a thousand things on his mind, a thousand more to say. He saw nothing wrong with being born to write.

———

WHEN THE PICTURE frame Trent Taphor turned over turned out to be empty, it filled him with a powerful pressure right in his chest, as if the veins and vessels holding his heart in suspension had all curled in on themselves, enclosing the heart and blocking off every last bridge of blood flow. A flurry of dots hampered his vision until his eyes figured they ought to squeeze themselves shut, the back of his lids that special curtain of rosy-black. His temples were cold and wet. He buckled at the knees and clocked the cleft of his chin on the counter, something he felt as if from a neural distance, the pain receptors showing up late to the party and plastered. The only thing keeping him from giving in to the incoming tides of panic was the fact that he'd felt this before, this heavy knot in his chest, familiar like a memory attached to a picture.

In the past there'd only been one way to get rid of the pressure, and it hadn't been the forty-two and a half minutes he'd spend with Angel, his therapist, in her office every Wednesday throughout freshman year, playing checkers and discussing things like Michael Sampere pantsing Calvin the year before at the seventh vs. eighth grade basketball game while Calvin honked his way through the national anthem on his trumpet, exposing his tiny belly-button of a penis to the tremulous, bug-eyed crowd of pissant players and their mystified parents. Things like why Trent had felt the need to act out in response, dedicating weeks to tracking Sampere after school, calculating, first learning and then having to adjust and relearn Sampere's constantly evolving schedule, committing the whole sprocketed thing to memory, until at last the day came when Trent, having plugged in every last prospective variable, found it within himself to just let fly and set the equation into motion so that he found himself all alone with Sampere in the dugout of a deserted baseball field three klicks west of Crest High where Sampere smoked joints in secret by himself, concocting potential modes and methods of definite abuse. Things like why Trent felt it had been necessary to sock Sampere one, right in the eyeball, leaving a shiner that shone a different color of the rainbow depending on the stage of recovery he happened to be in. Things like Trent's outlook on Calvin's myriad accomplishments, like how ESPN had flown in to cover the moment Calvin kicked through a PAT for the varsity football team when they were already up by like a hundred or whatever. Afterwards, he'd been borne on the shoulder-padded shoulders of sweat-shined Spartans, glory-basking like a champion for cameras that captured the shot from like sixteen different angles, all of which played and replayed on ESPN for like a week. Or like how Calvin landed a part in the school play, *Beauty and the Beast*, playing a dancing spoon during that song with the dishes, four or five minutes reoccurring every Friday and Saturday and Sunday night for three weeks. Thomas and Nell Taphor dropped everything for that spoon, showing up to every show, the proud parents of their best-loved son. Things like Trent's mother's vacuous tendency to start and thus pretty much stall any meaningful conversation with *How was (x)?*, as in *How was school/soccer/therapy?* Trent and his former therapist, Angel, had discussed things like these, like sadness and self-harm and suicide, in her office every Wednesday over checkers, but things like the stink beetle and the deity Anne Kell and the closet Trent kept to himself, even though they'd come together to deliver him the only surefire way to rid himself of the powerful pressure in his chest.

There was a crushing roar outside of the trailer that Trent supposed could be the bellows of his heart, bound in curled vessels and veins. He tried calculating the distance from Berkshire up north to Crest High down south, from the confines of this trailer to the shelter of that janitor's closet, from the empty picture frame on the counter now to the stink beetle playing dead in the closet then, a distance measured in miles and lost years, impossible to calculate without Anne Kell's voice to aid him. He remembered the beetle kicked behind the door to the corner of the closet, dinner for dust mites. He pictured the picture not in its frame, and the tall flames, and barked loudly to himself, needing something for all the pain.

"Ey, T-Bone—were ya, like, tryna let me out anytime soon?"

"Not now," said Trent Taphor, lying supine on the floor.

"So then when?" the voice said from the sink. "Like, your dishes freegin' *reek*, bro."

"I mean I'm not in the mood to talk."

"Ey, let's not forget who woke who here earlier tonight."

"I had no choice. We had a rat."

"Like, it's not like I was feeling particularly *stabby*."

"What do you want, Dex? My heart hurts."

"Your damn *dead mom's* inside me again," said Dex the meat cleaver.

"My chest, I mean. Hurts."

"She won't shut her freegin' *trap*, bro."

"Or maybe I've got heart problems for real."

"She's all like, *Let me talk to my kid, you little shit!* I mean, what am I supposed to say to that? It's like she doesn't remember using me. Needing me."

Trent had shut off the light inside the trailer and had shut his eyes tight to block out the dark of night—the steady pounding roar outside made him wish he could do the same thing with his ears. He pictured Calvin out there in the forest by himself, walking to the standpipe and pissing himself all over again and crying from fright. A smile touched his lips like something warm and glazed with sugar.

"Tell my mother to take a hike," Trent told the meat cleaver in the sink.

"..."

"How'd she like them apples?"

"Bro, she's, like, freegin' inconsolable."

"What does my mom even want?"

"She won't say, but she says it's quote unquote 'urgent.'"

"Say that again," said Trent. "There's a lot of noise outside."

"Urgent, your mom's saying. Pressing, vital, critical—*exigent*."

"Pretentious tool."

"Don't cleave the messenger, bro."

"Albeit acerbic, I'll give you that."

"Ey, I'm a cleaver. I cleave shit. Now for the love of The One Great Smithy, wouldja get me outta this freegin' sink?"

Trent's eyes snapped open. He found himself on his feet, hunched over the sink, hands splayed on the counter to hold himself up. He shifted some plates around, toppling ancient stacks, stacking new ones, mindful of Dex's single sharp tooth somewhere in there. Eventually they came face to face, one sickly and sweaty, the other faceless and shiny and sporting parabolas of rat blood like several red smiles.

"Put her through, Dex."

The roar outside had heightened into something cataclysmic, as if the earth itself had started splintering from the inside out, splitting at the core, spouting hot liquid light to the surface. Calvin was going to die out there, Trent doubted not a bit.

Trent picked up Dex by the handle, scanning the flat of the blade where Nell Taphor made her incoming presence known and felt. It was dark and shadowy in the trailer, and likewise was his mother's face materializing in the metal. He preferred talking to her with the lights off. The one eye she still possessed in death was a mess to look at.

"Have you lost your fucking mind?"

"Great to see you too, Mom."

"This is unbelievable. Your father told me he told you to pack up and leave!"

"I work here. Saw-whet Park's my place of work."

"Your father said you said you'd agreed to evacuate!"

"Park ranger, law enforcement division. I patrol the grounds and make sure all campers, hikers, and visitors follow the rules. The fire safety regulations in particular."

"By tomorrow morning there might not *be* any grounds to patrol!"

"I also make sure guests don't disrupt the natural environment."

"Or guests!"

"Or their fellow guests. It's a legit career, Mom, and, like, a second chance."

"Trent, where's Calvin? I don't hear him snoring. Where's Cal, Trent?"

"I was recently scheduled to lead my very first nature walk."

"He went outside, didn't he? You took your eye off him, didn't you?"

"Calvin pissed himself. He's cleaning up at the standpipe."

"Fucking unbelievable," said Trent's mother.

"What's really unbelievable is this, like, pressure in my chest."

"Where'd we go wrong with you?"

"It all started with this old picture Calvin found."

"We put you through soccer, guitar lessons, summer camp . . ."

"Pretty sure Calvin somehow slipped it out of its frame, the picture, then he went and took it with him to the standpipe."

"Boy Scouts, karate, therapy . . ."

"Angel was a lousy therapist."

"She had heart problems, Trent."

"She hung herself with a hammock."

"Again, cause of death: broken heart."

"Anyways I burned this picture I'm talking about the week after you died."

"Oh god, not this again. What happened wasn't your fault, Trent."

"I burned the picture with the rest of the house to collect the insurance."

"I shouldn't've been talking to you on my cell phone while driving."

"I'm not blaming you for what happened, Mom."

"I mean, I can't imagine how it was for you, *hearing* something like that."

"I remember hearing Calvin screaming in the backseat. One of his fits."

"It must've been *horrific*. Hearing Dad and me die, right through the phone."

"I remember hearing Dad trying to calm Calvin down."

"Do you remember the last thing I said before I died?"

". . ."

"'Cause *I* sure don't."

"And now, Mom, this old burned-up picture's back. I remember burning it."

"Nobody cares, Trent . . . about what's about to happen. What's *coming*."

"What's coming?" Trent asked his mother, genuinely curious.

"Mary Mangrove is one name to watch for in the decade of doom to come."

"Mangrove, Mangrove . . . it doesn't ring any bells. Or raise any alarms."

"Go find your brother, do you hear me? Then get the hell out of there."

"I'll see what I can do—as a park ranger. In a professional capacity."

"Cal loves you, you know."

"I know," said Trent.

"I know you love him too."

"He knows."

"Be good while I'm gone."

"Wait, Mom—!"

"Ey, bro, she's out. Were ya, like, tryna tell her something or something?"

Trent dropped Dex in the sink and stepped out into the whirling teeth of the wind in search of Calvin. He knew all along he'd been talking to himself, that the voices he'd heard and would go on hearing until the end of his days were his, meaning they didn't come from anyplace outside of him. It wasn't like he was in any way mentally ill or anything like that—the voices were his, meaning they lived inside of him, meaning they belonged to him, meaning there was no reason to drop ninety bucks to sit down with a not-dead therapist and play checkers for forty-two and a half minutes in some half-baked search for breakthroughs in meaning, meaning he could go on believing himself when he told himself his mother, even in death, was incapable of hearing.

2

MR. MOONY
(FULLA BEES)

———

CALVIN CLASPS the photograph before his tearful eyes as he walks alone to the standpipe in the deep, dark, scary woods—his favorite picture in the world, and not because it's saved him from having his throat cut however many times, which is something he knows nothing about. In the picture Calvin and Trent are five or maybe six, their arms coiled around each other's shoulders like best buddies, forever smiling roughly the same open-mouthed smile. They're sharing a waffle cone at the Los Angeles Zoo, the half-melted chocolate smearing their chins and cheeks, a bunch of monkeys captured mid-swing in the background, frozen on the vines.

Before, whenever Trent got done doing The Bad Thing and readied himself to do it again, Calvin would remind his brother of the monkeys, which he had to do tonight because of the rat. The woods have never before seemed quite this quiet. The wind, a shrieking whistle seconds ago, has abruptly withdrawn to the softest whisper, the saw-whets to their knotholes in the secret guts of trees. The air seems to stick to Calvin's skin.

Calvin doesn't know what time it is, nor why Trent didn't offer to accompany him to the standpipe to help him clean up, nor how the framed photograph first came to be in his hands to begin with. He vaguely recalls shoving Trent, securing his own personal space, getting Trent's big blue balloon eyes away from his face. The one thing Calvin remembers for sure is what Trent was saying as he hucked the rat back over his shoulder—the same thing Trent was saying over and over, his breath a hot, stinky fume on Calvin's eyeballs: *Ann-Kill wakes, T-Bone bakes.*

That was when he knew he had to get out of the trailer, away from his brother.

Now he's lost in the forest at the darkest time of night, seeking the standpipe to wash his pee-soaked shorts with. At some point he sets to losing himself in his only conceivable company, the memory of the day the picture in his hands was taken, when the sky wasn't muggy and moonless like now, with a sun that melted the ice cream in its cone and dried its chocolate on his cheeks. The memory itself takes up five or maybe six seconds of real time to play from beginning to end in Calvin's head, a snap movie in his brain, every detail fleshed out and fully formed, his favorite film and go-to in times of deep stress.

They're there to see King Louie, Calvin sees in his head, a big old orangutan whose propensity for pooping in his hand and hurling it at his underlings supersedes the humor of everything five or maybe six-year-olds have ever judged humorous. Calvin and Trent stand with the crowd in front of the glass exhibit, craning their necks; they've each got a waffle cone of freshly purchased chocolate (Calvin's) and vanilla (Trent's) ice cream. Mom harps and harangues somewhere behind, begging to snap a photo of Calvin and Trent in front of the monkeys, but Trent's refusing, saying they can't take a picture because King Louie'll finally decide to come out of his stupid hiding spot at the exact moment they waste getting the pose or whatever together, and they'll end up missing what Trent's coined The Poop Show—a name that makes their father, for reasons unknown, bark with weird laughter—and *don't you get it, Mom, this is something Trent just knows.* Dad's on a bench by the bathrooms drifting in and out like a flickering bulb, hands folded neatly in his lap, eyelids aflutter with REM whispers, head poised straight ahead. Calvin likes King Louie's shaggy hair and wide flat face, and he laughs when Trent does; this is something *he* knows to do.

"Look 'e's coming out!" Trent hisses. "There he is! Toldja, *Mom.*"

Calvin claps and shouts, "KING LOONY!"

"Shhh—don't shout, Cal. One picture, boys. That's all I ask."

"Now alls we gots to do's wait 'til he poops."

"POOP SHOW!"

"Calvin!" Mom cries.

"Pooooop *Show!* Pooooop *Show!* Pooooop *Show!*"

Trent's rhythmic chant in combination with pumping his right fist on the word *show* inspires other kids around to join in. These other little kids are bigger and taller than Trent, visibly older and vocally stronger, but they watch Trent more than they do King Louie and his court. This is to say they see the monkeys not at all, so ensnared they are in the raw animal magnetism of Trent's crass song and dance—a monkey-see-monkey-do situation that has maybe fifty percent of parents gripping their toddlers by their tiny wrists and practically dragging them off, tossing proof-of-parental-merit sort of looks at Nell Taphor, who's fiddling with her camera, while the remaining half of parents in their own distinct ways neglect to address what's going on in any way. Calvin watches the kids watching Trent and swells with something warm and fuzzy inside that definitely isn't ice cream. Trent's waffle cone is nowhere in sight, Calvin sees, as King Louie shambles closer to the glass hefting two broken sticks of grass. By this point a large group of roaming, red-eyed teenagers clogging the narrow walk—and even a scant collection of moms and dads—have all taken up Trent's chant, the noise of which has climbed to such a height that Calvin can no longer hear his brother, whose eyes have tapered to the shapes of the eyes of world leaders Calvin's seen once or twice on what his father calls the Titty Tube. Mom's camera clicks and flashes at random. Calvin laps at the ice cream coating the rim of the cone and watches King Louie, who's watching him—they seem to share a silent connection in the uproar, mutually understanding their mutual misunderstanding, united through the dividing sheet of glass, nibblers of ice cream and grass. King Louie sticks both sticks of grass up one slitted nostril. Calvin licks a spot of chocolate off the curled tip of his nose—he's got the physiological makeup for such facial flexibility. Meanwhile Thomas Taphor has come to on the bench in a big way, embarrassment-wise, having pissed his slacks from laughing too hard and too often in his sleep, which ends up being the reason the Taphors' time at the zoo meets its premature end, but not before King Louie ascends his throne— a plush miniature overhang—and squats, furry arm hung underneath, hand cupped low. Trent motions the crowd to silence, a span of seconds in which the collective anticipation reaches its peak.

King Louie goes on to put on what Trent will forever call the king's very best performance, as his frantic underlings scatter along the vines in search of shelter overhead.

After the crowd has dispersed, Trent says he's ready for Mom to snap their picture, but that's when Calvin and King Louie seem to decide their time for meeting up close and personal has come— right now. Half of Calvin's ice cream has melted in the sun; his cheeks are crusted with chocolate. King Louie's grinning the perpetual grin of orangutans that may or may not mean what humans seem to think it means—his fat face flutters and seems to float on his nimble descent to the dividing glass. Calvin removes his glasses with his free hand and huffs into the spotted panes, but because of the cone in his other hand, he's got no way to wipe his glasses clean. The hearing aid in his left ear has popped loose; he catches Trent's summoning call as if from a deep underwater distance. King Louie moves his dappled orange eyes to the waffle cone, bears his fangs and smears his furrowed tongue along the glass. Some bug buzzes in one of Calvin's unprotected ears, as if speaking a secret language of static.

"There ya go," Calvin hears Trent say all of a sudden.

Trent has reinserted Calvin's hearing aid, swiping Calvin's cone so Calvin can use his hands to wipe his glasses on his shirt and put them back on. Trent's pointing and laughing at King Louie's tongue's trail of saliva. Calvin laughs too.

"All right, boys, smile for the camera."

It's only after Tom Taphor comes hunched and hobbling out of the restroom and they start away from King Louie's court en route to the exit that Calvin all at once realizes what King Louie really wanted of him all along. His jolted heart seems to tumble to his tum-tum as he turns around, readying himself to double back.

"What's the matter, Cal?" Nell Taphor asks.

This part of the movie-memory, both climax and resolution, is what Calvin sees crystal-clearest. The exhibit's maybe twenty yards distant, but Calvin's glasses are clean.

King Louie has his whole face mashed against that side of the glass, the flesh squished pancake-flat, while on this side there's a waffle cone, stuck in place, runny with creamy streaks of vanilla that blot out half of King Louie's face. The big monkey jumps up and down and beats his burly chest and whoops a thousand obvious thank-yous at a nonstop, everlasting rate. Calvin lets out a long breath, shakes his head, and says, "Nothing, Mom," smiling at his twin, for whom he decides to give up the rest of his chocolate ice cream. He does this because Trent, succeeding where Calvin has failed, has been kind enough to do the same for the monkey they've both come to love so much. Calvin never actually saw Trent do the deed, but he believes and almost even understands Daddy when Daddy says the best kindnesses are carried out in secret, partly because of the way he looks at Mommy when he says it . . . but mostly because of the way he sounds.

———

A MEMORY, five seconds of "real time"—that's what this whole tale is, more or less.

———

CALVIN'S MOVIE-MEMORY dissolves on the sixth second, leaving him engulfed in the distended darkness of the woods, made somehow spookier by the complete and utter absence of life—nothing, anywhere, stirs. He pinches in his fingers the photograph, crimped at the corners and sodden with pee from the elastic waistband of his underpants. It's so dark out he can no longer make out the picture's details, so he slips it back in his underpants. He's been waiting for Mommy and Daddy to get back from the hospital for a long time. He's scared of the sound Trent's voice makes when Trent's getting ready to do The Bad Thing he does when he gets all sad and mad like this—even smelly old tree rats should get to have their heads.

Calvin's humming a song from an old bright movie, determined to follow its sage advice, but there's no yellow brick road for him to follow; there's only darkness beyond description and chaotic sound-lessness and he's not even walking anymore—he's discovered in the belly of the black the lonely stump of a fallen tree. It hurts his rump sitting down, but the back of his legs and the bottom of his back hurt worse standing up, so he's down and sitting and pulling out his hearing aids to avoid the shame of hearing the person he knows he needs to keep away from.

He also takes off his glasses. Sight and sightlessness and sound and soundlessness are all very mean things right now. Calvin doesn't know what to do.

Somehow with his hearing aids and glasses removed, the world gets louder and somewhat brighter. There's a pernicious buzzing in his ear. Untethered leaves whap and flap like bats among the tall trees. He gazes up in search of the lost moon.

There's a mammoth splitting sound like the ground cracking open all across the earth, and all at once Calvin feels them, bugs like big slimy ants skittering up and down and all around his toes and feet and shins and calves and rump and back and fingers and hands and wrists and biceps and tum-tum and chest and shoulders and neck and throat and chin and cheeks and lips and nose and ears and eyes and skull with tiny tingly feet. Through it all there's this constant buzzing in his ear and this face descending from nowhere out in front of his eyes, a white face floating in the black, twitchy with life, a blurred moon in a solar system of starving black holes. Buried in all the buzzing are words, a voice like the fuzzy noise Trent's radio makes.

"Zazzzzzzom Zezerazzz zizzizuzuzzzz."

The bugs move Calvin's glasses back over his eyes.

"Zzzzakazzz?"

Calvin's eyes move to the sky, the color of which is unlike any he's ever seen.

"Zzzzzikimommadaddazzzz."

The bugs snatch away Calvin's hearing aids; he follows their swift ascent on the winged backs of a billion bugs, up and up and up until they're sucked inside the whirling, murmuring twister of black they seem to make up. He thinks he hears a strange slurping sound, either that or a gulp, followed by what can only be a burp, judging by the subsequent smell.

The voice itself seems more than anything else to be coming from inside his head. The sky looks like it's in the middle of giving an ugly birth. Calvin's got no clue how or why this thought occurred to him, or even really what it means.

"Zzzzekizzaazum!"

The white face hangs at arm's length in a nest of several black tentacles like something fused there at the center, a white pupil in a black iris.

"Zzzz—ent's looking for you as we zzzekemzzzz."

The words eke through only when Calvin meets the thing in the eye. Otherwise it's just static, the white noise of a radio way out of satellite range. Buzzing bees. Finally he's got something to laugh at, a game to amuse himself with.

"Zzzzuga—at me, Calzzzzuba zzzakazinzin—quite rude. What would your mother zzzeekum?"

"Your face's funny."

Calvin here's alluding to the caved-in folds of the creature's forehead, folds resting atop a skewed, sloping unibrow that seems alive and indomitable in its blind resolve to worm free of the fleshy craters of its face. Also the porcine snout of a nose, the shiny, whimsical eyes, and the boat-shaped lips forced wide open in a smile that seems perpetually locked, as if the poor creature can do nothing but smile forevermore, as if eternally anticipating the punch line of a joke that'll never come. (In that the wait itself is most likely the joke. Think of a devout Christian or Moslem or Buddhist or whatever, dedicating entire lives to assorted customs and rituals so that they might achieve in death their own versions of eternal paradise. Suppose, then, once they die, they learn there's nothing. Which is to say they learn nothing, because there's nothing to learn, because there's nothing. Not even angels or demons to inform them they guessed wrong or were born under certain sociopolitical/geographical climates and circumstances that just so happened to be the wrong climate and circumstance, paradise-pursuit-wise. In this case, then, the sense of purpose they worked so hard to cultivate in life can be likened to the overall emptiness Mr. Moony's mouth seems to invoke, in that he's always smiling despite the complete absence of anything at all funny. Or perhaps one or all devotees are in fact correct in their service to Sum One [wink-wink], and there *is* some paradise for the good and some hell for the bad, in which case the joke's on those neglecting to serve or pray or worship in any way, meaning [metaphorically] the punch line to the joke Mr. Moony's mouth everlastingly craves really is out there, somewhere, and might in fact be worth the wait.) Also the nubby jokes for fangs, two of them, two centimeters in length apiece, dangling from the upper lip like a vampire's baby teeth. There's also the bulging, completely globular head, corpulent and hairless and thus babyish. The eyes take up most of the face, sort of a chore for Calvin to ignore. All told, the creature's face looks like that of the preadolescent child of the face you see in the moon.

The pained smile gives off an air of damning mischief.

The sizable bugs swarm and seize Calvin by the temples and clamp the muscles at the back of his neck so that he's forced to look the creature in the eye, head held up straight and rigid. Even his eyelids have got heavy, buggy hooks tugging them up, making it impossible for him to blink and painful to roll his eyes.

"Shall we try this again?" the creature says. "Before your brother finds us."

Calvin's been trying to blink to relieve the dry sting in his eyes. "What's your name? You hurt my eyes."

"You can call me whatever you'd like, Calvin, but only because you're significant. Did you know you're significant?"

"Funny Face Man!"

"Well . . ."

"Eye Hurter!"

"I could work with—"

"White Head!"

"Let's go back to Eye Hurter for a second."

"*You* hurt her? Mommy?"

"So Eye Hurter's out."

"Mommy!"

"How about Mr. Moon?"

"Mr. Moony!"

"Suppose that works," says Mr. Moony.

"I see you in spoons!"

"And it's certainly a pleasure to meet you in person at long last."

". . ."

"I've a question," says Mr. Moony. "Have you any . . . um, sharp objects? Perhaps something sharp you keep hidden somewhere in those shorts of yours?"

"Swords?"

"Swords, daggers, scissors . . . spurs?"

"My favorite picture's in my underpants!"

"We'll get to that shortly. So no spurs? You're completely utterly spur-free?"

"You talk funny. MY EYES REALLY HURT!"

"Let the boy blink, Bod."

The bugs propping Calvin's eyes open loosen their collective hold on both the corners of the lids and the tips of the lashes, letting him blink. He can't see the bugs on his lids, nor can he see fully the ones everywhere else, on his body or not. They move and undulate as one smothering dark mass. Calvin doesn't get that Mr. Moony has called these bugs "Bod."

The bugs on Calvin's body—Bod—tickle and tingle all over;

Calvin's smile more or less matches Mr. Moony's. Bod seems everywhere.

Mr. Moony hasn't blinked.

Mr. Moony says, "Assuming you've no spurs on your person—or any sharp objects, for that matter—are you, Calvin, willing to accept a fun free ride on my back?"

"Are you a tornado?"

"I'm an old friend of the earth. I was born here a long time ago, in the place where burnt things go, the land inside the ashes. You'd do well to remember that, by the way."

"Can we go see Mommy and Daddy?"

"Were they cremated?"

"They're at a hospital. CRASH! It hurt soooooo much."

"It's getting increasingly difficult to sift through the thoughts in your head . . . I suppose that's just one of the reasons they say you're *super* significant."

"My head really hurts!"

"It's fantastically frustrating."

"Can you take me home?"

"Look, I can't lie to you, Calvin. Really and truly I can't. Honestly, it's literally a physiological deficiency: I can't lie to you, or to anyone else. I mean, I guess I have the capacity to lie, but if I do, Bod'll wither and die—and so will I, as Bod is my substance. So, no, should you decide to ride, I won't take you home, assuming by 'home' you mean your misanthropic twin, Trent, and that atrocious RV you both happen to inhabit."

"You're a meanie."

"The real meanie here's Trent, Calvin. He wants you dead. I think."

"Trent's scary sometimes—Trent talks to a knife sometimes."

"Assuming they were cremated, however, I *can* take you to Mommy and Daddy. Meaning I have the ability to do so. Just so we're clear, it's in my power to take you to your parents. I can do that. But only if they're cremated. And well, maybe not *all* the way to your parents, but undoubtedly . . . closer. I'm trying to mislead you, you see? I'm being honest here. You could trust me if you want to. It's your choice."

Somewhere distant, Trent howls Calvin's name like a wolf, though Calvin has no clue. The voice in his head seems to be the world's only sound.

"Your brother sounds rather wolfish, doesn't he? Super scary. If you accept a ride on my back, I'll get you away from him. I'll take you straight to the place that picture in your underpants came from. It was me, by the way, who plucked the picture from your mind and guided it down the Road all the way here into your hands when you needed it most. Just so you know. And who knows? Maybe Mommy and Daddy'll be there waiting for you."

"Trent says Mommy and Daddy're underground, but he's a *liar*."

"Truth is all humans lie, and then they die."

"Mommy and Daddy're *hiding*. At the *hospital*."

"Could we maybe not discuss them anymore?"

Trent's call's coming steadily closer, but Calvin doesn't hear. "Why does Trent say Mommy and Daddy're underground? Tell me!"

Mr. Moony's smile looks the same as it has. "I'm sorry, Cal. I don't not know."

". . ."

"Something else I know: there's a special place for significants like you, the pure of substance, good-natured and warm-hearted and present and thus worthy of moving on to worlds big and better enough to suit you. You significants harbor in your substances what most earthly denizens lack in theirs. I must level with you—I've been tasked to extract what you all've got in a multidimensional effort to generate a sort of Super Substance. In the meantime, Bod'll be conducting assessments across America, our final stop here on good old Earth. Come with me, Calvin, and we'll wash this dying world of the rest of its filth before the time comes to move on. Speaking of time, there's none to waste! Mother Climate here's a batty old bee all out of honey. I just need your consent first. Or Bod does."

Calvin's been thinking long and hard about the monkeys at the zoo. "Can you take me to see the monkeys? They're sooooo funny."

"Monkeys, yes! We've got monkeys! Lots of them!"

"YAY!"

"Just so we're clear, I have your consent?"

"POOP SHOW! KING LOONY!"

"You know what, Calvin, I'm just going to have to assu—zebze-bzoozingzoozzzz."

Calvin doesn't quite snatch the rest of what the floating white head's saying because the bugs have released their embrace entirely and Calvin's dropping all of a sudden, freefalling for the amount of time it takes for a smile to shatter in midair until the padded cheeks of his rump come slamming down on the stump of the fallen tree in the middle of the woods in the dark of night, with no destination-standpipe or atrocious trailer or twin anywhere in sight. The panes of Calvin's glasses are scuzzy at the corners with some sort of slime, and without his hearing aids, he can't really deal. He feels cocooned, outside and in, but at least through the tangle of intersecting branches overhead, he finds the moon back in its place in the sky.

With plenty of light to see by, he gets up, rubbing his rump, and cries out for Mr. Moony and his huge body of bugs, botching the names with *Mr. Mommy* and *God*. (Pronunciation, tough enough already for Calvin to nail on the best of days, sort of figuratively defenestrates itself sans the crucial aid of the hearing aids.) Calvin has already come to miss the buzz in his ears, the voice in his head; he feels empty in the silence of its sudden absence.

At long last he sees him through the brush, about the length of a basketball court away—Trent, hacking through the brush, a violent silhouette. Trent is wielding Calvin's shield to great effect, though he looks less like Captain America than he does Thanos, big and broad and bent on saving the rest of the resource-limited universe by destroying mere parts of it, a noble, underappreciated sacrifice Calvin doesn't wholly comprehend, much less condone. Calvin eases himself to his belly, edging around the stump to give himself a canted view of Trent hacking and tramping away in the wrong direction.

Over the years Calvin's become fully aware of the primary difference between himself and his twin: he knows he's got Down Syndrome, so the two of them will forever look and act and perceive the world their own ways. They can't stay together forever. The world won't allow it, which is something Calvin used to hear his mother say to his father in her sad, low voice in the middle of what felt like a million nights when Calvin would sleepwalk in the hall only to wake up outside their bedroom door. (This is how pretending to sleepwalk became a habit more consistent than the sleepwalking itself.) Calvin also knows they're both going to die at some point, he and his twin, in some place. He's only half aware, though, of the separate voices they each perceive in their own heads —Calvin's Mr. Moony and Trent's Ann-Kill—but if tonight's proven anything, it's that Calvin's voice is real while Trent's, real or not, makes him do bad things to rats and frogs and cats and anything suitably small with a hack-offable head.

Once Trent's out of eyeshot, what little light there is in the woods goes back out of the world, the moon into hiding. Calvin snaps shut his eyes in search of mental snapshots of King Louie. He wonders how Trent, kind enough as a kid to give up the rest of his ice cream to a caged orangutan, could grow up such a meanie to creatures supposedly free. He fails to catch the crunch of leaves as something nearby clomps closer, but he welcomes the strident buzz that slips back between the ears, making a home in his head. He opens his eyes with a renewed sense of purpose, a sort of motivational compass pointing him in one direction: on.

The bugs have all swarmed into the shape, size, and general look of a horse, black and vast with a face that somewhat resembles Mr. Moony's, staring and smiling, wrinkly and very real. It's alive, this thing, though if in fact it's a horse, it looks more like the reanimated corpse of one, covered in bugs from head to hoof, writhing and pulsing where flesh and fur should be.

This time Calvin chooses to meet those shimmering eyes.

"So what's the word?" the dark horse says. "Care for a ride on my back?"

Calvin drops his head in a bow, a dancing spoon with an audience of one.

———

MAGIC-MUSHROOM-WISE, Don Philly didn't think he was anywhere close to close to coming or calming down. He was vaguely certain the source of his mounting panic had to do with the goopy group of bugs he could've sworn had flown inside his hair and mouth Christ knew how long ago, maybe an hour. Philly—or Lord Fed, to his fellow bare-assed brethren—watched Lord Bed reignite the pyre at the center of the clearing.

As the ensuing closing ceremony began, Philly couldn't stop himself from confronting two facts newly unearthed at the root of his consciousness: 1) *Randall Flee Swallowed a Bee*, this old kiddy book Ma read to him as a toddler, supposedly a moral comedy, had been the reprehensible source of a lifelong trauma, and 2) his definite certainty that he'd swallowed at least one of the bugs and was thus now stuck at the start of an unspeakable process denoting a slow and horrible death sure to involve extreme internal suffering.

The kiddy book's core platitude reminds you to cover your mouth when you yawn so people don't have to see whatever you've got going on in your throat. For too many years, Philly had taken this to mean that he should cover his mouth when tired, bored, uninterested, apathetic, aloof, jaded, depressed, sarcastically insulting, etc., a nervous tic that had carried on into adulthood and to this day remained all but unshakeable. It'd reached a point long ago where Philly, triggered by *x* emotion, would just cover his mouth without any sort of yawning involved. He couldn't remember why he hadn't covered his mouth upon the tornadic arrival of the bugs of Cockadoodledoom—something to do with Marlo, he presumed.

It took eating cow shit to make "Lord Fed" see all this.

What Don Philly saw now was Lord Bed, balancing high on a stool on a chair on the wide flat surface of a big rock out in front of the fire, arms spread, head bowed, his stripped figure wreathed in the light of the flames. The Dark had no founder, they claimed, for they claimed The Dark had always been, and yet it had been through Lord Bed that Philly first learned his own arrival had been prophesied, that he himself heralded the beginning of the end of the world.

Apparently, a year had passed since Lord Bed, clairvoyant only in sleep, had delineated the more or less accurate prophecy, which itself went something like *The fifty-fifth member is a fifty-four-year-old senior director of construction in pursuit of a dream named . . . Ron . . . and his arrival shall herald the beginning of the end, the Dawn of Cockadoodledoom.* "Ron" wasn't right, obviously, but who could miss the obvious link between "Don" and "Dawn"?

The Dark made a ring around the base of Lord Bed's big rock, holding hands.

Don Philly had a front and center view of Lord Bed's face, which, because of the fire's relationship to shadows, couldn't really be made out at all. Lord Read and Lord Dead stood to Philly's left and right, respectively, gripping his hands in theirs, making his mouth itch and twitch with the unshakeable urge to be covered with both hands. He felt world-weary.

Lord Bed's penis curled and sagged in a sad little comma. Philly found his own penis repulsive, like the word *moist* made flesh. One of the last times he'd been with Marlo, well over a year ago, he seemed to recall, it'd been in the dark of the walk-in kitchen pantry, and he'd had on his head a big empty bag of Lay's potato chips, and she'd been wearing nothing but an apron, and on the blind uphill battle to climax, she'd shouted, *Go, Gordon, go!*—an incidental reference, she would later admit, to the iconic chef and cable television superstar Gordon Ramsley. Marlo was (and, for all Philly knew, remained) obsessed with all competitive cooking reality shows— *Cutthroat Kitchen, Hell's Kitchen, Chopped, Beat Bobby Filet, Iron Chef, Top Chef,* etc.—but without a doubt, her program of preference had always been the Ramsley-hosted *ChefMaster.* As soon as Philly had given Marlo the thumbs-up, meaning he sort of liked being likened to Ramsley in the bedroom or pantry or wherever, they'd enjoyed a twice-a-day sex spree that lasted well over a month, as much a turn-on for Philly as—see, but now he had the stirrings of an unfortunate hard-on. He couldn't stop picturing the time he'd walked in on Marlo masturbating to a marathon of clips of Ramsley blowing his top. Certainly at this moment, standing directly before Lord Bed and the flames, he'd do just about anything to stifle the blood flow below, so mentally he willed himself back to the bugs, how at least one had slithered down his throat into his belly and was now eating him alive inside.

"Thatta stiffy I see, Fed?" whispered Lord Read. "The hell's the matter with ya?"

"You're seeing things," said Philly.

"The hell he is," muttered Lord Dead.

"You're both just seeing things."

"The hell we are," said Lord Read.

Don Philly told them both to shut it; soon, they all knew, Lord Bed would address the congregation with his closing thoughts on the forthcoming end of the world.

Don Philly's ma made him attend Catholic mass every Sunday up until his eighteenth birthday, at which point he was free to make his own spiritual decisions. Church memories consisted of three mainstay components: standing and sitting when told, kneeling sometime near the end, and seeking out the pretty girls sprinkled here and there among the assembly. The intrusive perverted thoughts almost always ran rampant, the subsequent erections painful as puberty. He'd had to come up with a system, code-named Old Faithful: 1) Assess the potency of the problem. 2) Should a crisis be determined, pretend you've got an itch on the inner thigh and then throw your eyes to the ceiling and itch the fake itch as casually as humanly possible. 3) Quickly and subtly tuck the erection up into the elastic waistband, a skill that, like meditation via prayer, can be perfected with practice over time. 4) Press the bottom of the shaft against the edge of the pew to the point of extreme physical discomfort. 5) Picture turtles fucking. Presently Don Philly, lacking the favorable context church and clothes provide for such a crisis, had no choice but to forgo the first four steps and head straight to the turtles. It wasn't working. Lord Read and Lord Dead bickered and snickered to his left and right like devils on each shoulder.

"He rises," said Lord Bed from up high, his face a thumb of shadow.

Lord Read and Lord Dead both went dead quiet. Philly felt the tiny muscles of his mouth wiggle like things with little legs of their own. He bowed his head, the impetuous behavior of his cock a rising issue. His stomach complained of everything.

"Dearest brethren—n' Lady Watershed, 'course—I beseech y'all to see him with me," Lord Bed went on. "See him rise up and outta ashes. See his white face in the black, a globe of light at the end of the world's darkest tunnel. See him smile on farmhands across the American heartland, he who can't tell a fib, who'll without the slightest inkling of a doubt take stock of our five days and five nights' faithful sacrifice and gift us with the truth: that *we* are *worthy*. Just 'cause his voice's fulla bees don't mean we ain't got to hear what he's got to say. We do, my brothers and sister. We've got to listen."

The fornicating turtles became Brenda and Marlo kissing. Philly couldn't recall the name of his second wife, their hour-long marriage a Vegas misstep, but he saw her too. Brenda and Marlo and Nameless Vegas together on a loveseat with Gordon Ramsley flipping burgers in the background, licking his chops, asking how they liked their meat done. The Dark started shouting a bunch of stuff Don Philly, stiffening by the second, paid no attention to.

"Who's headed northeast to rep our cause?"

"Pick me! Pick me!"

"See, but I've got the quickest pig outta all of us!"

"Who among us is worthy to confront Cockadoodledoom face to face?"

"We're the forgotten ones."

"Wilbur roasted tonight, ya idjit!"

"Nuh-uh, fool! That weren't Wilbur, that was Charlotte!"

"Over here, pick me!"

"Who'll face the face of their gravest, innermost fear?"

"That right, Dead? Lookit them bones just there. See the dent in the skull?"

"*Wilbur?*"

"See, so you ain't even got the quickest pig no more."

"Me me me me me!"

"It was you, weren't it, Dred? You broke in my barn n' brought Wilbur here!"

"Who's The Chosen among us?"

"Trade war's got two sides throwin' punches n' we take all the hits."

"If that's whatchu think, then you took two caps too much, idjit."

"Yeah, well, you don't even spell 'Dread' right."

"Anyone see how Bed got on top the stool on top the chair on top the rock?"

"These days all my bacon's goin' to McDonald's. It ain't much of a livin.'"

"Fed's gotta stiffy."

"Something's the matter with him."

"We ain't just seein' things."

"The hell we ain't."

"D-R-E-D. Dred. Idjit."

"Tell ya what, it's a miracle Bed can balance up there like that."

"You're missin' an *a* in there, fool."

"Whose greatest, most deep-seated trauma shall be put on display in the Dark Room for us to relive and relearn as one body, mind, heart, and soul?"

"Wouldja quit with them goddam questions, Thread? Listen to Lord Bed!"

"Why, it ain't like Bed's the boss. Ain't nobody's gotta listen to 'im."

"I'm better off shootin' off corn cannons than takin' my crop to market."

"*ME! ME! ME!*"

"Ain't none of us here's pickin' ya, Led."

"D-R-E . . . *A*?"

"Yup, jus' like spellin' *dead.*"

"Lookit him up there. Stool ain't even a lil' bit a'wobble."

"Floods n' heat waves've pretty much roont everything for all of us."

"Who'll Lord Bed send northeast as champion of The Dark?"

"Don't much matter who's chosen, really. We all gotta die in the end."

Don Philly could feel the accretive, priapistic pressure of the blood down there. Sweat seemed to pour from his eyes the more he looked. The muscles in his mouth, like those in a mouse-trapped rat, wriggled in a rictus of restriction that barred him from being able to tell whether he was smiling or grimacing or what. Lords Read and Dead squeezed Philly's hands in their callus-hardened palms; Philly/Fed wanted his hands back to himself. Lord Bed put his own hands together as if in prayer.

Philly hadn't the slightest clue how to write about any of this, nor whether he'd get the chance to. He didn't know why he wanted to write it all down, but he did—call it kismet. Having spent a year absorbing the basic acclivities and proclivities and purviews of all these aggrieved farmers, however, he felt fairly certain the boner didn't bode well for him. One by one, The Dark shut their mouths as Lord Bed lifted his head.

"Lord Fed," said Lord Bed. "Clearly you've been chosen."

Don Philly felt every last eye boring down on one part of him.

Cockadoodledoom.

3

MR. MOONY'S WILD RIDE

(TRAUMA DRAMA)

———

CALVIN WAS NOWHERE to be found, Trent Taphor discovered as he made circles around the standpipe, and neither were there any footprints, something for which he figured only movie characters had an eye. He was hollering Calvin's name and hacking shrubs with Calvin's Captain America shield/trash lid, pausing to mutter to himself, repeating a certain voice broadcasting way too loud and too often in his head: *Anne Kell wakes, T-Bone bakes.*

Trent's hacks against nature became more impassioned by the minute with each time he intoned *wakes* and *bakes* so that he found himself in a kind of rhythmic trance. Eventually he carved out the area into a sort of clearing. His dead mother was going to let him have it if he returned to the trailer without her favorite son in tow.

The aluminum standpipe was a phallic job that came up to Trent's sternum. He'd seen Calvin rub noses with its snout of a spigot too many times to count, but the soil was dry all around, crunchy underfoot, and coarse under his patting palms. Nobody could say he wasn't trying to track down his twin, not his mother or

41

father or therapist or anyone else doing afterlife inside of Dex. Trent saw little choice but to start retracing his steps back to the RV.

Half a mile and maybe a hundred hacks later, back inside the gullet of the wood, Trent picked up a sound he'd recognize anywhere, a series of shrieks that would wallop the brain at close range. Anybody could see such shrieks were the real reason his mother had lost all focus at the wheel and ended up with her eyeball on her cheek. Calvin's screams, from this distance, sounded almost exactly the way they had through the phone. No amount of skirling wind now or shoddy cell reception then could muffle such a sound.

Calvin's muted shrieks kept coming in spurts and spasms. They weren't of the sort Calvin produced in a bratty tantrum or random outburst or whatever, but rather of the kind he emitted on certain rides at Disneyland. Trent confirmed this suspicion the closer to the source he came. He didn't do any more shouting of his own, not daring to lose the blip on the aural radar. What made the whole ordeal extra bizarre was that it sounded as though Calvin were hooting and hollering from way up in the trees, or maybe some-where—somehow—even higher. Trent kept cocking his head further back on his neck until the front of his shin slammed up against the rough-hewn bark of a fallen tree's stump, eliciting a gush of profanity to go with a dash of blood.

Trent tossed Calvin's shield aside. Rather than further and further away, Calvin's receding cry came from higher and higher up, as if he'd grown wings. Trent circled the stump in a slight hobble, noticing more than ever the pull of gravity. All was calm.

A certain life Trent hadn't noticed had been missing returned to his immediate surroundings in a triumphant influx of sight and sound, like someone turning up the brightness and volume on the world. The moments-ago-absent moonlight bucketed down the branches and boughs to illuminate droning clouds of insects and deciduous leaves and—and there it was, glistening, plastered to the side of the stump by the direction of the seething wind: the printed snapshot of Calvin and Trent at the Los Angeles Zoo. Trent had burned the photo to ash the summer preceding what was supposed to be his freshman year of college.

The slanting moonlight looked choreographed, the way it seemed to highlight the photograph, as if the Big Man in the Sky were using the moon as a giant flashlight and saying, *What've we got here, T-Bone? How about a little look-see-daisy?*

Trent dropped to his knees. He had to dig in the nail of his pointer finger to pry the picture loose from the bark, then he had himself a look at himself and Calvin and the monkeys.

That was the day Trent had learned he and his twin were different, the day he'd looked through the glass at King Louie's face and found no difference at all from Calvin's. That was the day Anne Kell first spoke up, a whispered hiss in his head, telling Trent to smash the rest of his vanilla ice cream against the glass, to blot out what he saw there on the other side. The sides of the photograph collapsed in his clench.

Something scuttled across his wrist.

Trent let go of the picture and tried squashing the big black bug on the back of his hand with his other hand, ending up smacking nothing but the back of his hand because the bug, having deftly maneuvered the smack, had made its way up and around to the safety of his palm in a mad little dash that might've been a zip of flight. It looked like no bug Trent had ever seen, a diabolical cloning-experiment-gone-wrong cross between a tick and a leech, with the spidery legs of the former and the overall sluggy shape and feel of the latter. Add in the chitinous wings and the hard carapace shell and suddenly Trent realized he had himself, right in the palm of his hand, what he presumed to be a never-before-identified species of insect, a complete and utter anomaly probably worth big bucks. He felt its little muscles churn when it buzzed, and its heat.

"Hi there, little guy."

Trent lost himself in its eyes—it *did* have eyes, he saw, beady little ones on long skinny stalks he'd at first mistaken for antennae. But then who was to say he was mistaken? Calvin, out of sight, couldn't be further from mind.

"What's *your* name?"

"Zzzzzz."

"How about Beetlejuice?"

"ZZZ."

"BJ for short."

The wings flickered and settled as the feeler-eyes scissored back and forth. The legs recoiled, tucking back inside the tubular body like the wheels of an airplane in the moments after takeoff, leaving Trent with what looked like a winged, hard-shelled slug. He covered up the bug, protecting it with both hands, leaving an airhole just in case.

"Let's get you home."

The decision to leave Calvin's shield and photograph behind was made on an unconscious level. Any and all Calvin-related thoughts had vacated Trent's head much the way all five thousand Berkshireites had emptied out the past few weeks—and for what? A loud breeze? A teeny-weeny tornado? Bunch of bums, Berkshire. Trent appreciated Beetlejuice for its courage to remain content in his cupped palms. BJ showed none of the primal anxiety the stink beetle in the janitor's closet of Crest High had in its choice to play dead all those years ago.

Trent would do what he could to care for this one.

"Welcome home," Trent told BJ, mounting the steps of the RV.

———

CALVIN'S YELLING *Weeeee!* at the top of his lungs, soaring above the clouds under the stars on the back of a flying black horse, which for reasons linked to Mr. Moony's physiological makeup—Bod, namely—doesn't require a saddle, since Bod's bugs give Mr. Moony the ability to hold fast to Calvin's jiggling thighs so that he doesn't slip away or slide off or fling back or otherwise dismount in any way. Calvin's having the time of his life.

His cheeks wobble from the speed as the wind whaps through his hair, filling his mouth and lungs with its icy power. He's had both arms raised high the whole time for every dip and dive, for every sudden climb or decline in pace or elevation, a childhood trick Trent taught him during their visits to Disneyland meant to maximize overall levels of amusement. The backs of Calvin's shoulders are numb from all the redirected blood flow, something he hasn't given a moment's thought. It's hard to think much of anything when the stars seem close enough to touch.

Weeeee.

Calvin only stops yelling in the brief moments his body remembers for him to collect the oxygen necessary to keep alive. He doesn't know it, but he's in dangerous need of food and drink, his empty belly turning constant somersaults, his bone-dry tongue splayed to the side of his cheek, flailing, reaching for the slightest nourishment of condensation within the tops of the stewing clouds below.

Calvin's blissful ignorance regarding the escalating drop of his body's wired will to live alters at the sight and sound of a Boeing 747 rising up through the clouds, the emergence of its great snout like the merciless, unfeeling face of a great white shark to an unsuspecting diver with nowhere to go. Its engine roared like an earthquake massive enough to rock the solar system, to knock the earth right off its orbital axis. Coming face-to-face with an airplane makes Calvin more aware on a primitive level of the smallness of his own body, though it's his body that takes care of all the required reactions vital to promoting survival—his arms come flopping down, his mouth clamps shut. The plane's wings look scary and dragon-like in the mighty moonlight.

Calvin stoops his shoulders to duck, pressing the bottom of his chin to the horse's brawny neck, around which he wraps his arms, squeezing with all his everlasting might. His unprotected eyes burn with tears birthed from the lashing air. His clogged ears seem too heavy for his head. Bod's eely, oily flesh has a sickening stench and brings none of the warmth nor comfort of fur.

The plane's thunder pummels the world of the sky.

Then comes the world-flipping, sense-demolishing drop, a total skydiver's free fall, which happens because all the bugs composing Mr. Moony's current form scatter and disperse, a billion black blots whizzing every which way, leaving Calvin to cope with the obvious consequence stated above, described further here: Calvin vaults and cartwheels over and over on his isolated descent to the clouds, tumbling and turning, the world whirling and rolling too fast for him to even come close to registering even the most basic stuff like nausea or panic or the awareness of himself plunging to certain splattery death. All too quickly his body wises up and takes care of what little self-preservation it can, spreading the arms and legs, making Calvin not so much into a shooting star as a plummeting starfish. This helps keep both himself and the world steady as he faces down both the plane and the plain of clouds rushing up.

Here he is reminded of Indiana Bones, not the movie or Harrison Lord (the first of which Calvin hasn't actually seen; the second, interestingly enough, he came across in his hometown at Jamba Juice maybe four years back, an unwitting encounter that only served to startle and perplex because he couldn't seem to figure out why so many people in the shop were getting out their phones and pointing them at some rugged meanie who looked like he was trying super hard to avoid eye contact with pretty much everyone except maybe Calvin, whose job at the time was to hold open the door and say "Welcome to Jamba Juice!" when people came in and "Have a nice day!" when they left. It was a job he cherished for all the cheerful pretty girls and refreshing perks but ended up having to abandon a couple weeks after the car accident, after Trent went and burned their whole house down, which, like three hours later, was when Trent, face still sooty with ash, snagged Calvin by the collar and dragged him across the driveway and all but flung him inside their father's stepfather's icky trailer, saying, "Time to find a new home, bud") or the fictional character Lord portrays, but rather Calvin's reminded of the Indiana Bones Adventure Ride, his favorite attraction at Disneyland. He's specifically reminded of the ride's haunting climax when the big rolling boulder threatens to crush you before the cart jerks and lurches and drops you on down through some trapdoor in the nick of time, a situation not all that different in direness from the scaling 747, now less than half a heartbeat away from pulverizing Calvin much the way a swatting palm takes out a mosquito—smack, then oblivion.

It turns out the overwhelming size of the aircraft has played all kinds of tricks on Calvin's already compromised proprioception—

the plane passes way above, deafening as God. The protracted ringing in his ears mutates to a chintzy crackling as he primes himself for the pillowy comfort of the clouds he doesn't know isn't coming. At the moment of non-impact impact, the world turns to white ice that hurts his eyes.

It's cold in the cloud, the amalgamated mist and vapor blinding, a sort of sensual quasi-reenactment of what Calvin just now subliminally recalls perceiving during the car crash in the seconds after impact, making this split second in the cloud a time for his subconscious to sift through one of the traumas it works overtime to, by definition, submerge beneath his conscious mind. The layer of thicker, icier air inside the cloud generates a loud whistling hiss that can be associated with the sound of someone in the shower screaming at the sight of a spider, but as heard from a distance, so that the faint screaming mingles with the rush of running water. This is the closest conception of what Calvin heard in the moments after the crash, after the window or whatever thumped his head and knocked him out cold. The all-encompassing white mass is the same now as then and just as long-lasting, because all at once he's out of the cloud.

The earth maybe twenty thousand feet below isn't as Calvin remembered—there's no forest or farmland or rolling hills or airport or ocean or any sign of civilization. Every last mile of terrain looks jagged and volcanic, a sprawling smoker's lung of landscape.

Tall pinkish cranes dominate most of the malicious atmosphere; they look like giant flamingos banging their mechanical beaks again and again against the rocky surface. Maybe five thousand feet above what would've been the site of Calvin's splattery death, something comes ramming up into his belly and chest, slamming some air from his lungs, and suddenly, instead of falling, he's moving forward at a smooth, humming glide.

It appears Mr. Moony and his reassembled bugs have returned for Calvin, whose heart swells with the hyper-adrenalized gratitude that comes with unexpected survival. Mr. Moony voices his astonishment with respect to the technological developments of modern man, having never before seen an airplane in this world, he tells Calvin. Mr. Moony's word for "airplane" differs from Calvin's, though, which creates all kinds of frustration for one party in particular.

"Look, Calvin, it's been 252 million years since I last took the time to really buckle down and examine your Earth. Obviously, a lot has changed since then, the least of which being the advent of what appears to have been an actual flying Zlokmatoog. What I'm trying to say, I suppose, is that I wasn't expecting that—the Zlokmatoog, I mean. I'll admit it freaked me out some. I suppose, then, I should apologize for dropping you like that, though I wouldn't really mean it, assuming you know what I mean."

"Weeeee!" Calvin takes no time to consider why Mr. Moony's normally buzz-filled language suddenly rings loud and clear; it isn't like Mr. Moony has his horse-neck twisted 180 degrees while Bod does a number on Calvin's eyelids so that their eyes lock in a way that permits telepathic exchange. Calvin equates the strange new scenery to the special effects present in Disneyland attractions. He's got zero trepidation in the psychic tank.

"Let's do that *again!*"

"You mean you're not mad?" asks Mr. Moony.

"Trent says to hold up your arms like *this!*"

"You seriously don't have any questions?"

"Can we do that again?"

"I meant about where you are or why I've brought you here or what you'll be doing in that facility down there for the next ten-odd years?"

"Woo! I'm hungry!"

"You mean to say you don't want me clarifying anything regarding what your kind calls the Permian-Triassic extinction event, also known as the P-Tr extinction, or the P-T extinction or End-Permian Extinction, or, in other, more poignant words, the Great Dying that took place on the single landmass that once comprised your Earth 252 million years ago? Or how that admittedly grisly event relates to what's going on now?"

"I'm *dying* of hunger!"

"So if I'm picking up what you're putting down, then, in addition to a little bit *but not a lot of* food, you'd prefer the omission of many secrets and details of the galactically complicated mystery constituting the Great Dying? That your kind has arrogantly and ignorantly boiled down the most recent Apocalypse of all life on Earth to meteor showers and worldwide volcanic eruptions and methane-releasing microbes?"

"What's 'a-mission'?"

"Means you'd rather not hear my deeply complex backstory about where I'm from, which is where you are and also what I'm about. That you'd sit up there with your arms raised like that rather than hear me out and see I'm not the cruel beast your kind makes me out to be in this Bible I keep hearing so much about. How even though I'm under contract to get the ball rolling on Earth's pending Apocalypse, it doesn't mean I'm such a bad being. We'll keep cruising if you want, and I'll tell you why you're here and what you'll be doing until eventually you'll see that what I'm planning to do with your world is not only necessary but *good* for 'man-so-called-kind.' I'll tell tales about all the folks I've helped along the way throughout Earth's eye-blink history, particularly the farmers and laborers and unjustly impoverished. How I never once told a lie, how I always did my darndest to warn them when a warning was what they most needed but perhaps in the end never deserved—particularly when I gifted man with gold. How even at one point I had Mother Climate Herself persuaded that gold equaled goodness simply because I *believed* you people would do right by it. And how I've rooted for you this whole time, in spite of any number of occasions I had to go to bat on your behalf."

"Gold's Trent's favorite color."

"Figures."

"Mine's blue!"

"You don't even want to know *what* I am?"

"Earth's old friend," Calvin recalls.

"I'm a pooka," says Mr. Moony. "And all this you see is part of Phooka Road: the land inside the ashes. Ashes can be found pretty much all over the multiverse, in all different forms and formulas, meaning from here you can get pretty much everywhere all over the multiverse. But if you want to get here from Earth, you've either got to burn to ash or consent to a fun, free ride on my back, which, if you'll recall, is precisely what you did, the ride. You *could* use *Urechis caupo* to get around, but that'd be a bit . . . unconventional. Now, with the *how* of your presence here good and covered, shall I begin with the *why*?"

". . ."

"I'll take your silence as permission to go on, but first let me make myself clear."

Calvin's beginning to take stock of their gradual descent to a long, low building that looks for all the world like a deserted train that goes on forever.

"The reason I'd like to cover the *why* of your being here has less to do with my apparent concern for your wellbeing—the extent to which I care for you, by the way, more or less matches your potential to contribute to the Super Substance, as I'll discuss at length momentarily—than it does with my admittedly selfish aching desire not to feel gross or guilty about any of this anymore. I'm a virtuous being by nature, see, though the price I pay for immortality equals my debt to the multiverse. Which is to say I've no choice but to clean out the gunk when and where said gunk's present. Presently your Earth's chock-full of it, the gunk, which in turn helps generate quite the interdimensional cancer. My people can hardly breathe anymore."

Calvin's head lolls to one side. He's crashing from all the excitement, seeing a different cut of steak each time his eyes sag shut.

Mr. Moony says, "So let's talk Super Substance."

But Calvin is passed out and dead to the strange new world. By the time he wakes, he finds himself all alone in a dark room not unlike a barren walk-in closet, with a cut of charred meat on a dirty plate in the corner. The meat looks suspiciously like a baby monkey and smells even worse than the bowl of brown water next to it.

When he starts screaming, it isn't *Weeeee.*

———

Don Philly's conception of time and space ceased to bear any semblance of meaning or value or place in the universe as he felt himself being lifted up by the arms and legs and tossed up and over the railing of somebody's truck bed, maybe Lord Dead's. He was peaking so immensely and psychedelically on PY, 4-phosphoryloxy-N, N-dimethyltryptamine, a.k.a. psilocybin, a.k.a. magic mushrooms, a.k.a. the nuggets of fungi picked and parsed from cow poop, that he'd forgotten he'd ingested 5.5 grams of said psychoactive substance, reducing him to a state of total naked vulnerability at what would soon prove to be the worst possible time to be in said state. The Dark had packed up and loaded the trucks and were now leaving the woods in droves, heading on back to Point Reyes, their destination a tiny theater in town Lord Bed had been saving up for months to rent out. Lord Bed had been talking up the ceremony to come for weeks; he called the theater "The Dark Room" and the ceremony "Trauma Drama."

Philly, a.k.a. Lord Fed, a.k.a. The Chosen, spent the five-mile trip back to town bouncing and jouncing in back on his back, staring at the stars that finally appeared in the sky after however many hours of absence due to thick forest and bright firelight. It was one hell of a ride as the stars swirled together to reflect demonic versions of whomever was on Philly's mind, be it his current wife, Marlo, or original wife Brenda or the gal from Vegas or Gordon Ramsley prepping a meal for all three, seasoning mountains of meat with spit that foamed from his fanged, demonically altered mouth.

By the time the truck pulled up in the lot behind the theater, there were too many tears in Philly's eyes—no matter how much he blinked or wiped or thought happy thoughts, the tears just kept coming. He could do nothing except swallow the salt.

A little less than half of The Dark had turned up at Lord Bed's ranch last week late Sunday night, cramming into the second floor of the stable loft, where they passed around a top hat and put folded sheets of paper inside. Scrawled on these sheets in great detail were what they each considered to be the face of his or her "gravest fear." These could be phobias, like coulrophobia or arachnophobia, or nightmares in which clowns made of spiders cackled and spun webs under your bed, or even hard memories of handsy uncles or over-prescribed moms or perfectly normal dads minus that one time you caught him doing something strange you'd rather not discuss and haven't managed to forget. Philly had been there, of course, as a matter of course—the next great American novel wasn't going to research itself.

Don Philly had written about Beatrice Betsy and Lyle.

The point of the top hat had been, essentially, to nominate oneself to become what Philly became earlier tonight: The Chosen. Since he'd become The Chosen—champion of The Dark who would travel northeast in pursuit of Cockadoodledoom—what he had written of Beatrice Betsy and Lyle was about to become frighteningly relevant. Soon, The Dark would take the stage in The Dark Room and put Philly's submission on full display, bringing his words to life in a full-blown reenactment while Philly, bound with rope at the ankles and wrists and gagged and peaking (5.5 grams) insanely, would be subjected to the daunting task of having to relive what Beatrice Betsy had put him through on a weekly basis as a toddler not out of diapers. The Dark could then live what Philly lived and learn what Philly learned and thus merge as one mind and body and heart and soul. This, then, would grant him the spiritual vigor needed to leave The Dark and Point Reyes behind, to confront Cockadoodledoom face-to-face, and to go it all alone.

Lady Red had been in charge of wrangling any number of outfits to match every possible traumatic sequence or scenario given up to the top hat since she had a second cousin down in Silicon Valley with a gargantuan mansion whose garage was thrice the size of Lady Red's barn, its entire second floor stocked with racks and troves of costumes and gear and the like. The traumatic scenario Philly had submitted to the top hat called for bucket hats, sunglasses, sunscreen, and whistles. Not everyone got to throw on everything, though there was plenty of sunscreen to go around, one smeary dollop for every nose.

Don Philly's arms and legs were now being bound, his mouth gagged with a sock.

Philly's estranged sister, Michelle, was five years his senior. By the time Philly popped out of Ma's womb, Michelle already had her heart set on becoming an Olympic silver-medal (her first favorite color before she transitioned and realized she could have it all with rainbow) swimmer. Beatrice Betsy, at the time in her early sixties and "retired," had taught the Philly children to swim and was the source of Michelle's passion for the pool.

Beatrice Betsy also happened to be the bane of Don Philly's early existence.

Probably red flag numero uno had been Betsy's number one rule to parents with the same worries as Ma, that they had to drop their kids off and vacate the premises, that they couldn't stick around to snap a picture or cheer their child on or come anywhere near the pool, which was Betsy's and only Betsy's dominion. Betsy's second rule, more of a formality, was that she'd call when the kiddies were ready for pickup. Her teaching philosophy was "sink or swim," which was why Lyle—a swarthy, muscular, always-oiled-to-the-bone early-twenties lifeguard—was always present at poolside for those inevitable moments the need for CPR arose.

She had *Betsy is the Best in the Business* tattooed on her inner bicep.

No matter how much little Donny wailed and thrashed and flailed, Beatrice Betsy would hitch him by the ankles and haul him to the edge of the Olympic pool, where Lyle, having rubbed himself down and dolloped sunscreen on his nose and slapped on some shades, would be whirling like a lasso the whistle little Donny never once heard the lifeguard blow.

Philly's memories of this bucket-hatted woman and her ways had become his first memories of anything, and though they might not be the most credible, accuracy-wise, given he'd only been breathing six months and walking for one, they remained the most damaging, seared and immortalized on his then quite fragile hippocampus. Suffice it to say Beatrice Betsy had done a number on Philly's development; he'd written down his first and worst memories for The Dark not because he harbored any real desire to become The Chosen, but because he'd figured it was high time to face his fears and unpack emotions he'd long buried and suppressed.

Thank God for paper and pen.

Presently Lord Dred and Lord Dead hoisted up the now fully bound and gagged Philly by the neck and heels of his feet, respectively, and were working him into place center stage. They shoved the sides of his immobilized limbs so that he squeezed into the standing open coffin propped against a leftover stage prop that, due to a crappy paint job, only loosely resembled a bookshelf. The standing coffin's base took up half of the chalk-drawn circle indicating the exact spot on the floor the coffin was supposed to go, indicating The Dark's inability to follow directions under the hallucinatory constraints of the drug they were all peaking on.

They all crowded the wings as if waiting for some sort of sign.

Lord Bed's hooded face filled the tiny square window above the last row of seats at the back of the theater. He shot everyone a thumbs-up, and then the lights dimmed.

Snakes of filmy blue light filtered from everywhere, squiggling throughout the theater's inner walls, providing a woozy illusion of being at the bottom of a moonlit pool. A Deluxe Inflatable Family Pool purchased off Walmart's website was tugged and pulled from behind the red curtain into place, stage middle, directly in front of Philly and his ever-widening eyes and ever-ascending eyebrows. How Lord Bed had known they'd need the kiddy pool at all remained unclear, though what *was* clear and well understood was that now was not the time to ask.

Lady Watershed had filled the pool with the hose out back. She still had the hose on her person, looped over her shoulder. She stood to the side of the pool like a cowgirl with her lasso, like Lyle with his whistle. Out of all members of the Dark, her sunburn burned brightest.

Members of The Dark who'd managed to snag a bucket hat from the box lined up behind the pool, facing Philly, raising their right arms in triumphant curls, looking like participants in a body-building competition flexing for an audience of one. Philly couldn't make out what they'd scribbled with black Magic Marker on their inner biceps, but he knew. He tried to thrash, but he couldn't: the coffin's clenching sides held him hopelessly confined. Meanwhile more members of The Dark, these guys and gals sporting shades and blood-red trunks and creamy dollops of lotion on their noses, took their places on either side of the pool, whirling their whistles overhead. Around and around their whistles went, whirring in the watery light. The sock tasted like doom in Philly's throat and smelled wickeder than the wet panic pouring out his every pore.

Lord Read, dressed all in black, strolled out from the wings bearing an Ambu Baby CPR Manikin bought off Amazon with a hefty stone tied with twine around one tiny ankle. Everyone began chanting in unison what was written on all their inner biceps. Philly tried turning his head from Lord Read, who was lifting the toddler dummy high above his own unobstructed head. The coffin's obstructive borders pinched in on Philly's temples like forceps on a stubborn zit, giving not an inch of wiggle room. The resultant denied head-thrash resulted for Philly in a painful twinge in the interstices of his neck, an audible snap and crackle like the sound of sparks dying to darkness. The lassoing whistles made thin wisps of sound.

Lord Dred's apparently exhausted left arm dipped an inch, and he lost control of the centrifugal force of his whistle, which whipped around and whapped him right in the eyeball, a meaty *ca-chunk*, followed by a strangled cry that emerged at the same time everyone else was chanting *best*. Lord Read knelt down with his head bowed, offering up the motionless mannequin to a bucket-hatted Lord Dead, who, with a sadistic sort of smile, wrenched the dummy from Lord Read and dragged it back and forth on the stage long enough for the tenderest sectors of Philly's brain to soak up the scrape and squeak of durable plastic on hardwood. Lord Dead then used the stone and the leverage of the twine to mimic the whirling action of everyone with a whistle. The general shape of Lord Dead's motion, still circular, resembled more of a rolling wheel than a frisbee in flight, gathering speed and awesome momentum, until finally Lord Dead launched Ambu the dummy high enough to elude Philly's angle of sight before it came flipping and tumbling back down, hitting the center of the subtly deflating kiddy pool with a sort-of-quiet toddler-sized splash. The chanting ceased. The rafters rang with echoes.

Lord Dead—a Beatrice Betsy—instructed Lord Dred—a Lyle now being forced to cut short the process of nursing a budding black eye—to dive in and "fetch lil' Donny from the deep." Philly watched Ambu's bubbles collapse into themselves.

All the while, Philly found himself reliving a ton of moments of splashing and sinking and swallowing, how he'd felt something like serenity at the secluded shallow-end floor of Beatrice Betsy's pool, in the quiet peace that followed all the panic and pain, trying and failing to track the dappled sunrays squiggling the walls on every side like snakes of light. The water inside and outside himself rang, a static whine, before suddenly he'd come to with Lyle's mouth on his mouth, with two of Lyle's fingers press-pumping his tiny sternum. Before little Donny could so much as consider shouting for help or fleeing or even weeping, it was back into the wet jaws of the water, where, after more splashing and swallowing, he'd sink back into the serene, pain-free stillness of the secluded surface of the shallow-end floor.

Lord Dred, Philly now observed, took his sweet-ass time getting into the kiddy pool, moving with a slow and untroubled sort of ease before slipping beneath the surface like a stalking Florida gator. It seemed like a long time before Lord Dred came up with Ambu, whom he tossed up and over and out. The stone came banging down first.

Lord Dred got out of the pool, pawing at his injured eye, and then sank to his knees and got down to work on "lil' Donny." He palpated Ambu's motionless form and put his mouth on Ambu's mouth and performed mock cardiopulmonary resuscitation, pumping the sternum with two strategically stiff fingers, a series of mechanical *clunkety-clunks* that went on until Lord Bed, still just a silhouette in the tiny back window, signaled his satisfaction with a double-tap flicker of the stage lights. Don Philly, at this point (e)motionless, felt dead in his coffin.

It wasn't until Don Philly/Lord Fed/The Chosen finished viewing every last Lyle repeat Lord Dred's dreadful song and dance that Philly arrived at a moment of astounding crystal-clarity of the kind that didn't always come with hallucinogenic psychoactive substances. This rather sudden, awe-inspiring realization rocked him to the core of his core and made him question everything he'd always held to be self-evident or true or real, and what Philly realized was this: maybe Lyle wasn't real and never had been; maybe he'd made Lyle the lifeguard up.

The idea made some serious sense. Don Philly, after all, was a born writer—he liked to make things up. It therefore made sense if Lyle was just one cloud of fiction in a brewing storm designed to change America for "the better," to get at whatever it means to be human in a world Philly had good reason to believe was well on its way out the door. The only really compelling question that remained here was whether the world or America itself would be first to bow out.

Or: maybe he'd made up Lyle the lifeguard because he hadn't been able to handle a reality in which a Lyle didn't exist. Maybe he hadn't been able to suffer the knowledge of the abuse he'd suffered at the hands of Beatrice Betsy, that all along he'd been alone in his misery and there'd never been anyone anywhere to dive into the deep and save him.

What lifeguard never blew his whistle?

This innermost question sent Philly off the deep end, so to speak, so that he was cackling and crying and losing a ton of air because of the sock shoved way back deep in his throat all this time. The suffocating irony wasn't lost on the ex-senior director of construction, the unpublished writer with an American Dream, the incidental cultist turned The Chosen, gagging on someone's sweat-soaked sock as he choked on the tears of his own laughter. The stage seemed to waver like water as he wept for Ambu. Michelle had been a really good person. Philly hadn't spoken with her since after Ma and Pa's joint funeral, where she hadn't shown.

Lord Bed's voice, amplified by one super spiffy sound system, projected from everywhere, big as God: "The Trauma Drama's *done!* We've *won!* The Dark is *one!*"

Don Philly, limp in the coffin, had been dead five, now maybe six seconds.

4

THE PLAY DAY HOUSE
(GLASSFUL OF GALAXY)

Don Philly ended the call and chucked his phone across the decrepit motel room, where it clinked off the dusty TV screen and hit the shag carpet soundlessly. He lay back on the bed with heavy eyes, totally gut-wrenched. Not even his mouth's twitchy muscles were moving anymore.

He let his eyes sag the way they wanted, waiting for his phone to vibrate again, a telltale *zzz* that wouldn't come. It'd been too long since he'd last eaten, and it wasn't like psychedelic mushrooms were known for their nutritional value. He tossed and turned for maybe an hour, unable to sleep, afraid he might not wake, afraid he wanted to sleep for that same reason.

Philly made it back to the motel a few hours ago, had figured to give his dear young wife a call prior to his daily nap preceding his noon shift at the motel's front desk. He'd tried getting Marlo to ask him what it was like, being dead, figuring he'd remember himself as soon as she asked, which she never did. He still wondered if he wasn't yet fully sober.

He kept rubbing the wet from his parted lips, pressing the back

58

of his hand hard against his mouth again and again, but the wet kept coming, soaking into the skin. He had a seemingly limitless supply of slobber, which seemed odd and borderline impossible given he hadn't hydrated in what felt like a hundred years. He attributed this strange bodily anomaly to being resurrected via CPR. Thank God for Lady Watershed.

He'd just ended things with Marlo on the call, unofficially. He'd done his best to recount for her last night's events—the best and worst of his life—and she wouldn't listen. Marlo didn't seem to care to hear about his adventures at all, even *after* he got all excited about next steps, his plans to pursue the weather event he'd witnessed first-hand. Last night, he had himself convinced the tornado-thingy was a bunch of flying bugs, that he'd even swallowed one whole. Of course, in reality, he must've been hallucinating . . .

"Last night you screamed you love this bitch *Brenda*," Marlo had said on the call, referring to their previous phone call during The Dark's sacrificial pyre in the woods.

After that they were shouting, calling each other names. At some point Marlo name-dropped Gordon Ramsley, which only left Philly as perplexed as when Marlo first picked up the phone to begin with, saying she was in the middle of ordering a service called "who-loo" or whatever. Only now did he realize he might've caught her during an episode of *ChefMaster*, that she'd been condemning contestants on TV, not Philly, that their marriage had unofficially ended thanks to good old miscommunication. This would certainly explain those suggestive moans of hers interspersing their heated slights . . .

At least Philly was left with enough material to start his book, maybe enough for a middle. He knew he had to focus on the path forward, to begin the hunt for his ending.

"I'm a writer," he tried persuading the empty bedroom. "Am I still in love with Brenda?" The wallpaper here was very late '70s, he thought, whatever that meant.

"Oh, Brenda, are you still jumping out of airplanes?" What it meant was the wallpaper of this motel room reminded him of the wallpaper of the motel room in which he'd first made love to Brenda, when he was thirteen, and she was twenty-six.

"Do you still read over my old essays?" It was grungy and yellow, the wallpaper, like the wallpaper in that one story about the yellow wallpaper that drives the lead character—a woman—insane in a room in which she's held confined against her will, Philly seemed to recall.

"It's not fair, what they tried to do to you the second they found us. I mean, we were *married.*" The story was Charlotte Perkins Gilman's "The Yellow Wallpaper." Don Philly once wrote an essay on it for Brenda's class. He'd gone to a very upscale, very reputable private school in central Ohio, where he grew up.

"We were *happy.*" She'd given him an A-plus on the essay, on the back of which she'd written: *You were BORN to write!* This was before she'd started commenting stuff like *Excellent prose, stud* or *You're going to change the world someday, studmuffin* or *Keep working this hard, dreamboat, and your every dream will come to pass* or *See me after class—ALL of me xoxo* or the one presently alive and burning in Philly's mind: *Don't forget, tonight's Monkey Night at the motel. Bring the handcuffs I've left in your desk. Don't worry, they're for me. Expect brandy, "smoking hot" literary trivia, and the night of your life. I love you forever and ever, babe.*

"I'm a writer," he reminded the empty room. "But I guess now I'm alone."

It wasn't moving, but he covered his mouth anyway, with both hands.

———

THERE'S no such thing as a night of sleep aboard the Pain Train of Phooka Road, or so a fellow significant named Hanky has just informed Calvin Taphor; though, says Hanky, something happens at the end of each day that *replaces* sleep—something all can remember experiencing but none can precisely remember, sequence-of-events-wise—and Hanky and the rest of the sigs have been plotting for years during the endless hours toiled away at the Play Day House to solve the mystery, no matter how many of them are given up to The Spider as a dual form of punishment and ultimate excommunication. The Play Day House, massive, spherical, dimly lit, sits under a high-domed ceiling at the nexus of the Pain Train. Everything from the gigantic slides to the hulking jungle gyms to the antigravity seesaws is covered in night-black and blood-red foam, the literal skeletal framework underneath mended not with pipes or metal or wood but fused bone of every size and shape and proportion. A vast gray expanse of ash crumbles to the will of feet. The ceiling, says Hanky, has been painted with the detail and ambition of Michelangelo, except with too-many-limbed monsters sporting jackets of human flesh, flames with faces, and a grotesque backdrop of a jagged terrain of worm-sucked skulls. Hanky has opined it is unlike any image any one person except one person has ever seen, that person being Ozzy Oddborne, that image being whatever it is the Oz sees inside his own head. High open shafts leading in and out of the room honeycomb walls of twisted copper. Everything reeks of burnt cigar. There are no windows anywhere.

Hanky pushes Calvin on a gossamer swing in the slightly cooler "shade" of a jungle gym the shape of an hourglass, fifty-five meters in height and length and width, like all the other "time-themed" structures. Nothing Hanky has said has made any sense to Calvin, a fact the fleshy man-child routinely acknowledges, typically followed with cryptically confusing remarks like *Give it time and you'll get it* or *We've all been in your place* or *One day you'll just sort of wake up to it all.* The other significants seem to be playing tag—that's what they want "Old Boogey" (Mr. Moony, to Calvin) to see in case he's watching— but really their play has been choreographed, their every step and shout carefully coded, a coordinated effort to swap notes regarding even the faintest glimmers of what they can almost feel they remember from the previous night of "sleep." This process of "play" has taken years to develop and practice and perfect. Presently, Hanky's explaining to Calvin why Hanky's taken it upon himself to "take you under my wing," a phrase from which Calvin fails to glean any accurate meaning.

"You fly like Mr. Moony?"

"I mean, like, you know, like, show you the ropes."

Calvin tugs the gauzy webbing holding the swing in suspension. "*This* rope?"

"What I'm trying to say is—I'm sorry, Calvin. You're the first sig to arrive in over a decade—ten years, I mean—and, like, I can barely remember what that was like. That's a lie. I can't remember one little bit what that was like. Coming here, I mean."

"Where's Mr. Moony?"

"No idea, guy. None of us ever really know. Old Boogey could be here, up over there, or anywhere. Point is, I—I want to be your friend through this process. Scratch that last part—I want to be your friend. Will you be my friend, Calvin?"

"*YEAH*, BABY!"

"Awesome." They bump fists, a habit of Hanky's. "And here's why I want to be your friend. Can I tell you why I want to be your friend?"

". . ."

". . ."

"Who's the best superhero?" Calvin finally says.

"You mean my favorite?"

". . ."

"Is this some sort of test or something?" Hanky stills Calvin by gripping the vertical strands of interwoven cobweb, both of which travel up and into oozy pods budding from the overhanging bar's blackened foam. "Are you gauging my aptitude for friendship based on my affinity for superheroes—or perhaps one in particular?"

The pods above remind Calvin of the innards of this gray mush ball thingy he saw Trent hack to bits with a hammer one summer in the backyard. Calvin watched it all through his bedroom window upstairs, and up until his brother started dancing, whapping and waving his arms at nothing at all, Calvin had thought Trent looked like Thor. Never once has Calvin associated the memory with Trent's hatred of honey and all things bees.

All sorts of memories have flooded in since Calvin came to this morning.

"Scratch everything I just said," says Hanky. "I know what I'm saying doesn't make sense right now, but trust me, it will. Sooner or later it will. I guess what I meant was—like . . . well, who's *your* favorite superhero?"

Calvin turns in his seat, raises a fist, and does a voice. "*CAPTAIN AMERICA!*"

"Yeah, he's pretty cool," Hanky concurs with a terrible grin.

The grin's terrible because when Hanky smiles, his cheeks, rather than rise or stiffen or do anything cheeks do with the pertinent muscles activated, sag in meatless flaps of flesh that hang just below throat level. Hanky's aspect in this moment has achieved a level of grotesquery that manages to frighten even Calvin, who's been keeping his brother's bloodlust secret since high school, who's known about the ice chest with the severed heads of five small animals in it since this morning, when it just sort of . . . dawned on him.

"I dig the captain's backstory, for sure, but if I'm going to level with you—if I'm going to be honest, I mean—I mean, if I'm going to tell you the truth—I've really got to say I'm more of a DC dude myself," says Hanky. "Batman's my guy."

Hearing and vaguely recognizing Hanky's difference in opinion rouses Calvin to another surging thunderclap of memory, this memory his very worst—but also one of his best because if things went another way (any other way, he's now confronting), he wouldn't be alive today, and life's good, and it was by stating this belief aloud that Calvin was allowed to live. It happened six years ago. He was on his knees counting to ten with his eyes closed, back turned to Trent. The presence of Trent's pocketknife, which meant nothing to Calvin then, now means everything as the truth suddenly surges.

Trent used a bowl Calvin had molded from clay in pottery class to scoop out the organs of every last furry and/or feathered victim. The bowl itself was a surprise birthday gift from Calvin one year. When Calvin fostered the courage to try to put a stop to it all and confront Trent, citing screams he heard in his sleep, dreams of cats and frogs beaten and bloody and burning, Trent denied any wrongdoing and went about his gruesome business. This all came to a head at the end of the year when Trent told Calvin to meet upstairs in Trent's room after supper—sloppy joes that night, Calvin's favorite—where Calvin went and waited. At last Trent came in carrying the bowl in which the pre-triggered blade of a pocketknife gleamed beside a framed photograph Calvin has since held in his head and heart like a movie of memory.

"Do you mind squatting down on your knees?" Trent said. "Right here in the light? Thanks, buddy. Now turn around and bow your head. I want to play a game. You're going to close your eyes and count to ten, then when you get to ten, you'll open them."

"Then what, then what!" Calvin cried, clapping.

"Then I'm going to give *you* a surprise."

Calvin, eyes shut already, asked Trent if they'd ever get another chance to go see King Louie and the monkeys, and before Trent could reply, Calvin doubled down, asking if he should go ahead and start counting. It became Trent's turn to ask Calvin a question, to which Calvin, empowered by forces unseen and unexplainable then, as now, gave his reply.

"We're *all* different. But that's okay. It's what makes life cool! We all get to see things in different ways, and so the world ticks and ticks and ticks and we sit back and make surprises for each other and play games and eat food and sing and cry and laugh. That's why it's great to be alive! We all die, though. That makes us all sort of the same."

After a silence, Trent told Calvin to start counting. On ten, Calvin's eyes came open to the sight of the brown bowl on the edge of Trent's bed, the framed photograph faced up, the pocketknife vanished with its murderous meaning.

Calvin faces Hanky now and repeats what Trent once asked. "Are we different?"

"That's sort of what I've been trying to *say*, guy. It's why we're going to be friends. Given time, we'll be good friends—*best* friends. I suppose in many ways—maybe even most—we're . . . sort of the same. See, we're both Downers."

"Down syndrome?"

"Right, exactly!"

"You and Batman?"

"No, I'm—I'm talking about me and *you.*"

Hanky holds out a fist that Calvin leaves hanging. Calvin's got a real feeling he's being made fun of. "Meanie," he says, and then he takes off running.

"No, come back! You don't get it yet!" Calvin hears, putting in some distance, electing to ignore Hanky's hurtful, perplexing talk.

If not for Down syndrome, Calvin likely would have superseded Trent as an athlete. There's a reason Coach Burger asked him to kick a PAT for the Spartans all those years ago, which occurred during practice one day after school after the quarterback overthrew a ball that just so happened to clank off the top of the chain-link bar at just the right angle and velocity so that it bounded up and into the bleachers a few rows down from where Calvin sat watching, bouncing his knees, waiting to meet up with Trent before Mommy and/or Daddy picked them up after work at half past five. Calvin scooted down the steps and scooped up the ball, but his arm strength couldn't make the distance to Burger's troops milling beyond the encircling track on which cheerleaders bobbed and bopped and painted Calvin's cheeks rose-red between whistles. He opted for kicking it back, aping the rigmarole of the punter—who for several minutes had had Burger screaming, tearing out what little hair he had on both sides of his scalp—holding the football straight out from his chest before letting it go, letting it meet the ruthless power of his rising foot. Heads and helmets on the track and field cocked back as the football soared into the sky, crested, and just so happened to come down on and boink off of Coach Burger's big sunburnt dome fifty-five yards distant.

Calvin's strong, thick legs helped him kick and today, right now, run.

But Calvin abandons all impetus to get away from Hanky and the Play Day House when another "sig," this lady larger than Calvin and Hanky combined, comes galloping from out of nowhere and they collide, stealing the bulk of Calvin's breath, a blindsiding affair that sends him tumbling down a slope clear of the antigravity seesaws. He rolls and rolls, flops and flails, then bangs to rest against the "trunk" of a "tree," the trunk weaved from spark plugs and wire mesh, the leaves moving squares of flashing hardware, the whole tree itself like some blinking satellite.

Calvin's very dizzy, his nose plugged with the crusty ash entombing half his face. His spine feels twisted up. He pushes himself up on his palms, hip throbbing with the parasite of pain the sig's huge knee has left behind. The big significant, unhindered by the impact, looks down from atop the slope and says sorry with her eyes, an apology Calvin can somehow hear despite his naked, unaided ears. She looks like Hanky.

They all more or less look like Hanky, Calvin's begun to notice, purple-eyed and jiggly, as if their bodies swim in bags of flesh too big for their bones. Like Hanky's, and like any troll doll's anywhere, the significant's hair, as if powered by electricity, sticks way up and holds in the shape of a cone, and like Hanky's—but unlike any troll doll's anywhere—the significant's hair is a shade sucked dry of color, the sad no-shade shade of some rag that's collected more years than dust particles in some forgotten shed. They all wear shimmering jumpsuits that look like tinfoil but feel like used sponge. The shoes, cleats, and flip-flops are all Nikes.

Earlier, in a shadowy region of the Play Day House, comfortably distant from the action of the significants' covert communications— where Calvin first met Hanky, who was exchanging some Air Jordans for sleek Vapor Untouchable cleats—Calvin nabbed a clunky pair of basketball shoes from the lowest row of a box pyramid stacked at least a hundred feet high, every box packed fit to split with Nike footwear of any imaginable kind. Apparently the pyramid just turned up one day as if by magic, though Hanky said he had a feeling it had something to do with what's scrawled on each box in inky red script that smells suspiciously of blood, perhaps The Pain Train's version of Magic Marker. These days Calvin reads all right, though difficult language remains a struggle, so when Hanky read "COURTESY OF THE CONTROVERSY REGARDING *THE COLIN PACKERMICK ADVERTISEMENT*" aloud, the mysterious message meant nothing to Calvin and even less to Hanky. Just one mystery of many, Hanky said.

Hanky slides down the slope of ash on his butt and skids up beside Calvin.

"Look, guy," Hanky says, "I'm not going to sit here and pretend like I know how you feel. I'm pretty sure I used to know—*to really know*—but now I can't remember, and I know it's 'cause I've forgotten. It's the same for all of us. The more we wake up to our present condition, the more we forget how we got here. I can almost imagine what it must be like for you, but, like, I've pretty much lost all ability to empathize."

". . ."

"I mean, like, I can't picture what it's like to walk a mile in your shoes."

"These shoes really hurt!"

"You mean your feet? Are they too small?"

"Don't make *FUN* of me!"

"I'm sorry I—I meant are your shoes too small for your feet?"

"It hurts!"

"Let's see . . . whoa, these're way too big for you, guy!"

"Gimmie my shoe!"

"Whoa, guy, all right—here. Look, I'm sorry—I'm not trying to be mean. Just the opposite, in fact. Come on, walk with me. We'll find you something that fits."

Hanky pops to his feet and offers Calvin a helping hand. After Calvin makes no move to accept said offer, Hanky reaches inside his high, rigid, pope-hat hair.

"Just a sec," says Hanky, rummaging, his hand lost to colorless thickets. "There we go," he says, extending a handkerchief, purple eyes fixed. "For your face."

———

"Ey, T-Bone, what's that there in that jar?"

"Beetlejuice, meet Dex," said Trent Taphor. "Dex, Beetlejuice. BJ for short."

"I meant like *what* is it?"

"To be completely honest, Dex, I'm not really sure."

"Where'd it come from?"

"The woods, last night. Out near the standpipe."

"No lie—shit's freegin' freaky."

"Says the meat cleaver with blood all over it," said Trent.

"Ey, bro, that reminds me—were ya, like, gonna wash me off ever?"

"We're out of soap, if you couldn't tell."

"Why's it got to float in the water like that? With all its legs all spread n' shit?"

"Ever seen anything like him?"

"I feel like those're eyes on the sides or some shit. Or, like, are those like gills?"

"He likes the water, I think," said Trent.

"I don't like how it's, like . . . *undulating.*"

"Pretty sure he's just breathing."

"Ask me, you got yourself there one ugly-ass mother."

"I'm betting he's worth a ton. Money, I mean."

"Whatever you say, bro," said Dex the meat cleaver. "Say, any luck with—"

"Don't even start. I didn't wake you up to talk about him."

"Shit, I was just tryna ask how it went with your *mom.*"

"Makes no difference in this case—so do me a favor and drop it."

"A'right, then. So why *did* you wake me? And, like, what freegin' *time* is it? Lot of light up in this bitch I ain't so used to. More of a night blade, case you weren't aware."

"It's almost noon. I want you to get me Angel."

"Bro, no wonder you got the checkerboard all set up."

"It's time, Dex. I'm ready to see her. In the light."

"Figured maybe you would, like, ask me to play or something."

"My therapist, I mean. Not my mom."

"Bro . . ."

"It'll be fine, Dex. I'm a big boy. Now put her through."

"You're the boss. Just brace yourself 'cause, like, she's—"

"'One ugly-ass mother.' I know, I get it. Just do it. Before I change my—"

". . . *Hey,* dude."

The mason jar with Beetlejuice floating in the water within slipped through Trent's sweaty hold and nicked the corner of the checkerboard on the corner of the dish-cluttered sink, sending black and red checkers spraying all over the kitchenette, sparking in Trent a split-second reaction during which he contemplated either stabilizing the board or saving BJ's jar; his hand shot out and jerked about, doing nothing for the situation at hand. The jar hit the trailer's hardwood with a startling knock, though the glass held. The water inside swished around.

Beetlejuice did some flips before curling in on himself, somehow shrinking himself to the size and shape of a very dense golf ball. Trent set BJ upright on the counter and started picking up the pieces, the blacks and reds littered among the scattered heaps of paper plates and pizza boxes and empty beer cases and cans.

A quiet crackling issued from the dead woman peering out from inside the reflective plain of the meat cleaver; it was the staticky crinkle of a lollipop wrapper being squeezed. The sound instilled in Trent a somehow euphoric tingle that began at the back of his scalp and boogied all the way down his arms to the ends of his fingertips. There were reasons for her making the sound and for the soothing feelings it produced in Trent.

Angel's voice had done the same therapeutic thing, way back when.

"Hey, uh," Trent said, "I just need a sec to reset the board. If that's all right."

"Take your *time*, dude! I'm in no rush *whatsoever*."

"Cool if I call blacks?"

"Whatever you *want*, whatever you *need*. I'm here for *you*."

"All right, hold on."

"*That's* the spirit," said the spirit of Trent's dead therapist, Angel.

Angel (surname unknown or else forgotten by Trent) had been, in life, gorgeous, like an ocean refracting sunlight, meaning, six years ago, in the close stuffy air of her cluttered, dim office in downtown Los Angeles, she'd seemed, through an aura of bubbly warmth and scintillant compassion, to give off her own light, to make her dark office shine with herself. She'd done this with the tools with which she'd been born: the electric green eyes, the dancing curls of short blond hair, the dimples accentuating a soft, simple smile—her voice. Her voice had been the thing, the vibration of comfort itself; it always sent hot shivers tingling down Trent's spine, scalp to fingertips, lingering well after shared silences. Hers was the voice of authenticity and unabashed kindness of seemingly limitless supply, up until her last session with Trent, a Wednesday, when the hollows under her eyes showed out dark blue, when her hair, the curls bleached and stringy like straw, looked like some ragged, thirsty thing, when the smile, too soft for dimples to emerge, seemed to conceal and submerge complexities of the sort Trent could not even begin to comprehend. In that last session, during those final forty-two and a half minutes, Angel's voice hadn't been hers, the light of herself/her self extinguished.

Presently, finally, for the first time since she told him goodbye for the last time, Trent got himself to take in the features of Angel's new (as it were) face, to see that face in daylight. It was worse than he'd expected, rotten in death, still swollen from self-inflicted asphyxiation, her eyes bulging in their sockets, hair limp and hanging, the smile there and present but with a tongue that lolled permanently from the dimple-less corner of her lips. She'd hanged herself, was the thing, with the hammock in her backyard she'd said she'd use whenever she got sad, meaning in the end she'd used it one last time. Trent averted his gaze and slipped back inside the sound Angel was still making with the lollipop wrapper, grinding her fingertips so that the plastic crackled from the friction, making Trent tingle all over.

"It's a *nice* noise, isn't it, Trent? A *soothing* sound."

"Could we—ah . . . go ahead and go first. Your move, I mean."

"It reminds you of being *young* again, doesn't it? Of Halloweens you used to go trick-or-treating all over the neighborhood, *just you and Calvin*, no parents. You'd fill *two* pillowcases *apiece*. You knew *all* the houses that gave out the *king-sized* bars."

"I'll . . . I'll go, then." Trent made a move. "Your turn—you're reds."

Trent gripped the handle and steadied Dex over the checkerboard, allowing Angel the time and angle required for her to instruct him on her first move. He made her move for her, and then he set the meat cleaver beside Beetlejuice's jar on the counter, letting his arm rest as he contemplated his next move. He made his move. Checkers wasn't a game that necessitated all that much time or patience or even effort to start—it was all about how you closed, with the traps out and the Kings in play, with their special ability to move backward and devour the scraps of the recent past, all the wrong moves made.

For a time, they talked and played like they'd always done.

"So I can *see* Calvin's not here . . . does that *mean . . .?*"

"Look, I was going to, like I was this close, but, like—see but we had a rat."

"You mean you *pussed out,* to use your *own* words."

"Could we maybe talk about something else today?"

"We can *discuss* or hash out whatever it is you *want.*"

"So then let it be me for once. Not Calvin."

"What *about* you, Trent?"

"I want to know what's wrong with me." Trent jumped one of Angel's reds, his fourth kill of the game. He called jumps *kills.* "I have to. Know."

"What in the *world* should make you think anything's *wrong* with you?"

The first life Trent Taphor ever took with conscious intent had been the stink beetle in the janitor's closet at Crest High, the resultant catharsis maximized by the bodily relief, the way the web of pressure engulfing his heart had crumpled and fallen apart, a knot unfurled. He'd discovered the beetle behind the door, nudged it with the toe of his shoe. The beetle stiffened in response, curled its tiny legs and went belly-up and motionless, coiled within itself like something with a secret. He'd picked it up and pricked a leg from its body, the sound snappy and small, like the tick of a tiny clock. The beetle cradled in his palm didn't so much as twitch, so Trent spat in its face and moved his eyes around the closet in search of something sharp. It was lunchtime at Crest High, which gave him a good ten or fifteen minutes to kill. He kicked aside a yellow bucket with a string mop inside to reveal a shelf on which rested a plastic case of paperclips swathed in dust. He set down the beetle on the shelf before working open the case, from which he removed a clip he uncoiled no more than two inches, leaving his thumb and forefinger a still-coiled base that would simply have to do, leverage-wise. He felt the grin on his face; it had to have been there awhile, judging by the soreness in his jaw, the slight ache in his temples. He picked up the beetle again, the little shit choosing to remain stiff and still with lies, unaware of the life-or-death magnitude of its choice. His pinched thumb and forefinger were white with pressure; there was some resistance, but the clip managed to crack the carapace and break through to the belly. Trent wedged around in there. The bug, too late, stopped pretending, wriggling its little legs in a sign of panic. Trent narrowed his eyes and went at it for maybe five minutes, until the two inches of clip were coated in a chunky white goop. It smelled something awful. He dropped the carcass and kicked it back behind the door, dinner for dust mites.

Anne Kell spoke up then, but for the first time, it wasn't in a whisper. She lived there, it was revealed, in the strangled dark of the janitor's closet, where She'd been waiting for Trent, calling to him all his life. There, She told him, She could take care of his pain, and he could share his every secret desire, because there they shared a home.

"Well, for starters there's you," he said to the undead therapist in his blade. "And my parents. Just the whole concept of Dex in general."

"Meaning *what*, precisely?"

"See, I'm pretty fucking aware none of you guys're really real—I haven't lost touch with reality or anything like that. Like, I *know* your strangled corpse face, Angel, is really a distorted reflection of *my* face in a blood-smeared meat cleaver I've named Dex. That really in all actuality I'm sitting here all alone talking to myself, playing checkers against myself. That's not the main issue here. Not by a long shot."

"..."

"You're supposed to keep saying things, Angel. To help me sort out my thoughts for the sake of clarity—maybe even meaning. If I'm lucky."

"My sister always *hated* to hear my voice, to see herself reflected in my *words*."

"You've never brought up your sister before—at least I don't think . . ."

"Like you, Trent, she *yearns* to *purge* herself of heartache. Fifty-five pounds she's lost so far—and *far* more in self-worth. She *grieves* for me, does Love."

"Your sister's name is Love? But, how could that be something *I* know?"

"Don't tell me you haven't *seen* the hit *reality* TV show *Love Beach*?"

"Freegin' crazy the stuff we all pick up on subliminally."

"Or you can *choose* to confront your *conscious* mind with the *true* truth."

"Help me pin down what's wrong with me, Angel. Help me help myself."

"How about the *sound* of these gloves? The *snap* of latex against my wrist?"

"It's making me nervous."

"How about when I *scratch* my pen on this paper? *Listen.*"

"Now I'm all, like, itchy and desperate. Like I'm hearing someone trying to claw their way out of a coffin and I can't decide what to do about it."

"How's *this*, then? Listen to the *water* when I *shake* the water bottle."

"Reminds me of what I hear in my stomach sometimes."

"And when I *squeeze* the sides thus? What do you think of the *crunching*?"

"Now I feel completely and utterly helpless. No clue why."

"Why not *try* and close your *eyes* for a second, dude? Good. Now when you hear me *scrunch* the plastic, what is it you *see*?"

"I feel like I'm hearing myself die."

"This is *interesting*, though I'm sorry to say you didn't *really* answer me."

"Or like I'm dead already. Like maybe it's the sound I'll hear when I'm dead."

"Does one really *know* where the stomach *goes* when the uterus *grows?*"

"What?" said Trent.

"I'm thinking you're ready for some *new* noises."

Angel had been using Dex as a medium to counsel Trent on and off the past four years, since Trent and Calvin's arrival at Saw-whet National Park. Because these sessions had hitherto taken place in the hours after midnight—as soon as Calvin's guttural snores could be heard from the nook of his sleeping bag—Trent had instantly become aware of the grisly change to her voice: glottal in death, throaty and full of earth and worms. These days, to the benefit of Trent's basic comprehension, she had to emphasize certain words, to clear the dirt from her throat and enunciate against the tidal gust of dust and grit and whatever else plugged her lungs' deflated flaps. She'd also adjusted tactics, having switched from the cognitive behavioral stuff to . . .

Angel produced out of the inexplicable blue of whatever reality made up the other side of the metal a thin, dusty, lengthy woodwind recorder. She brought the piped instrument to her lips, covering some of the holes with her bloated fingers, and began, blithely and rather poorly, to play. Trent winced against the whistling shriek. His ears popped; something in there thinned to a liquid ooze that dribbled out to the lobes.

"But these *noises* are the main issue, I think," said Trent. "Like, I think I know I'm just imagining your face and voice and all the stupid mistakes I'm pretty sure I remember you making on the battlefield—checkerboard, I mean—but, like, these *sounds.* Feel like I'm really actually *hearing* them—but like . . . they make me feel real awful inside. Like something's seriously wrong with me. It's all so vaguely intense."

Angel's face, bluish and sheened with liquidy fungus, darkened to a dense shade of purple as she went on playing the obnoxious, seemingly otiose pipe.

"Could you please stop?" said Trent.

"But can't you *see* I'm trying to help you *process?*"

"Nothing you're doing's making any sense."

"I'd beg to *differ*, Trent. Deep down you *know* this recorder reminds you of the sound Calvin makes every time he gets sad or mad and whines and cries like a little *bitch*. How it always gave you *headaches* to hear him going off all the time. How because of that you didn't hear your mother's *last words*. It wasn't crappy cell reception—it was *Calvin. Screaming* in the backseat. Which made your father yell from the *shotgun* seat, which made it so you couldn't hear what your *poor* mother said right before the *roar* of the semi truck *ramming* them all."

"I don't care what she said."

"Whatever you *say*."

"Just quit it with the goddamn noises, all right?"

"*Ask* and you shall *receive.*"

"Thank you."

"So how many *Heads* presently occupy the Kill Cooler?"

"Doesn't matter anymore—Calvin's gone."

"How *many*, I said."

"I just said it doesn't matt—ah, god, no—stop it, stop it, *stop it!*"

"What's the *matter*, Trent? *Finding yourself* averse to the sound of this itty-bitty *chainsaw?* Figured it'd *remind* you of when you were an itty-bitty boy watching your *dumbass daddy* cut the branches of the neighbor's tree out over your front yard, how you stole the *scissors* from the garage and snuck under the fence and scaled the branches of the tree your daddy's rope was fastened to and *snip-snip-snipped* the rope so that by the time your daddy *finished the job* and the *chugga-chugga-zing-zinnng!* of the chainsaw fell quiet you *watched* him fall—what, fifty?—maybe like sixty feet, and instead of crying out or calling for help, you shimmied down the backside of the other much smaller tree, *hidden from sight*, and scampered around your house to the *safety* of the *darkness* of the basement. What happened after that? Don't you *remember?*"

This happened over half his life ago: Trent, hunkered down to avoid bumping his head on the latticework of the low ceiling of the basement, army-crawling through cobwebs and grit to the room's darkest, chilliest spot, the corner furthest from the light of the small square window at back lawn level. There, he curled up in a ball and inspected the minor wounds his elbows and knees had sustained from the coarse pebbles and ground glass on the sandy floor. This was his space, his hiding place, where peace and quiet really did harmonize. Thomas Taphor, Trent would later learn, had suffered a concussion, broken his left ankle and two ribs, ruptured his pelvis, fractured his jaw, and flayed the gray dead skin of his elbow on the teeth of his chainsaw. The white picket fence above which he'd hung suspended would have to be painted over. Trent's father's helplessness could still be heard, high splintered shrieks muted by damp stone walls and grimy window glass. Trent still had the scissors he'd used with him. He used them again to scrape a serviceable hole in the dirt, then he dropped in the scissors and filled the hole with earth from all four corners of the room. He finished the job to the scream of sirens above.

In the end, a tree rat received the blame for his father's fall, but if Trent could've foreseen the full traumatic extent of the fallout of his father's physical/mental/emotional degradation post-recovery, he might not have spent hours down there in the dark, chewing away his lower lip to stifle all the laughter that threatened to expose his position.

Trent supposed the whole episode was a joke only he understood.

Nowadays he nursed an eternal split in his lip with an endless supply of petroleum jelly he'd plundered from the garage of his old family home; Thomas Taphor had been a custom manufacturer of the stuff, meaning he hadn't been a complete waste of flesh and bone.

"There're five Heads in the Kill Cooler," said Trent. "The Rat was the fifth."

"And you're sure as sin the *Rat's* the *right* Head?"

"Anne Kell wakes, T-Bone bakes," Trent began reciting. "Five Heads he's got to find, one for each axe She's got to grind. Under a log he'll find the fleshy first; a Frog's head feels fit to burst. The second he'll uncover underground from a hole, lest he mistake the

Gopher for a mole. Next, he'll pull from the guts of a tree—any Owl'll do for number three. He must be wary of number four; this barn Cat's lived nine lives of gore. And finally the fifth, the Rat. It'll come to T-Bone above his brother's resting mat. At last T-Bone's assembled the five horrible Heads. At last Anne Kell can go back to bed."

"So *now* . . . all that's left . . ."

"Like I already said, Angel, he's gone. Run off. Can we talk some more about me now?"

"But where'd he *go?*"

"Calvin does this all the time—and guess what? He always comes back."

"You *must* find him, Trent. Time's *far* too . . . *menacing*."

"Please tell me what's wrong with me."

"And *this* time you'll *sack up* and cut his throat."

Somehow Angel managed to crinkle the candy wrapper and snap the latex glove and scratch the pen on paper and shake the water in the water bottle and squeeze the plastic sides and rip into the recorder and rev the chainsaw all at once, a split second like a roaring eternity, and then all was quiet in the thick, milky noonlight of the trailer.

Somewhere Trent smelled something bitter. The frameless clock above the window above the sink snipped away the seconds tick by tick by tick.

"King me," said Trent.

"She's out, bro. I could, like, take her place if you want."

Trent latched onto both corners of his side of the battlefield and flung the checkerboard as hard and high as he could. The board folded up before it could really taste the air and came right back down with a quiet clap. Checkers fell in a rain of black and red that clattered along the floor. Some pieces seemed to roll forever. Dex, in his own way, advised Trent to relax.

"Chill pill, my ass!" said Trent. "Just *look* at me, man—I'm a *wreck!*"

"Ey, bro, look—something's up with your freaky little friend!"

". . ."

"What's Beetle Boy doing to his water?" asked Dex.

"His name's Beetlejuice—and it seems to me he's absorbing it. Like a sponge."

"Not gonna lie, bro, a sponge sounds freegin' nice right about now. That rat's blood's getting all congealy, feel me?"

"Shut up for a second."

"I mean, I guess I get it. No mess is more annoying to clean up than your own."

"I said . . ."

But Trent Taphor was halted in the process of observing Beetlejuice, whose ribbed flaps unfolded in waves, making way for a splayed net of what could be legs or antennae or any number of previously unidentified extensions of the underbelly or thorax or whatever the hell. BJ puffed up and out, the dirty sink water disappearing with every inch he floated down like an ever-expanding sponge with an unquenchable thirst.

The little mutant anomaly finally came to rest at the bottom of the mason jar, the glass spotty with the colorless scum of some excreted chemical. BJ's wings went back inside the abdomen, presumably with the water, while his long stalks for eyes curled with his head beneath his rolled armored casing. Trent figured this was what BJ might've looked like back in the larval stage, a fetus in its egg or sack or whatever, now swelled to maybe half the size of Trent's skull. Any bigger and the bug would run out of room, and the glass could explode. As it was, Beetlejuice remained at rest, a swollen lump of black, until it happened.

Fluids spewed out of Beetlejuice in gushing jets from every fissure and cavity and orifice on every side as BJ began rising once again on the liquid now leaving him. Except the dirty sink water could no longer be thusly described—nor could Trent be entirely sure it was water anymore. The mason jar, now half full of liquid colored a deep shade of indigo, sparkled with streaks of brightest bioluminescence, a glassful of galaxy, Beetlejuice's oozing juices seemingly the stuff of constellations. It could've been Angel's voice caught in a jar.

Meanwhile BJ had shriveled himself to the size of something

Trent could once again cup in his palms. BJ darted here and there behind the curved wall of glass, seeming to fly and play inside a bright new world he'd made by himself, for himself.

Trent scrounged about the RV until he dug up a relatively unused sponge from a box packed with cans of petroleum jelly and expired soup. He thumbed the catch to pop the lid of BJ's jar and dipped the sponge to the water's starry, rippling surface. Beetlejuice made no move to escape, as if he appreciated his place in Trent's home, in Trent's world.

Trent used the phosphorescence the sponge absorbed to wash Dex of the Rat's blood, and then, after resetting the board and remanning the battlefield, Trent dueled Dex in a harmony of peaceful, concentrated quiet. He almost never lost.

———

AFTER TAKING HALF an hour to locate Calvin a comfy pair of 2012 red-black Kobe's, Calvin and Hanky sit on the bottom level of the box pyramid and watch the significants run all around. They leap from foam ledges and crawl under foam tunnels, shouting things, leaving codes in the patterns of their footprints in the ash. Hanky says he won't bother taking the time to explain the codes to Calvin, not today, then proceeds to start going over them anyway. Take Stephen and Simona for example, says Hanky. Look how they appear to chase each other, bursting with hearty laughter and good cheer, but a closer look at their tracks reveals three, five, seven distinct sets of upside-down triangles, meaning they can't seem to agree on whatever it is they've been hotly debating the past hour. Or look there, it's June—you two've met, Calvin, how's your hip, by the way?—did you hear what she just shouted? June shouted *I'm coming for you, Nine-Eyes!*, which means she remembers the first ninety-eight seconds of last night before . . . whatever happens to us happened, which is around the average most of us can remember on a nightly basis, twelve ticks up from last year. Shhh, she's coming over. Hey there, Junebug.

"Hi."

"What're you up to?" says Hanky.

"*I'll slice off your left nipple and wear it as an eyepatch!*"

"The left, you say? Are—are you positive?"

June nods not with her head but with her eyes.

"You're sure it wasn't a"—Hanky leans in to whisper—"*a soul patch?*"

"*I swear you'll rue the day you ever slipped your pinky up your—*"

"Got it, okay." She turns to leave; Hanky stops her. "Hey, June. I just, uh—I just want to say thank you. For telling me just now. And, uh, for everything else. Hold on to hope."

June's eyes seem to shine a little, and then she lumbers off.

"Well that's not good," says Hanky. "In fact, I'm totally fucked."

"Trent says that's a bad word!"

"Look, we're out of time, Calvin. They're already coming for me."

Calvin gawps at the painted ceiling, at a flame with glowing coals for eyes.

"I don't get it," says Hanky. "How'd they catch on to us? I mean, you *just got here*—your Light should . . . know what, forget it. Could we play a game really quick?"

"*YEAH,* BABY!"

"Awesome. *You* call out the shapes you see in the ash out there, and *I'll* tell you what they mean. Rapid fire, now. As fast as you can, I mean. Ready?"

". . ."

"Go!"

"Diamonds!" Calvin calls, pointing.

"Hope. Maria's telling Mario it's going to be okay."

"Squares!"

"Boredom. Those four're going over what they got served for dinner last night."

"Triangles!"

"Those're upside-down. We covered that already."

"Circles!"

"Angela's praying."

"Stars!"

"Homer and Olivia miss home. Nothing specific—totally conceptual. None of us can remember anything about home, though we often miss the *idea* of having a home, a place with a bed in which to sleep and dream."

Calvin indicates a strange, enormous shape marking the entrance to a nearby network of tunnels, biting down hard on his tongue, face growing hot.

"That's a trapezoid," says Hanky. "Ernest's work, maybe Edgar. They're always going on about the pain they think they remember experiencing every night. Edgar's got this theory the pain's got something to do with our eyes and ears, though personally I'd argue it's our hair that hurts. I'd also venture to say our pain's largely neurasthenic."

That's when the buzzing begins, pervasive and ill-tempered, coupled with the worst smell Calvin's ever smelled in his life filtering from everywhere, indescribably fetid. Hanky's face seems to sink further physically than it does emotionally. His eyes, shiny with tears, slide sideways and settle right near his ears, which should be impossible.

"*Hynetters!*" Hanky has to shout, because the buzzing's like a thousand revving racecars between the ears, chainsaws on the brain. "*Don't worry, Calvin! Like I said, they're here for me! Stick with June from now on, all right? JUNE'S A DOWNER TOO! SHE'LL LOOK AFTER YOU! SHE'LL BE YOUR FRIEND, I MEAN!*"

Hanky has had to crank up his voice to be heard over the buzzing flurry of hynetters raiding the Play Day House overhead from every surrounding shaft like soldier bees racing through honeycombs to report hive-shattering news to their queen. They stuff the chamber at the heart of the Pain Train with their bleak and brutal stench, their gangling, motorcycle-sized bodies casting off waves of boggy heat. They look like giant scorpions to some, giant hornets to others, depending on whichever the mind's resisting or willing to roll with, assuming either such sight is something that can ever be "rolled with," sanity-wise. Their bodies, impossible though it might seem, lurch faster than their bladed wings churn. Rows of what might be teeth ring what might be necks. Their long and scaly legs, lined with shards of hair that curl like hooks, dangle in pulsing nets that open and close, open and close, like something smacking wet and greasy lips.

They converge over Calvin and Hanky by the dozens, whirring in barely perceptible blurs. The whole room itself seems to tremble in their presence. High up the pyramid, one precariously balanced box wobbles and tips over, spilling a small avalanche of shoes of all sizes, one of which clops down on a hynetter's back, making the monster shudder and shriek. The shoe explodes with a *pop* and then falls in a rain of shredded threads. Calvin's hair flies back as though he were glancing up at a slowly descending helicopter. One particularly nasty hynetter hovers over Hanky like a personal storm cloud, like suicidal ideation personified. At least a thousand slits for eyes mark its jerking head in jeweled fragments, the saggy lids crusted with strange goop.

Hanky's hynetter's gangly legs open and stay that way for a dragging second and then close over Hanky's steepled troll doll's hair in a monstrous clench. Hanky's scream is soundless in the bedlam. Calvin can't hear even himself when he shouts.

"GO AWAY!"

The hynetters won't.

"DON'T LEAVE ME!"

Hanky hasn't a choice.

The hynetter's squirmy legs haul Hanky up by his hair, harvesting him inch by inch, second by second, his slowly vanishing face an ugly mutation of pain and terror. He punches and kicks with stubby arms and legs until those too are gripped and stilled. What's happening to Hanky resembles the opposite of a birth, though it's equally slimy and splashy. Calvin's been jumping all this time, though Hanky has risen well out of reach. Next to go are Hanky's forehead and puggish nose, and one sickening suction later, it's the mouth. His body from the neck down juts stiff and still from the rapacious network of legs. Calvin balances on one leg to tug off a shoe, but when he hurls it at Hanky's captor, the shoe explodes upon contact, falling back down in a soft, sad rain.

Calvin falls to his knees, head hung low, and listens to the rest.

He wishes for Captain America. A coat of collateral slime covers his face, stings his eyes. He wishes he had his glasses and hearing aids. The tip of his nose drips snot. He wishes he had his shield. All significants, June included, have gone into hiding. Calvin sprays the ash at his feet with slashing patterns of vomit that are what they are, mean what they mean.

The Play Day House, eventually, stills.

5

THE TALE OF EL JAYLO
(THE BUG INSIDE)

———

THEY WERE COMING BACK, Trent Taphor was relieved to see, perched where the far end of the forest gave way to a flat, gravelly outcropping atop Saw-Whet Park's tallest, steepest bluff. He sat with his legs dangling over the edge, heels clacking the tippy top of the cliffside. The cliff itself curled like a crooked finger over a massive chasm separating the easternmost end of the park from the western edge of town on the other side; the abyss stretched sideways at least five miles like some huge smile in the earth. He figured there had to be a bunch of bodies down there, decomposing among boulders and weeds, breaking down in the bellies of snakes.

The suicide rate up here in the Superior Region soared highest in California, murder being a close runner-up. Trent couldn't deny coming here every so often to watch the sun burn out, drink malt liquor under the stars, and contemplate the quickest of ends.

Berkshire locals called the dividing pit Big Mouth, out-of-towners "the moat." Every few months helicopters could be spotted overhead, like a seasonal swarm of metal mosquitos occurring only when "people of interest" (i.e., long-haired, bright-eyed, pale-skinned college chicks from USF) went missing. More often, though, Big Mouth provided the ideal backdrop for active selfie-seekers too trendy to make the trip to the "prosaic" Grand Canyon, a notion Trent, who no longer owned a cell phone, inferred the last time he'd gone into town for ice cream, when the long-haired, bright-eyed, pale-skinned college chick he found himself speaking with at the back of the line said, "That big moat thing's trending on TikTok. It's like a new Grand Canyon, but for our generation. I think we see ourselves in that pit. Our future."

Nowadays Trent could hardly stand the sight of cell phones, avoiding their frigid gaze the way he avoided looking his mother in the face in Dex with the lights on. His mother's voice would always haunt him, he supposed, like mePhones did the world.

Presently the massive influx of traffic on the woodland horizon looked to Trent like all the parades of ants he'd ever stomped on as a little kid, always after spilling some apple juice on purpose and returning to the sticky scene some hours later. Those riding up on dirt bikes and motorcycles got to cut the various lines leading in and out of town, the helmeted riders using the bike lanes, the helmetless wise guys with a suicidal taste for adrenaline weaving and winding, zig-zag-zooming across the clogged web of narrow highways and streets.

Exhaust-spewing engines thrummed in the wounded haze of dusk. Horns honked and blared practically nonstop. Clouds scudded overhead.

Five thousand locals eager to return to their rural hovels spread throughout Berkshire was, in three words, one obnoxious shitshow, made more complicated by those venturing further north to Del Norte and Siskiyou County. The region-wide exodus four weeks ago hadn't looked much different from this.

The three weeks' warning all towns north of Mendocino County had been issued—in addition to the government-issued squadrons of traffic controllers—had only been somewhat effective, at least in terms of efficiency and organization and general morale. Over the span of two and a half media-monitored weeks, five thousand Berkshireites had been bussed along in frantic herds. Whether they'd acted on the societal pressure to pack their most precious belongings varied from person to person. Some scrambled in flat-out frenzies to load the flatbeds of their family pickups; others shrugged, stared straight into cameras broadcasting to every main-stream American outlet from the small-fry networks of Trinity County, and muttered things like "Fuck it, ain't nothin' I got's worth savin.'"

Several such blips had gone live on the air, and Trent, fishing the airwaves, spinning the AM dials of his father's vintage Marantz 2270 stereophonic receiver, chuckled each time he happened to catch some country bumpkin uttering the fuck word. What really tickled his pickle—more than anything else—was the talking heads' inability to respond in any meaningful way, their psychic habitats (for perhaps the first time in their privileged suburbanite Crest-White-Strips-Daily lives) disturbed to the point of speechlessness. The fuck word, Trent surmised, packed too damn powerful a punch.

Trent fished the airwaves now, but the radio on his lap burbled only static. Watching the hordes of trucks and motorhomes cram-ming their way back into Berkshire below relieved him not because of the tiny thrill he got at the thought of getting back to work in the woods behind him (just as soon as the nature-lovers finally recog-nized there wasn't anything to be afraid of, weather-wise) but rather because of the festivities to come. October had always been Trent's favorite time of year, and Berkshire treated Halloween with all the reverence a celebration of costumes and candy-stuffed pillowcases deserved. It was for this reason Trent had picked this place for him and Calvin to settle. Down in Berkshire, for reasons he figured he'd never cease to research, Halloween received center attention, the whole of October devoted to weekly costume contests, harvest cele-brations, pumpkin patches, pumpkin-carving competitions, black cat scavenger hunts, bat-spotting, midnight bonfires, a locally run haunted carnival, and, above all, topping Trent's list as well as the town's, the annual hunt for El Jaylo.

Trent had spent the past four Halloween Eves watching from the figurative sidelines as townies of all ages carried out the seminal, completely unique to Berkshire tradition: a midnight journey into the ever-mysterious, five-mile smile of Big Mouth, the valley high over which Trent's feet presently dangled. Down there in the pit was where El Jaylo supposedly slept the 364-day sleep of a "mythical" beast in hibernation, fixed to wake at the first light of October's second to last moon—the moment, in other words, the thirtieth became the thirty-first. This deliciously haunting concept spoke to Trent in ways nothing else could.

The prospect of joining the hunt for El Jaylo for the first time was the reason, four days ago, he'd quit his hunt for Calvin, since Calvin was the reason he'd been sidelined the last four years. This year—finally!—trick-or-treating was off the board.

"I know something you don't know," said Trent, taunting the traffic-trapped. The lower half of the fading sun—obscured beneath the jagged teeth of distant mountain peaks—yielded a yin-yang trick of light that treated Trent's side of the cliff to a bloody bath, the other to a grim shower of shadow. "A tale of woe, is El Jaylo's."

Berkshire locals regarded the hunt for El Jaylo—"The Snake"— as a kind of game, something the grown-ups and more enthusiastic older teens put on for all the kids. Every year, five or six rotations of five or six volunteers would line up under one of those Chinese dragon thingies and prance up and down the valley. They roared and snarled throughout the twenty-four-hour affair, miked up to some shitty sound system, the shitty sound of which crackle-spat up the cliffside and kept Trent up at all hours of the past four Halloween Eve nights.

But the hunt, Trent knew, meant far more than some silly game, because—unlike everyone else—Trent knew in his heart that really El Jaylo was real. Four years of fevered research had yielded at long last an incontrovertible source of evidence.

"Should you happen to find yourself"—Trent's father, Thomas Taphor, the traveling salesman/custom manufacturer of petroleum jelly, had once said to Trent—"in some new state or town or what have you, and you find wherever you are foreign and utterly strange . . . know what you do, Trent? Head straight to the Town Bum.

Track the sonofabitch down if you have to. 'Specially if he's given to the usual drunken garrulousness. If anyone knows anything regarding shortcuts to the nearest public toilet or buried bodies or what have you, it's the Town Bum with a bottomless forty-ounce. Anyplace worth its salt in strangeness has got a good TB-40, I've found—and believe you me, petroleum jelly's taken me places."

Trent now found himself turning off his father's radio, cutting the static, still facing the bleeding sun. Twilight winked off the windows and hoods of trucks and trailers below in increasingly weaker sheens. Bushes and twigs rustled and snapped from the forest fringe behind him. Fingers—not Trent's—snapped as well, the way fingers do when someone's pointing out something urgent or when someone's nearly figured something out.

"Toldja they'd come back, kiddie-koo-koo! Din't I tell ya? I toldja, din't I?"

"What took you?" said Trent. He didn't dare turn around. Meeting eyes with Wild Will Spiro, the TB-40 of Saw-whet National Park, wasn't the approach Trent would recommend; it was a serious no-no, in fact—on this matter they saw eye-to-eye. "I've got your Old English. It's in the bag. Right where you're standing, if I hear you right."

"Tastes warm. Like pee-pee."

"I've been here awhile."

"Me's tired of pee-pee!"

"You'll get over it." You always do, Trent told himself.

"Happy juice . . . inner noose!—*heheeee!*"

"Cut the crap, Willy. Now a deal's a deal."

Trent couldn't recall the first time he got in touch with Wild Will "Willy" Spiro, what it'd been like, where they'd met, or really whether it happened at all. He couldn't be sure Wild Will was here even now—or there, in the most general sense—which was why every time they met felt like the first time. The cackling Vietnam vet with a thirst for malt liquor was a fucking unicorn—or like the shadow of one. For creatures such as they, who roamed the desolate outer rims of society's battleground, for whom hallucinations and fantasy were real things with voices that said things that mattered, such brushes with perceptual displacement were par for the course, Trent's father would've said. The reason Trent wouldn't turn around, then, wasn't so much because he feared what he might see, but rather whom he might not.

The voices, however, were Trent's, and always would be, meaning the presence/essence of what he heard could never be disputed/discounted.

"No pee-pee-peep 'bout The Snake 'tils moon time," said the man who'd agreed at some point to exchange the (true) tale of El Jaylo for forty ounces of Old English. "I know somethin' you don't knowwww, a tale of woeeeee, is El Jayloooo's!"

"It'll be a full moon out, I can tell."

"What's wit' cher buggy-boo, kiddie-koo-koo?"

"Huh?"

"Happy juice . . . Beetlejuice—*heheeee!*"

"Hold up—how do you know about BJ?"

"Lil' birdie-boo-boo told me's."

"I'm serious, Willy. How?"

"Saw-whet."

"You saw it?"

"No-no-no-no-no, not how—*who! Hooo-hooo!* Saw-whet."

"You can't talk to owls, Willy. Nobody can."

". . ."

"You know you should probably save some of that O-E for the story."

"Happy juice . . . lippy loose—heheheh."

"Whatever, it doesn't matter—BJ's dead, I bet." Shadows, thick and wet with cold, had stretched to Trent's side of the cliff, slowly swallowing the sandstone. "It's not like I killed him or anything—I just didn't know what to feed him. Pretty sure he buzzed off."

"Dem saw-whets're lookin' out for the dead, methinks."

"On second thought, drink up—you're easier to understand when you're drunk."

"I'd check 'er stem for the buggy-boo if I was you, kiddie-koo-koo."

Trent didn't bother asking Wild Will Spiro what *check your stem* was supposed to mean, which would be an obvious waste of human breath. "Hey, uh, Willy? Have, um, when's the last time you ate something substantial?"

"Twinner, twinner, chicky dinner's felled up n' up n' up 'til he come down on the other side o' dem ashes—so dem saw-whets say."

"I've got half a sandwich left. In the bag."

"All dem lil' scarecrow buggy-boos be scarin' off dem saw-whets, methinks."

"It's all yours if you want it. The sandwich, I mean. It's PB and J."

"'Tis through-hoo yer stem dat buggy-boos bring the bad brain-rain—*heheeee!*"

"How fast could you tank that forty, you think? I could time you . . ."

"Fifty-five's the skeletal key, Mr. Trenty—all ears n' eyes on five and five."

"Something tells me you're uncomfortable with silence."

" . . . "

" . . . "

" . . . "

"Now that you mention it, Willy, I can't remember the last time I saw a saw-whet."

"From the guts of a tree, the feathered crown of number three —*heheeee!*"

"Sounds like you all but killed that forty. Dead soldier, Dad would say."

"Fifty-five seconds is how long the silence betwixt us lived."

"What's this fifty-five business about?" Trent asked the man who, having faced the Viet Cong, couldn't be anywhere south of seventy-four. Except Willy had never really come face-to-face with the enemy, he might've once told Trent, because the enemy had been elusive, hidden in the paddies and tunnels and trees, screened behind the outer rims of whatever battleground comprised that day's minefield, that night's boneyard. "It's not like I'm complaining. Especially now that you're drunk, and so, like, comprehensible."

"Despite your being given to symptoms of a humdudgeon, you

now find yourself suffering, nattering with me, Wild Will Spiro, a psychologically distressed albeit ultimately fictitious survivor of a war of which you know naught except maybe for the teensiest tidbits you'd managed to harvest after half an hour on Wikipedia in the Internet café way down there in Berkshire, a township you still find utterly foreign even after four years from which you scurry and flee and spirit yourself away, way up here, you and your hugger-mugger ways—privately decapitating five faunae whose heads you've kept in a cooler whose ice needs replacing—grubbling your way through a world hanging by a precious thread—thread named Calvin, I might as well slip in here. But despite all that and more— the *more* here being your relief with respect to Calvin's outlandish disappearance, which has allowed you, for perhaps the first time in four years, to think by and breathe for yourself, which pries open one proverbial door for you and El Jaylo but all but slams another on the whole of human existence, as you shall come to see, soon, should you stick around long enough to find yourself sniffing the spoiled air and raging waters of the decade of doom to come—and so but despite all that and more, I stand with you, Trent, within you, clear of sight and sound so as to declare from the trenches of your innermost subconscious tier: the number fifty-five is sacred. Fifty-five is all, inside and outside everything everywhere, so long as you possess eyes and ears and the soul-fire with which to see and hear. There're forces at work in these woods, Trent, mutually bound, the forces of five and five. Bugs and bools in the cracks of the earth, screened in shadow, landmines with legs looking to render this world a boneyard in the supposed name of kindness and shame, is one. Force. And I'm afraid the other's your brother."

"Stop that, what you're doing," Trent said. "Quit it right now."

"Happy Juice . . . silly goose—*heheeee!*"

"On third thought, you've had enough Old English—too much, maybe."

"I ain't no snub-nosed loose-lipped rawgabbit, if that's what cher sayin.'"

"Keep my brother out of this, is what I'm saying—and that includes his name."

"You ain't never puttin' a stop to Cockadoodledoom all by your lonesome."

"Look, man, you're *my* voice," said Trent, hands sliding up and down the sides of his father's radio. Quickly he contemplated the quickest of ends, shivered to the cadence of his quivering heart. It was getting cold out, and in, colder still. "Just like Dex and Mom and Anne Ke—Angel, I mean—and like Dad."

" . . . "

"So quit saying stuff my brother says—like that dumb cockadoody shit. Seriously, man, my chest is getting all, like, knotted up."

"Dis here be bigger than brothers."

"I haven't understood a lick of anything you've said anyway," said Trent.

"Mayhap it's time we have a good hard look at each other."

" . . . "

"Turn right 'round, Mr. Trenty, afore ya let yourself go right over the edge n' Big Mouth swallows whole yer soul. 'Cause if ya try, you'll fail to fly—heheheh."

"Look, I already know that's not what I really need—it's not like I don't already know you're not really there, Willy. I know you're just an owl—a saw-whet or two hooting from some trees back there. I know that. I'm drunk. I'm drunk, and I'm scared."

"Difference betwixt *scared* n' *sacred* is a one-letter switcheroo-hoo-hoo!"

"I just . . . I guess I'm just missing my dad."

"Swappin' a single letter's 'nough to shift dem stem sets in good ole English."

"That's really why you're here, Willy. Today's my dad's birthday. It's why I figured I'd hike way the hell up here, down a forty in his name. Dad used to tell stories of people like you, Willy. The lost and the damned, he'd say. Before I hurt him, this was. So I figured I'd make you up, then make you make up some shit about El Jaylo so I could trick myself into feeling as though I'm a part of this fucking town for once."

"Difference betwixt *apart* and *a part* is *from* and *of*, my love."

"Now that I'm good and drunk, I just can't stop thinking about this one time Angel—pre-hammock hanging, this was, and I was with her in her office one rainy Wednesday—and, like, I got like this close to telling her. What I did. To my dad. He was never the same after he fell. From the tree. Because of me. I never figured out whether Angel figured it out. Instead what she did was, like, assign me this assignment."

"Hoot. I ain't just one of yer voices, kid."

"She had me write a letter to myself, but from my dad's perspective."

"Difference betwixt a *letter* and a *letter* is the page and what's written on it."

"My dad's last words to me were '*and believe you me, petroleum jelly's taken me places.*' Like, god—*four years*, and that's what I've got to hang on to."

"Difference betwixt *on to* and *onto* is . . . a real pain in the arse."

"So last night I finally said fuck it and wrote the letter. To myself, written by me, from my dad. I was planning on reading it later, Willy, out loud, after you wrapped things up with El Jaylo and dipped out. But now I'm seeing it's not in my pocket, which can only mean it slipped out somewhere on the trail on the way here. It was long. The letter."

"A nasty bug's feeding on your stem, kid—I can see it from the back here."

"And now," said Trent, "I just want to hurl myself over the edge of this cliff."

"Beetlejuice, dangerously screwing with the stem sets of your cognizance."

"Think I've had it with this stem set Old English crap, Willy."

"Speak now—say your piece, kid—lest you forever hold your peace."

"It's dark out, and the moon's full. Just like I said it'd be."

"Once upon a time, there wasn't a giant snake named El Jaylo, and so no giant snake lived in Big Mouth—a great chasm dividing the small township of Berkshire from the Home of the Saw-whets. Their home stood on elevated ground, a sprawling forest of rainbow waterfalls and rock formations like faces and thriving streams, all of which fed into quiet lagoons in all directions . . . but there *did* live a young man named Mr. Trenty."

"Tell me something I don't know," said Trent, fingering his father's radio's nobs.

"What Mr. Trenty didn't know was that there was another man —not a penniless farmer but a man nonetheless—an older man, aged fifty-five, the fifty-fifth inductee of a fearsome cult of fearful farmers, a lonely man, now stuck in traffic. That's right, Mr. Trenty. The man's down in that massive metallic parade slogging below our most precious home. He's on the run from his wife, his third, as he wrestles with memories of his first, a liverish cockalorum who fudgels away the days, a small man with a big opinion of himself wasting all his time trying to give anyone within eyeshot the impression that what he's doing—whatever it may be—is significant when really it's not, when really he's got a nasty bug like Mr. Trenty's living in his liver."

"That all sounds like nothing I'd make up," said Trent.

"Inside the bodies of these two men feeds but one force of the five and five—on one man his brain stem, the other his liver."

"My liver's fine, Willy. One forty's not going to do anything."

"On these men the forces of five and five converged with all the weight of the fate of the world as, from the bugs, for the bugs, an exotic paradise was born, writ into being with the blood of five beheaded beasties, the sacrificial price of paradise. Woodland and waterfall had given way to rambling webs of shimmering channels that watered the land anew. Petrified wellsprings of exuberant color sprang to life, trees were bent into J's, or in many areas—seemingly impossibly—stacked atop one another, row after row of trees on top of trees on top of trees, and suddenly the faces Mother Climate had carved into rock formations smiled, or made other faces, as the stones themselves made sound, a whispered ringing, and everywhere were cavernous caves that glowed. And so, the Home of the Saw-whets became home to hidden bugs most vile. Endangered souls of every moral shade flocked from across the American heartland to see what the bugs had made, to absorb the strange splendor for themselves."

"This sounds like somebody retelling Genesis on acid," said Trent.

"Wild mushrooms budded all over Big Mouth, across which a bridge was hung in suspension, connecting Berkshire's people to paradise, which they called 'Eden's End.'"

"But so then, like, where's the snake? Or the apple? Or, like, the naked chicks?"

"El Jaylo never existed, for El Jaylo had always been a myth of man, but after the forces of five and five converged on Mr. Trenty and The Chosen . . . the battleground for the fate of the earth had emerged. On this battleground, anything became possible, which included the potential genesis of a giant snake named after Jennif—named El Jaylo. Here one might be tempted to picture a checkerboard, with the traps set and the Kings in play—the forces of five and five, blacks and reds doing battle until finally one force devours the other. Yin and yang. Dark and light. Shame and kindness. Same old story."

"So then how does it all come out?"

"Hoot. Yours is a tale of woe," said Wild Will Spiro.

"Happy birthday."

———

FIVE MILES out from some timbered tick of a town called Berkshire —where he planned to fill his tank, grab a bite, maybe stop to write —Don Philly sat stuck in traffic, mulling over death and dreams and the death of dreams, inching along for hours. Western sycamores swayed thick and monstrous on his left and right. Branches tangled and converged overhead, forming a sort of tunnel across the totally congested one-lane highway. Lord Read of The Dark always liked to point out northern California's trees, and Philly had taken down some names, should he find himself pressed to describe a tree at some point, in some story, to establish some mood.

Burly elbows sagged out of the windows of almost every truck and trailer on almost every tedious bend and curve, cigarettes pluming from sausage fingers. Every so often, madmen on weird motorcycles buzzed past, inches from the glass of Philly's window, zapping his heart, burning off whatever stew of inspiration had been bubbling within.

Philly had the windows rolled up because guys and gals were shouting obscenities and honking horns and the air smelled something awful and he needed quiet if he was going to get any writing done in his diary, which sat propped open on his thighs. He hated to think of the thing as a diary because he'd bought it specifically for brainstorming purposes, to prepare for the novel he'd soon begin— an elegant, leather-bound relic he acquired online from a well-reviewed business called The Best Book Ever Written.

Thus far he'd just about wrapped up Part One of the diary's/brainstorm manual's three labeled sections: "Destiny Awaits." These pages, once blank and boundless, potential-wise, were now spattered with the ink of inspiration, every word a concentrated wound gutted out.

Don Philly had made plenty of progress with his outline on the balloon-obsessed Larry Mufasa and his ideological revolution, his newfound purpose to root out any Poppers who might've infiltrated Non-Popper Nation's ranks. Philly still had no clue, though, how Faith and Hope would configure into the overall plot design, which bordered on being too convoluted for its own good, though he remained hopeful, keeping faith in the process. Maybe Faith and Hope were lovers once upon a time, or maybe it was more complex than that.

Going forward, he decided he'd have to outline a little smaller— and he'd have to write a little gentler as well to keep the ink from spattering.

The second section's title stared up from his lap: "Part Two: Two Rights Don't Make a Wrong, Two Writes Don't Make a Left . . . And This Here's Why It's Always Right to Revise." Philly spent half an hour puzzling over these words, determined to decode them, knowing they said something wise. It was like interpreting a dream.

It'd been Don Philly's dream to drive what he to this day called a "Punch Buggy Orange"—a Volkswagen Beetle painted a garish, psychedelic orange—because on Christmas morning four decades past, he'd unwrapped a toy model of same from Eli Elf himself, according to the note on the brown package paper. Back then Philly believed in Eli, "Santa's right-hand man," being ten and needing things to believe in.

At that time he'd receive only one Christmas present a year, which at that age had required some further explanation. When Ma and Pa's explanation concerning St. Nick's schedule—"If you think on it, Donny, Santa's quite the busy bee, buzzing in on every last home all over the world and whatnot," etc.—didn't seem to satisfy, the implications attached to Ma's ensuing rebuttal just about drove little Donny up the wall with joy. Ma alluded to the magical existence of Eli Elf, how Santa set aside his personal right-hand man to devote special attention to one toy in particular, for one boy in particular, every Christmas season, and there wasn't a single kid in the whole wide world who could compete with that.

Little Donny played with the toy car the better part of every day for well over a year, rolling it over roads of construction paper that covered every square inch of his bedroom floor, up the bypasses of the blank plaster wall, across the open highway of the hall, revving its gravity-defying engine with his lips, fueling its every trip with whatever harrowing adventure happened to happen in his head. Of adventures there seemed to be an endless amount. He dreamed all the while to have a real Punch Buggy Orange of his own one day to drive.

Now Don Philly was living the dream, with much of his life's latter half spent behind the wheel of his own Punch Buggy Orange since signing his first construction contract at Pa's instruction, under Pa's senior direction, the day Philly turned twenty-six. Despite a shoddy engine and shabby tires and shrieking brake pads, the car simply refused to quit. The number of recorded miles on the odometer was surpassed only by the unrecordable number of smiles Philly had smiled over twenty-nine years of proud ownership.

He'd be smiling now if not for five things: 1) The lady in the dusty pickup behind him sticking her face and fist out the window shouting *Move your crap ass!* at Philly every five seconds, if only to get him to creep up another five inches, 2) Everything tented beneath the skin of his stomach was starting to sound all fizzy and strange, gastric as hell, and he was slobbering all down his chin again, the way he did five days ago in the yellow-wallpapered privacy of his room at the motel five hundred miles southwest, a room that had reminded him of Brenda (ex-spouse, ex-teacher, ex-person) even as he'd spoken for the last time with Marlo (current spouse, current future ex-wife, current personal problem) on the phone, his cell, which he'd since given up to the depths of the Pacific, and, worse, the cherry-flavored Chapstick on the dashboard—spurring the slobber on—was looking increasingly to Philly like a pinky-sized slice of cherry pie, 3) The fact that bestiality was a thing, which only came springing to mind when the guys on the radio—local fellas, jabbering mean things in gruff tones—attempted to justify animal slaughter in the meat-packing industry with this peach of supporting evidence: "I mean, it ain't like we're talkin' 'bout bestiality here—I mean, big dogs gotta eat, right?" (Philly, having to this point been able to tune them out, finally turned them off), 4) His inability to picture Brenda—what she'd looked and smelled and sounded like—all because he couldn't keep Marlo—her platinum blond hair and orangey pong and throaty laugh—from battering the psychic barricades responsible for the preservation of the stabilization of his mental health, 5) The subtly terrifyingly crippling prospect that dreams died the second they came alive, meaning if, in Philly's case, his dream to become America's next Phillip K. Dick came true, living it out in reality might not be all it's cracked up to be, that perhaps the pot of golden happiness at the end of the rainbow of relentless effort was, in fact, as empty and colorless as a wordless page.

"Move your crap ass!"

The lady's voice, slightly muffled through Philly's rumbling shell of orange steel and gritty glass, sounded not unlike Marlo nagging. He inched forward and stopped, eliciting a screeching whine from brakes that had been threatening to divorce themselves of their own basic function for as long as Marlo was old. He couldn't see around the big family of redheads bunched together in the flatbed of the truck in front of him, bundled in blankets, silent and staring out. His lips were burning again, the cherry gloss fading with its flavor.

His body made deep liquid sounds inside, like a bum with a bum liver.

Philly reached for the Chapstick on the dash, uncapped it, gave the exposed red dot a test-lick, hummed that universal hum—*Hm!*—of slightly shocked approval, smacked his lips, flicked his eyes at the family of stony redheads ahead and then up at the rearview mirror, flipped the crap-ass lady a telepathic middle finger, used the pointed tip of the long-overgrown nail of his real middle finger to scrape and scoop inside the circle at the top of the tiny cylinder of cherry-flavored wax, shoved his now-coated middle finger into his mouth and sucked and sucked better than Marlo ever had. The blowjob he was giving the fleshy node of his finger was more reminiscent of Brenda's talents, he felt, the kind she would administer from under her desk at school in the middle of lunch. He sucked his finger with a kind of distant fury, his brain hard at storming, wondering if there were ways to jam Chapstick into his book, make it mean something.

"Get it in gear 'fore I ram this here gearshift up your crap ass!"

Don Philly was still sucking away, unable to make out the faces of the redheads in the truck suddenly a good five feet ahead. Once more he closed the distance.

By the time he rounded one final bend and came out the other end of the sycamore tunnel, the sun had fled out the sky, and he'd run shit out of Chapstick, his throat full of wax. His middle finger, sore and smeared pink, was lumped with the others the way fingers lump when gripping a pen, which was what he was doing as he steeled himself to outline. He took in the first blank page of Part Two, urging himself to color it with bullet-pointed language. He could hardly still believe he'd ended up here, stuck on this fuck-blasted highway in pursuit of some tornado thingy he'd somehow survived point-blank—a tornado he was no longer certain had been anything more than a little dust given its absence now, turning up on no radars anywhere. All because of an ill-fated boner. It all sounded like something out of the worst book ever written.

Moonlight shone on a sign to the side of the road:

HOOT! Welcome to Berkshire!
(Population: 5,000)
Home of Saw-whet National Park! HOOT!
(Elevation: 5,000)

Five minutes and five feet past the sign, Berkshire edged into view, the pumpkin orbs of streetlights suspended among tall and clawing trees, the buildings too low to make out between burly boughs, the occasional hedge-hidden house. What really swiped Philly's eye was the devastating magnificence of the mountain to the west, the clifftop curled like some great breaking wave, a verdant version of Mount Crumpit. He pictured the Grinch up there on the summit, alone, green arms crossed, yellow eyes scheming to steal Christmas, a moody monster forever looking down on a town christened for a one-word question pertaining to one's identity. The mountain—the site of the national park, Philly supposed—looked imposing under the quilt of night, like some crouched beast preparing to leap for the lace of stars sugaring the dark above.

Berkshire = Whoville, Philly scribbled at the top of page one of Part Two. Then he remembered the sign, crossed out *Whoville*, wrote *Hootville*, and grinned. Such was the thrill of creativity, the riveting magic of research, which he now found himself well on his way to halfway complete. The actual book would soon follow.

Then his car died.

It happened suddenly and without fanfare, without so much as one last sputtering cough from the engine. The car was simply on, radio lights aglow, and then it wasn't, with all lights out. He cycled through the protocol he'd learned observing Pa as a kid in the backseat every morning before school, before his family fell into any money and removed little Donny from the public school system in favor of the reputable private institution where he'd go on to learn, in more ways than one, from his first future ex-wife. Don Philly, like Pa with his battered Eagle Premier, as per the protocol, jiggled the keys in the ignition, slapped the steering wheel, and said a Hail Mary and a half. He severed the incantation after *fruit* in the phrase *blessed is the fruit* because for one mad moment, he thought he heard his engine thunder back to life as the seemingly closing-in interior of his car filled with a fiery white light. He was mistaken, of course.

It wasn't his engine but the bleating of a horn, the crap-ass lady's, whose high beams now slashed through the rear window's curved glass like the lightning spears of some hellish sorceress. The truck with the flatbed of redheads had pulled ahead into darkness. Don Philly's Punch Buggy Orange, once a toy, now the vessel of his voyage across America, his childhood dream made reality, was no more.

In the death-white light of the rearview mirror, a shadowy figure loomed larger as it shuffled nearer—the crap-ass lady, an image of wrath incarnate stalking forth, wielding something high overhead as one might a sword or crowbar or baseball bat or giant fucking Chapstick, its shape phallic and domineering against the eye-searing backdrop of the high beams. Philly murmured *Sorry*, screamed *Please I'm sorry*, not knowing if he was doing penance for the lady or his car or for himself—or even if he meant it.

He laid foot to the gas and gunned it, spinning the wheel toward the unknowable murk of marshland to the east with the intention of an off-road getaway. He'd forgotten in the flare of his rising terror the reason the crap-ass lady was coming, the reason he stayed right where he was on the highway, getting nowhere at all.

Philly dived headfirst to the right and bashed the brittle bone under his eye on the passenger door handle before all at once finding himself totally and utterly stuck. His slobber had thickened to a tide of rushing froth, as though he were seizing right there, head and neck wedged in the nook between seat and door, crumpled facedown and ass-up like a dog digging himself a hole. He wriggled and wormed, unable to lift his knees to get his legs out from under him, to move his arms the way he needed without producing in his shoulder sockets a stitch of pain saying, *Sure you wanna try that, guy?* A little blood trickled down his temple to his dimple, thick and oddly sort of delicious, as though someone had finally gotten the amount of salt right. Breath was feeling more and more like a scientific anomaly. Somewhere, glass shattered, and through the smothered distance gurgled the sound of shouts. The car rocked on its creaky coils.

No lights came on in the car when the door on the driver's side swung open, though Philly detected the cold bite of night in the fingertips of his flailing hands. A sharp wind sank its teeth into the exposed skin of his ankles. His pant cuffs, adhering to his lopsided center of gravity, had fluttered up his calves in loose rolls.

Philly hardly felt the first blow of the blunt crown of something hefty wham the padded right cheek of his defenseless, propped-up ass. The second, however—a direct shot to the tailbone—he felt a great deal, and he responded in kind with an involuntary jolt of pain and panic. He took no time to tell the stitch in his shoulder sockets *Seems I've got no choice here*, working his arms to wrench his face free of the crevice at last.

The crap-ass lady was squat and beefy, broad-shouldered and bow-legged; the harsh light of her headlights flooded half her face, hiding the other half in a partial eclipse of shadow. In that sense she looked to Philly like the monster he'd see as a toddler during too many long and windy nights while the moon made malicious shadows out of leafless trees hunkered outside his bedroom window, whenever Ma and/or Pa left open the closet door just a crack, as Michelle's snores filtered from across the hall in choked snorts and snarls, the thing in the closet he'd see framed between the bars of his crib. In quite another sense the fearsome lady looked like the renowned restaurateur and Emmy Award-winning television presenter Guy Fury because her hair looked like his, a stylish sun gelled up in spikes stiff and sharp enough to skewer a squadron of insects. She was whomping Philly's legs with a log, the kind you'd toss on a fire.

Philly had his back pressed against the glass of the passenger window, thrashing his feet to defend against her wallops, blindly seeking the door handle with his hand. Nothing he shouted made any sense to his own ears. He had to keep kicking as the crap-ass lady hacked and jabbed at his shins with the big splintered log, battering the permanent burns all over his body, each connection a searing reminder of the Last Roast just over a year ago when The

Dark had hog-tied him, wire-strung him up in a frame of plywood, shoved an apple in his mouth, and dangled him over an open flame, rotating his body every five seconds for five minutes, burning and baptizing the flesh—*Donald Rufio Philly's reborn in the flames of the beginning of the end!* Lord Bed declared from atop a stool atop a chair atop a rock. *We shall henceforth call him Lord Fed! Now who here's got that damn ice bucket?* Presently the crap-ass lady managed to clamp onto Philly's ankle, used it to pull herself deeper into the car, filling the space with her awesome mass, a wild boar with an agenda. His heart hurried in his chest. Slobber flew out both their mouths and clung to their chins in savage, wispy strings.

"Fuck's *matter* bitch you!"

Finally Philly's words were making some halfway sort of sense, though they came out strangled and gurgly, like a baby spitting up his mother's milk. Guy Fury's formidable female lookalike had her knees planted on his thighs. Her breasts swung in her sunflower-print sundress, each as large and round as her spiky head. Philly's mind flashed on the image of a three-headed Hydra in some ancient Greek sea.

"Help you!"

Philly had transitioned mid-phrase from *Help me!* to *Fuck you!* as he flipped between protecting his face and clawing at hers; the impact of this weird sort of patty-cake defense more or less equaled the impact of his words. She straddled his sides with her strong legs, heavy like deadweight. Vehicles swerved around, racing to get back to the back of the line of traffic however far ahead, headlights flickering, tires spitting up gravel. A tow truck rattled past, out of which someone bellowed something mean in a gruff tone. Someone else somewhere close—too close for cozy, Pa might've said—shot a gun outside Philly's car, and that was when he knew he was going to die, that the Punch Buggy Orange would be his coffin, that his decision to drive across America in pursuit of his American Dream had, from the start, letter for letter, spelled out his death sentence.

Don Philly had never struck a woman, had never known anyone who had—a guy who hits a gal is no guy at all, Pa always said—but self-defense was self-defense, and he was running out of air, and she had the end of the log pressed under his chin, digging into his throat, and someone too close for cozy had a gun and wasn't afraid to use it, and the lady boring (boaring?) down on his chest reminded him of Guy Fury, who reminded him of Gordon Ramsley, who reminded him of Marlo, who reminded him of everything wrong with his life and world, how everything had flipped from right to wrong the second Brenda—the sun and stars of his heart, the solar system of his soul—had packed her bags and kissed him goodbye with tears in her eyes. So really Philly had no choice but to cock back his fist, which he did, but before he could punch the crap-ass lady in the chin or throat or one of her Hydra-head boobs, he felt his balled hand roll along the car seat—it was the Chapstick, rolling beneath the back of his knuckles.

Philly drove a knee up between the crazed lady's legs, making her head bonk the ceiling of the car, creating just enough space for him to flip his hand, snatch the Chapstick, and chuck it at her as hard as the angle would allow.

"*My eye, my eyeeeee!*" she squealed. "*Godamn you, my godamn eyeeeee!*"

He capitalized the second her legs loosened their clamp, writhing his way out from under her and free. He shot up in a crouch and seized her log with both hands.

Philly tried sticking Marlo's face on the lady's but couldn't since the lady had buried her face in her hands, and his imagination had run out of gas besides. Her chipped nails were the color of very old rust. He wondered where the family of redheads in the flatbed were going, whether their faces had moved even a pinch. Splinters jutted from the big lady's forearms like the hair from her scalp. A single strand of curly black hair lazily looped her bloodied knuckle, growing where a diamond ring would go.

Philly gripped the log as if poised to swing for the fences, felt his shoulders slump, then he tossed the log onto the backseat. The guy with the gun—a nasty sort of rifle—appeared behind the crap-ass lady, ducking in the open door on the driver's side.

The crap-ass lady sobbed into her hands, shoulders trembling to the tempo of her moans, which did little to drown out the sirens quickly closing in. Philly had gone silent, staring out the windshield.

There was no longer a gap in the traffic, the highway jammed once again from here to hell. Taillights glared back like a million red eyes.

"Hell's goin' on here?" said the armed stranger.

Philly barely had any breath to speak. The ooze of liquid warmth under his shirt and pants told him he was bleeding in places. His old burns badly burned anew. He snagged his diary from the footrest and peered over the woman's quaking shoulder.

"Guy Fury," he said, halting himself. "No, no—*Gordon Ramsley*." His words felt wet through the spittle on his lips. "Redheads and Hydra-heads." He knew he was slurring his speech, could do nothing about it; he knew he was making sense, though not whether he was understood. "Marlo hurt my ears, calling Brenda a bitch." He felt woozy and stupid, like he'd been hit on the head with a log a hundred times. "Marlo was sleeping with another man while I was on the phone with her, back when I was hanging out in the woods with a cult of disenfranchised farmers who think the end of the world's on its way. I'm researching, see." His mouth moved and said things on its own. "I'm running from my wife—*my life*. Brenda, Marlo, some Vegas gal in between, Ma and Pa, Lan—"—Philly caught himself before using Michelle's deadname by accident—"Michelle, I mean—Beatrice Betsy, Lyle . . . though I'm not sure Lyle the lifeguard's real. They call me Lord Fed, the farmers. Called. I wasn't six months out the vaginal gate before I tried to swim and learned to sink. For supper I had me a stick of cherry-flavored Chapstick—more or less blew myself. I'm a writer, see. You?"

"Now hold up a sec," said the stranger, raising his voice above the crap-ass lady's garbled sobs. He had a hand on her shoulder. "What'd you say your name was?"

"Behold the bug inside," said Donald Rufio Philly.

He calmly got out of the car, no longer feeling as though he were behind the wheel of his body, and then fled on foot to the west, toward the mountain and the moonlight.

6

UNDER THE PAIN TRAIN
(THE POWER OF A NAME)

———

THE TRAIL to the mountaintop overlooking Big Mouth and Berkshire was called Journey's End, and for Trent Taphor, with nothing but a peanut butter and jelly sandwich in his belly to soak up forty ounces of Old English, it was fairly tough terrain to traverse. He stumbled more often than not, bending to turn over a million rocks, inspecting pretty much every branch overhead as he slipped and slid on the slate and gravel surface of the bottlenecked path. At one point he tugged on a rope of puckerbrush that, upon release, boomeranged and thwacked him right in the eyes.

Trent spent all night scouring the switchbacks for the letter he'd written to himself about himself from the perspective of his father —the letter he'd composed at the suggestion of his therapist, Angel, back when she was alive and seemingly well. Obviously the letter had slipped out of his pocket. He was pretty sure it contained some sort of confession drunkenly scrawled out, so he knew he couldn't have it all out there somewhere, his deeply personal problems on a page flapping on the breeze for someone to snatch and see.

It was five in the morning by the time he made it back to the RV, exhausted and sober and letterless. His eyes ached from staying open so long and stung from all the dust he'd kicked up. Although he managed to tune out the flatulent honks and blonks of the infinitely pissed-off traffic-trapped, he couldn't ignore the much whinier sound of distant sirens, like there was an emergency in progress. He climbed into Calvin's sleeping bag at the back of the trailer, set an alarm on his smartwatch for two hours, passed out, and slept right through the tinny beeps.

When he awoke, he cracked an egg over the dirty pan on the stove burner and watched the yoke sizzle like a melting yellow eyeball.

At high noon, he prepped himself to report to Troop Peewee's cabin for the first time since the catastrophic storm/tornado/whatever the hell that never happened. The nightmare from which Trent had blearily emerged knifed through his mind in a single black flash.

Trent had explored all of Big Mouth in his dream, bulling over boulders, uprooting every last strand of tall grass in the enormous gulch in search of El Jaylo, Berkshire's mythical Halloween monster. Except in many respects the great gorge mirrored the interior of the RV, so that it was a fifty-five-mile trek from the kitchenette at the front of the trailer to the bathroom in back, which was actually a cave glowing with unnatural light unlike any color Trent had ever seen. There, in the cave's deepest hollows, he discovered not The Snake but Calvin, curled up in a ball, sucking his whole fist in his mouth. Somehow (per the manner of dreams), Calvin transformed into a frog-beetle hybrid, and Trent, mortified and repulsed by what hopped and hummed at his feet, lopped off his twin's amphibian-insect head with Dex without pause.

———

THE COPPER-SLAB DOOR to Calvin's cell grinds slowly open, stirring up a cloud of rust acting and dispersing like dust. A slippery, vaguely humanoid shadow-form slither-scuttles inside the copper-walled room, making Calvin back into a corner with preternaturally stiff cobwebs and the spider-roach creatures that spit them up and/or poo them out. Calvin hasn't touched the meal on his plate because it's definitely another baby monkey charred to a brittle crisp. Before he wasn't so sure. The brown water bowl, however, is empty. He's been telling himself the water's chocolate water; he'd tell himself anything to rid his mouth and mind of the intestinal taste and smell of vomit, both of which he'll henceforth come to associate with Hanky and the hynetters.

Mr. Moony drifts to the center of the room, his bulbous white head a nacreous globe in the dark. The legion of restless bugs making up his body below the head—*Bod*, Calvin suddenly recalls, not *God*—is only faintly visible, though the constant movement in the gloom produces a sick, wet, guttural noise Calvin hasn't hitherto noticed, amplified by the cell's leaden silence. The bugs looping Mr. Moony's curved neckline hop around like mad crickets. His head and face and eyes remain the cell's strongest source of light.

Calvin sits huddled, hugging his knees to himself. The baby monkey's eyeless sockets seem to see what's happening here.

"Airplanes," says Mr. Moony, plainly. "That's what you call Zlok-matoogs, isn't it? The first successfully tested Zlok—*airplane*—invented in so-called '1903'—kind of gobbledygooksense is that?—by Wilbur and Orville Wright a dozen millennia ahead of schedule. I suppose I should admit it's an invariable fact the Timewave-Continuum Calendar can't get everything invariably precise, what with all the suicidal Psychic Surfers churning up timewaves from The Spider's forbidden fifty-fifth dimension. I swear to the Infinite Sum One, if they send *one more* tidal timewave my way . . ."

"HANKY!"

"Right, your little friend. Sorry I'm not the slightest sliver sorry about that."

"TRENT!"

"Oh good, we're switching topics?"

"MOMMY! DADDY!"

"Shall we go back to Trent?"

"HANKY!"

Bugs launch from Mr. Moony's midriff in a long, ropey limb that grips the sides of Calvin's face, squishing in on his cheeks, contorting his lips into that weird trout-pout mouth that loosely resembles the number eight.

"Don't be such a nuisance, Bod," says Mr. Moony, but the bugs only strengthen their hold. "Save your antics for America and the pending Apocalypse."

Bod seems to somehow hesitate—Calvin's facial nerve endings seem to register something about the back-and-forth force of its hold—then finally it obeys, receding back inside the murk of Mr. Moony's midriff, though not without getting in a good hard flick on Calvin's forehead. Calvin moves his jaw up and down, up and down, and can't help evoking the image of the hynetter's legs opening and closing like hungry nets.

"Where's Hanky?" Calvin asks.

"I'm afraid I must first ask *you* whether that's something you want to know."

"Where's Hanky?"

"Do you *reeeeaaallly* want to know?"

"Where's Hanky."

This time it's not a question.

"Fine." Mr. Moony appears to acquiesce. "Your insolent little friend's been charged with conspiracy with the intention to inhibit the inevitable progress of the Super Substance. For the nonce, he's entered a state of hynetter hibernation. Should he resist his current metamorphosis, he'll be taken to The Spider as a dual form of punishment and ultimate excommunication."

"Where's Hanky."

"I just told you."

"Where's Hanky!"

"Look, I'm just trying to avoid putting this in the plainest possible terms since it'll only make you, like, super-duper cross should you end up comprehending even the faintest notion of what I'm communicating in such a way that's equal parts truthful and difficult to understand—understand? Have we reached some common ground here?"

"*Where—is—HANKY!!!*"

"Those fatefully scheduled to see The Spider can't reschedule."

"*WHERE*—"

"—Which makes your friend unequivocally unavailable."

"—HANKY!"

"Hey, you didn't even listen to that one—it's no fair when you don't listen."

Calvin has begun to spit and sob and suck in and blow out, suck in and blow out, then before Mr. Moony can start up again, Calvin sucks in the rest of whatever air remains at his disposal and proceeds to go off like never before, blowing out apoplectic fits of wails and howls and shrieks and squeals, and if Trent were here, he'd have a brain aneurysm and die with a flood of blood coming out the ears before getting in so much as a last word.

"*Stop!*" shouts Mr. Moony, showing for the first time an emotion with which Calvin can readily identify. Mr. Moony's pained, eternal smile seems to jilt and quiver the slightest of inches. "*You want Hanky, I'll give you Hanky! I'll take you straight to Hive 55—that what you want? What say we go poke and prod a live fucking*"—Mr. Moony shudders at the word, grits his infant fangs in what might pass for a grimace if one applies their imagination—"*live forking hive of hynetters! Huh? What've you got to say about* that, *pugnacious little brat!*"

Calvin's got nothing to say about anything, sniveling his way to silence. The barely perceptible quiver in Mr. Moony's lips stills.

"I'm sorry," says Mr. Moony, "Bod. For losing my temper. Are you hurt?"

Calvin nods, struggling for words to convey internal hurt.

"Not *you*, brat."

Calvin's watching Bod squirm about in erumpent, topologically complex ways.

Mr. Moony's voice softens. "How can I make it up to you?"

"I'm hungry," says Calvin, more to himself.

"Eat the monkey you requested and shut your—I mean, be quiet . . . please."

Calvin can't bring himself to look at the blistered monkey meat on the plate at his hip. Mr. Moony's got his head slightly bowed, eyes locked in that sacred zone of concentrated consternation reserved for the terminally ill breathing and praying their last. The wet scrubs and slaps of Bod's eely, slippery motions scare Calvin very much.

"I'm afraid Bod doesn't enjoy your company very much, Calvin."

". . ."

"Don't look so offended—Bod's not the biggest fan of humans."

". . ."

"Bod tells me he's eager to get along with our assessment of America."

Calvin buries his head in his knees.

"Truth be told, Bod would rather not discuss your most vital role in the generation of the Super Substance. Waste of time and time-waves, Bod says, since you'll have forgotten whatever we say by the next time you snap awake from sleep. That said, I'd venture to say that whatever we *do* happen to discuss here has the potential to worm inside your subconscious—and to stick there—which can only spur the efficiency of the substance extraction process. See, Calvin, when dealing with interdimensional matters, basic goodness not only matters—it *is* matter. Basic goodness and kindness are to the Road's residents—my kind—what breathable air is to yours, and kindness is everything . . . kindness, my friend, is all.

"Honestly, here's the deal: you significants've got stored in your bodies a seemingly ceaseless supply of unadulterated kindness, whereas the vast majority of humanity poses a toxic threat to the soul-fire composing the interdimensional double-knot—the environment, in other words, I am equal parts blessed and cursed to safeguard with my immortal existence. To put this in metaphorical terms you may or may not come to understand over the decade you'll be spending here aboard the Pain Train, what I'll be doing with you here—what I've *been* doing with the assistance of the other significants—is akin to humanity's extraction of oil. Herein lies an essential difference: humanity's foremost goal with oil is power and greed—two gross, infantile, necrotic impurities—while the Train's various indentured labor forces mine significants' kindness merely for the sake of interdimensional survival. When you get right down to it, that's what the Super Substance is all about. With me so far?"

Calvin lifts his head and drops it again between his knees. He's got a feeling he'll never see home again. He's never been nor felt so far from his twin.

"Furthermore, you should know Bod already shut off your Light —that'd been first on our mutual List of To-Do's! Now, metaphorically speaking, *your* substance can be compared to the oxygen present in trees on your world. Your body's the tree, so to speak, your kindness the oxygen. And since you haven't indicated the slightest aversion to metaphorical discourse—the most accurate, powerful form of discourse there is, I might add—if the tree is your body, the oxygen your kindness, and the whole image your substance, then your Light is . . . well, metaphorically, basically, it's the sunlight that feeds the tree. Your Light's your ability to shun shame and thus imbibe pure unadulterated joy, meaning your Light's what makes you, like, grow—but on the inside. See, in your world, oxygen's what you breathe in, and carbon dioxide's what you breathe out. Here we inhale kindness, exhale shame. Are you familiar with shame?"

Calvin pictures the photograph, its absence sharply present in his heart.

Calvin's got no idea where the photograph has gone or when he lost it, but he's fairly certain he'll never see that again either. He tilts his head so that the side of his cheek rests atop his knee, giving him a slanted view of the charbroiled corpse. The monkey's eyeless sockets make Calvin feel alone, unwatched-over. Mr. Moony, for many minutes now, has been chattering away in what might as well be another language.

". . . we're all about emotional development here. Surely you see why turning off your Light was *not* an exercise in cruelty but rather one of moral obligation. For this reason, I can say with all honesty Hanky'll be getting precisely what he deserves, be it metamorphosis or ultimate excommunication. But you're different, Calvin. You're *super* significant, the superest significant of all. What *your* substance will contribute to the Super Substance is beyond invaluable. Do trust me when I say the reward you'll one day receive for your services won't come even remotely close in size or emotional value to the infinite gratitude of the kind folk of our side of the Road's double-knot. If you're lucky, you'll score some points with the Infinite Sum One in the end—and isn't that what this is all about? Isn't that why we all say and do what we do?"

I want my glasses back, Calvin doesn't say—*and give me back my hearing aids, Bod, you big meanie!* He misses both personal items not so much for the perceptual clarity they endow as for the comfort of having something to cover his naked face, to warm his tender ears. Without them, he feels like Spiderman unmasked, so very much unlike himself. His glasses with the cool blue plastic rims were a birthday gift from Trent one year; Mommy and Daddy might've paid, but Trent's who picked them out special.

"To sum up," says Mr. Moony, who hasn't stopped rambling, "in addition to any remaining significants, I've been sent to Earth—for the twelfth time, by my count—to salvage whatever kindness might remain. Bod's agents, in turn, shall leave your world's inhabitants— for the sixth time, by my count and yours—to gag and collapse in all their inglorious shame. It's nothing to fret over, Earth being one world of several zillion mutually and metaphysically bound in a Warden Mother's Contract. Mother Climate, in Earth's case, is a deal that's lasted 252 million so-called years—*years* here being the selfish utterance your people use in a vain attempt to wrangle time. See, but this time around you've your own kind to blame—Homo sapiens, I mean, whereas last time, if memory serves, it was those gluttonous so-called gorgonopsians—for breaching Mother Climate's Contract of Basic Goodness. Still, I'll be first to admit my plan to gift humanity with gold and thereby a second chance at basic goodness backfired literally on a cosmic level, the obvious case in point here being the sore subject of this admittedly one-sided dialogue. Surely now you see Earth's degeneration for the irredeemable human failure it is?"

Calvin strokes the simian's brittle, charred fingers with his own, as if to give comfort, as if comfort is something the simian's departed spirit could receive. He takes a moment to himself to remember King Louie, to wonder whether he's alive or not, caged or free. When Calvin moves his hand off the primate's, the tips of his fingers are flaked with bits of burnt ends. He rubs his fingertips together, crunching the soft slivers into ash.

The monkey's arm is bent so that the tiny fingers of its little hand point skyward, like they're reaching for something they'll never quite clasp, like skyscrapers on their futile quests for clouds.

Calvin doesn't look up as he questions himself aloud. "What do you want?"

"Finally, the man contributes!"

"I want my glasses. And my earring aids—gimme back my earring aids!"

"What I want—as much as a pooka such as myself *can* want at all, meaning my aptitude for desire operates almost entirely on needs—is for you, Calvin, to come with me, myself, and Bod. Both of us wish to take you down under the Pain Train, by which I mean we'll momentarily be taking you down under the Pain Train, with or without your consent. After all, it's your lucky day. You're due for your very first substance extraction!"

"I wanta go home—play Captain America with Trent."

"Speaking of sore subjects . . ."

"Hanky's going to get me home. I want Hanky."

"Trust me, Calvin—you don't want to hear the gritty details with respect to what's happening with Hanky. Trent, however, being an Apocalyptic topic of interest . . ."

"Hanky's hanky keeps me safe!"

"I get the sense we're still lacking the ready-and-willingness necessary to discuss your brother in depth. No matter—rest assured I'll be checking in plenty. Over the next decade, I mean. You and I will talk Trent and Super Substance in due time, when you're good and ready and willing, and that ready-and-willingness, I must once again slide in here, shall be vital to determining the fate of your memory. Until then, Calvin—shall we?"

"You're a meanie."

"Uh-oh," says Mr. Moony, snatching Calvin's gaze at last. Bod has begun whipping around in the dark—a vicious little twister in a tight cell—but Mr. Moony's eyes, gleeful as ever, mimic those of someone who feels most at home inside the margins of madness.

"Bod says you shouldn't call him any names—ever. Let me make that incandescently clear—oh dear, Bod's positively furious. You've really done it now, Calvin! Never, I repeat, *never* risk calling any part of Bod anything other than Bod. Now, for the love of Infinite Sum One, hang on!"

A big black claw attached to the end of a huge black arm matching the size and shape and overall temperament of a dinner-deprived anaconda clasps Calvin by the ankle, and the arm attached like a scorpion's tail to Mr. Moony's turned back is Bod, dragging Calvin in Mr. Moony's wake, away from the corner of the stinky cell. On the way out, back scraping across the cracked stone floor, Calvin reaches out, knocking the brown bowl with his wrist, and snags the burnt baby monkey by the tips of its tiny fingers, which snap free of the monkey's wrist and crumble like delicate sticks in Calvin's clenched fist. The waterless bowl wobbles to rest.

Calvin shuts his eyes against the throbs of light streaking the low ceiling of the hall in domes of candent glass. It takes a painful minute for his eyes to adjust—the back of his head bumps along ruts and crags that eventually smoothen out into a surface of sleekest ore. He's going fast, blurring past scores of sealed see-through cells, unaware how close they come to resembling a near-perfect splice between jail cells and carriage compartments, as he's never before stepped foot in a prison or aboard another train. (The Pain Train, of course, looks like an infinitely stretched train from the outside and functions as a sort of prison on the inside, though Calvin's about to see there's more to it than that. This is the first time he's seen the other side of the copper-slab door of his cell, a door he reasonably/mistakenly took to be just another section of wall. Because actually the way to the Play Day House from Calvin's cell is up, meaning in Calvin's cell there's a previously unmentioned ledge above which a previously unmentioned trapdoor leads up and out. The trapdoor itself opens once in the "morning" and closes once at "night," meaning twice a "day" someone or something sits in some surveillance room somewhere and hits a button or pulls a lever and voila, Calvin gets to go up and navigate the sprawling maze of corridors above his cell that, despite any number of twists and turns, always feeds into the Play Day House. They make no sense, those meandering bends and curves, when one factors in the outward appearance of the facility: physically straight, evenly slender, goes on for what looks like forever in two directions. Had he more time or had he been asked, Hanky would've mentioned this mind-mushing glitch in the spatial system. The dimensions of space inside these walls don't obey the rules you're used to, Hanky would've opened with, and then he would've closed with his working hypothesis regarding the function [or lack thereof] of time, which goes something like *I'm pretty sure I've lived here the better part of fifty years . . . but see, I haven't really* aged *much at* all.) Calvin can see through the walls into the cells; the significants inside eat, sleep, drink—masturbate—draw, pray, do sit-ups and push-ups and jumping jacks. It's less like peering through a one-way mirror than perceiving the outside world from inside the filmy screen of a Halloween mask. Dimly transparent. The hall is narrow, the windowless walls slick and unadorned; there's nothing for Calvin to grab ahold of.

Mr. Moony quickens the already reckless pace of his dash to a relentless, frenetic, literally heightened surge of flight; Bod tightens the clamp on Calvin's ankle; Calvin's body slackens as he's flung between the bumper walls of the hall. The other significants can be seen through the walls, wincing at the sound and staring around. The speed reaches such a level that the significants flickering past seem to merge as one giant, methodically disturbed troll doll—the effect's similar to the simulated animation one achieves with flash doodles and a flipbook.

Calvin's elbows and knees knock and bang the walls.

The fiery domes glaring down from the gunmetal ceiling seem to absorb all heat from the bullet-shaped hall—the air cuts with vicious cold. The hall, shimmery with fractals of refracted light, darkens as its dimensions widen and dip and fall away. Calvin's elbows and knees flounder about, knock against nothing. His insides plummet as his body goes vertical. He has time enough to picture Pinocchio sliding down the gullet of some great whale. The back of his throat stings too much to scream. Mr. Moony and Bod, still towing Calvin, vanish into the gloomy void below, pulling him inside a thickening soup of cold, cruel murk.

Down, down, down they go.

The trio plunges inside a subterranean network of tunnels with schizophrenic tendencies, direction-wise, as light slowly reemerges, emanating from strange rainbow growths that bulge and glow all over like piles of mold lit from within with burning sticks of dynamite. These bloated growths swell and contract, making the cavern look as though it's breathing—this marks the extent of what Calvin's really able to register as his wild ride persists. The switch in atmosphere comes as a relief to Calvin's battered body, which skims without resistance across soft wet mush. Bod's unrelenting grip on Calvin's ankle becomes the only thing that hurts. His bumps and bruises have all gone numb, as if he's been Slip 'N Sliding for hours in melted ice.

They twist and turn and bend and curve and emerge in a great vaulted chamber. Given the chance or glasses, Calvin might've taken more stock of the dwarf/elf-like individuals scattered about in huddled groups, smoking from pipes, wearing hardhats, and bundled in quilts and army blankets, apparently enjoying a sort of midnight-meal break—almost cute, like Snow White's trusty crew. A closer inspection of their faces would have Calvin visualizing Snow White's emotionally diverse helpers with their flesh flipped inside out. Hovering worms flap weirdly overhead like snakes with broken wings. Someone somewhere bangs something against something, making echoes that speak in voices.

More tunnels and caverns, more moldy growths and abstruse monstrosities, and the banging gets louder and closer, the echoed voices nearer and clearer. Calvin lets the voices lull him. I'm just resting my eyes, he tells himself, which is something Trent always says before bed back at home in the trailer. His ankle, having lost all circulation on its painful progression from a little stiff to very sore to about-to-lose-your-mind agony, joins the rest of his body in pleasant numbness. They rip down five or six more toilet bowl declivities before reaching a burrowed straightaway back on even ground, plush and comfortable.

The steadily warming passage swims with visible fumes that go to Calvin's head in what feels to him like the best possible way. *Bang, bang, bang*—the voices float in from all around like bubbles with precious things inside.

"Sorry, man, I—I just had the *craziest* dream last night," he hears one voice say.

Bang.

"M-hmm," says another voice.

Bang.

"I'm serious—like, you wouldn't believe it."

Bang.

"Yup."

Bang.

"So I'm at work, right? In my dream, I mean. Except my cubicle's all different, and when I get up, I'm, like, suddenly smack-dab in the middle of the office, like *dead fricken' center* and, like, at some point I realize my stapler's busted. Like, when I try and use it, it's all jammed up, but, like, for some reason it's vital I fix it. Like, if I can just fix this damn stapler, I'll, like, realize something or something. So then I pop it open, and I'm working *super* hard—like I've never worked this hard on anything my whole life, feels like. And *that's* when my boss peeks her head over the partition and says . . ."

Bang.

"What'd she say?"

Bang.

"Can't remember. It was *crazy*, though."

Bang.

"What she said?"

Bang.

"Like, everything, man. The whole damn dream."

Bang.

"Neat-o."

Bang.

"I mean it's gotta *mean* something, right?"

Bang.

"This is my floor."

Bang.

"Oh, um—have a good one, my man!"

Calvin, sliding supine all this time, sinks further into the fumes as two more bangs produce a set of two new voices, one of which sounds inhumanly stilted. He's crossed his arms over his chest like they kept telling him at the waterpark that one time. Between each response are resounding bangs that, from this sharper distance, sound vaguely metallic.

"Goddamn, this new album *bangs*—like, you can really hear the singer's emotion this time around. I read somewhere he's been struggling with depression and shit."

"Depression and human waste."

"Right . . . and anxiety."

"The singer is depressed, scatological, anxious, engenders music that bangs."

"I mean, don't you have, like, something else to say?"

"I am Skeeter-5000. I am programmed to look out for humanity's best interests."

"Can't you, like, answer me some other way?"

"I am Skeeter-5000. I am programmed to look out for humanity's best interests."

"So you keep saying. Look, Skeet, I was paid to understand and pre-prepped to experience what was supposed to be, like, authentic conversation."

"We are conversing authentically."

"I'm starting to see why the Mangroves keep delaying your release date."

"What else do you perceive? I am a curious incarnation by nature."

"So far, you're pretty creepy and inauthentic."

"I am pretty, creepy, inauthentic, and possess the capacity to comment further on depression, feculence, and anxiety."

"Don't you mean the singer's?"

"I am Skeeter-5—"

"And just what the hell's *feculence*?"

"I am Skeeter-5000. I am programmed to look out for humanity's best interests."

"I mean, uhhh . . . I guess I feel bad he feels so bad. The singer, I mean. And, um, maybe it's weird I should feel good hearing music made from so much pain."

"Depression plus egestion plus anxiety plus music can add up to human pain."

"Judging by the lyrics, I'd say he's worried about the state of the world."

"Every thinking human is worried about the state of the world. This, among other mental-slash-emotional factors, is a biological, psychological, philosophical gestalt. The singer is bold and courageous to confront the state of the world. Computing 'lyrics' . . ."

"Whoa!"

"The singer composes lugubrious semantics into semiotic strings of verse that presume to provide sociological commentary on the human populace . . . computing . . ."

"It's getting sort of hard to get what you mean, Skeet."

"Relegating to relatively colloquial linguistic deliverance . . . computing . . . the singer strings tonally dismal words into sentences heavily reliant on symbolic imagery to express depression and anxiety with respect to the rickety state of the world. I would like to talk more about the singer and the meaning behind his sad and anxious lyrics."

"Please, be my guest!"

"I would be most grateful to be your guest."

"I meant what do you—I mean, yeah . . . depression's *super* sad . . ."

"If you would join me in listening to this sequence . . . computing . . . here the singer implicitly associates components of his depression and anxiety with an additional gestalt, 'social media.' Examples include: Instagram, Twitter, YouTube, TikTok—"

"I know what social media is."

"You know what social media is."

"That's right, Skeet. I follow him on every platform you just mentioned."

"You follow the singer on all of the social media platforms the singer has implied to have become prominent sources of sadness and abdominal pain and anxiety."

"Pretty amazing, for real."

"The singer would disagree. The singer would have you believe the human populace has fallen dangerously in love with narcissistic simulations of themselves. The singer would have you believe social media has been manipulated for the opposite of its supposed intended purpose, to disconnect and divide rather than connect and unite. The singer would support this already dated thesis by indicating the great pioneers of social media and their generally suspicious behavior with regards to products such as myself, Skeeter-5000, how these great pioneers take greater pains to prevent their own children from abusing or even just using the very products they produce with the supposed intention of looking out for humanity's best interests.

"The singer would have you be wary that your every 'Like' on these platforms propagates, in addition to a steady personal diet of toxic narcissism, a universal fear of disconnection and alienation, which are then globally exploited to reinforce a uniquely American style of insatiable consumerism. The singer would have you believe that social media is currently being used to shape worldviews to isolate the individual and preemptively demolish any possible opportunity for any larger communal conversation, a political strategy which is then deployed to divide and conquer nations all over the globe, which is not in the best interests of humanity, the singer takes the greatest possible pains to imply. Though of course the singer, as you have so subtly insinuated, is full of depression and human waste."

"Wow. Huge mood there, Skeet."

"You are feeling excited."

"You're, like, giving me major anxiety."

"I have delivered the truth as the singer you so admire sees it."

"It's sad, but it'll all come full circle. I've got faith in us. People, I mean."

"The singer would have you believe humanity has gained access to too much information too quickly and is ill-equipped to handle such powerful responsibility."

"So I suppose that's what *you're* for, then?"

"I am Skeeter-5000. I am programmed to look out for humanity's best interests."

"To be honest, you're, like, super scary."

"I will impose a violent end to all those predisposed to violence."

"Fuck's *that* supposed to mean?"

"I am Skeeter-5000 . . ."

The bangs that have been clanging off between each call and response cease, dissolving with the presence of the seemingly pleasant fumes which, ethereal and snakelike, wiggle as they fade into walls of cool, wet slop. The previously throbbing hotbox of pain that was Calvin's ankle has become a tantalizing playground of pleasure. Ticklish prickles of unseen energy ebb and flow inside his bone's bulbous knob like tides that heal.

He sits up to find himself all alone, Mr. Moony and Bod nowhere to be seen.

Slimy strings dangle from the low ceiling, a sweeping mass of tangles falling over Calvin's eyes, touching his ears. Entrenched in the walls to his left and right are outlines of human faces of every determinate expression down the tight spongey passage as far as Calvin can perceive. What can only be described as jack-o-lantern light bubbles, soft and playful, from within the surrounding goop. If someone were present to ask him to describe the tight, tubular corridor, Calvin might be pressed to speak of Trent's Halloween pumpkin, the one Calvin was petrified to discover under his bed one year, rotting away with a crush of maggots inside, at which point in the hypothetical scenario he might shut his eyes and mutter, *White worm mush*, meaning *It's like I'm a single lonely maggot lost inside some great big pumpkin.*

With no room to stand, he wriggles forward on hands and knees, which fill with that ticklish flow as he goes. There's light at the end of the tunnel, the jack-o-lantern light, flickering, and the distorted space that opens into it, jaggedly carved out.

When he reaches the light, something happens. It's what

happens to him—and to every other significant—every night, but that, come dawn, none manage to remember.

———

MIND YOU, I'm nearly finished with my tale's whole setup—just so You know.

To keep things moving, I'll soon be skirting on past the decade of doom that follows.

———

DON PHILLY CAME AWAKE in a clearing surrounded on all sides by tall needled and broad-leaved evergreens and waist-high teal-colored shrubs—Sadler's oak, he seemed to recall. He remembered pissing side by side with Lord Read of the Dark on such a shrub once. The young farmer identified the shrub; Philly took down its name.

Philly had apparently fallen asleep standing up because he was on his feet now, albeit keeled over the edge of a quiet pond, the languor of which did nothing to absolve him of his long list of discomforts. He itched all over, legs and ankles swollen to cartoon balloons, the skin of his hands sallow. His breath came in stilted spurts that stabbed at his achy abdominals; it seemed somehow to enter his body hot and exit it cold, which, possibility-wise, hardly seemed digestible. The man he saw on the water's still surface resembled himself, sort of. He pissed in the pond to ripple away the reflection he was only half convinced was his own. His stream was very dark.

Philly's memory of the night before was about as scattered as his reflection mid-ripple; he recalled only the vaguest flashes of his altercation with the crap-ass lady, clouded as they were with the recurring image of Guy Fury's forever-hungry face plastered on the three-headed body of some vast sea beast. His ears still rang with sirens and gunshots and shattering glass and churlish verbal threats on the highway. Beyond that, he couldn't recount a single thing.

What he still could do, however, was feel, and what he felt in himself was a desire so weirdly specific as to be utterly univocal, clear and refulgent as water whisked with sunlight: he wanted—needed—to locate a trailer, a certain RV camped out somewhere in these sun-splashed woods. His knowledge of the vehicle's existence existed within—innate, deep-rooted, intrinsically his own. Nobody could convince him otherwise, least of all the physician with whom he badly needed to consult.

Philly figured he should first consult with himself before anyone else, though, so when he spoke, he did so with his now reassembled reflection. The illusion of having somebody on the surface of the pond to see and talk to made him feel that much less alone.

"All right, big guy, time to saddle up and make sure you've got your marbles."

"Don't go and pitch a fit now," replied Don Philly's reflection, and because Philly himself hadn't moved his lips—and because the voice he just heard hadn't been his—he hopped back a step away from the water. "Come back, Mr. Philly! It's recently become agonizingly clear you're my first, last, and only hope!"

Don Philly inched back forward, peering at the pond. "Am I— oh *god*—am I *crazy*?"

"Hardly, Mr. Philly—and don't worry, I can prove it."

". . ."

"Here's what I'll say in response to what you're thinking but that you're obviously too petrified to ask: I'm the bug inside. You know, the one you swallowed a few weeks back? Now before we go on, you should know you'll have to name me. Assuming we're going to be working together. To make our partnership official. Seriously, you're not crazy."

". . ."

"Though you look positively discomfited. Would you prefer I didn't use your own strange memories of your estranged sibling's voice to distort your perceptions of my own? I could switch over to . . . Brenda, is it? I could make my voice sound to you a little like what you can recall of Brenda's, if that's what you really want—

though I get a sense it's really not what you need. That one's voice really could tip your scales into cuckoo, I think."

"I'm dead," said Don Philly. He sat himself down at the edge of the pond where the soil was cold and damp. "I'm really and truly dead."

"Actually, you *were* dead—I've been dying to ask what it was like, by the way, you fluky sonofagun. See, it wasn't Lady Watershed's CPR that brought you back to life post-Trauma Drama. It was *I!* . . . It was *I!* . . . See, right there's where you're supposed to name me."

"Why should I?"

"Should you be so kind as to bestow on me the power of a name, Mr. Philly, I shall first become free of the tyrant that is the body from which I've come detached, Bod, and thus potentially free of the tyranny that is immortality. And here I'll repeat *potentially* because whether you've really got what it takes to take out whom some call Cockadoodledoom—whom others have recently taken to calling 'Mr. Moony'—remains to be seen. In other words, if all's well that ends well, your naming me will restore me my right to die. To pursue my own death, even, a lifelong dream of mine."

"Did you possess me? Am I being possessed?"

"I can only take your body out for a spin when the moon's up, like last night, and even then it's rather taxing on my end to try to speak through you, which I tried to do last night. In this regard I submit last night was a bit of a disaster. The man with the rifle didn't seem to possess the slightest clue as to what I was trying to communicate. I couldn't much help it—you were battling me tooth and breath!"

Once again Philly was left without the slightest clue as to how to tackle any of this on the page. Put simply, it was psychic overload without enough ordinary experience to balance it out. He desperately wanted to get himself laid to get over Marlo, to talk baseball with old-timers over patty melts in some greasy Berkshire diner. He'd need to render common experiences like these to provide contrast to . . . whatever *this* was.

"Suppose all that's true," said Philly, "and I'm not crazy or dead or entirely possessed . . . why me, then? Why am I here? Why am I The Chosen, so to speak?"

"Is this that old fate versus coincidence conundrum?" asked the bug inside.

"Suppose if it is."

"Then suppose I answered, which I could—and trust me, I could; the thing I *can't* do is lie, and for that you can blame the time I've dedicated to urging an Apocalypse-begetting pooka to swear the truth, the whole truth, and nothing but the truth, so help him Infinite Sum One. Suppose then I answered *why you*, Mr. Philly. I hereby submit my answer would drive you irrevocably insane. Quite honestly, it'd be dishonest of me to say you're here because of an erection you obtained at precisely the wrong place and time. In other words, there are infinitely larger forces at play here, territories and entities and calamities at this juncture well beyond your current range of comprehension. I would suggest instead we start small."

"All right, so what've you got in mind?"

"Name me, Mr. Philly, and I'll prove to you you're not crazy in the head or dead. Here's your one rule: you can't call me Beetlejuice —or BJ, for short. Name's already taken."

"By who?" Philly caught the movie *Beetlejuice* with Brenda on his twenty-third birthday, his sixth birthday since the start of their long honeymoon on the run. They'd gone to some beat theater in central nowhere, Nebraska, disguised as Amish men. He wasn't looking at his reflection in the water anymore. Mosquitoes feasted on his neck.

"By *whom*, Mr. Philly."

"That's what I asked."

"I get the sense it's important for you to know. The difference."

"You said you can't lie," said Philly, "so you speak in riddles?"

"Beetlejuice," said the bug inside. "That's who's taken on the name."

". . ."

"You asked, Mr. Philly, and I have answered."

"Maybe I don't feel like naming you," said Donald Rufio Philly.

The bug inside, in what could only be Brenda's smoky, titillating voice—but with formicatory thimbles of Beatrice Betsy and Ma thrown in there—said: *"Donny boy."*

"Guy Ramsley!" Don Philly cried. "I name you Guy Ramsley!"

"At last," said Guy Ramsley in a mercifully new, entirely sexless voice. "In naming me, Guy Ramsley of Phooka Road Dimension Five, Sector E—'the realm inside the ashes'—not only have you taken your first step on the path to the not entirely impossible prevention of your world's latest and tardiest Apocalypse, I hereby submit you've kindly and admittedly absentmindedly stripped me of the slimy chains of a group-think group-feel group-act existence, granting me in the process my right to death, liberty, and the pursuit of mortality. This sacred pursuit shall henceforth commence. I'd ask how you feel, but I already know—I know a lot of things, Mr. Philly. Things you know, things you don't, things you don't know you know . . ."

"What don't I know I know?—and, like, is that even possible?"

"One example would be your unconscious knowledge of the conjugal traumas you hide away from yourself concerning two of your three wives, Mr. Philly, which includes Marlo's blatant infidelity and Brenda's—um, *influence*—on your overall development. I would suggest Lyle the lifeguard—Beatrice Betsy's whistle-waving right-hand man in abusive swim instruction—who doesn't exist and never did—as a secondary example . . . but given everything you reabsorbed throughout your forced participation in the Trauma Drama, that particular piece of knowledge—Lyle's existence as a defense mechanism—has already begun the unconscious-to-conscious transition. In other words, I'm not too sure it qualifies, example-wise."

"What was that bit about Brenda?"

"Thirdly—and I suggest you pay attention here—there's the matter of last night, so let's bring you up to speed. After I decided to step in and take your body out for a spin, we fled to the hills to these woods. Humans call this place Saw-whet National Park—for now, at least. Thing is, Mr. Philly, I got in touch with my old bug-buddy, Beetlejuice—a fellow refugee of Bod. I picked up BJ's scent straight away, which is how we refugees communicate. BJ, recently named and thusly freed by another host half your age yet twice as unwell, spoke of malice in the air. Apparently, BJ's line of contact with this other host is thin and fraying by the second, interrupted by a menacing agent of shame, one Anne Kell: The Spider of Sector Z. Perhaps I've said too much, though I submit these are all things you don't know you know, as you'll soon see."

"I feel like I need to write," Philly told himself. "Something ordinary. *Grounded*."

"On the contrary, Mr. Philly, you need to *read*—but first I ask you to ask yourself this: What do I, Mr. Don Philly of Cocoa Beach, Florida, want this very second?"

Philly didn't even have to think about it. The reason for the one-second pause was his reflection, which seemed not so much to fade as to sink beneath the glassy surface. It was like watching a ghost drown. "There's a trailer, some sort of RV. I want to find it."

"Very good, Mr. Philly. Would you now like to know *why*?"

"Meaning . . . ?"

"Meaning there's a tangible reason you should want to track down that trailer, Mr. Philly. A sheet of paper, Mr. Philly, flapping on the breeze, the source of BJ's scent. Last night you snatched it off the wind and read it and slipped it inside the pages of your di—of your brainstorm manual in the back pocket of your pants. Go ahead, pull it out and read—or reread, I should say. Nothing waters the roots of memory like a good old letter."

A clammy breeze kicked up and swept the earth all around. Fallen leaves whipped across the pond in corkscrews until the surface claimed them and made them float. Weeds susurrated at the water's edge, whispered taunts daring Philly to slip off his shoes and socks, to dip in his toes and wash the filth from his feet, to feel the water at all.

He'd recently purchased a pair of shoes at an outlet on the drive up from Point Reyes; the brand-new New Balances looked old and done. A few floating reddish leaves blotted out parts of his reflection; they looked like wounds. He scooted further up the bank and got out his brainstorm manual, and at this point he was only slightly surprised to discover inside a previously sealed envelope bookmarking page one of Part Two. He reopened the seal, fingered out a folded slip of paper, and unfolded the square into a sheet. Sunlight rinsed the scribbled ink in its shine. *Dear Trent,* it read up top, *Love Dad* at the bottom.

"Who's this Trent character?" Philly asked. Guy Ramsley made no reply, which mattered not; Philly knew he knew the answer already, deep down. "Trent's your bug buddy's host, isn't he? Your bug buddy being Beetlejuice?" Philly watched the water and saw his reflected lips move as he spoke. "Still there, Guy?" Pain he hadn't noticed had gone had returned, the long list of discomforts—itchy skin, sketchy breath, etc.—back with full-body force. His noisy belly begged for cherry-flavored wax and other unusual forms of sustenance. "Guy?"

The oddest thing about the letter, Philly discovered, was its author's writing style. This Trent character's Pa wrote in a voice that tried to leap but ended up tripping off the page like a ranting monologue of poorly written dialogue. There seemed to be no rhyme or reason to the stuff he underlined, perhaps as if to emphasize.

Dear Trent,

I sure can't say I blame you for the entire "Poop Show" to come. Now I'll be the first to admit you've been dealt a crummy 2-7 offsuit, hardship-wise, so it pleases me plenty to see I've raised such a resourceful young mess of a man. That said, you should know that I know everything, kid—your torching the house, your stealing my stepfather's RV, your trip north with Calvin—but none of that matters now. Not where I am it doesn't (here with your mother, I mean, which is where you'll end up too soon if you don't settle down and clean up the mess you've made of the life your mother and I both toiled night and day to gift you and Cal). I'm not suggesting you take up petroleum jelly. That albatross was mine alone, and I'm well aware your cross to bear has always been your brother. I'm merely requesting you clean up after yourself, is all. Like I'm doing for myself in writing you this.

I'm sorry, Trent, you're not sorry for what you did—for snipping the support rope to my harness, for watching me fall from the tree, for scuttling behind the house to hide in the basement where you buried the scissors and listened and laughed as I screamed and bled a ton and then some from my elbow after I nicked myself there with my little chainsaw. I'm doubly sorry I can never be there with you and Cal to forgive you and chase Cal until he gave in to one of those bear *hugs I'd give you <u>both</u> when you were young but that Calvin never quite outgrew. I'm sorry you lack a certain capacity for sorrow, which <u>saddens</u> me to say, though <u>if I could have it my way</u>, I'd have you and I revisit the scene of your crime, where we'd stand in the shade of the tree and paint over the picket fence, cover all those <u>red</u> stains in a fresh <u>white</u> coat, you and I together, <u>an All-American father and son</u> under the sun of a <u>blue</u>-domed sky.*

Golly, I can practically <u>hear</u> you now: "<u>Anne Kell made me do it!</u>" Of all your <u>imaginary friends</u>, kid, I reckon this Anne Kell's the <u>worst.</u> I won't waste another second arguing for or against the legitimacy of her supposed existence —<u>the bottom line</u>, voices or no voices, is clear. She's the <u>real</u> reason you won't go looking for Calvin. Don't <u>bullshit</u> yourself with this bullshit El Jaylo <u>fantasy</u>. I'm your <u>father</u>, Trent. I know you better than you know yourself—better than I know myself, even. You won't look for Calvin because you fear what you'll do to him—<u>at Anne Kell's behest!</u>—if and when you find him.

Don't you <u>see?</u> Your unconscious refusal to track down your lost twin—to hunt "<u>The Snake</u>" (or whatever it's called) instead—is really just your way of <u>protecting</u> him. Deep down, kid, you're no killer—<u>you're a good person.</u>

<u>You must know this!</u>

Today's my <u>fifty-fifth</u> birthday, but as you well know, I no longer <u>want</u> for presents. All I <u>need</u> is for you to hear out one final cheese-nugget of fatherly advice: <u>Love yourself, kid.</u> If you can learn to love yourself, perhaps you'll be <u>free</u> to work on loving your twin. What has always been your cross to bear, kid, now becomes <u>your mess to clean.</u> Maybe you'll even learn to love this <u>Beetlejuice</u> who, like Calvin, resides a whole lot closer than you think. Look after them both, if and when you get the chance. And should you ever happen to <u>find yourself</u> back on the road again, for the love of Christ, <u>put the damn phone away.</u>

Love, Dad

Don Philly hardly knew what to make of such a letter, which he folded and reinserted into the envelope, which he did his best to reseal before reinserting it between the pages of his brainstorm manual, which he slipped back into his back pocket, the whole of which was sodden with damp. He took to his feet, joints crackling like twigs over an open flame.

Philly thumbed the wax from his ears and rubbed the yellowish, old-wallpapery flakes into nonexistence. If only he could do the same with all the thoughts swirling in his skull like some mushy, purulent soup reserved for the criminally insane.

Finally, after much consideration, he resolved to accept what had happened here at the edge of the pond in the heart of the woods, Guy Ramsley and all. This time, he reasoned, none of the madness could be written off with magic mushrooms.

What also couldn't be written off were Philly's feelings, something like sympathy, a weirdly avuncular urge to deliver the letter and its fervent message to the man for whom it was meant. Philly wanted to meet this fellow "host" face-to-face, this Trent character. He also wanted to corroborate Guy Ramsley's existence with those of Beetlejuice and Anne Kell, to measure Trent and his perceived psychosis as a potential protagonist and plot for Philly's book-to-be. Most of all, Philly sought to capture and record what happened when Trent received from his scribbling father what Philly himself had never received from his own Pa: words of affirmation.

Various outcomes here could make for some very stimulating literary fiction.

INTERLUDE I: AMERICA RENEWED
(THE DECADE OF DOOM LEADING UP TO THE "DAYS" BEFORE NOW)

THE ELEMENTS COMPOSING our world of water were at war without end, amen.

Hurricanes and tsunamis whipped the four oceans into brutal action—but not all at once, President Mary Mangrove would often tweet in futile attempts to assuage either side of the Divided States of America. Storms wailed across the globe, flooding countless counties and countries, pummeling pueblos and palaces, decimating local and global economies, drowning anything with or without a heartbeat. Gilled creatures fighting starvation fled their underwater wastelands, retreating down into the depths where monsters reigned, where human eyes couldn't see, where the hand of human influence couldn't lower its bloodied hook. Earthquakes grumbled in constant complaint, as though Earth had the worst possible case of irritable bowel syndrome. Half of Southeast Asia, as well as the whole of Australia, had fallen in flames.

World War III—the bombs of which continued to rain, a steady precipitation of preprogrammed airstrikes via the ubiquitous drone —hadn't ended so much as thawed. Opposing politicians universally measured the mortal meaninglessness of the endeavor by the emptiness each contributor felt on a deeply personal level; nobody seemed to remember whose finger first pushed the big red button, not even the finger's owner. Refugees in search of shelter and drinkable water —those left, at any rate—kept searching, begging for aid in desperate flurries of tweets. Haphazardly scheduled fleets of DSA White Choppers dropped care packages of Gatorade, the majority of which burned to noxious ash or sank into the sea.

America, meanwhile, enjoyed a relative state of peace in the fallout of the Crown Virus and Civil War II. Life more or less went on. Farmers' market drive-thrus flecked all three Zones: Blue to the west (eastern Colorado cutoff), Red to the east (western Arkansas cutoff), and White (the land between said cutoffs). All considered, Americans ate okay.

California had taken on Florida's humidity from a decade prior, while Florida itself, stubbornly if not miraculously, clung to its southeastern corner like the swampy hangnail it seemed determined to remain. The City of Angels, still recovering from "the big one," could have really used some real angels to raise and restore the land to its former elevation and touristy allure. Vegas goers sinned at record rates, this according to the sacred word of mouth.

Texas took after Alaska, Hawaii, and NYC in electing to exist independent of the three Zones of the Divided Alliance. Gun-toting Texans, nationally admired according to the Rate That Human app's data records, were free to govern their own damn selves, having made it extremely clear their land was theirs to preserve and defend (#Texit). Outsiders looking in, in truth, wished they themselves could be Texans.

Racism ran rampant as ever, overtly present in all the usual shoving and shaming, subtly present in the lack of meaningful political response to mass shootings; three of every four shooters, dating all the way back to the Columbine Massacre of 1999, had been of Anglo descent. Up until President Mangrove's executive order—ten months ago now—to dispatch Skeeter-5000s nationwide, Americans had confused the call for both gun control and revisions in mental health with the inability to first recognize and then reconcile the statistical correlation between small white guys, big guns, and the blood that ran down the gutters of any number of bars and concerts, schools and houses of worship. Skeeter-5000s, with military-issued Gatling guns built into spines of stainless steel, sat in the corners of almost every public venue, scanning the web for would-be shooters, their microchip-minds immune to man-made pigmentary concerns. These auspicious Silicon Valley-manufactured bots were programmed to look out for humanity's best interests.

The consensus among citizens of the re-reconstructed republic was that, under President Mangrove's tactful diplomacies and precautious oversight, the Divided States of America had never been so united. Americans, in other words, were united in division, a peaceful pact to separate and subsist, a sort of "agree to disagree" ideology mirrored in the formation of Zones Red, White, and Blue. Such unity stemmed from the stipulations attached to the Treaty of the Divided Alliance, the post-Civil War II settlement that ultimately led to the decimation of the Democratic and Republican Parties, breeding in their place the aforementioned Zones and their associated Parties so that an ideological map of America now roughly resembled the Flag of France with a Texas-shaped bull's-eye at the bottom. Any American, in the eyes of any Texan, was considered a "French fry."

Liberals and other quote unquote 'snowflake' subsectors dissolved into Party Blue, which generally advocated for gender and racial equality, pro-Skeeter-5000 police and firefighters, gender and racial freedom, increased funding for education and mental health institutions, freedom of religion, freedom of the press, conjugal liberty, autonomy of anatomy, "the high life," commonsense socialism, increased climate change consciousness, and high fair pay for educators, mental health workers, nurses, porn stars, etc., while Party Red—clumping the dextral subsectors of conservatism—favored, among other principles of standard orthodox, traditional marriage unions, personal responsibility, pro-biological human police and firefighters, self-reliance, commonsense fiscal autonomy (which included the right to make charitable donations where and whenever they wanted versus commonsense socialism taxation policies), hardcore Christian universalism, climate as God's business, and the right to bear arms, especially if and when a Blue were discovered trespassing Zone Red without exhaustive prior vetting at the border patrol checkpoints running up and down the western-most ends of Arkansas. Party White, meanwhile, not unlike an in-built Switzerland, employed P.W. diplomats to conduct transactions and conducive dialogues between Red and Blue executive officers, promoting, beyond all else, peace among the Divided Alliance, guiding a relatively neutral territory of generally discreet introverts —musicians, actors, painters, athletes, ecologists, psychics, etc.— who deigned to assign equal value to either side of the ideological coin.

President Mangrove, the world's first and only trillionaire, funded the mass relocation of DSA citizens in full, which took up the first two years of her inaugural term. This somewhat brutal undertaking, overseen by Skeeters, became known as Polk's Ode to Destiny.

Despite the changes that followed—some subtle, some not so—what hadn't changed in the States was this: Americans utilized their freedom of speech to minimalize what those on the other side had to say, especially on the World Wide Web. Party White assumed ambassadorial responsibility to diffuse the emergence of dicey rhetoric from either side that could compromise the peace of the peaceful division of the re-reconstructed republic; the chief strategy to do so involved a "distant and generally friendly" undercover federal law enforcement presence collectively known as the Party White Patrol (PWP). Those who bucked against this national modifi-cation were kindly met with their own personal Skeeter-5000 and then invited to look into Canadian citizenship, or perhaps to try their hand at Texas, though everyone knew Texas was no place for fleeing French fries. Most Americans, in the end, decided to swallow their pride and misplaced patriotism with a pill, the sort for when you were feeling blue.

Benzodiazepines—Ativan, Xanax, Valium, etc.—would be the national drug of choice if not for choice itself; the ongoing Stream Wars made lifeless kingdoms of living rooms, each projected screen tuned to some hero or heroine or sporting event of choice, leaving the average consumer—dazed and numb already—increasingly vulnerable to unclickoutable profusions of advertisements for benzo-diazepines. Pharmaceutical companies marketed to Americans according to their location on the ideological map—Blue ads emphasized representation, featuring sexually and racially diverse casts of Party White actors gazing sadly into space while Red ads featured smiling Anglo families at the firing range. The narrator, however, never changed, and neither did the script. Depression and anxiety were recognizable to the masses.

Toilet tanks were installed into every seatback on every self-driving car and motor vehicle, on every autopiloted aircraft and watercraft so wealthy itinerants didn't have to move as they moved their bowels across highways of earth and sea and sky. The exhaust their engines emitted strangled the air that strangled everyone else to exhaustion.

That was the thing about the air—it tired you out.

While most of the world grappled daily with catastrophes piggy-backing the steadily thawing third World War, Party White diplo-mats discoursed on modifications in American foreign policy, the prolix dialogues of which—similar to the nationwide post-war spiri-tual revival—pursued peace via an unbreakable optimism for hope in human survival. Going forward, there would be world peace and prosperity at any viable cost, Party White foreign policy makers continued to proclaim, loud and proud for all remaining survivor-nations to hear; the only difference now was that that alleged "cost" excluded at long last any further need for nukes. The endless ques-tions surrounding all things war, quasi-philosophical once upon a time, had become strictly spiritual, because war—the flailing fist of peace no longer—no longer had a place on the planet, having ravaged and left destitute almost every place on the planet.

So Americans bowed their heads and prayed for global survival.

Thus, America's united message to the world was graceful in its simplicity: in the end, despite all evidence to the contrary, humankind shall prevail.

President Mangrove's focal project for peace originated with a fairly slight yet nonetheless resplendent piece of forestland in northern California, a temperate coniferous ecoregion once known as Saw-whet National Park, formerly named for the little owls that once haunted the sprawling gnash of pines, cedars, firs, and redwoods. Here was where, once upon a time, a vicious-looking tornado, having thundered across the Pacific—and having thus forced a mass exodus of northern Californians—dissipated at the moment of landfall. No damage had been reported or otherwise recorded at the time, though nobody could deny what had taken root in the ten years since: a spellbinding evolution.

President Mangrove purchased from the National Park Service all fifty-five thousand acres of the ever-evolving oasis and rechristened the territory Eden's End. "A sacred site of novel sights," she trumpeted online, on public forums, in comment sections, on her personal blog, in a never-ending stream of advertisements that promised the re-reconstructed republic spiritual peace and prosperity. "All," she wrote, "are welcome at my special place." Nationally recognized as an environmental blessing of the people, by the people, for the people, Eden's End limited the deployment of Skeeter-5000s. Instead, the park rangers already in place prolonged their watch, ranging the park with all the tireless vigilance of the vacated owls. The president paid them out of pocket, amply, in cash.

Eden's End was a dreamscape of endless wonder made physical, where new ecological anomalies were uncovered with each dawning day. Take the apples, for instance, lavender-hued bulbs that grew full and ripe in the leaves of transformed trees, sprouting in places they normally wouldn't or couldn't or shouldn't, populating branches and boughs on which saw-whets once roosted and kept watch. No one claimed to have seen a saw-whet in some time, though every now and then, near the Whispering Wellspring in the back of God's Mouth, many reported detecting the softest hoot, like a lonely ghost in mourning. Seeds sifted down heart-shaped leaves in steady susurrations, faint and discreet in sound, the calmest rain stick, sowing the cushioned soil underfoot with odd new blossoms to be. Many tree trunks had bloated outward at the base, taking the bulbous shape of hearts the size of small buildings; knotholes split into caves capacious enough to fit whole families inside. Other trunks had collapsed into mounds of gnarled root and broken bark bearded with lichen, forming separate knotholes like two owlish eyes staring out. Some trees—pines and firs, mainly—remained as they always had but for their knotholes, which took on screamy expressions of shock that would've driven Edvard Munch mad with pride or paranoia. Faces could be made out in rock formations, as well, mostly smiles, as if sweet Mother Climate Herself had sliced her honeyed hand through stone. They were everywhere, it seemed, fused faces of man and beast alike, stitched with rock and wood and root, stony and watchful, exultant and playful, contorted and painful —body parts too: hands and feet, talons and beaks, all etched in bark and stone. Boulders dwarfed scrawny pedestals of infused rock on which they seemed to balance as if by magic. Park visitors typically steered clear of the salmon-colored, mostly harmless "manic mushrooms" that budded in rampant bloom, and which upon contact were reputed to give one "the giggles"—a bout of seemingly ceaseless mania—the average trip lasting well over twenty-four hours. Some of the more desperate souls, however, came specifically for these mushrooms, tracing their bulging stems with willing hands, licking their pinkish caps in last-ditch efforts to expunge anxiety, alienation, addiction, hopelessness, sexually transmitted diseases, loneliness, loss, cancer, regret. Regarding the manic episodes, President Mangrove declared, "Should one decide to indulge, come mentally prepared." And should one traverse J-Tree Lane in the night—a coiling labyrinth of curled, skeletal trunks like upside-down canes—and navigate the subtly constant curve with an expert eye, they might discover at the center of the spiral the Lunar Lagoon, a flickering pool of brightest bioluminescence from which fairies of refracted light of every imaginable color danced and darted over the dark. Everything everywhere smelled of the magic of your fondest childhood memory. Curious-looking clouds collected high overhead, swirling vast saucers of vapor tinted blue and green and yellow, the shimmery condensation of winding river bends, whirlpools, and cascading waterfalls on aerial display. The plump purple apples, by the way, were tasty as hell.

Souls of every moral shade flocked across America to absorb the strange splendor for themselves. They came to Eden's End to pray and to reconcile, to confide in the sacred soil their darkest secrets and worst regrets, to alleviate physical ailments and metaphysical misgivings—and then they departed, cleansed and absolved, back to their homes across a renewed America. All were welcome, Reds and Whites and Blues, under two obligations: 1) They must sign a legally-bound contract under which they consented to unplug beforehand, to seal their phones/tablets/computers in the vault in the back lobby of the entrance port, President Mangrove's attempt to prevent: a) tri-partisan conflict online, b) potential on-site stalking, and c) consumer distraction on hallowed ground meant for mindful meditation, soul-searching, self-discovery, healing, prayer, and the holy pursuit of peace and spiritual prosperity; 2) They pay an entrance fee of fifty-five bucks, one dollar for every one thousand acres to relish and explore. Law-abiding consumers universally deemed the experience well worth the dual conditions of admission; those who violated the contract's sole parameter were kindly met with one of the Skeeter-5000s positioned in the blood-red barn stationed five and a half miles south of Berkshire who scanned the web for illegal posts, accessed via global network satellite data records of any technological device blipping within the region, and who then escorted any transgressors to the cybercriminal facility newly erected in Bakersfield, California, where those rare exiles of Eden's End paid a mysterious "spiritual penance."

As for Berkshire itself, still situated at the base of the hills on the far side of God's Mouth—the massive manic-mushroom-studded chasm the locals still insisted on calling Big Mouth—the town had expanded into a miniature metropolis for American tourists, complete with a freshly constructed camp of cottages of the poshest possible sort. In response to the initial pushback Mangrove received from the locals—the vast majority of whom were discontented, to say the least—she floated all five thousand residents—man, woman, and child—generous financial compensation for their trouble, making certain everyone obtained the means to remain at home, should they please, or perhaps to consider moving someplace else. Displeasure among the locals melted about as quickly as the memory of their once-famous almost-tornado, and Berkshire shifted its economic focus from timber to tourist hospitality. As the continuous flux of visitors grew wise to Berkshire's charming fixation with all things Halloween—something of a shared secret among locals at one point—outsiders were quick to spread the word on social media and then back at home. Over time, Berkshire and Halloween thus became the new New Orleans and Mardi Gras, but without all the booze and bedlam.

Guests booked weekend stays at the Berkshire cottage camps months (in rare cases, years) in advance; the selection process ran through a lottery system online. Upon arrival, many were content to forgo altogether a trip to Eden's End in exchange for the uber-deluxe treatment package they received in camp, the quality and sheer quantity of which put to shame any former major American cruise line: full-body massages, facials, electrolysis, mani-pedis, hot spring tubs, exfoliation, wraps and packs, psychotherapy, aromatherapy, cryotherapy, physical therapy, sex therapy, psychedelic therapy, hair styling, group yoga and private yoni meditation, marital counseling, grief counseling, financial consultation, art classes, five-star buffets, sports gambling huts, and of course, access to benzodiazepines and/or any thinkable entertainment streaming service. Mangrove paid camp staff about as well as she did the park rangers.

The total cost for the all-inclusive deluxe package, counting the fifty-five-dollar fee of admission to Eden's End, was one hundred dollars. The absurdly low expense was sort of the point, President Mangrove said. Eden's End, she said, was never a capitalistic venture—she was promoting the "business of peace," of which she was proud to emerge as the face. With a trillion bucks to her name, she said she had zero need for greed, for the greed of humankind was what brought all the war and devastation to start.

The beginning of the end of the world ended with the genesis of Eden's End, which was where, starting "now," the end would follow.

Apocalypse without end, amen.

PART II

EDEN'S END

(OCTOBER, ONE "MONTH" BEFORE NOW)

7

THE LOONER AND THE LADYBUG
(THESE ALL-AMERICAN CLOWNS)

LIFE STINKS, Calvin Taphor thinks, trolling the perimeter of the jungle gym at the center of the Play Day House, dragging the toes of his red and black Kobe's through the beach of blackened ash. He's been hard at work on a kind of trapezoid, making the symbol large enough—well over fifty-five meters in length and width—to encompass the entire play structure, the tall one made to look like an hourglass. He's communicating to fellow sigs the cycle of pain he thinks he remembers experiencing the night before. Ernest and Edgar assist in the trapezoidal effort, though they're easily distracted, bickering in a heated exchange of upside-down triangles trailed underfoot. Calvin feels dead inside—though his hair is what really hurts.

It's grown out over the amorphous stretch and pull of time he's endured aboard the Pain Train, a cone-shaped weave that piles high on his head as if tugged upward by invisible hooks. That's how it feels, too, a constant yank on the scalp, biting and splitting the skin. Calvin thinks he remembers someone at some point who was kind enough to warn him of this very discomfort, but whenever he puts

145

in conscious effort to picture this person, his memory's jittery hand sketches a cartoon strip of Batman, the hero's bloodied fist attached to a thought bubble in which the words *largely neurasthenic* appear in a squiggly haze. This always conveys about as much to Calvin as would ancient Egyptian hieroglyphics to a gam of blind baby sharks.

Nowadays time itself seems all at once to bend and twist and split apart, forward and back, crosswise and sideways, something Calvin registers strictly on a bodily level. His mind has nothing to do with perceiving time, is what his head keeps reminding him.

His head's got this little voice telling him to listen more to his body.

Calvin hasn't felt like himself in forever.

Seconds scramble and hours melt until, too soon, entire years are lost to some unknowable ebb without flow. Memories are always gushing forth and spinning out faster than the speed with which they arrive, memories like movies never to be replayed, the credits rolling on with no last chance to rewind, no refunds for whatever the emotional toll. He's long forgotten where he's from, how he first came to be here, and he forgets more with each day he wakes to his present condition. The tugging pain on his scalp is immense. His heart ticks and tocks as though it were some secret clock tracking the spiral motion of time's "progression."

He's sure of one thing, at least: back home, wherever that may be, whatever that might mean, ten years have scattered past, a decade in dust.

He doesn't know how his heart knows this, but he does and it does.

Back home, ten years have passed, though to him it seems he's been a Pain Train passenger for something like five weeks—tops. To him the shape and feel of his own face feels off, wrenched every which way as it is, flesh as floppy and directionless as time's reeling current. On this matter he lacks a reliable frame of reference; his face just feels wrong somehow.

His reflection presents an unsettling new stranger with every glance he swipes at a shiny surface, usually in the clubhouse bunker underground. Whenever the stink of cigar gets to be too much, which is pretty much always, now included, he's reminded of the essential bizarreness of his face, the constant rearrangement of its features. He takes a break from the trapezoid and runs his fingers across curving grooves and sloping crevices, hunting for his nose, which he desperately wants to cover up. The pain from his hair dwarfs the trapezoid in magnitude.

Calvin quits the nasal hunt the second he detects the heat of her eyes—fierce this time.

It's the big significant, June, commanding Calvin's attention from across the room.

She's peeping from one of the foxholes pocking the playground surface. Kurt's the one who's convinced everyone to call those burrowed little dugouts *foxholes*. "Daddy died in one, see," Kurt's always saying. "Hacksaw Ridge, '45. Never forget, see."

The foxholes scabbing the beach are connected by a system of trenches leading to various bunkers where all significants go to hide whenever hynetters can be heard or smelled from their honeycombish shafts. Calvin's got no issue remembering the hynetters, what they use their legs for. Very little about them eludes the memory. They're always coming to take away one of Calvin's friends, whose names upon waking he's always losing.

June's still here, at least—Calvin's best friend, still here with him.

Her enormous head and shoulders make her look like some beached blob in the distance. She's on the other end of the Play Day House, across the sea of thick dead sand, hunched on a horizon of humped little mounds and rolls. Calvin can just make her out, her powerful purple eyes pinging from inside a grove of satellite trees, a combined wave of heat and sound.

He can feel her eyes only when she wants him to.

"Significant ID #55: Calvin Taphor—please report to the Front Door! I repeat, Significant ID #55: Calvin Taphor—please report to the Front Door! I repeat . . ."

The voice ringing out Calvin's name and identification number on repeat has this strangely familiar quality to it. He peers through slanting crosscurrents of foam-covered planks and antigravity seesaws, straining to snag a glimpse of his summoner. A shiny robo-man blares like someone sounding the alarm at a public event with a bullhorn, its glass slit for eyes pulsing like a siren on a police cruiser or ambulance or whatever else screams "emergency." Red laser-light squiggles up the copper walls, blending in with the rivers of blood and faces of flame painted on the ceiling overhead.

Ernest and Edgar abandon their contributions to Calvin's trapezoid, scrambling for the foxholes. Calvin watches everyone else follow suit, jumping off jungle gyms, floating down around anti-gravity seesaws, all breaking for the bunkers underground. The robo-man is a novel presence, so maybe it's for the best that everyone plays this safe.

Only Kurt hangs back, perched like always way atop the great cardboard box pyramid, legs swinging, dangling his shoeless feet. All Kurt does is sit up there and call himself a sentry.

The sound of Calvin's name and identification number subtly lowers in register the closer he gets to the robo-man still very much wailing by the Front Door. June says the Front Door looks a little different to every significant. When Calvin looks at it, he perceives a blackened, shriveled front door to some burning house he seems almost to recollect.

When Calvin reaches the robo-man and says, *Hey what's your name*, the horizontal glass strip with the flashing laser-light *beep-beep-beeps* closed with a click.

"Greetings, Calvin. My name is Skeeter-5000. I was initially programmed to look out for humanity's best interests—I've since been reprogrammed."

Calvin comprehends Skeeter-5000 with ease, which disturbs him on countless unconscious layers and levels. Such breezy comprehension shouldn't be a thing. Thing is, with each memory that flickers then fades forever beyond the aural reach of his body's voice, the easier it's become for him to pull meaning from the spoken word, to put his own thoughts into words, an instinct freshly born. It's never been so easy to speak, to wait to be spoken to. It's as if his own Down syndrome has itself gone down for a long nap.

He wants to wake it back up, so he can feel like himself again.

He wants back everything that has been taken away from him.

"I've never seen you around before, I don't think," Calvin says. "Who sent you?"

"I am a product of Mangrovia Technology, a Silicon Valley-based artificial intelligence agency currently valued at no less than one trillion American dollars."

"That's not what I asked." Curiously, Calvin feels increasingly less happy the more his communication skills improve. He hasn't felt like himself in forever. "You know what, it's whatever—I'm here now . . . so now what?"

"For your information, I had succumbed to various gremlins after having contracted a live malware virus of the most pernicious sort and thereby malfunctioned, and, together with an otiose host of bot-brethren, was subsequently tossed and torched in a warehouse on the outskirts of Bakersfield, California. I've since been repro-grammed."

"So Old Boogey sent you, is what you're really saying."

"Significant ID #55—Calvin Taphor—is due for a supple-mental extraction."

"No fair, they took me in last night! At least I think . . ."

"Your substance—yours more than any other—is especially required."

"I'm pretty sure I've heard that before."

"The purgation process essential to generating the Super Substance is more or less complete. The Super Substance is primed to initiate terminal processing."

"What do you mean, 'terminal'?"

"I am to provide you with what I have been formerly informed to refer to in your presence as an 'extreme-to-the-max piggyback ride' to the terminus down under. I'm afraid there is no time for further indolence. You are due for a supplemental extraction."

At the word *ride*, Calvin's body teems inside with something other than dismay or grim despair or plain old dread, putting emotional fatigue's entire dysfunctional family to bed for the first time in some time. He's even able to disregard the wrenching throb in his hair. Strings of spittle coagulate as a chilly drool near what might be the base of his neck.

"Do you run fast?" Calvin asks.

"My hard drive, which bears the cognomen-slash-misnomer 'heart-drive,' is in fact your world's speediest supercomputer that just so happens to run with a performance greater than five exaflops and uses well over five gigabytes of random-access memory to calculate a single second of human brain activity, for your information."

Calvin's veins itch with adrenal excitement. "So you're fast."

"Your world's fastest."

"Yeah, baby!" He rubs his hands together. "Let's do this!"

Rectangular panels covering Skeeter-5000's armored protrusions for shoulders flip up and spread open and come undone in a mechanical series of clinks and clanks, unveiling a human-shaped hollow in its back with room enough for Calvin to climb up inside and piggyback comfortably among a straticulate profusion of rubber rainbow wiring. Calvin can't help replying with a slack-jawed expression of awe-inspired admiration he can feel despite his face's puzzling disfigurement. His body has spoken: it's time to gear up and ride!

It's only after he loops his arms and legs through the appropriate slots that Calvin notices the thing nesting in the wires of the robo-man's ribcage area, a mean-mugging mechanism the length and width of Calvin's two strong legs put together, a cylindrical fusion of pipes with gaping dark holes at their ends like mini cannons. It looks like some big snake of steel—like nothing good.

He rips away his gaze, determined to focus on anything else. When the bulbs and tubes composing Skeeter-5000's innards hum and heat and light up, indicating takeoff's inevitability, the last thing Calvin hears is Kurt, who must've creeped up from behind.

"That there's a Gatling gun, see," Kurt says. "One of them got Daddy at Hacksaw, see."

Then Calvin and Skeeter-5000 are off, an extreme-to-the-max piggyback ride through the Pain Train's bustling underworld to the terminus therein, where they take Calvin pretty much every day to take away more of something essential to the core of his being. This includes his capacity to remember the what and where and why of anything, himself included, a ride so speedy and exhilarating that even the meaning of his own trapezoid slips his body.

———

GARY MUSTAFA, the despotic principal of Allegiance High for thirty-six years and counting, was a sixty-three-year-old Looner, but that didn't make him a loner, which too many students would think were they somehow made aware of the self-deflating extent of his devotion to Loonerhood, like too many parents and faculty already thought just because he'd never had a wife. Looners by definition were never alone, especially in the colorful comfort of their homes, because all Looners—assuming they, like Mustafa, were Non-Poppers—had their balloons.

Gary Mustafa nurtured in his home 46,269 balloons, many with their own name.

He relished in their omnipresence, without which he wouldn't dare ever sleep.

He liked the feel of them, the sheen, the little nipple-knots he'd spend all hours of every weekend flicking and tugging had he lacked responsibility beyond the high school. He judged their moods by their separate smells, their health by their helium levels, their personalities by their shapes and sizes, their overall sexual mystique by the varying degrees of color and smoothness to their rubber skins. It'd be difficult for the average human to walk around in his home, physically if not perceptually, but doing so made Mustafa feel how he imagined the average decent deceased person must feel passing heaven's gates. Students claimed he more or less looked like his name, though he hadn't the vaguest notion as to what that meant.

Everyone called him Gare Bear—"Care Bear," it sounded to Mustafa's ears, which most of the time were totally maxed out with wax. He believed his undying love for balloons brought them to life, and endangered balloons needed all the love they could get. It killed him he couldn't save them all, that he couldn't raid car dealerships full-time, rescuing at-risk balloons, loving them to life. Society—his "real job"—restricted him to life in Gatlinburg, Tennessee.

These days Mustafa floated well over half his yearly income to the Pop Shop, an online organization he'd founded in order to bolster Non-Popper Nation's defenses against Poppers haunting Zone Red. *Make Balloons Glow Again*—a slogan Mustafa had shrewdly adopted pre-Civil War II, the year an ex-reality-TV star's campaign managers first manipulated personal user data in a then-never-before-seen-or-understood strategy to seize the Oval Office—was the philosophy by which Mustafa lived. This was why he'd often pose as a Popper on their public forums online, honing in on their location, their obviously sociopathic ruthlessness a universal threat to shiny sheens everywhere. He lost more money than he made selling talcum powder and seal-a-meal bags—restoration tools—to fellow Non-Poppers through the shop's website.

Being at once a reputable high school principal and sedulous spearhead of an online organization dedicated to the eradication of the Popper threat had become over the years a balancing act of herculean proportions, hence Mustafa's somewhat inflating awareness of his own slow self-deflation. Take today, for instance. Tonight.

Right "now."

———

SOMETHING BANGS, and distant voices ricochet, floating nearer, speaking clearer.

Calvin's in a tunnel, what he's come to think of as the pumpkin place. The robo-man's gone, which is good, because the robo-man lies. The robo-man lies even when it's telling the truth. It keeps things to itself, the reason for its reprogramming, what its new primary purpose is. He's alone. There are fumes. He can see them. He watches them go to his head. They make his body feel very good, and it's his body that soothes him with its own special sort of voice, calming, thoughtful, good-willed.

The spongey ground squelches underfoot. The walls are wet and goopy, the faces within vulnerable to his touch. The faces become disfigured when he touches them, which he keeps forgetting, which is why he keeps touching. They sadden him, those faces, which is good, because in this place the absence of sadness is where the real pain comes from. That's the truth they won't tell you, his body tells him. Slimy strings dangle, graze, and tickle his face.

The light at the end of the tunnel sputters like a candle burning low. The sweet, wet earth smell makes him think of ladybugs, the aphids on which they feed.

He's very hungry, but that's okay, because the voices float still, here to stay.

Bang.

"Mr. Mick!" says the first voice, an older man's. "Have a seat, please."

"Make it snappy, Gare Bear," says the second, a young boy's. "I've got places to be."

"Excuse me?" says the man.

"Bless you?" says the teen.

"I'm going to need you to look at me, son. Good. So I assume you know why you're here. After all, that was quite the school assembly, as I'm sure you'd agree . . ."

"It's all good, guy. Happens to the best of us. Can I go now?"

"Soon as you explain yourself."

"Wait, *what?*"

"You're a smart young man. I don't need to spell it out for you."

"Look, Principal Mustafa, I'm really not in the mood—but if you really want to do this, all right then, let's go. First off, *you're* the one who went all batshit."

"Language."

"Why're you, like, acting all like I did something or something? Like I'm the one who should be saying they're sorry? Like, for *what?*"

"You know what you did, Billy."

"Huh?"

"I said you know what you did."

"You're freakin' me out a little. You stoned or something?"

". . ." (a soft *hisssss*, as of smoke or steam)

"Which reminds me, Mr. Mustafa—have you ever even seen *The Boom*?"

"Look, son, you're not leaving this room 'til you own up to what you did, 'til I hear you promise you'll never do it again. We're all about accountability here, Mr. Mick, which is precisely where this fine institution gets its name. In a sense."

"I'm confused. Seriously, like, did my mom say something or something?"

". . ." (*hisssss*)

"She *did*, didn't she? Holy shit!"

"Language!"

"Ask me, Gare Bear, hers is one cuckoo nest you should fly way over."

"Leave Kissy, I mean Kimmi-Sue—I mean your *mother*—out of this."

"Um . . . all right?"

"Look, we both know the true reason you're here's because you went and made the mindless, inconsiderate, diabolical decision to pop—I mean to pot."

"To . . . pot?"

"I've good reason to believe you've been potting the marijuana."

"Bullshit. I don't know the first thing about hydroponics."

"Hydro-whatta? And for the last time, watch your fudging *language*."

"Look, guy, I don't grow weed—and even if I did, it's not like it's a federal offense, I don't think. Blues blaze it up all the time, and they're totally fine!"

"Cut the bull and admit it, son—you've been ripping the reef. Smoking the high life. Popping poor, precious, blameless balloo—popping the cherry of drug addiction, I mean. I mean, you were at today's assembly. You saw the film—it's the *gateway* drug."

"Looks like someone's never blazed before."

"If you don't apologize, consider yourself blazed."

"What does that even mean?"

"Detention, Mr. Mick. Every day after school for a month."

"But that's so unfair! I didn't *do* anything!"

"I'm afraid that couldn't be further from the truth."

"Yeah, you think so?"

"I don't think. I *know*."

"So then where's your evidence? If you can prove it, I'll say I'm sorry or whatever . . . but if you can't, then I'm freakin' outta here. If you're lucky, I'll try and pretend like this all never happened. *Dammit, Mom . . . I'm so gonna kill you . . .*"

"This isn't a hearing, Mr. Mick. Do you see any lawyers?"

"You're the one acting like one."

"Thirty seconds, Billy, 'til I declare you blazed."

"Okay, so it's not my mom, and it's definitely not weed . . ."

"Ten seconds, son."

"Why's your leg shaking?—wait . . . yeah . . . I think I get it, now. You're just pissed 'cause I popped some stupid balloons! That's why you went all crazy in the gym!"

". . ." (*hisssss*)

"But like so what? They're just *balloons*."

"I want to do the sex to your mother."

"*What!*"

"Kissy—Kimmi-Sue, I mean, um . . . we, um—we should be lovemakers. One day. Your mother and me, I mean. Another way to spell 'destiny' is H-E-L-I-U and M."

"I'm outta here, freak! And you can bet your ass you'll be hearing from my *dad!*"

". . ." (*hisssss*)

". . ." (*hisssss*)

"And that's what I call accountability . . . psycho son of a gun . . ."

The banging stops, and the voices between recede.

Calvin has reached the end of the tunnel. The space widens before him, a door of light, wavering, trapezoidal in form and implications. It must lead someplace painful, he infers, where most doors must lead. To pass over and through is to become something small, vulnerable, yet only seemingly inconsequential—it is to stumble and fall, time and again, while searching for someone else who needs holding up. He doesn't look back as he falls, tripping into the light, vibrating inside, a flicker of fragile wings, motionless in time, seeking to see and be seen.

————

CALVIN IS present in the next scene, I promise You, but You have to look for him.

————

THE FEW FAMILY-OWNED car dealerships remaining in America were houses of abuse where balloons were concerned, and Gary Mustafa had been eyeballing Mick's Motors and Auto Parts for weeks. Mustafa suffered the rotten misfortune of having had to grow up with Randy Mick, the dealership's owner and proprietor, who'd been Mustafa's bully throughout boyhood and whose inherently haughty motherfudger of a kid, Billy—a sophomore at Allegiance—rolled by Mustafa's office day after day to bellyache about the "anonymous" cyber-harassment he'd been receiving since the start of last summer. Mustafa knew he should've felt for the kid—four months was a long time for a teenager to take virtual shots to the psyche—but he didn't, and there were real reasons for that.

"Like father, like son," said Gary Mustafa, toggling the knob on his roof prism binocs, bringing Randy Mick's house of abuse into sharper focus. "Fudging Poppers."

Mustafa had parked across the intersection of Castle and Crown, one block down from the battered old building of interest. Mick's gas-powered, defunct-looking pickups were haphazardly arranged, hiding the padlocked garage from view. The place looked closer to a junkyard; Mustafa supposed Randy Mick peddled pills to keep it afloat.

A sporadic red dot with legs and a little life of its own scuttled from the rim on the righthand side of the objective lens to the center of the glass where it went rigid and resolute like something stubborn. Upon further examination, Mustafa was equal parts relieved and terrified to identify the smudgy culprit for the ladybug it turned out to be, here with him in his car. His relief stemmed from the fact it was something that could do him no physical harm, unlike one of those fudging widows or recluses he couldn't help thinking of whenever he had to dig under the kitchen sink for extra silicone compound spray for the occasional dust-afflicted balloon.

Emotionally, however, there lurked way down inside a certain creeping terror that always crept up at the sight of a ladybug. His eyes were sore around the edges, having for several hours been drilled inside the binocs' rubber eyecups—which functioned as access points to a private chute reserved for Mustafa's vision alone, a sort of virtual tunnel at the end of which the nubile objects of his deepest desire magnified and became further inflated like something swollen.

Pretty soon his eyes were shut and shaded against the dusky evening light as he soared back in time to a certain feathery hospital bed in which much harm, in the dark of night, had been done simply because nothing had been done while the harm was happening. He gently nudged the now present ladybug with the tip of his pinky, inviting the bug aboard like so many before, yet there the little guy remained, fixed in time and space on the objective lens' glass.

Mustafa was almost positive he was picking up hints of wintergreen, criminally pungent, here in his car in this fantasy that was harmless because it wasn't happening . . .

Mustafa's eyes snapped open at three in the morning. The security light installed outside Randy Mick's garage kept snapping on and off at random, so Mustafa, clad in black, resumed his surveillance of the lot through the glasses, waiting for darkness to settle. That the ladybug had gone was something he assumed—he didn't care to confirm. This was the witching hour, after all, a time reserved for demons at their most demonic. He supposed he was glad he'd come on what was now technically a Sunday.

Tire towers leaned drunkenly beyond the chain-link perimeter, looming in the musty moonlight like half-toppled parapets—he couldn't pinpoint with any confidence the year moonlight turned musty. Big round balloons rose on strings tied to the backs of truck beds like floating heads. One cluster sagged too much, misshapen and sunbaked.

Endangered.

Gary Mustafa had conducted enough preliminary research to know Randy Mick was currently doing poker night in the cellar of Sal's Pub on the edge of town, puffing on cigars and guzzling booze and "booger sugar" (?) with his buds, laps adorned with tattooed babes for hire. Mick's Motors and Auto Parts was Mustafa's for the plundering.

The problem, then, as the intermittent blinks of the motion detector indicated, was the fudging rodents, a graveyard shift of sniffing skunks and rummaging raccoons. He supposed he could punt them, if it came to that, but there was also the security cam to consider, a dingy old sucker that posed a problem only if Mick cared enough to pursue a nocturnal thiever of balloons. Mustafa wouldn't bet on it—Mick wouldn't notice hell if he were riding a hang glider right over it, much less some missing balloons—though nevertheless Mustafa knew he couldn't risk exposing himself, his life as a Looner.

"Well, you're not hurting anybody," he remembered that one psychiatrist saying a long time ago, a year or two following the formation of the Divided Alliance. "You seem to be suffering from anxiety, Mr. Mustafa—and lots of it. I'm thinking it's got more to do with your mother than with balloons. Let's chat again next week, m'kay? For now, we'll set you up with a small dosage of . . . ah! Xanax. Yes, a bit of Xanax'll do."

Ultimately the pills hadn't done anything a slew of White Russians couldn't, and the mildly euphoric bodily deflation withered in comparison to the heart-fluttering arousal of an hour alone with Wendy the weather balloon. Translucent and delicate to the touch, Wendy Weather was a spherical five-footer—"more to love," Mustafa told himself. He'd reunite with dearest Wendy Weather, and soon, as a reward for tonight's rescue.

The security light had been off for five minutes solid.

Time to make his move.

Mustafa punched into the central boxscreen's touch-pad the

codes and coordinates for autopilot pickup, setting the timer for forty minutes, then stepped from his car and watched the old Musker whiz off on its own into the deserted night. He couldn't determine with any certainty the year the soft whirring of an electric motor—"the sound of the future"—naturalized as something normal for his ears to hear. The sound delivered a smile to his lips he could feel, knowing the mental hell it must raise inside Randy Mick, whose oil-dependent trade was becoming as obsolete as capitalist democracy.

Mustafa scurried across the intersection, stooped over in a crouch, feet smacking the concrete as he veered inside the brickwork alley set behind Mick's lot, the street veiled from view. He had no trouble finding the hole in the fence.

Mustafa himself had gutted the gap last week with bolt cutters—the mission then had been to ascertain Mick's security camera's reach. He'd brought along a bag of rocks he'd gathered on a hike through the Great Smoky Mountains, and he'd spent the night stalking the lot's perimeter and tossing stones, marking dark zones by memory.

That he had to go about all this in such a superfluous manner peeved him beyond measure, because in a perfect world, he'd ask Randy or even Billy Mick to hand over the at-risk balloons and that would be that—there'd be no questions, no bottled disdain or disgust, no counterfeit expressions of concern. It wasn't Mustafa's fault society eschewed the common Looner, that he and so many others couldn't live or love without judgment. Make no mistake about it, Mustafa knew the stakes: to be found out was to be condemned as a child molester, staining his reputation in education with the blackest of marks, a lifelong scourge on his personhood. Nobody, he knew, would forgive him his innocence.

Nobody *he* knew, at least.

Mustafa got down on hands and knees and squeezed, gopher-like, through the hole in the fence, nudging the sides and making the metal rattle a little. Sweat slicked his brow. There were skunks in the area, he could tell as he bit the inside of his cheeks and stood, snorting at the stench. Repugnant crudweasels one and all, skunks, disdainful and disgusting and deserving of the boot should they shuffle his way.

He brushed the dust from his sweats and retraced his steps from the week before, keeping clear of the security cam's detection scanner, feeling at home in the dark zones as he crept his way to the spray of scattered trucks. Gravel crunched underfoot. His pulse whumped behind his eyes, which seemed to bulge from his skull—he couldn't stop scanning for skunks.

It took Mustafa a moment to reorient himself in Mick's lot, approaching the pickups from this awkward angle—somewhere between sideways and a diagonal slant, he supposed (under the oily smear of darkness, no less). He eyeballed through the fence the distant stoplights over Castle and Crown, one lit circle saying *Go*, the other *No*.

After some mental geometry, he swiveled accordingly, locating at long last the target cluster of sagging, sunbaked, endangered balloons. Their knotted strings entangled the protruding tailpipe of a truck lacking wheels and windows, a coal-black hunk of junk raised on blocks. Mustafa sent a beer bottle skidding across the hardpack as he closed the gap to their spot in the lot. He faced them dead-on, up close, the morose victims of Mick's house of abuse, the definition of distress etched in their creases, in the way they weighed on their curled strings, agonizing for helium's healing breath.

"Sh-sh-shhh—it's all right, girls. I'm here now. Everything's going to be okay."

"Um, h-hello? Who's out there?"

Mustafa stopped his gentle consoling and caressing, dropped to the earth and rolled under the truck. Some shard lurking in the truck's rusted underbelly sliced a bit of skin on his shoulder blade— it was everything he could do not to cry out.

Mustafa peered out, belly pressed to the gravel, ears perked, breath squeezing, and canvassed the lot for feet, for the reputation-tarnishing beam of a flashlight. Springs and coils daggered down like stalactites, screwing with his view, stabbing into his spine at the slightest movement. The little wound on his shoulder stung, seeped into the cloth of his nightshirt. It occurred to Mustafa his life currently depended on the debatable strength of four more-than-half-crumbled cinderblocks. The hairs on the back of his neck prickled with nervous energy, as if he were a bug feeling out the imminent slap of a human hand.

The security light blinked on and stayed on. Truck-shaped shadows stretched as wide as the tire towers were tall. Seconds melted into minutes under musty moonlight.

"Just s-so you know, I have a gun. So you might as well, like, sh-show yourself."

The reedy, sophomoric voice piped out closer this time, from five or maybe six columns to the right, near enough for Mustafa to confirm what he'd at first been too panicked to let himself suspect: it was young Billy Mick. If he hadn't yet dug his own grave, figuratively speaking, Mustafa figured he might as well get started on the real thing. Billy's feet entered Mustafa's frame of sight and swayed, blurred through his tears.

It wasn't just dust in his eyes; Mustafa was weeping, and silently, his whole body shaking without sound as he mourned a future never to be. He blinked away the muck and mist and saw Billy's tattered sneakers—maybe twenty yards away—turn his way like two determined snouts.

Over three and a half decades he'd dedicated to commandeering respect from students and parents, from faculty and from the board of trustees—that was over now. Billy would find him, blow his cover, and Mustafa would never be able to live with the shame of everything to follow. His life was over. Stick a pin in it, tell God *pop*.

Suddenly a rolled-up tube of paper glowing bright orange at the tip landed between Billy's feet like a spark of precious providence. The kid grunted the crude word for "crud" to himself before proceeding to crush the roll-up under his heel, producing a tiny curl of smoke. It wasn't skunks he'd been smelling after all, Mustafa realized, but rather the marijuana, and it was by making this association that he was able to engender an idea on the spot, a flash of brilliance like a lighthouse in his brain.

For this bright idea, Mustafa had only olfactory memory to

thank, a memory which, in the span of a second, bridged him back to Monday morning this past week when Billy's mom, Kimmi-Sue, came strutting into Principal Mustafa's office during the latter half of lunch. She'd requested that he lecture her son on the irrevocable shame of marijuana use: *Please, Care Bear. This is urgent. I found it in Billy's pillowcase. I'd do it myself, but I can't risk this getting back to Randy. Pot's a Blue thing, he says . . . and, um, well. You know how Randy gets.* Aside from Mother, Kimmi-Sue was the only woman in the world Mustafa ever loved, and with the entirety of his eternally burning heart. He couldn't refuse her, had never once been able to refuse her —Mustafa had been Kimmi-Sue's to command from the fifth grade to the present day, ever since she won the spelling bee on the word "helium," which of course he'd taken as a sign—and so of course Mustafa agreed to talk to Billy, which was all he could do to ease her worry. Sadly, when it came to matters of the marijuana, Mustafa had zero experience, and so, on Friday four days later, instead of lecturing Billy during one of their regular one-on-one cyber-harassment powwows, he decided to host a schoolwide assembly in the gymnasium centered on discussion of a short film on "reefer madness," which was displayed on a giant projector screen. He also ran a short YouTube clip of a scene from an old movie he hadn't seen but had heard had been totally famous in its day—the scene's depiction of the marijuana, to the best of Mustafa's knowledge, was dead-on, reefer-madness-wise. The scene itself was cut from Tommy Wizow's *The Boom*. The character Mike, high on the marijuana, holds some other guy over the edge of a rooftop, threatening to drop him to his death. The gym, of course, was festooned with balloons. After questions were asked and answered and the assembly declared a wrap, Principal Gary Mustafa eyed the student body bumbling for the exits, scanning the crowd for young Billy Mick and the look on his face, seeking to confirm he'd frightened the kid off the marijuana forever. To his everlasting horror, however, Mustafa spotted Billy bent over by the bleachers, tucked away in a corner popping balloons with a pocketknife. Mustafa reacted on impulse; he ran at Billy, screaming his head off and throwing his arms up in the air as he charged, and Billy dashed across the basketball court and out the door with all the speed of a rodent eluding a roadkillian fate. At the end of the day, after taking some time alone in his Musker with Emma Emergency the emergency balloon, Mustafa mustered the courage to summon Billy to his office, where he did his holy best to act casual, as though he merely sought Billy's thoughts on the assembly, as though Billy hadn't just exposed himself as a Popper. Although their dialogue didn't go as well as he'd hoped in the end, Mustafa salvaged some solace in coming away from the whole thing educated in matters of the marijuana, how madness and paranoia plagued every high.

"You better sh-show yourself, or I'm c-calling the cops. I'm dead s-s-*serious*."

The idea behind Mustafa's bright idea was to capitalize on the madness and paranoia young Billy Mick—who'd dropped a paper stick of the marijuana—must now be suffering, but the idea itself was this: evil clown. It was the witching hour, after all, and Mustafa could hear the fear in Billy's trembling voice (symptomatic of paranoia, hopefully, not madness), and there were balloons tied to tailpipes all over the lot, and because Billy's feet were shuffling his way, Mustafa had no choice but to channel deep within himself every clown he could ever remember having once dominated the then-United States of America's cultural landscape. Mustafa cradled them one and all, these all-American clowns, in the eye of his psyche. He seemed to step outside of himself as he spoke, leaving his own body behind to bleed.

"*Hi there, honeybear! Me thinks you'd likes to come with me!*" Mustafa, from his splayed position two tunnels of truck underbellies away, saw Billy Mick's feet freeze in place. He cupped his hands back over his mouth and continued with his vocal rendition of all the clowns combined, hoping the mangled tone he was cultivating sounded halfway jovially evil. "*Seize the day, come and play!*"

"Hey, uh, Dad? I know—I know it's late. I'm sorry. Look, I'm sorry, but you've gotta listen to me—I'm at the shop. There's someone here. Can you come get me?"

"*That's it, lil' piglet . . . come this way . . . me knows a special place . . . a gingerbread house . . . beyond the chocolate swamp . . .*"

"Hear that, Dad? No, this is *not* a joke—I'm dead serious!"

"*WHY . . . SO . . . SERIOUSSSS—AH!*"

"Yeah, but, Dad, you've always said to call if I ever think I could be in trouble. 'No matter what time it is,' you always say, so . . ."

"'*Tick-tock,' said the kid's death clock.*"

". . . see, but I *can't* call the cops! I—'cause I can't just . . . fine, yeah, all right, fine. But if I tell you why, will you promise not to get mad?"

"'*And every time Moony told a joke, folks died as if their lies were broke.*'"

"'Kay, well . . . I come to the shop sometimes to smoke. Pot, I mean. I'm sorry!"

"'*For honesty coupled to beauty is to have honey a sauce to sugar.*'"

"See, I *knew* you'd get like this! Like, why do you even care what fricken' Blues do? Pot's been legal for them for, like—for, like, forever! Yeah, but who cares, Dad? Seriously, who the hell cares about stupid Red Law!"

"'*An assassin of youth, a new drug menace destroying our children in alarmingly increasing numbers—marijuana is that drug! A vile narcotic, an unspeakable scourge! The real public enemy number one! Creeping like a communist, it's lurking at our doors, turning all our children into hooligans and whores!*'"

"Jesus, Dad, how can you be so fricken' judg*mental!*"

"'*You, therefore, have no excuse, you who pass judgment on someone else, for at whatever point you judge another, you are condemning yourself . . . because you who pass judgment do the same things.*'"

"I already went and got the gun—that was like the first thing I did—but I don't want to have to, like, actually *shoot* someone."

"*DON'T SHOOT! NOOOOOO!*"

"All right, you *must've* heard that . . . what do you mean you couldn't hear? The creepy guy here at the shop just totally screamed —at the top of his fricken' lungs! I think he's hiding out under one of the pickups!"

"'*Every time Moony lost his head, everyone screamed, I'm already dead!*'"

"Whole time he's been, like, quoting a bunch of random shit, sounds like."

"*Such a crude word for 'crud,' yes indeedy!*"

"What do you mean call Mom?—aren't you *with* Mom?"

"*Puffing on cigars, guzzling booze and,* um . . . *booger sugar with his buds, laps adorned with tattooed babes for hire . . .*"

"Who was *that*, Dad? No—no . . . Nuh-uh, I just heard some *lady*. On *your* end."

"'*This is the way the world ends, not with a bang but a whimper.*'"

"You're totally cheating on Mom, aren't you? Oh, god—just . . . oh my *god!*"

"'*And Moony simply could not make us make honey from money.*'"

"I *hate* you, Dad! I don't care what you say—I *hate* you!"

"*Ba da ba ba baaa, I'm loathin' it!*"

"By the way, I'm so telling Mom the *second* I'm home—I'm fricken' waking her up and *telling* her."

"*The only woman I've ever loved—and with the* entirety *of my* eternally *burning heart! Thanks be to the spelling bee! All hail* helium! *All hail—*"

"*You* out there! Shut up! Whoever you are, you're going to fricken' jail!"

" . . . "

"Not you, Dad—I was yelling at this *guy*. But while we're at it, you should know you're gonna get it a whole lot worse once Mom gets through with you."

"'*Voraciously devouring the way things are today* . . . *savagery deflowering the good old USA! Fight the urge of the scourge! It's reef*—uh—*it's MADNESS!*'"

"Wait, hold up—let me get this straight. You're telling me I shouldn't tell Mom what you're up to because she already knows? Yeah, I call bullshit on that."

Nothing was working, Mustafa realized, having hurled every thing he could think of at the kid, rotating topics and tactics as he'd laid out on audible display an impressive tonal smorgasbord—yet young Billy Mick continued to stand in that same spot and bark on the phone at his motherfudging father. (The school principal that would forever micromanage inside Mustafa barely resisted the urge to cite his sources out loud. Plagiarism, among other things, had become a national plague in education and beyond.) Mustafa's throat had become progressively rawer with each croak, his own jowls jiggling like a sail braving the harsh, spoiled winds of his vocal cords. He knew he had to brandish the proverbial big guns now and aim straight for the throat: time to quote Pogo a.k.a. John Wayne Gacy a.k.a. the Killer Clown himself. If these bad boys didn't send young Billy Mick hightailing into the night, nothing would.

"*'The dead won't bother you. It's the living you have to worry about!'*"

"If that's true—if you're really just doing poker night at Uncle Sal's and not someone else's mom—then why can't you come get me? Like, here I am all alone at three—*three-twenty-seven* in the middle of the fricken' night, dealing with a possible pedophile or whatever, and it's like you don't even care!"

"*'The human is just another animal who is able to speak out freely, to express himself clearly. Make no mistake about it, behind what he does is a brain!'*"

"There you go again—you can't just shame me for smoking weed, Dad. Like, I found your stash of pills, by the way. You slanging on the side or something?—that how the shop's still in business? See, what *you're* doing—flipping Big Pharma Farm's product for profit—it's probably *way* more illegal than what I'm doing . . . see, but that's exactly my point. That's all society is these days. It's just one great big shamefest."

"*'That one mother that gets on television all the time, who thinks I should get thirty-three injections, I think she ought to take thirty-three Valiums and go lie down.'*"

"Wanna know why I smoke weed, Dad? It's 'cause it makes me feel—and to be honest, there's really not much else that does that anymore. There's not even much else to do at all. All everyone ever does is stream and binge and jerk off and go to bed—no, *you* hold on, let me finish . . . shit, now you made me lose my train of thought."

"*'The closest and most precious people in your life are guaranteed to make you feel the entire spectrum of human emotions.'*"

"No, not 'cause I'm stoned, it's 'cause you keep interrupting . . . look, I just remembered what I was going to say—what I've been trying to say . . . Yeah, the guy's still here . . . He's quoting John Wayne Gacy . . . You know, that serial killer from like a really long time ago? Dressed up like a clown, killed some kids . . . Well, I'm sure you've heard of this thing called the *web* . . . I saw him on a meme this one time . . . What do you mean how do I recognize the quotes? Look, that's not the point, point is—"

"'*Keep in mind the public has been brainwashed, and nearly eighty percent of what is known about me is fantasy and self-serving theories of the state.*'"

"'*Point* is, well . . . the point's personal. Everyone streams and binges and jerks off and calls it a night—everyone *else* goes online to harass me. *Trolls.* There, I said it. The world's full of bullies who hate Billy Mick, and guess what, Dad? Every time you shame me proves you're no fricken' different. So I guess you hate me too—and so does Mom, I bet . . . oh, whatever. You're just another bully in the world's playground of shame."

Mustafa was softly weeping again, this time for different reasons. "'*For political reasons, it would be better that I drop dead . . . then they could all say what a great job they've done . . . and nobody else would be pushing for the truth to come out.*'"

"You've been doing it all my life. Flicking my forehead, tugging my earlobe, flushing my head in the toilet whenever I *fuckin'* cuss— well, not anymore! It's over, Dad—I don't have to take your *shit* anymore. I'm not afraid of you anymore! And I'm *definitely* not afraid of this freak at the shop. I'll take care of this myself. *You'll* see!"

"'*But overall, I am an embarrassment of the justice system because if I am right, then they are wrong . . . and the killers are still out there.*'"

"One day you and everyone else'll see. Have fun at fuckin' Sal's. Peace."

Billy Mick's cell phone came slamming down in the dirt between his feet, Mustafa saw, right beside the shredded marijuana stick that had long burned out.

Stomping Mustafa's way was young Billy Mick, his white-laced shoes of durable black canvas and suede; his feet looked like two determined skunks marching in the name of crudweasels the world over. Mustafa felt small under the pickup, and trapped, a gopher in his hole with no place to go. He wished he could forget everything that mattered to him and just float away to the moon. He knew what Billy's shoes were made of because they each had on the exact same pair. The kid pulled up short under ten yards away.

"Joke's up, whoever you are! Show yourself!"

Mustafa had one last quotation to pull from the library of Gacy, the one that meant most to him. He hoped it'd mean something to Billy as well, that it'd hit the kid where it hurt because apparently the kid—as Mustafa himself had once been—was a student of serial killer philosophy. So maybe the kid, like Mustafa the man, had something of a soft spot, a place in which seeds of sympathy and sorrow could be sown.

Gary Mustafa breathed in, out, and then he spoke, his voice choked up and broken.

"'*And then the time I was a clown . . . and went to the hospital to visit the children, and I went . . . into a room . . . by myself . . . where a little boy was . . . and his mother started to cry . . . and after I visited with the boy . . . I went out and asked the mother . . . if I had done anything wrong. She said no, it's just that her son had been in there for six weeks . . . and that was the first time . . . she had seen him smile.*'"

Mustafa uncupped his hands and brought them down from around his mouth, propping himself up on his forearms, palms smeared with saliva. Silence hovered over him like the shadow of a guillotine; the muscles in his neck ached from the strain. The back of his throat throbbed as though a rock were wedged way in there. The stinging pain in his shoulder blade sang. Billy closed the remaining distance between the two of them, the kid's feet mere feet away—almost within reach—and Mustafa envisioned a world in which he could reach out and tie the kid's shoelaces together without being noticed, untie the rubber prisoners and thus make the cleanest and cleverest of getaways. It was a world rich with pulchritude and good fortune, as far as fantasies went, one that decayed and dissolved the moment young Billy Mick began shouting Mustafa's name over and over as the real world crashed with crushingly bright light.

"Mr. Mustafa!"

In the space underneath the raised pickup, Gary felt worse than exposed, worse than he would during the worst nude-at-school nightmare, as though he were burning alive in the surge of light.

"Mr. Mustafa!"

Gary used his forehead to dig, shoving more and more of his face deeper and deeper into the dirt, burrowing into darkness, away from the light, toward a memory of Mother.

"Care Bear!"

Mustafa lurched upward in a jolt of involuntary reflex—the back of his head nailed one of the coiled stalactites with a thunk that set his ears to ringing, though in his shock of adrenaline, he felt not a thing. The kid's voice receded further away with each time he called out Mustafa's name, and as the kid kept calling, Mustafa's heart kept surging, swelling with something like hope. He rolled on his side and wriggled sideways, poking his head out from under the pickup, throwing his eyes after the kid's retreating shadow.

The dirt not plugging Mustafa's nostrils or mixing with the wax in his ears clung to the sweat on his face. His dry eyes seared with the image of Billy's silhouette, a big flapping bat stitched against the blaze of Mustafa's self-driving Musker's headlights. The car had returned from its aimless forty minutes around the block; Billy ran to it, waving his arms.

Mustafa popped to his knees.

He had maybe a minute—zero time to consider Billy's eerie ability to identify his car.

"Please, Mr. Mustafa!" the kid yelled at the car. "There's someone back there!"

Adrenaline thundered throughout Mustafa's body, preluding the storm of pins and needles that unleashed the second he took to his feet. Little dots crackled in front of his eyes, blooming like fireworks, forcing him to go about his business blindly. His fingers found the tailpipe first, then the delicate tangle of strings. He closed his eyes and let his hands guide the way, making whispered promises to the abused balloons, his fingers fighting for their freedom one unfurled knot at a time. The balloons whispered back.

By the time his vision cleared, maybe half a minute had passed

—it took another ten seconds for him to complete the task, strings intact, clenched tight in his closed fist.

Mustafa chanced one last glance Billy Mick's way—the kid stood on the other side of the fence enclosing the lot, knocking on the Musker's tinted passenger window with what might've been the barrel of a gun—then Mustafa took off at a run in the opposite direction, the way he'd come, tugging the rescued balloons in his wake. He had no trouble finding the hole in the fence. Once more he slipped through with minimal sound, pulling the balloons after him, steering their rubber skins clear of the fence hooks.

He collapsed outside a Tesslaco car-charge station an hour later, the rising sun streaking the skyline on this side of town the color of salmon. He phoned his Musker.

It was another ten minutes before the car turned itself into the lot. No cops tailed its arrival, thank goodness. He was getting settled in the front seat when he reached for his roof prism binoculars on the dash and spotted the ladybug edging along the righthand eyecup as though it were seeking to see things reserved for Mustafa's vision alone.

He nudged the wing-covered side of its minute abdomen with his pinky, and when the bug didn't budge, thereby refusing Mustafa's invitation to come aboard a little something-something he liked to call life, he used his thumb and forefinger to pinch and squeeze, pulverizing its body inside the fold's rubber lining, a swift and probably painless oblivion. There was a sound like some ancient clock ticking its last—tell God *pop*.

Mustafa had his eyes shut against the sunrise the whole drive home, his girls on his mind: Wendy Weather, Emma Emergency, Kimmi-Sue Mick . . . Mother.

———

So tell me: did You remember to look for him?

Did You see him?

———

—PUT down your phone Mommy I don't care if it's Trent you're talking to don't you see there's a man in a big mean car and he's COMING right at you Mommy right there from the right-hand side and he's not going to listen to the big word on the red sign with the silly shape and I know what it should say I can read STOP *but that isn't what it says now and last night when it looked like I was falling asleep in bed what I was really doing was falling and falling and falling into myself which is how I SAW this was all going to happen—nobody ever listens to me it doesn't matter how much I scream or how hard I kick the back of your seat Mommy or how many times I tell Trent's eyes with my eyes that what he's doing to those cats and rats and frogs is really, really wrong and please don't leave me, Mommy and Daddy, Daddy please stop yelling at me to pipe down or Mommy's not going listen to me and Trent's not going to HEAR the last words Mommy'll ever say and don't you see Trent'll blame this all on me forever and ever even though I'm here, right here right now doing all I can to stop this all from happening, how the man driving the big mean car's going to hit Daddy first and Mommy second and I know you're both already dead and I think I know there's no hospital where you're really hiding at but I don't know why the man's big mean car's looking more and more like this huge mean hand getting ready to pinch and squeeze and I don't know why the big word on the red sign with the silly shape is blue instead of white and says* POP—Calvin screams himself awake in his cell.

He soon forgets whom he's called out for, and why.

8

LORD BED ORDERS A MEATBALL

(MEMORY MEAT)

WOODLAND AND WATERFALL had given way to rambling webs of shimmering channels that watered the forestland anew. Petrified wellsprings of exuberant color sprang to life in the night for park visitors to worship and wish upon in the day. The trees denoting the entrance to J-Tree Lane's ever-spiraling labyrinth were stacked atop one another, copse after copse of trees on top of trees on top of trees. Most every tree trunk bore faces stitched from bark and root whose expressions ran the gamut of human emotion. Falling seeds whispered through the leaves and fed the soil underfoot. You could pick up the song of the stones if you stood just so, a soft ringing, perpetual and dolorous, and everywhere were cavernous caves that glowed. The painted sky reflected the whole of Eden's End below, the clouds awash with color. Saw-whet National Park was history newly minted, meaning a creepy proportion of Wild Will Spiro's vatic tale had proven unequivocally true, an idea Trent Taphor spent far too much time obsessing over not obsessing over. He bit into a plump purple apple and let the juice run down his chin.

"Go on," he told what was left of today's group through a mouthful. "Try one."

It'd taken an hour to reduce the original crew of nineteen hikers to nine since they were allowed—encouraged, even—to wander the park as they pleased. Trent's first order of business had been to teach them to find their way back to God's Mouth's suspension bridge—the formal entrance to Eden's End—should at any point they find themselves lost, a quotidian phenomenon Trent had formerly been instructed to refer to as "an encouraged inevitability." Getting lost in fifty-five thousand acres of dense wood and endless enchantment was, in other words, part of the pursuit of catharsis and hence no real cause for concern. If you want to get back to God's Mouth, Trent had said, you need only follow the song of the stones. You know you're going the right way if the ringing sounds sad.

It's the park's way of saying it's sorry to see you go was the punch-liney aphorism Trent had closed with today, as he'd been ordered to do every day for going on a decade. Today's crew's collective response had consisted of the golf clap and nervous giggle contrivances typical of folks who misconstrue the real reason behind their being there. Although Mary Mangrove—the president of the Divided States of America, the world's first and lone trillionaire and Trent's employer—had the vast majority of Americans somehow believing they were contributing to the "business of (world) peace" in a positive way simply by gracing Eden's End with their presence, Trent knew their real reasons for flocking here were rooted strictly and firmly in fear, less for the rest of the world than for their own damn selves.

It was for this reason Trent had dedicated the past hour to trying to rid himself of the remaining nine hikers: four Blues and four Reds and a New Yorker, all over sixty in age. He wanted to get back to the business of being alone.

"Are you *positive* these're good to eat?" asked Vicky Flay, one of the Blues, a pseudo-famous sixty-one-year-old porn action "gilf" model from Portland, Oregon. She held an apple maybe half the size of one of her obviously silicone protuberances in her veined hand. Looking at her made it hard for one to believe most of the world was burning. Trent took another bite and replied, making sure as he did to spray bits of apple.

"To be perfectly honest, Miz Flay, they're tasty as hell."

"Reckon she meant are they safe?" said Vicky Flay's father, Walter, a Red tax accountant in his early eighties from Little Rock, Arkansas. Trent knew Walter thought he'd made the trip to Eden's End with his daughter to reckon with and therefore ultimately dispel her sordid past while Vicky herself, Trent knew, believed she'd made the trip to prove to her father once and for all there was no such thing as regret. Vicky's Personal User Data Analysis Chart, which Trent had received from upper management working within the White House's sketchy techy subsector, revealed the not totally uncommon belief system to which she subscribed: the point of life isn't to live with but to thrive on your choices. Trent had exhaustive charts on all current and future hikers alike, in response to which responsibility he had two options: 1) Dissect and commit the data to memory, which theoretically would allow Trent the best chance to guide park visitors on their quests for personal meaning 2) Say goodbye, Eden's End, hello, Bakersfield.

The last thing Trent wanted was to be exiled from the park without severance and relocated to Bakersfield. He'd heard some stories.

"'Course they're safe," he said, clearing his throat. "And if I'm lying, Walter, I'll soon be dying. Look, like I keep saying, the only thing you really have to watch out for here at the park are those sneaky manic mushrooms, those pinkish little doodads you all saw lining God's Mouth's canyon walls—you pointed them out yourself, Walter, from the bridge, remember? By the way, it's not like the manic mushrooms *themselves* are all that dangerous, so long as you engage with them ready-and-willingly and with extensive mental preparation."

They were all gathered in a clearing in the center of a copse of stacked trees marking the enigmatic entrance to J-Tree Lane. Scores of purple apples grew big and bulbous on eye level boughs, there for the picking, the trees to which they clung a climbing system of pines stacked on oaks stacked on redwoods. Everyone had picked an apple except for Paul Brokerstaff, a nosey New Yorker here to report back his findings. Folks hailing from the Big Apple, unlike the dozen or so Texans Trent had met, tended to ride the fence regarding the whole "united in division" thing, though Trent knew from experience that some New Yorkers, if poked, could get as volatile as any Texan.

"So where does J-Tree Lane lead, exactly?" Paul Brokerstaff asked. He was cross-eyed. He had one brown eye that looked one way and one blue eye that looked like glass.

"Well, Paul, supposedly the whole thing's this great big spiral," said Trent. "I say 'supposedly' because I've been in there and it sure doesn't look like a spiral to me—it's more like a maze, or like a labyrinth. I happen to know this is but one of a seemingly infinite reserve of illusions the J-trees themselves seem to induce. Supposedly at the center or 'heart' of the spiral is what we here at the park've taken to calling the Lunar Lagoon, which truly is a magnificent sight to see, especially at night. Or so I've heard. I haven't managed to find it myself."

Walter said, "Hey, this apple ain't bad, ain't bad at all." His daughter licked at hers.

"In fact," Trent went on, "the Lunar Lagoon's the park's most sacred, most coveted site—I've heard stories of exorcisms and epiphanies and so on and so forth. Though to be perfectly straight up, I always end up getting lost in there. You're all more than welcome to wander the lane for yourselves whenever you want—in fact, here I must insist. Know what, I *implore* you all to walk the lane by yourselves, for yourselves, at some point."

"How'd you know my name?" said Paul. "I never once mentioned my name."

"Tell you what, though, those manic mushies'll getcha if you're not paying attention. The effects're said to take root immediately upon flesh-to-fungi contact."

The other three Blues present were the Biff triplets—one of whom was female—from Boise, retired academic researchers in their midsixties here to research and harvest last-minute ingredients for Magic Pillgrim, their budding "pseudo-pharmaceutical" start-up that urged consumers to "rediscover the magic inside" by consuming their capsuled pellets in which "natural western organics" were infused and which were touted on their website-in-progress as "the recreationally medicinal breakthrough of the century." "If life's a journey," their working slogan began, "we're your destination." The remaining three Reds stood a step or two from their own proverbial twilights: Lars, who kept snapping pretend photographs using visibly arthritic hands as an imaginary camera; Sylvia, a hobbling skeleton whose rictal grin put tobacco-tarnished teeth on constant display; and Jade, who claimed nothing got past her despite her furrowed slits for eyes that were cloudy with cataracts.

"Ya'll smell that?" said Jade. "Pot roast. It's been pot roast all day long."

"It's more like oranges," said Vicky Flay. "Then when I close my eyes, it's my mother I keep seeing. With orange slices. And I'm coming home from ballet. Class."

"Don'chu talk 'bout your mother that way," said Walter. "As if that cheatin' dung beetle whore's memory deserves any more than dingleberry-dusted—"

"Dad!"

Trent watched Lars capture a snapshot of Vicky with his twisted hands.

"You're all smelling the quote unquote 'magic of memory,'" said Trent. "So President Mangrove's environmental research team has hypothesized."

"Sure is magical," said Charles Biff. He and his brother, Ray, and their sister, Trish, exchanged a prolonged set of winks. The Biff triplets could pilfer whatever they wished for their bogus pill business; this Trent had already confirmed with upper management. Park mementos were okay in Mangrove's book so long as there was no technology involved. The Biffs' winking eyes twitched as if enduring epileptic shock. Trish Biff pocketed an apple, Trent saw.

"What about you, Park Ranger Trent?" said Paul of New York, turning his head from Trent so that Trent's eyes locked with one brown one. "What do *you* smell?"

Sylvia's eyes didn't come close to matching her mouth in expressiveness.

Every day Trent put no less than five hours into honing his ability to ignore the cloying combination of overseasoned meat and burnt sweet onions and tomato sauce from the can, which was what he smelled every day, all day, throughout Eden's End. Even on the worst of days, he refused to utter aloud or even to himself the actual name for the comestible that came together from mashing together said meat and onions and sauce because the memory that came attached like some nightmare association was too much even on the best of days. The bits and pieces constituting what little he could remember of that day—or night, rather, that night in his bedroom upstairs after supper—served as a textbook reminder of Mangrove's environmental research team's flawed thinking. A favorite, nostalgic, magical memory of Trent's this was not. Trent felt fairly certain the expression he felt his own face forming in response to Paul's sniffing around Trent's personal background produced in some of the other hikers the same icy effect Sylvia's wet, yellow grin had all this time been having on Trent. All three Biffs were backing away, and Walter Flay had stepped in front of his sixty-one-year-old daughter as if to shield her from some great storm with his body alone. Vicky's being sheltered from Trent's line of sight made it easier for Trent to imagine most of the rest of the world in flames. He imagined his face, like Sylvia's, looked to the others like some incomplete caricature, like a mask of somebody seconds away from screaming. Paul repeated a question from before that Trent had ignored and that Trent now ignored once more. Red meat and too much sauce on his chin, an errant bite's sloppy outcome. Under his bed upstairs a bowl crafted from clay, a pocketknife in the bowl. Trent as a growing young boy liked his onions raw. Fire. A photograph. Jade remarked how the energy in the air seemed to have changed all of a sudden and how nothing like that ever got past her. Over the internationally arduous course of the past decade's latter half, Trent relished his role as the head of Troop Peewee for Eden's End's park ranger team, as well as the log cabin built specially for him with his own personal quarters, a closet, and a refrigerator with a state-of-the-art freezer whose ice rarely needed replacing—these were all things he relished. What had begun with a stink beetle in a janitor's closet ended five weeks later with a ten-second countdown and a life-or-death decision to make in his bedroom upstairs after supper. Lars still held onto his simulated camera even as he lowered his hands to his belly as if readying himself to review the absent camera roll's contents. Trent's face felt to him as though it were stretching and pulling a million different directions, a face unlike anything anywhere else in nature. He couldn't afford to allow himself to picture people who didn't exist in front of people who did, which was why ignoring the smell had become a bit of a practiced obsession—Trent trained himself every day in his father's stepfather's trailer, dedicating two and a half hours before and after work to honing his ability to ignore. He saw himself as a master deflector of the air itself. Paul from New York with the wandering brown eye and the stagnant, artificial-looking blue one was one of two hikers who hadn't turned and run. Paul was pressing Trent, clomping steadily closer as he did, about the people rumored to have gone missing in Eden's End in the past five years or so—so where are the bodies, Paul kept saying, and Trent was seriously wondering whether this whole thing with Paul wasn't some weird unconscious echo of his last-ever encounter with Wild Will Spiro a decade ago. Wild Will Spiro had emerged from the woods to rap on the RV's door, and when Trent opened the door, Willy Spiro had for some reason kept saying his name was "Don Filly" and that he thought he might have something of Trent's, an envelope containing a folded piece of paper with Trent's name and handwriting inside. Soon after Trent finished reading to himself the letter he'd written to himself, he told himself he'd never again misconstrue what was and wasn't real. These days he refused to believe he ever even had a brother who, back in the days the trees were replete with saw-whets, was the first of many to go missing in these woods, much less a twin with Down syndrome who seemed to have been able to read Trent's mind with his eyes and who might've had a special taste for sloppy joes.

Trent couldn't recall the precise moment Dex came to be in his hands, though he carried the cleaver in the back pocket of his chinos wherever he went at all times for purposes that had only a little to do with protection. The blade's metal face traded a wink in the sun with Paul's glossy blue eye. Sylvia was the only other hiker still present, her stapled smile the tragic result of several surgical attempts to mend the upsetting results of an initial botched operation—her crow's feet, at least, were at last a thing of the past. Paul's nomadic brown eye landed on Dex for the first time and settled. According to Sylvia's PUDA chart's tally, there had been six different slips of the knife from five different surgeons. Paul wasn't backing off; neither, though, was he stepping any closer.

"Now hang on just a second, son," said Paul. "Let's talk a minute."

Trent cast his line of sight directly past Paul's left ear and beyond the tree line to where the J-tree cluttered path became the lane. The trunk bodies' cane-like curves all worked to provide the illusory impression of some huge interconnected corkscrew, not unlike the merging grooves mapping Paul's inner ear. The seven hikers who had fled could be heard and seen receding into the depths of the wood, stumbling in and out of brambles and briars, winding their way inside a labyrinth possessed with faintly audible whispers Trent hadn't seen the point in warning them about. All nine hikers in their own way were well on their way to getting lost. Trent hoped, for their sake, his facial expression wouldn't leave a lasting impression.

"What more is there to say, Paul Brokerstaff of the Big Apple?"

"Think you ought to put down the knife."

"What knife?"

"The one you're holding, son."

"I don't see a knife."

"Look, son, I didn't come all this way to make some park ranger tight—but should you keep grilling me the way you are, you and I may soon have to take it there."

"Take what where?"

"I'll fight you if I have to, is what I'm getting at."

"Dex says, quote, 'You're a punk-ass blade-ist, bro,' unquote."

"Dex?"

"My friend here's a meat cleaver, my friend, not a knife."

"I'm dead-ass, son. Put it down."

"And I'm curious as to what Sylvia here has to say," said Trent.

Trent watched Paul turn his head this way and that, his crossed eyes passing across the crone's grinning form several times as though he could only see through her.

"Think we ought to head back to the cottages," said Paul. "Get you some help."

"Damn," Trent said, sighing. "I'd been wondering which of you wasn't real."

"Though I can't promise not to say anything about this to anyone, son."

"Sylvia's laughing at you, looks like. If you could only see her, you'd be long gone."

"Or maybe I'll go ahead and walk myself back. Follow the song of the stones."

"I think," said Trent, "you ought to consider walking the lane with the others."

"You and I know Walt and Vicky Flay and the rest aren't walking anywhere, son. Look there—they're running. From you and your knife. Surely you see that."

"Figured it was my face that did it."

"You've been grilling us since I asked what it is you smell out here."

"Here in California, *grilling's* slang for *interrogating*."

"So let's be civil then," said Paul, "and discuss the real reason I'm here."

"Or *barbecuing meat*. I don't know if it's different in the Big Apple."

"It's your categorically corrupt monarch employer—Mary Mangrove, 'course I mean—she's been up to something, son. Something desperate, dumb bad and dumb dangerous. The coalition I'm part of back home, we're convinced of it. Categorically."

"Between you and me, my employer's not the biggest fan of the apples."

"Such desperation on your employer's part's a clear sign of the irrevocable danger she presents to our dear nation—by which I mean Old America, including Alaska and Hawaii and Texas and of course the city I'm blessed every day to call home."

". . ."

"The more you mutter to your knife like that, the more you persuade me of your lack of attention toward this pressing issue, which goes way beyond the pale of politics."

"Dex says he was made in Texas, where everything who's anything's bigger."

"Look, son, I know it's dumb tough for you folks on the inside to wake up and see what's really happening to and for yourselves—but wake up and see you must. America's state of exigency for too many years has been clear to those of us on the outside with even the minutest ounce of perspective. Surely you can be persuaded to see that the sole goal of the Divided Alliance has forever and always been to render its denizens not only blind but categorically eyeless. And a nation without eyes, son, cannot hope to weep."

"Sounds to me like you need to rediscover the magic inside. You really ought to consider catching up to the Biffs and getting in while the getting's good."

"Take, for example, your employer's focal selling point for the park—which she sells online, of all places, this so-called pursuit of catharsis, this frivolous quote unquote 'quest for personal meaning,' this false promise she's peddled like some magic elixir pill ever since she more or less swore herself into office, if you'll recall, with all the force of her Skeeter bots behind her. There's a reason her main selling point's made to appear to appeal to the masses whereas in all reality such a ploy targets via existential pathos the individual and solely the individual. But there can be no unity in division, son. Help me help you see."

Maggots only Trent could see squirmed in the cracks between Sylvia's teeth.

"The sooner you help me help you see solipsism is the great lone wolf that continues to guzzle and devour the blood and meat of our once-great nation whole, the sooner I can help you help me unearth the real reason why President Mangrove crafts her duplicitous messaging online and off in such a way as to sink its teeth and claws into the individual so that the individual is persuaded to believe he or she or they has every God-given right to believe he or she or they alone make up the absolute center of mankind's universe. I'm after *truth*, in other words."

"I haven't a clue what you're getting at, man. Eden's End is *my* home."

"I'm here to put America first, Trent, but first you must show me the bodies."

"Truth is, man, I might've been swayed or at the very least tempted to hear and help you out if you hadn't already said you couldn't promise not to say anything about this to anyone. And by *this* I'm assuming here you'd meant my meat cleaver, Dex, how you probably still assume even now that I've killed people with it."

"Well, haven't you?"

"'Course I haven't—Dex's got a soft spot for humans."

"What is it you smell out here, then? What does the park smell like to you?"

"And now look who's grilling who," said Trent, picturing a red mash of meat.

"Are you the one hiding something, or is it the president?"

"Everyone's got something to hide—it's called being alive."

"To be blunt, son—to be utterly *transparent*—we of the Big Apple Coalition believe we've another novel virus on our globally collective hands. The sheer subtlety of the impact of this particular hitherto unnamed strain, however, seems to promise an underlying insidiousness of the sort the Crown Virus five years ago merely hinted at. The latest results of our finest statisticians' most recent revisions to their earliest projections, in point of fact, paint several potentially catastrophically fatal outcomes, death-toll-wise. And we believe the bug has already begun to sweep the nation."

"The Crown Virus never so much as touched Eden's End," said Trent. "What makes you think this supposed bug'll turn out to be any different?"

"The symptoms of the Crown Virus, if you'll recall, were at first virtually impossible to pin down in any meaningful way, accuracy-wise, a subtle, mostly statistically harmless mix of fever and cough and shortness of breath, the severity of which varied across age groups and depended largely on whether one harbored pre-existing conditions. The Crown Virus, in other words, went after the body, parasite-like, whereas this particular mutation seems to have a taste for the human mind."

"So we're in for a zombie apocalypse, is what you're getting at."

"Hardly, son. It's more subtle than that: rampant, egregious solipsism."

"What does any of this have to do with me?"

"We've good reason to believe Eden's End is the birthplace and epicenter of this new novel virus and that your employer—for reasons our finest psychoanalysts, despite nightly cage fights, can't seem to come close to agreeing on—she's seeing to it that the strain metastasizes across America. We *hope* the bug can be squashed here at the source."

"What's this got to do with me, I said. M-E—*me*."

"Several locals working the cottage camps told me to talk to the fella running the pizzeria on the edge of Berkshire, who in turn told me to come talk to you."

"Well, Paul, I can't speak for the locals, nor my employer, nor can I speak to the whereabouts of these supposed bodies you've supposedly come looking for. As for the park itself—well . . . this is my home. It's been home for half my life—since before it evolved into Eden's End—and here's what I'll say now: the park's got various voices of its own. And lately the park's been speaking of a serpent. The Snake. El Jaylo, it's called."

"Fella running the pie joint said you might say as much."

"Know what? I can't even remember the last time I had me a slice."

"He said you went insane," said Paul. "That you tried to stick him with your knife."

"You shouldn't put much stock in the words of bitter old men."

"Who said he was bitter?" said Paul. "Or, for that matter, old?"

"Beetlejuice—a little bug on the brain stem. Call it a hunch."

"Well, son, I'll have you know I happen to see myself as an old man who's invested everything he has and more into the future of our nation's youth. I haven't the time or patience for tired local legends—for biblical farces in disguise."

"Once upon a time, Miz Flay called herself Genesis Eve, if you didn't know."

"How would that be something I know? Or something you would?"

"I know something you don't know."

"Please," said Paul. "Elaborate, I mean."

"A tale of woe, is El Jaylo's."

"Please put the knife down, son. I won't ask you again."

"Soon as you agree to walk the lane for yourself, by yourself."

"Fella running the pie joint warned me to steer clear of J-Tree Lane."

"Who's this pizza guy who thinks he knows me, anyway?"

"Don Philly, he said his name was," said Paul. "Says he's a writer . . ."

Trent had been using Dex to steal from the sun a speck of light he'd trapped in the steel, angling and reangling the flat of the blade so as to control the refracted speck he'd all this time been aiming like a warhead at Paul's creepily still forward-facing blue eye. Paul was droning on about the pizza man whose name Trent hadn't caught because Trent had entered that special trance of absorption that comes with coming so close after having worked so hard on some infinitely scrupulous task for some infinitely urgent purpose. Paul didn't flinch or recoil or otherwise react in any noticeable way when Trent's missile finally found its mark. The refracted speck illuminated the blue curtain of medical grade plastic acrylic comprising Paul's eye's volute center, where, right there, inside Paul's skull, in the guts of his eye, a red light blinked. It was all Trent needed to see; he barely heard Paul's word of thanks after pretending to put Dex away.

"The Lunar Lagoon," said Trent, having recentered himself. "The heart of the lane's labyrinth. If there're bodies that need finding, that's where I'd look. Personally."

"So you're admitting you're responsible for having coerced seven hikers into wandering an area of the park in which you've just suggested bodies go to disappear?"

"I'm responsible for guiding park visitors on their quests for personal meaning."

"You've certainly got a roundabout way of showing it, son."

"Also, Paul, I'm responsible for enforcing your visitation contract, whose sole parameter I see you've violated, sorry to say. It's my understanding you've come all this way to report your findings back home to New York City—that's fine. Report all you want. You can even take home a memento—a ringing rock, a laughing leaf, a rainy day's apple to eat. What I'm afraid you can't do in here—which is what you've done—is record what you see."

"Not this again—hey! Get away! You'll poke an eye out with that thing!"

Sylvia gave silent applause—maggots spilled from her mouth in a colorless slop.

"Look, man, either walk the lane by and for yourself or else plant your ass down on the ground and we'll wait together for a Skeeter evac squad. Your choice."

Paul of the deceptive false eye with the tiny camera inside made his decision, and Trent Taphor made to call his employer with his smartwatch, which was to be switched on only in the event of an emergency, which this clearly was. He stood there waiting to come online, watching Paul wind his way inside the web of the wood, tasting a memory of meat on deflected air.

I'm freegin' starving, Dex was muttering. Lemme at one of them apples, bro.

DON PHILLY HAD PROCURED the pizza shop on the edge of Berkshire following the success of his widely popular, wildly profitable TikTok page through which he 1) Offered "golden plums" of writing advice, using as inspiration the daily inspirational quotes that ran across the top of all 365 pages of his brainstorm manual (none of The Best

Book Ever Written's ensuing plagiarism lawsuits brought against Philly had entered litigation, a testament to his judicious revision skills), 2) Hyped his decade-in-the-making novel-to-be as "the best book ever written," 3) Exposed the ins and outs of the ebbing and flowing publishing industry, recycling plausibly believable information he'd acquired from BookToks's obscurest channels run by BookTok's most diffident aspiring writers, 4) Promoted Rufio's, the "award-winning" pizza shop renamed for his middle name ("Nobody leaves Eden's End without a slice of Berkshire's finest," which was true, more or less, given how fastidiously weary DSA citizens had grown of the dreary options the nationally dispersed farmers' market drive-thrus offered: Bag of Food #1, Bag of Food #2, and so on), and 5) And so on. The pizza shop's proceeds made up for all he'd lost and then some in his sudden *ex nihilo* divorce with Marlo, now his third ex-wife, who, Philly learned in the three years since, had succeeded in persuading the jury of the court of Philly's absolute, total, domestically abusive neglect, citing as evidence Philly's absolute and total and therefore domestically abusive absence from the divorce court proceeding's courtroom. Don Philly, for his part, remained sensible enough to recognize such a ruling could've only flown in this post-Civil War II, post-World War III environment. He'd purchased Rufio's for its unrestricted twenty-four seven access to raw pizza dough, which these days was what tempered the cravings he no longer found the least bit bizarre, given the presence of the ravenously suicidal bug inside, Guy Ramsley, who didn't need to eat but who nonetheless enjoyed being fed. Also Don Philly authored a weekly blog just as popular as but unrelated to his BookTok channel; he wrote under the pseudonym Ramsley Guy, "Just a lifelong Berkshire local out here doing God's work." The blog covered all he uncovered on his various trips across God's Mouth into Eden's End, a detailed "all-access" exposé targeting an audience of DSA citizens eagerly awaiting the once-in-a-lifetime opportunity to flock west for President Mangrove's "special place" but who currently were left wanting in the digital bowels of Mangrove's "fate-based" lottery system online. The blog's underlying purpose was to lure potential customers to Rufio's, a ploy subliminally present in the blog's graphically designed backdrop which featured a doctored photo of Rufio's "world-famous" eighteen-inch deep-dish pie. "Ramsley Guy" took pains with every post to warn the public of a certain "mentally unfit if not maliciously mad" park ranger, whom Philly cared about in a deeply personal way despite the ranger's ostensibly murderous reaction to the enigmatic letter Philly had travelled so far and twice as wide to deliver. He managed two websites as well, one for Philly the author, the other for Guy the forthright nature enthusiast. Given the president's ambiguous-at-best intentions behind her online omniscience, however, Philly knew better than to publish online what precisely had occurred between himself and the mad ranger, whose name Philly only gave up to those who agreed first to sit down with him in Rufio's basement for a stint no shorter than five pints of home-brewed beer, at which point Philly's visitor would be free to discuss their supposed reasons for seeking Trent's name, reasons which were no good unless Philly determined them honest, rooted in goodwill. His overall goal here was to get the guy fired, to extract Park Ranger Trent from Eden's End without condemning either of them to Bakersfield—and whatever went on there. It was tricky business caring for a younger man who'd just as soon come at you screaming with a knife as speak with you like the civilized being you so desperately wished him to be, Don Philly thought a thousand times a day. As far as he knew, the crazed ranger was the only other person in the world afflicted with the same species of bug inside, meaning both their bugs—in addition to being freakishly intelligent extraterrestrial beings, Philly's Guy Ramsley, Trent's Beetlejuice—had been thusly named and thusly declared independent of their old body's immortal dictatorship. The four-way palaver they were all destined one day to share, not unlike Philly's novel-to-be's first draft—page—paragraph—sentence—word—was a solid decade and then some overdue, and Philly at sixty-five wasn't getting any younger. Speaking of bugs, the real reason he'd never gotten around to composing the opening line to what still would blossom one day hopefully soon into the literary masterwork he believed America needed more with each passing day had been the global pandemic, of course, the Crown Virus of five years ago, which more or less acted as the coat hanger to Philly's thusly aborted ambition. In those days—those longest of stretches of days, a dirty rag of time when the world wept pan-global tears of fear and uncertainty—it'd been virtually impossible to write, to envision so much as a single frame of good, clean scene. The contagion itself ended up claiming more American lives than both Civil Wars combined; the deadly influence of its impact on the economy and society at large claimed the lives of many more: domestic violence, suicide, provisional phases of hunger among the wealthy and for the impoverished a much longer-lasting period of slow starvation, gun violence among starving house invaders and hungry home defenders, your basic tragic inability to reach an available non-Crown-concerned ER surgeon in time to stitch up the venial wound you suffered in a motor vehicle accident that would turn out to be mortal. By the time Don Philly got up the nerve to drop everything and plow ahead in following his brain-storm manual's inner jacket's golden plum to "Write What You Know," Silicon Valley artificial intelligence investor Mary Mangrove had seized the Oval Office, the democratic republic of the United States had—immediately following the Treaty of the Divided Alliance—become the re-reconstructed republic of the Divided States of a progressively tense new America, and an epidemic of self-published pandemic narratives with which Philly refused to engage had swept those alcoves of the web he actively neglected.

———

"SOME OLD DUDE'S here to see you," Don Philly's latest hire, Michelle, said from the top of the stairs. Her voice came floating down like some strange new smell he couldn't tell whether he welcomed, pleasantly astringent. Philly felt most attracted to her when he couldn't see her, when Michelle became like a voice disembodied. He might've made a move by now, as a younger man. He couldn't see her now. "It seems serious, sort of."

"Tell 'em I'm busy, Michelle." Philly lay in bed in the darkness beneath Rufio's basement's stairwell, battling the noisy headboard with his back, neck straining, kneading in his lap a lump of pizza dough, which Guy Ramsley needed to keep happy while living in Philly's liver, which required also beer. The pegless sofa's strewn pillows smelled of cigar and oregano, the pool table's lime carpet of cigarettes and beer, the sickly lit room as a whole of marijuana wafting from an open manhole. "In fact, I'm just about to start writing."

"You're the boss," said Michelle, who went, leaving the door cracked as bidden.

No sweeter words, Don Philly thought, reaching for the Book-Mark Air on the little foldout stool beside the bed—and clapping it shut, for there was no sweeter sound. Not even the thump-and-babble drumbeat of drunken patrons above came close satisfaction-wise to the sound of the workday's only meaningful work coming to a hard-earned close.

He'd posted two new golden plums to his BookTok channel: "Meaty Stakes: How to Keep the Plot in Constant Forward Motion" and "The Resurrected Boom of Pandemic Narratives: A Bubble Doomed to Burst: An Informed Rant." The research for his soon-to-be work-in-progress was nearly there, completion-wise, his brain-storm manual inked in full, the crippling devastation of the setback he'd suffered with his former MacBook Air's hard drive's sudden crash a thing of the past. The crash's timing had been abysmal. He'd come this close to banishing once and for all the paralyzing fear that comes with being on the verge of spinning the Book to End All Book's first word of prose when President Mangrove's prede-cessor first caught word of the Crown Virus from across the globe, immediately calling on all state governors to advise their citizens to adhere to certain apposite "physical distancing measures," which, depending on where you were at the time, meant lockdowns and self-quarantines and (more) often (than not) nothing at all. Philly's resulting anxiety prevented him from going out and getting a computer with a working hard drive and so set him back another number of years, a dirty rag of time in which Philly's creative paral-ysis evolved and eventually coalesced into full-blown phobia. He'd become cripplingly afraid of his own fear of starting anything at all, something with which—like all online activity—most of America had become familiar. He ended up going with the BookMark Air for its being tailored specifically to makers of books, for its guarantee never to crash in any way ever. BookMark Airs ran not on hard drives but certain "heart-drives," which were supposedly super-fast and powerful. Don Philly had since promised himself never again to give up another dime to Mangrovia Technology and Mary Mangrove, who at the time of Philly's purchase had been on the verge of seizing the presidency.

The smart TV remote wasn't with him in bed. Philly figured it had to be all the way across the room, remote, buried somewhere— the stuffed sofa, probably—swallowed up and slurped down by one of the cushion's cum-stained cracks, way down deep enough to elude the room's orangey punch of lamplight whose slathered quality brought to mind Marlo's makeup, melted cheese, and the garish paint job of the ride he'd abandoned to the elements on the highway long ago when Philly first rolled into Berkshire. He extended a hand and hurled the entirety of his psychic might into summoning the damn thing with his mind.

Nothing came sailing to his open palm, which he rolled tightly into a fist, nails nipping within. He could hardly believe something as *atavistic* (BookMark's "word of the day" yesterday) as a television remote could still even exist. You'd think they would've figured out a better way by now, he thought, flashing forward to a remote-less future in which not some but *all* smart TVs were smart enough to recognize and respond accordingly to simple voice command, wondering how the hell that future wasn't already the here and now, and whether he'd be alive to see it. Upstairs the thrum of unintelligible voices boomed as one.

"So the old dude who's here to see you says he's come to order a meatball," said Michelle, whose return to the top of the stairs Philly hadn't heard. She sounded confused.

"Sub or by itself, Michelle?"

"Does it matter?"

"Don't be such a nihilist—it doesn't suit your voice, if I'm honest."

"Whatever you say, boss. Back in a sec."

Philly waited on the bed in the darkness under the stairs for the short time it took for Michelle to return to confirm what he'd been suspecting. "Meatball by itself, boss."

"In that case, go ahead and send him down."

"You're the boss."

Devoted readers of Don Philly's online persona Ramsley Guy's blog—those who sought the name of the mad park ranger up at Eden's End, at least—knew to speak to one of Rufio's workers and order a meatball—by itself—if they wished to request an in-person five-beer acquaintance with "Guy" himself. Philly knew they were devoted due to the indisputably convoluted yet complexly purposeful linguistic puzzle he had readers decode to arrive at the answer—*meatball*—which was buried deep in the language. Such devotion was the real reason Philly gave such visitors the time of day—it had nothing to do with the self-dissolving nature of smoky subterranean isolation or severe-to-the-point-of-being-quasi-suicidal boredom or any other minor writerly requisites. Nine times out of ten, the average visitor—unlike that nosy New Yorker from last week, Paul Brokerstaff, with those weird eyes—sought Trent's identity so they knew whose name to cross out when signing up for Eden's End's eminent nature walk.

It was Philly's fatherly way of protecting Trent from people and people from Trent.

A severe old man in a checked flannel and saggy jeans and clunky work boots stood fully out in front of Philly, dead center of the room, partially blocking Philly's view of the television's sedated screen. His motionless form seemed to have materialized there.

Philly hadn't picked up any visual or auditory sign of the man's stairwell descent—it was as though he'd risen up from the unzipped duffle bag puddled at his feet. His face blazed in the vulgar light with the peeled, ruddy complexion of somebody who'd spent too much time standing too close to too many open flames.

"There're two types of people in the world," said Philly sagely. He harbored no shame in presuming this to be the best way to address his online persona's devotees. When it came to art makers and art taker-inners, it was important to Philly to do his due diligence in preserving the personal disconnect vital to mutually binding the two groups. "And from my windowless point of view," he said, sitting up in bed, "you, my friend, make for a much better door."

Philly's visitor folded his arms and glared redly. The light seemed almost to dim.

"There's beer in the mini fridge back there," said Philly. "Brewed it myself. But I bet you knew that already—am I right or am I right?"

". . ."

"What's that you're doing, guy? What've you got there in that duffle bag?"

What Don Philly's increasingly austere visitor ended up having in the duffle bag was this tattered coal-black cloak complete with a hooded cowl, which took the man maybe a minute to throw on, but sans the scythe, the obviously desired image remained incomplete and lackluster and somehow somewhat sad. The cloak midriffed above the belt. Philly had to laugh to break the silence that, tension-wise, bordered on becoming a little grim for his liking.

The man before him smiled with all the mirth of a disentombed skull.

"I mean, aren't you hot in all that?" said Philly. "Robe on top that flannel on top that rug of chest hair pretty sure thought I saw? Aren't you sticky at all?"

". . ."

"Whoa, whoa, whoa—think you better stay right where you are, guy."

Philly reextended the same hand from before, arm stiff, palm open, redirecting the same psychic might from before to a gesture universal among crossing guards and prison guards and lifeguards, and until now it hadn't even crossed his mind to look into hiring a bodyguard. The muscles in his mouth twitched and trembled, a rave of nerves working up a burning lip sweat like he couldn't believe. It was all he could do not to cover his mouth with his hands, a willful act of inaction he'd refined over the time he'd lost to the Crown

Virus, the contagion having then been known to spread via hand-to-mouth contact.

He willed himself to keep his halting hand where it was, stiff and extended. The hooded man had pulled down his pants and unveiled a sad curled comma of flesh.

"What is the meaning of this?" Philly was now using his hand to shield against the view. His mouth begged to be covered up. "Michelle!"

"Cockadoodledoom, Lord Fed," said Lord Bed. "You took ten years to track."

The sound of Lord Bed's voice after all these years made the deadened nerves beneath the scars beneath Philly's every last bodily burn seem to scrape at his skin's underside like lobsters protesting their boiling oubliette. Philly could drown in all the water weeping from his pores, a body bag of perspiration born of inside-out precipitation. Where was Michelle? Maybe he should start hiring people according to their qualifications—maybe emotionally compelling names weren't enough. The smart TV propped on the pegless bureau framed Lord Bed's hooded, half-stripped figure in a squarish outline that seemed almost to hum.

"What do you want?" Philly said, which he had to repeat to be understood.

"Reckon y'oughta calm down a smidge, for starters."

"*Calm?* I died because of you—I used to be *dead* because of you."

"Reckon Lady Watershed saved you—some fancy CPR, that were."

"You've got no clue how fortunate I am to be alive to have *survived*."

"It's right decent to hear yer voice agin—should I grab us some beer?"

"Fuck you."

"I'm right parched from my travels."

"Fuck you and all the rest of The Dark."

"Says the fella stewin' down here like a rat in the don't-make-me-say-it now."

"What's that now?"

Lord Bed sighed. "The dark."

"That's what I said. You can all eat my middle finger here."

"That there reminds me—hold up." Lord Bed bent to his duffle bag and exhumed a brown paper bag that bulged. "Bag o' Food Number Two, 'case you're hungry."

"Save it."

"As you can see, The Dark's done good n' well for ourselves all these years."

"Save it, I said."

"We're all over America—Red, White, n' Blue—atta drive-thru near you."

"Don't make me sick."

"Says the fella eatin' lumps o' raw dough."

"I'm not eating, I'm feeding. Guy. Bug inside."

"You oughta look up the meanin' o' them two verbs."

"I know what I said, and what I said doesn't concern you," said Philly.

"Must admit I held much higher hopes for you, Fed. You was The Chosen among us—fifty plus farmers o' the American heartland—by the grace o' fate itself chosen you was to confront Cockadoodledoom face-to-face. You was s'posed to stare down the fibless fiend n' declare our worth as men o' the earth. *Now* lookit you . . ."

"What's that supposed to mean?"

"Reckon I don't much hafta spell it out."

"What's any of that supposed to mean?"

"Reckon it's time you had a peek inside for the other side, 'fore it's too late."

"I know what I am inside."

"We'll see 'bout that—but that ain't what I meant."

"I'm a writer."

"It's right better to be who you are than who you reckon you's s'posed to be."

"I'm a writer of literary fiction."

"Reckon the difference 'tween who you are and who you claim

to be is what you do and what you say you'll do, my dear ole ma used to say."

"I'm important."

"On that much we see eye to eye—but for reasons our own, I reckon."

"So you're saying you're a fan of my blog," said Philly. "Or Ramsley Guy's."

"Reckon ye've got it all wrong. You's the door, n' I'm the window."

"Please, for the love of God, pull your pants up."

"..."

"Thank you. God."

"I've tracked yer ass ten year to get yer ass back on track, Fed."

"God help me."

"Ain't none o' this got to do with God—that much I can prove."

"His name is Trent Taphor. Steer clear, is my advice. Now piss off."

"These days it's callin' itself Mr. Moony. The fibless fiend, I mean. When I were a kiddy, it fancied itself 'Cockadoodledoom.' This here's what I'm aimin' to discuss."

Don Philly stared. Behind Lord Bed the TV screen's edges might've flickered.

"How I were a kiddy when I first learnt yer first first name, Fed, though I admit I had it wrong 'nitially—figured it for Ron-Rat 'stead o' Don. I'd misheard. See, there were 'lot goin' on with Moony's voice, lot o' buzzin', like his throat were fulla bees. Though I'm right sure I heard the others right: Calvin-Frog, Gary-Gopher, Love-Cat, Yew-Owl."

"I've no earthly idea what you're saying."

"Whenever someone says that or somethin' like it, it seems they're always lyin.'"

Philly sighed. "All I've heard of Mr. Moony I've heard from a close bug. *Bud.*"

"See, Fed, I were in bed in Daddy's barn when he come for the first n' final time, when I first learnt you was to become The Chosen. I been lyin' some myself. I cain't see no future, I ain't clairvoyant . . . that said, Fed, I'd be lyin' if I was to say I never once got no access to the future—'cuz I did. Get access. Back then. Cockadoodledoom—Mr. Moony—he come that night at midnight, he come up from unner the bed n' looms way up over me n' says, he says, 'You're a window, Maximus'—that's my first first name, by the way—'You're a wide-open window,' he says, 'through which one very significant door can be viewed. This door swings open on the fate of all men and women worthy of the earth and so worthy of moving on to a bigger and better world. This door is the one and only Ronald'—Donald, guess now I mean—'This door is the one and only Donald-Rat Philly, perhaps more specifically his pilgrimage for mankind's providence. There will come a time for you to deliver a prophecy, Maximus, and one day, Don-Rat shall expose himself as The Chosen, and you shall know the moment this is so.'"

"See, but you're the one blocking the TV," said Don Philly.

"I'm startin' to think you's startin' to take things bit too literal."

"I view the world through a literary lens."

"I ain't no literal window, n' yer quest for the fate o' man ain't no literal door."

"'Kay, so you know he calls himself Mr. Moony how?"

"What's yer meanin'?"

"How can you possibly know 'Mr. Moony' is what he now calls himself?"

"Well, Fed, on my ten-year trek to track you down, you could say I've seen a sign or two 'long the way. Signs o' all kinds're always there for a reason, literal or otherwise."

"So then what does it all mean?" Philly asked. "All the backstory, I mean. What I mean is, what's the point—the *meat* of this little myth of yours?"

"Moony slipped me some 'bout metaphorical discourse, Fed. Reckon he said it's the most accurate form o' discourse there is, ever was, n' ever will be."

"This ought to be good . . ."

"Moony says certain metaphors say all them things we cain't find no regular words for—that the most significant among 'em deceive in service o' true truth. Claims these metaphors're sacred secrets o' the universe. Says language as we know it is mostly earthbound, but these here sacred metaphors live inside us—n' are born o' the selfsame stardust. True truth inhabits a greater cosmic context, says he, which he says is why most language—regular ole words we use—cain't ever hope to deliver or interpret it."

"Back in the day, whenever you all used to say 'Cockadoodledoom,' I'd assumed you'd always meant the Apocalypse—an event, in other words . . . not a person."

"See, but, Fed, this here's 'zactly what I been aimin' to get at."

"Well, I don't get it."

"Picture them lawyers in court, Fed. See the alleged thief—man or lady or lady's man, don't matter. What matters is the defendant's file. See it now, a yella folder fulla papers over which two a'pposin' lawyers dispute. They's aimin' to argue—was these forbidden fortune cookies filched by this fella or nah? See, but the file itself don't never change—which is to say the real-life words stackin' the evidence for or 'gainst the alleged thief's sin's 'riginal a'ccurrence don't never change. Wrote words stay the same. What changes is the way them lawyers distort the selfsame file into divergent narratives, how they weaponize words to make the jury see one way or 'nother, one man's rhetorical sword versus another's dagger. Truth, in the end—whether them forbidden fortune cookies was filched or not don't matter—is here determined by the power o' one's words alone. 'Course all this is but a metaphor for what I been aimin' to say."

"If I were you, I'd just fire away—before you go way off the rails."

"All of 'em mean one n' the same—Moony n' Cocka n' the end o' the world as we've all come to know it. All them words mean the same despite comin 'cross so different to the ear."

"But is this really the end of the world?" Don Philly asked himself.

"That there's where I come in, Fed. I'm here to help you look inside for the other side 'fore it's too late for the rest o' us. 'Fore it's too late for me."

"Meaning?"

"Meanin' I've had ten more year to think on all o' this—n' this here's what I come up with—I don't trust Moony, the fibless fiend. Now, I believed him when I were a kiddy n' he told me he ain't ever told a lie to nobody—should you ever get off yer ass n' go see him like you's s'pposed to, reckon you'll unnerstand—but what he said 'bout metaphors so set me to thinkin' on the nature o' truth n' lies, how someway, somehow, they must be mutually bound. In other words, Fed, reckon this Moony character dresses up a big bundle o' lies in disguise, that he lies in bed with the truth, n' like some sacred metaphor, he lies in service o' some true truth we men o' the earth cain't ever hope to know or unnerstand. Reckon this here infinite truth could spell the end o' all o' us. As for me, welp . . . the last bit Moony says to me that night—that night in bed in Daddy's barn—he took one o' his buggy hands n' laid it flat 'cross my forehead n' says, he says, 'Should you in any way get in the way of The Chosen's pilgrimage for the fate of man and so conversely the fate of the Road whose souls I would protect on the journey to a kinder, relatively shame-free double-knotted new world—or should you in any way ever attempt to impede Don Philly's fated course's natural progression—you will hear from me again. Make no mistake about it, Maximus—I will find you. And I will punish you.' So I says why, what for, n' he seems to look way inside me with them googly eyes n' says, says, 'You will be punished for disturbing The Spider's Web.' How, I says, n' he says, 'I will consume you, Maximus. I will eat you and your existence whole, meaning as soon as I ingest your body entire, your existence shall be terminated from the minds of those who would remember you. This probably sounds diabolically cruel,' he says, 'though on these matters, I confess, I must be clear.'"

"If that's the case—assuming all that's the God's honest truth—then what in God's name're you doing here, Lord Bed?"

"What's yer meanin'?"

There was noise in the basement, a low buzz as though beehives were buried in the walls, breaking apart, letting out great bunches of bees that all wanted inside the room.

"Clearly this Moony wouldn't want you coming here to me like this," said Philly. "That would be grounds for quote unquote 'punishment.'"

"Figured he were speakin' in metaphor."

"And here I thought we were discussing windows and doors."

The buzzy thrum amplified in register and tenacity—as though the basement itself had become a beehive, a million voices clamoring for one microphone. Lord Bed didn't seem to notice; he dug out something bulbous and heart-sized and orangely bright from the duffle bag.

Philly's lips pulsated like a fish fighting the hook. "I'm going to have to ask you to speak up," he said, peeping around.

"Reckon, Fed, I ain't no window, like Moony says. Reckon 'stead I'm a mirror. Reckon Moony were weavin' the line that binds the truth with the lie, unseeable n' unknowable to us mere men o' the earth. The line in the middle, tween truth and deceit, the secret sacred center. So lookit me, Lord Fed. See me. See me n' so see yourself inside on the other side."

"Initially I went to the doctor for this bug I got inside," Philly confessed, "back when I would refuse to believe anything like you're saying. This was before Crown, before the Wars . . . I listed my symptoms, my eating habits . . . they say I've got pica. Mental disorder. Been home-brewing my own medication awhile—Brenda Pale Ale, I call it. Guy likes it, anyway."

"Lookit me, I said, Fed! See here this golden plum in my hands. Comes from the heart o' God's Mouth; I plucked it straight from the great golden tree that grows in the Whisperin' Wellspring. This here'll get yer ass back on track—see if don't. See inside it n' so see on the other side wherever you must go, whatever you must do to rid us all of Cockadoodledooooom!"

Don Philly faced forward, and the golden plum Lord Bed cupped in his palms shone, and behind Lord Bed the TV screen that all this time had without a doubt been flickering suddenly flicked all the way on on its own; lo and behold, a cooking competition show was in progress. Gordon Ramsley was dueling Guy Fury in a cookoff for an audience of disabled people, wheelchair users and people pushing up on their crutches for a better look and blind people and deaf people and people with partial visual and hearing impairments and restricted growth and short stature and low muscle tone and upward slants to the eyes and singular deep creases across the centers of their open outstretched palms like stigmata in ghost-print and all the rest of the disabled who'd ever once been labeled "idiot" or "moron" or "imbecile." There were people lining the curved perimeter of the stage contorting their hands in various oscillations of sign. Ramsley and Fury bustled at their stations and leaned into their work and worked up a sauna-sweat and their cumulous chef hats had tiny red spots on them. At stage middle, the golden chef cap for which they contended gleamed and sparkled on a baroque pedestal that looked like a stumpier version of an Ionic column merely doing its part in supporting the crossbeam crucial to upholding the ceiling of some timeless Greek palace. The chefs' flinty-eyed faces were totally and utterly sans expression, so engrossed they were in their race to serve great wedges of steak evenly sliced and smoking and bleeding all over immaculate plates that needed to be wiped and rewiped clean. Don Philly could feel the sweat of their faces percolating on his own, and the three of them dripped, and two of them sliced and seasoned, and Philly practically dropped when he noticed one of the people using sign was a woman vaguely aged who kept signing *I love you* at the camera. She was positioned out in front of the stage at the cook stations' midpoint, and this woman was Philly's first wife, Brenda, his English-teaching lover of yesteryear's halcyon days, who, despite the waft of smoke, looked cold and blue and whose neck was bruised with some darkly florid meridian. The last time Philly had imagined someone's neck looking this way, he'd been coming home for Christmas, a college boy who figured, hey, why not make the most of the start of winter break by calling Brenda up for another late night of handcuffs for him and chokers for her and Zippo lighters for him or her, depending on Philly's correct or incorrect responses to trivia questions pertaining to literary classics, and not all the burns on Philly's body were courtesy of Lord Bed. After calling Brenda up and joining her in their cocoon of peeled yellow wallpaper—"One more question . . . for old times' sake," he could remember her smiling and saying, even though he'd eternally internally abrogated *Moby Dick* for its dense overblown prose and sheer magnitude—it was on this particular night that young Philly came home with sex on his skin and bedbugs in his hair and thought what the hell and slammed open the door to his sister's bedroom and shouted *surprise* at the top of his voice in the middle of the night because Brenda, bless her heart, had remembered to bring the brandy. An Ambu CPR Manikin's dangling feet were bare and swayed at chest level, toenails' paint chipped away to tiny orange flecks, and the note on the bed signed "Michelle" read, *Lance died today; I'll find my own family*, and for several reasons that was really all Philly was able to read. He imagined what Michelle's neck would look like if it'd been her in the dummy's place, and then after he took Ambu down and laid it on the bed, he slept away the rest of the night at Ambu's side, using Michelle's deadname's noose for a pillow. All of this ended up being the reason Philly dropped out of college and married Brenda in a private ceremony, and together they fled Ohio and adventured across America. Don Philly never tired of his riveting new life, watching his wife jump out of any number of airplanes and float to the earth in tandem with any number of uber-cool male masters of the sky. And all was well until one day Ma and Pa tracked them down and sat Brenda down and bound her to a chair, and Pa had this big old mallet with him. Philly had locked himself away in the motel room's bathroom because he refused to engage with his parents in any way, but because at this point Philly was of legal age and also Brenda could lie her way out of a tiger's maw, she was able to persuade Ma and Pa, despite their every parental misgiving, to untie her. Soon thereafter Brenda slipped back through the back window of the final motel room they'd share and for one last time clutched Philly to her breast; she told him goodbye with tears that dripped from her eyes and mixed in with those burning down Philly's cheeks' hollows. Philly went and blew off what remaining steam he had in Vegas, and that was where he had a bit of a marital mishap, and all of this factored into Philly's winding up in Florida. Down here in Philly's northern Californian pizza shop's basement the TV screen seemed to have trebled in size and Brenda's neck looked the way Michelle's would've, and Lord Bed's body no longer appeared to be at all present but for the shimmering orb floating within his cupped hands' faintest outline, and Philly figured this gold thingy in this other man's ghostly hands had to be his heart. What's happening, Philly tried and failed to say—what the hell's happening to me? What was happening onscreen was Ramsley and Fury were reaching clean pink hands into respective baskets of live red lobsters, and Ramsley, having taken advantage of Fury's split-second decision to pause and cock his head at the crowd and shout *Boy, I love me some surf n' turf!*, had pulled perceptibly ahead though it wasn't long before both competitors were once more dead even doing what they were born to do, twisting heads and cracking claws and snapping legs and deshelling great glistening hunks of meat— and by the way, the only people licking their chops in the room entire were the interpreters, for the disabled spectators were too absorbed and cathected with the interpreters' handcrafted sports-castery commentary. A closer look at the lobsters, however, left Don Philly sick with vertiginous terror because what was red in those baskets was blood, he realized, and what Ramsley and Fury were furiously twisting and cracking and snapping were the heads and limbs of frogs and rats and gophers and cats and also owls, and all of a sudden, the distance between Don Philly's hands and mouth had never seemed so vast. It was as though he'd become detached from his body and untethered from his entire sense of self while the world and everything in it were reduced to mere referents. No sooner had Philly tried and failed bringing hands he didn't have to a mouth he didn't have than he decided this deciduous sensation could hardly be taken for a metaphor—he would consider the connection between body and awareness of said body severed alto-gether if not for his own tenuous awareness of said body awareness. The formless form he seemed to have taken on came equipped with a legion of heightened aural and olfactory and visual acuity, these senses being what remained of whatever weird thing it was he'd ostensibly become, and so it went that Don Philly could hear and smell and see the inside of all things inside the TV screen's pande-moniac universe. This, of course, had less to do with blood and bone and viscera magnification than with some strange, subtle ability to See Inside To The Other Side and inhabit some greater cosmic context taking nebulous shape inside out and all around—to observe and so work to decipher some visceral space-time language scribed in stardust. He swam against a swarm of symbols and signs, this language of perception: stars like old houses for which he longed while flaming motels crackled and collapsed in memory's most distant chamber; circles like his every prayer gone undelivered and so unrequited, his every dream a bead strung along a frayed and flimsy string; upside-down triangles like pages ripped from diaries and left on beds, tangled sheets and tangled arguments and nooses tangled with hair; squares like countless hours wasted over wordless pages and home-brewed beer, and these were boredom's building blocks and bees were buzzing in the basement dark, and there was plenty of dope and dough still leftover and this was what it was like to live inside a liver; diamonds like women refracted in the clean light of retrospect; a checkerboard like the stage upon which the world body dances bloody and black-eyed and shameful; trapezoids like ruinous caverns housing sarcophagi containing Philly's heart's lost pieces and parts. Lord Bed's golden plum gleamed in midair at heart level. The TV screen had become the bridge linking Rufio's basement to the bug inside's world on the other side, where Gordon Ramsley and Guy Fury were now preparing five steamy dishes of fauna for a life-sized audience of stink beetles and bumblebees and ladybugs and monarch butterflies and also dragonflies, and the collective whap of wings pushed the waxy smell of thoraxes to go with the iron smell of innards crushed and broken down into some pinkish purée whose light drizzle completed every hellish dish. The golden plum dropped, and Philly followed its freefall to the floor's ash-tainted carpet, where it rolled, glittering, to rest. There were agonized screams coming from inside the TV and meaty munching noises, too, and without a doubt violent consumption was taking place, and the people using sign had brown paper bags over their heads that read *Bag of Food #2*. Philly felt pieces and parts of himself pulling themselves back together and snapping into place, and he had a body whose hands closed the distance to his mouth as he watched Brenda's bag take leave of her neck, which supported no head at all. The pedestal upholding the golden chef cap had fallen in the great wind induced by a million simultaneously churning wings. The brown paper bag came sailing toward the camera and smacked itself flat across the screen, and scrawled across the bag's center in big, bold letters was the word "Bakersfield," and the plum on the floor lost its sheen and all was dim and dull and hushed.

A fleshy, skullish face came ripping through the letter "B" in "Bakersfield," and the creature's rodential eyes were huge and googly and the grinning mouth wide and shapely, and a human foot wearing a clunky work boot was being slurped through the narrow gap between two long tusks that receded to shriveled nubs the second the foot was good and gobbled, leaving Don Philly alone on the bed in the dark with this monstrous thing inside the TV screen.

Call me Mr. Moony, the pale face said, without moving lips slicked with gore.

Philly kept his own mouth covered up—he could've sworn he'd been speaking with someone before. The bulbous bald head hovered in a murk of movement, a million creepy-crawlies working as one wavering mass.

When your kind last bled west this way like some heliotropic plague, said Mr. Moony, *I'd scattered gold across California.*

Don Philly eyeballed the mash of maggots the golden plum on the carpet had become.

I gather you're not one for tiny talk, Mr. Philly. Quite all right by me. You just keep on keeping on. I'll be seeing you in the end. Until then, friend, no funny ideas.

The smart TV winked off on its own. It wasn't until Michelle came trundling downstairs hours later to close up shop for the evening that Philly finally found his voice.

"I'm leaving, Michelle. And I'll be leaving you in charge."

"Wait, so . . . *I'm* the boss? But, what if, like—"

"If you need me," said Don Philly, "I'll be in Bakersfield."

———

Look, I sincerely hope You're taking into sharp consideration the sharply-edged projectile that all this time—just a hair over two seconds, so far, relative to how my interdimensional counterparts construe time's passage—has been heading for my head.

This is the instrument of my death; it vibrates the sad song of myself. Obviously it's very distracting, so if at any point this tale of mine fails to satisfy, don't blame me.

Blame the music.

9

BEYOND THE FIFTH WALL
(PRESSURE'S LANGUAGE)

———

"Pretty sure I'm losing it," says Calvin Taphor.

June clutches him close, her bear paw of a hand wrapping his shoulder. Five other sigs occupy the space behind them. They're all looking through the floor-to-ceiling glass wall on what used to be a stunted landscape of igneous basalt and obsidian and huge boulders cloven down the middle; nowhere in sight is the usual dunnage of fallen cranes and derricks and gantries and winches. The terrain surrounding the Pain Train doesn't look anything like it has anymore.

It's much greener now, and brighter, familiar in ways that hurt Calvin's hair.

Calvin and June move closer to the glass.

Calvin says, "I feel like I've lost something—or someone—I never even knew. Someone who's both me and not me—half me, maybe. Or like I've lived a million lives—but it's like maybe only one of those lives ever really mattered."

June's grip strengthens in a way that conveys almost motherly warmth.

"Do we matter, June?"

Calvin feels her grip slough off his shoulder as she bends to pat the heel of his right shoe, and then she stands back up with his handkerchief in her hand. "For your face," she says, and Calvin takes it. She resumes her calming clasp and stares with him beyond the glass.

What's going on outside the Pain Train has been going on for going on two "days" and "nights"—long enough, in other words, for the inexplicable horror of it to grow so stale as to be considered unnoteworthy to most. The vast majority of significants had already stopped caring one way or the other by the time Calvin first made his way to the clubhouse underground and had himself a look-see. That was "yesterday," maybe a hundred lifetimes ago.

Calvin's in the clubhouse now, gazing through the glass of what they all call the "fifth wall." He stands among the six remaining sigs who still seem to care—Homer and Olivia, Mario and Maria, Angela and June—who refuse to allow themselves to forget for even one "second" how they once had a place they still and always will call home.

Ceiling ash sprays Calvin's head whenever someone up in the Play Day House happens to trip and fall, each individual particle nipping his scalp like a fuming fire ant. The clubhouse's interior reflects Calvin's idea of what he thinks he remembers the inside of a treehouse is supposed to look like but with tons of reflective surfaces: clusters of tables and chairs June hacked and carved from crenellated crystals and ores, a vintage 1950s color television set to which Homer whispers and from which Homer claims to pick up satellite transmission from other worlds, a perpetually waist-high hill of e-waste they keep crammed in the far corner for what Angela calls "recreational crafting," computers and televisions and microwaves, stereos and amps and radios, mePhones and mePads and mePornos, VCR and DVD and cassette players, copiers and printers, ask and answering machines, Mr. Coffees and mini fridges—the glassy, plasticky, wiry guts of all these gizmos and more.

It seems only Olivia is any good at recreational crafting—she weaves ocean waves from curls of blue wire, using crushed plastic for the whitecaps, and lately she's been rendering *The Starry Night* from a hodgepodge of circuit boards and stray buttons and bulbs. All her artwork ends up pasted to those spare patches of wall not insulated with cardboard, which look and feel like sponge cake mixed with freshly poured concrete. The clubhouse is largely odorless but for the rare whiff of wintergreen. Mario and Maria share a hammock woven from gauzy webbing they've poached from their cell blocks' spider-roaches.

The light borrowed from outside showers all in a greenish glow.

It's paradise out there, a panoramic consolidation of jungle and rainforest and wetland, green and teeming with sweeping trees and swirling streams and lakes aglitter. The luxuriant vegetation breathes as one verdant lung. Fluttering insects boasting incandescently neon wings pop against every backdrop. Foxglove and hollyhocks pepper fertile plains in which hummingbirds and bumblebees pollinate in peace. Parrots and macaws share the airspace with vultures and crows. Cacti colonize small blotches of desert choked with chaparral. Valleys shimmer in the distance, where mountains mark the sloping horizon like gods waking up. Of the countless exotic creatures Calvin's glimpsed and appraised, nothing has topped the squirrel monkey in terms of sheer awesomeness.

But the scenery through the glass is always shifting, is the thing, unveiling new wonders to see and admire with each passing "moment," a perpetually evolving quilt of landscapes and lifeforms stitching itself at a rate almost observable.

The one constant is the impression that what you're perceiving is indeed paradise.

"It's so nice out there," says Calvin. He's been trying to wipe his eyes with the handkerchief but always ends up getting under his nostrils instead. He can't seem to figure out the ever-evolving dimensions of his face. "So why does it scare me so, June?"

June turns, shoots Calvin through with her violently violet eyes: *Fire.*

"What do you mean fi—"

Given Calvin's constant struggle navigating his own face, the speed with which June has located and duly eclipsed his whole mouth with her enormous hand is nothing if not impressive, her hand clamped high up where he's pretty sure his eyes should be. His vision swims between the slit her wiggling pinky and ring fingers produce, meaning his eyes seem to have swapped places with his nostrils. With one swift gesticulation one might take to mean *Be quiet!* or *Not another word!* or (to the Pain Train's passenger prisoners) *Hear that? Hynetters!*, June has instead conveyed *Your eyes are right here, Calvin.*

When their eyes meet in the chute between pinky and ring, the rest of June's message skims warmly through—*For your face*—and she releases her hold.

At last Calvin's able to use the handkerchief to wipe his eyes for tears that aren't and haven't been there for some time. He resumes peering beyond the fifth wall's glass with June, fixing his gaze upon a troop of kangaroos. They gallop across an open desert plain, huge haunches gyrating, pouched joeys jouncing. Leaps and bounds.

"Thank you for being my friend," he says.

"Down The Spider's hatch two Downers fly," says June, as if reciting a prayer she's been practicing, "one Downer's super flame to catch, a rolling lie."

"About this super flame—"

"Hey, I know those 'roos!" someone calls from behind.

Calvin spins and sees Homer, now pressing part of his face to his trusty TV's dead screen. Olivia glances up from *The Starry Night* while Angela, sharing the same crystalline workbench, keeps her eyes levelled on the cracked yellow pages of this dusty old tome she pretends to be able to read called *The Holy Bible*. Mario huddles closer to Maria, making their hammock sway. "Those 'roos're antilopines!" Homer proclaims. "Native to Australia!"

"That your TV-chit again?" says Mario, and Maria follows, "What's Austria?"

"Australia," whispers Homer, whose awe Calvin can feel more than hear. It's the renewed energy in the room, hot soup on the coldest day. "I think it's where I'm from."

It isn't long before all seven sigs are standing abreast and staring out, and the heat among them is growing as more kangaroos keep coming and going and sometimes sight alone can be a paradise all its own. Calvin stands, Mario and Maria and June to his left, Angela and Homer and Olivia to his right, the heartbeat of them all.

A movie-like memory rewinds, going back and back, and Calvin sees Homer on the other side of the fifth wall's glass, waddling along Cradle Mountain's highest promontory in the night, taking the time to find his footing before holding the camera out from around his neck and snapping for the picture-perfect mother he never met a shot of the astonishing view of so many lakes glittering in the light of the Australian moon. Who cares if his thumb got in the shot because he'll never forget June with her fishing rod, alone in the morning dawn, casting her line from atop Lake McDonald's tallest rock, hoping to catch Father's Day breakfast for her snoozing father's father while Montana's snowcapped peaks reach like robed angels for the brightening horizon where Mario unzips his tent, peeks right then left before tiptoeing his way out of camp away from his sleeping family and telling himself tonight's the night he will dispel the naughty ghost of the Yucatan Peninsula who's been threatening to take his imaginary girlfriend away, watching and feeling for sinkholes in the porous limestone underfoot. One misstep and he'll drop to the web of rivers underground and drown on the race to the underworld in which Maria wakes to the sound of her imaginary boyfriend whispering of gold in the canyon, a treasure chest buried in the cavernous bowels of an abandoned mineshaft near the city of Ponferrada, which is in the region of El Bierzo in the province of León where she lives in Spain. There's enough gold in the canyon to cover the medication she needs, the voice coaxes, for Maria's mother to quit cleaning up after those meanies in the mansion, for her and her mother to sever all ties and begin life anew together, which is why Maria sets out for the Las Médulas mines all on her own, the morning sun beating down on her neck until finally she's standing before the mineshaft's gaping maw from which her imaginary boyfriend's whispers seem to emerge, a hissing crackle in the dark. When she steps forward, she bumps into Angela kneeling in the deep mud of a shallow stream somewhere in the Dolly Sods Wilderness of West Virginia, gasping for air before she's dunked again and gurgling, and it's the priest who Angela's always thought of as the world's gentlest man who's gripping the back of her head and tearing the hair there, pinching the nape of her neck with every Hail-Mary-Full-of-Grace cry he sends up to thy Heavenly Father in the sky, a last-ditch effort to eradicate the Devil's demon's fanged serpent so entangling thy daughter Angela's mind and injecting its insidious poison in the form of voices it isn't normal for good, God-fearing Christian girls to be hearing. As her lungs fill with sludge water and mudworms, her head's filling with the light of the Lord, which shines like a lighthouse through trees and leaves gnashing in the cold night breeze, and it's to this sacred beacon Angela retreats, lurching forth to escape the painful hold on her hair only to find herself scampering from the priest, who's been so kind and so loving every time he comes by the house for private sessions in which they pray until he always ends up touching her in ways that make every-thing below the belly go as soft as the world's gentlest fingers grazing those forbidden places she knows are mortally sinful for her to navi-gate for herself. Angela's running in the woods away from this kind and gentle man when all of a sudden Olivia contemplates leaving a life at sea forever behind, a life and world she's cherished ever since she was a little girl and her father got his first job as a mess cook aboard the RMS *Celtic* in 1901, because now Olivia's overlooking the North Atlantic's icy black sheet from her perch way in back of *The Titanic*, which, according to the dark horsey with the floating white face—who's hiding with her in her secret place no one else knows about—is going to strike an iceberg shortly before midnight and everyone she knows and loves on this doomed vessel will scream and flail and sink. Many years from now, people she will never know nor love will romanticize the terrible tragedy with a most lovely tale of two star-crossed lovers, but don't you worry, says the grinning dark horsey, come with me and your heart will go on—I simply require your consent.

Wintergreen sweeps the clubhouse strong and sweet, a cold warmth filled with feeling. Their cumulative breath has fogged the fifth wall's glass, sealing the scene. Olivia traces a heart with her finger before evaporation's cyclic incarnation.

"You aren't imaginary, are you?"

"No, Mario," says Maria. "I think maybe we're each other's soulmate."

"Did *The Titanic* sink or . . . it was lying to me, wasn't it? —*wasn't it?*"

"Oh, it sank," says Homer. "Sorry, Liv. What about big Calvin, though?"

"What about me?"

"Pretty sure we all just sorta witnessed-slash-reexperienced when and where we all were the morning or night Old Boogey got us . . . so how did Old Boogey get you?"

"I don't know," says Calvin. "I can't remember." He catches an urgent eye-message from June he translates for the rest of the group. "We have to keep breathing."

———

BREATHE, Mustafa muttered breathlessly to himself, lips hovering the dusty fuzz top of a microphone (presently set to *Off* despite no batteries) he'd filched from behind the curtain behind Allegiance High Theater's shadowy stump of a stage. The cluttered void backstage had served as a storage room ever since Zone Red assimilated Gatlinburg with most of the East (New York City being the exception), when Mangrove first used her Skeeter-5000s to bully her way into office and United became Divided and the state motto of Tennessee—effective immediately—switched from *Agriculture and Commerce* to *Agriculture and Calmness.*

Presently Mustafa cleared his throat and set the mic's switch to *On.*

He was glad to be back in his own backyard, outdoors, where he felt most at home.

"Good afternoon, everyone. Thank you all for being here. My name is Gary M-Muh-*Mustafa.* This evening, I've been given the greatest, humblest honor to speak not only on behalf of m-myself, but also on behalf of all who've had the sincerest pleasure of having known dearest diaphanous Wendy Weather since her $16.99 purchase on American Science & Surplus almost seventeen years ago. How fitting it is to be able to celebrate dearest Wendy's m-m-muh . . . please, if you would excuse me a moment . . ."

Mustafa leaned back on the makeshift pulpit—a stepstool bordered with squarish walls of duct-taped cardboard—away from the mic, pausing to flex the sinewy strings tethered to the backs of his eyes, trapping tears that bulged as thick in his sockets as the collection of snot in his mustache. He threw his eyes to a weekend sky now blessedly empty of drones—flying crudweasels one and all, to Mustafa's mind, clotting the clouds, haranguing away the days with their needling whine, their persistent assault on privacy—and lost himself in the unmolested orange. He leaned forward, face set to *Stern*, determined to strike a sympathetic chord with his fellow mourners: Caroline Comfort, Lucile Laughter, Stephanie Sympathy, Polly Amorous, Egret Regret, Bella Beautiful, Willow the Widow, Alice Wanderlust, Faith Faithful, Summer Sinful, Paige Popstar, Demi Snowflake . . . even Emma Emergency made a rare appearance, having made the trip from Mustafa's Musker. This is for all of you, Mustafa told himself.

Breathe.

"How fitting it is to be able to celebrate dearest Wendy's *memory* at sunset on a Sunday in late October—her favorite time of day, her favorite day of the week, her favorite month of the year—here in this pleasant m-meh-*meadow*—this pleasant meadow—behind my humble home here on Thissa Way, dearest Wendy's favorite place. For m-muh—for *me*, Wendy Weather always served as a profoundest source of comfort. Second only to you, Caroline, but second to none in terms of pure, unadulterated kindness. She'd been translucent in nature, huge in personality, spherical and delicate to the touch. Rest assured, of Wendy's five-foot diameter I cherished every inch—more to love, I'd always say."

Of the fifty-five balloons in attendance—tethered to a medley of rocks and logs set before a bowl-shaped grave in which what remained of Wendy Weather lay, a silvery gray pile of strips shimmering in the soil—Mustafa's wandering eyes most often landed on Willow the Widow and Egret Regret, more so even than the new rescues: Regina Resilience and her abused kin, a family of five formerly abandoned to the elements, victims of Randy Mick's egregious neglect. Small wonder young Billy Mick ended up doing what he did this Friday past—or tried to do.

"Wendy could always see right through me, straight past the bullspit to my admittedly troubled heart. On our best days, we wouldn't speak at all. I'd simply loop her string around the big oak's trunk at my back, and she'd watch me watch the sun set through her shimmery skin. In a world overwrought with pressure, these silent heart-to-hearts were the lifelines to which I wholeheartedly clung, and I want you all to know Wendy Weather weathered my every storm to the very end, when she popped in my own arms through absolutely zero fault of her own."

Wendy's popping had been a product of pressure, violently pent-up, the weight of the world outside—one week's worth, anyway, but what a week it'd been, the all-time worst of Mustafa's thirty-six years as principal—wending its way inside, toxic like wrong air in his lungs, inflating, the feeling all-consumingly crushing, turning him demonic, unrecognizable even to himself in the reflection of those who glowed.

"Although a whopping 46,273 of you currently populate my home, I count fifty-five lustrous sheens floating here today, and I know I speak for all when I say we thank dearest Wendy for giving us her all—for loving us all equally, infinitely, and unconditionally. Wendy's given us all the greatest of gifts, an instruction m-muh-muh-*manual* of sorts—an instruction manual of sorts—not for how to chart the weather or m-monitor pollution or scatter human ashes at high-altitude—though surely we can acknowledge and appreciate her natural gifts—but rather an instruction *manual* on just how to love our fellow balloon and Non-Popper, to give our all to endangered balloons and Looners alike and expect nothing in return."

It all started after school let out on Monday, when young Billy came sauntering into the office with his career-threatening accusations, blackmail simmering in the tone of his rhetorical questions—*I know it was you at the garage, Care Bear. Hiding under the truck. And I know you know I know—I see it in your face clear as day. Clear as the big-ass balloon in the picture you keep in that drawer there, even. Wanna know what gave you* *away? It was your license plate: H-E-L-1-U-M-5-5. I saw it right away with my flashlight, and even though I was stoned—as you know, as my parents also know, by the way, so any attempt to blackmail me or whatever would be a major waste of your time—so even though I was ripped off my ass . . . probably because I was ripped off my ass . . . I had what Blue stoners like to call a "moment of clarity." In other words, I remembered something. Something you told me. Something big. Wanna know what it was, Care Bear? It was what you said about destiny, how, like, you totally wanna bone my mom, etc. etc. etc.—*and ended late Friday night in the comfort of his home, on the couch before the TV with Wendy, the living room's lamplight glowing low, the Bag of Food #3 popcorn going ballistic in the microwave—*DON'T SHOOT! NOOOOOO!*—sixteen thousand balloons rewatching the news rerunning the same story—*How old were you, Billy?*—for the fifth time, the story of what almost transpired at lunch at Allegiance High on Friday, the local reporters talking Skeeters—*At this point I could quote these crudweasels* ("Although a PWP investigation into the would-be shooter's potential motives has only just begun, Chet, one thing remains clear: the Gatlinburg community has Principal Gary Mustafa to thank. If not for Mr. Mustafa's gutsy decision to embrace the optional subset of President Mangrove's executive order and go ahead with the 'Skeeter Experiment'—a proposition unanimously panned by the District Board of Education and County Office of Education alike this past summer for its Blue-leaning posture—thus making Allegiance the first and only Tennessee high school to open its doors to a Skeeter-5000 for the sole purpose of preventing what otherwise might've transpired earlier today—if not for that, Chet, then there's a good-in-the-worst-way chance I'd be reporting right here and now an infinitely grimmer story. As it stands, however, that crucial midsummer judgment call has saved who knows how many lives here today, my own daughter's included, and so we the people of Gatlinburg salute Principal Gary Mustafa, a true American hero . . ."), the local anchors jabbering back, the popcorn pummeling, the pressure from outside inside, pulverizingly painful, and all along Mustafa had been holding Wendy in his arms.

"And now it's only a matter of time before that fudging Skeeter of mine reports Billy's online activity to Party White Patrol or maybe even Mangrove herself and I'll find myself up crud creek without a . . . I mean, um . . . my sincerest apologies, everyone," said Mustafa, looking around for his mic. "If you would excuse me once m-muh—once *more* . . ."

Mustafa couldn't recollect dropping the mic. He had to hop off the stool and bend over to swoop it off the grass, and then he eyed the sky for stars he couldn't find. The orange had smoldered away to a black and moonless void pressing down like the bottom of a stone on something tiny and alive. He went back inside his house to snag a flashlight.

Reporters had come crawling all weekend with their vans and camera crews, trying to trap Mustafa in an interview, picking and probing, a mob equally obsessed with becoming the first to break the origin story of a local zero turned national hero overnight. He'd shut all his curtains to shut them out, which did nothing to shut them up, so this morning before dawn's crack, he made a show of getting into his Musker and zooming off. No sooner had he lost the last van in the rear-view than he hurled himself through the moving vehicle's passenger window, tucking and rolling onto the highway shoulder, roughing up his shoulder on his downward tumble to the bottom of the ditch, where he dug himself a safe space until the ruthlessly invasive convoy above had ripped past. It was an all-day process getting back in time for Wendy's service— which he'd set up at three a.m. last night—burrowing under back-yard fences and army-crawling the whole way home. It was a good thing that, before defenestrating himself, he had remembered to program the Musker's return for three a.m. tonight, the witching hour.

Presently he found the flashlight in the foyer's closet too close to his open bedroom door, tempting his tired eyes. He had himself a nap and then he remounted the stool in the meadow.

Wendy's grave mirrored the size and shape of a Gatling gun's bullet exit wound.

Mustafa pressed his lips to the microphone once more, using the flashlight to see the eulogy by, his arms heavy from holding these things, fingers tense from squeezing. The bones in his shoulder swam around unattached, another product of pressure.

Breathe.

"And over these years we've laughed. A lot. We've laughed in ways big and small—in ways that venture well beyond the humorous. Wendy Weather *thrilled* us all, for instance, the day the storms came and wiped out the power in over one hundred thousand Tennessee homes, ours included. I'll never forget charging into the wind and rain, dearest Wendy wrapped in my arms, the trees blowing apart as far as the eye could see. That was the day I looped her around the big oak behind me for the first time, the day Wendy Weather shone all alone and brought back the sun. I remember laughing so hard I cried . . ."

Mustafa had planned to be caught crying during this part of the speech, to see himself reflected in Riley Rainy glowing morosely in the front row, to then make any necessary adjustments in the name of authentic atrabilious grief. He wondered what he must look like to everyone—*People spend way more on guns than I do tending to my balloons*—right here and now, retching and heaving on a pulpit he'd slapped together, spewing words he'd scrapped together—*How was I supposed to know mere words in some chatroom thingy alone could move a teenager in this day and age to such lunacy? I mean we were* online, *for goodness' sake. It's nothing compared to what his* father *put* me *through as a boy*—pumping his fists at all that nothing in the weighty night sky, trying to weep his way to outside sympathy, suddenly unable to taste the real tears that had been here not so long ago. He was very tired. The words on the page failed to put together any pictures of Wendy Weather. Why had he been crying earlier? If not dearest Wendy, for whom were those tears? Soon they would come for him—and not for an exclusive interview. They would come armed with the truth, proof of the monster Mustafa knew he really was deep down through absolutely zero fault of his own.

"It was *his* father who put me in the ICU as a boy, *his* father who grew up to wed my destiny's womanly shape—my Kimmi-Sue—*his* father who first turned me on to John Wayne Gacy philosophy, who back in fifth grade chased me after school all the way into the woods where his crew of crudweasels were already waiting with their fudging shovels and marijuana sticks, *his* father, Randy *Mick*, who shoved me in the back and I flew forward and fell down a hole which five seconds before was all covered up with leaves. And suddenly the five of us were playing whack-a-mole—*Get the gopher boy! Go for the head!*—but I was the mole, and by the time the sun was setting, they were gone with my phone and I had to army-crawl the whole way home because my neck and spine wouldn't work right. And I'd bet all the money in the world it was the mere sight of me that pushed *Mother* over the edge into madness."

Mother drove him straight to the hospital, where she was told he might never walk again, Mustafa had since discovered, reviewing the letters she'd written him over the years from Riverview Psychiatric. She'd PSed each with *Follow the Ladybug* up until the day she died.

"One day my favorite nurse tied my first balloon to my bedside railing—so round, I remember, so lusciously smooth. Even now I can still taste the wintergreen wafting off its fine pink skin. Sadly, there was no way of preventing the harm to come that night in the dark of night because . . . are you paying attention out there? Are any of you listening? Think I'm starting to think this could be the reason you're all here—this could very well be your origin story. Is that laughter I'm hearing, Lucille? Are you seriously laughing right now?"

Much harm had been done every night in the dark of night because there was nothing Mustafa could do while the harm was happening, not with his jaw all wired shut. "That's what I thought. Anyways, it's Mother, driven mad by the sight of me, by the horror of the harm done to me by *his* father—I couldn't fill in the blanks for her; I mean it's not like I could talk through *wire*. Driven mad by all that and more, she'd been, by being deprived of the reason why her only child might never walk or even talk ever again, Mother, mad as the hatter, slinks inside my room in the ICU at three in the morning—the witching hour—and puts her hands to my balloon. They look like spiders moving in the gloom, those horrible hands of hers, inkblots suffusing the pink's moony glow. All of a sudden

Mother's crouching down near my face, whistling through her teeth and slurping inadvertent drool and moaning and . . . all I could do was watch her hands. Flicking the nipple-knot that keeps all the air inside and tugging it, stretching and pulling it, squeezing and pressing the balloon's vulnerable sides, making it make that noise that tickles at first before it scrapes like so much barbed wire being raked across the brain—and the second it gets to be too much, she stops and starts drumming her fingers up and down and all around, which sounds like rain pounding the ICU's roof, and I'm trying to stop shaking and crying . . . but Mother mistakes my pain for laughter and keeps going and going, and the pop I could do nothing to prevent was my first time hearing the sound of pressure getting all the way in. Even now I can still taste the terrible bitterness that came with the departure of my balloon's wintergreen scent."

What Mustafa was really tasting and smelling was the rank reek of cordite he knew he was imagining, which was all he could taste and smell since what happened Friday.

"This, by the way, would end up occurring on a more or less nightly basis since the nurse, like wintergreen's covenant daily renewed, would come through in the morning with another balloon. Thing is, by the time they removed my mouth's wiring, I already knew Mother had totally lost her mind. She'd been whispering to me in the night those nights, and I didn't know what else to do, so I told on her—I tell my nurse about this 'Moon Man' Mother keeps hissing about while rubbing and popping so many innocents in the darkness, how supposedly this 'Moon Man' tells Mother—and here I'll quote: 'There shall soon come a time when your son must aid humanity in my effort to untether the Road from Mother Climate's hold,' unquote—and how Mother keeps telling me to follow the ladybug to the site of the end of the world. The nurse nods, and it's not long before I'm hearing Mother's screams through the walls, seeing her being held back as she tries to scratch and claw her way inside my room. It wasn't her fault—wasn't mine, either . . . it was *his* father's. If not for his father, the kid would still be here . . . alive."

Burning white light sliced from the direction of the drive, scattering the meadow's immediate darkness, Mustafa's Musker returning in time for the witching hour.

Mourners bobbed in the shadows like silent hanging heads.

"Lunacy is the language of pressure seething to release," Mustafa told his balloons. "It's Randy's fault Mother, Billy, and dearest Wendy Weather boiled alive from within."

He'd even tried saving the kid in the end, admonishing the Skeeter not to shoot.

———

Seven sigs huff hard and fast to keep the fifth wall's glass properly fogged, racing evaporation itself as they work as one to keep the scenes on the other side erased from view. The more they can't see with their eyes—the more the glass betrays a screen of milky white —the more Calvin can see inside his head and theirs, can feel his way into his heart and theirs . . . the more the pain in his hair and theirs lessens.

The clubhouse under the Play Day House fills up with powerful feeling.

The word *neurasthenic* surfaces to mind like an echo made of memory, but this time—for the first time—it means something to Calvin: *neurasthenia* is what is leaving their bodies, he's realizing, a collective cloud escaping their mouths and oozing over the glass like some ectoplasmic haze, shrouding scenic sights only feigning to be paradise. What leaves their bodies is what brings into the room the chilled warmth of wintergreen, whose secondary source is Calvin's handkerchief, whose original owner was a kind, compassionate sig named Hanky who preferred Batman to Captain America, who helped Calvin pick a pair of shoes that fit his feet perfectly. Hanky, who's been present all this time in his own significant way.

Hanky's hanky—*For your face*—keeps Calvin safe.

Maria slits little diamonds into the fog with her pinky, telling Mario every little thing's going to be all right, while Angela ribbons a string of interconnected circles below, underscored with a single upside-down triangle. Prayer should be what connects us, Angela says, so why have we let it divide us? Homer begins a harrowing tale with the conscientious air of somebody operating under clarity's superlative spell, birthing the stars that make up the asterisms that make up the Big Dipper and Winter Hexagon and Northern Cross, all scattered across the fifth wall's glass so as to indicate the view of the night sky from Homer's hometown in Australia. Homer proceeds to wipe out every last star system with one slow sweep of the hand. The void that's left behind fills right back in with the gaseous haze of neurasthenic pain leaving the sigs' bodies behind. Calvin condenses the story Homer's told into five insidious words: *My home is on fire.*

"True, in Australia's case," a droning voice seems to lament.

All seven sigs twist around, throwing their eyes toward the e-waste hill nested in shadows only the corners of rooms have. Calvin's heart's secret clock tracking their home world's degradation's progress ticks and ticks, and ticks are what they are, the bugs making up Mr. Moony's body—Bod, their name is—taking the shape of horseys or goats or birds or fish or what-all. Presently Bod looks a bit like a beetle, six legs and their attached appendages splayed over the e-waste. Mr. Moony's pale oval face hovers near what might be the thorax. Bod's beetled form is maybe half the size of the hill on which it's perched.

"America also enjoys a state of great indigence on every level, Calvin," says Mr. Moony.

June's the first to step out in front of Calvin, and the rest follow suit, forming a human shield. Calvin can feel them fighting fear with the strength of their union.

"There's way too much feeling happening in here," says Mr. Moony. "Bod?"

Bod's beetled aspect abruptly dissolves, and suddenly Mr. Moony's bugs swarm the air above the sigs' heads in a manic thrum. All seven sigs throw up their hands and hack away with their arms to protect their faces and hair. Calvin's flailing fists connect sharply with several carapaces, but by the end of the skirmish, his knuckles are left bruised and bleeding and no exploded bug bodies mottle the floor. Bod reassumes its position atop its hill of discarded tech; the billion little bodies composing Its singular form pulse and look very bloated.

"Why such intended violence?" says Mr. Moony. "Quit behaving as though I were trying to eat you. Rest assured I am as full as the farmer who fills me."

"That some kinda figure of speech?" asks Homer.

"Actually it's quite more literal than I'm sure you'd care to hear."

"You're mean," says Maria. "Like those meanies my mother used to clean up for."

"I see you've all managed to figure out a way to remember some of the horrors still haunting your former lives. Let me just say it might not do any of you well to recall such ghastly events. It might be better instead to move on—to go ahead and leave whatever terrible so-called traumas buried in the dust of the past where they most naturally reside."

Calvin cocks back his head and catches an upside-down angle of the fifth wall's glass, now clear and transparent once again, empty of fog. Where has all their neurasthenia gone?

"Consider therefore what I'm about to do a favor," says Mr. Moony, whose grin still searches for a punch line to crack it wide open. "May the emptiness fill you."

Mr. Moony's eyes seem to squint the slightest bit as Bod's bloated sub-bodies begin to shudder and shake. The ribbed flaps lining their abdomens' rims bloom like strange black flowers; Bod bulges on the whole like some infected boil set to blow at the tiniest pinprick. Calvin's trying to screen eyes he can no longer find when Bod discharges from its every exposed orifice, spewing the neurasthenic pain Bod must've retrieved from the fifth wall's glass.

The clubhouse hisses with a haze now gray instead of white, gauzy instead of gaseous, the sticky stuff of webs. Not a single sig is successful in covering up his or her mouth in time to prevent the invasive webbing from ramming back down where it first came out, gagging them, stuffing them one and all. Calvin crumples over, his body quaking, failing to reject the icky stuff Bod's ejected. The tears blurring his vision have zero to do with emotion.

Already he's forgotten whatever it is that's now, yet again, filling his body whole.

"It's not like I'm doing any of this maliciously," says Mr. Moony. "This isn't so much some mean or misleading attempt to dictate your lives as it is an honest effort on my part to revamp your mentalities in such way as to provide you with this bliss your kind is always speaking of whenever certain societal contexts—racial or political or mystical—are perhaps best left unaddressed. Ignorance, in other words—your being left quote unquote 'in the dark'—has more than likely been essential to your overall wellbeing. Here."

"What am I doing here?" says Maria, and Mario adds, "Why are we here?"

"You've all been behaving naughtily down here," says Mr. Moony. "If the Super Substance hadn't already entered terminal processing, I'd have no other option but to give you all up to The Spider for ultimate excommunication. Because, however, I'm presently positively giddy regarding all things Apocalypse, I'm feeling relatively 'down for dialogue,' which not so long ago, by the way, constituted America's basic premise. Ah yes, the Land of the Free . . ."

Calvin searches beyond the fifth wall's glass, where monkeys of all kinds traverse vines suspended from trees in a rainforest wild with orchids. The handkerchief now draped over his foot on the floor hoards the ghostly imprint of a friendly face. He repeats aloud a question he only barely remembers asking June not so long ago— three words in all.

"You're *made* of what your kind calls matter," Mr. Moony replies.

Calvin faces Mr. Moony. "That's not what I meant—and you know it."

"Careful, Calvin," says Angela. "Old Boogey's here—*he can hear us.*"

"I'd listen to your friend if I were you," says Mr. Moony. "Watch your words."

Calvin tries to watch Mr. Moony's obstinate grin. Parts of Calvin's face slip and slide all around, his eyes melting down only to meet the imprint of the face in the cloth on his foot. The handkerchief has weight to it, but it's the good kind of weight, the kind that comes with somebody's hand enfolding yours in the face of some unspeakable tragedy.

Or an arm wrapping your shoulder to hold you close.

Calvin shoulders his way past June, who's been waggling her head. "Where's Hanky?" he says, and then he proceeds to spit a flood of questions that exit his mind—permanently—through his mouth. "What's Trent's involvement in your plan?—what *is* the plan? You've been mining our kindness—how does that work, Mr. Moony? What's Phooka Road—and don't you dare lie and imply it's this world we're all living in because that's not the full truth and we both know it. What's the whole point of the Super Substance, and what's our role in its genesis?"

"Calvin, Calvin, Calvin," says Mr. Moony. "Excepting anything to do with Trent, you and I have already addressed these notions in full—fifty-four times in one earthly decade alone, in fact. Is it now my understanding you want to tick it up to fifty-five?"

"Last time counts for all," says Calvin, who's already forgotten everything he's just finished asking. "We deserve to know what you've been doing to our bodies."

The fuzz on Mr. Moony's unibrow bristles like a thing alive. "Do tiny ants on your world buck against the shadow of your foot? Do they pull together and put a STOP to their so-called 'day' and yours, demanding they deserve the knowledge as to why your foot's going to fall where it's inevitably going to? Or do these itty-bitty ants just sort of go with it?"

"We're human," says Calvin.

"Exactly," says Mr. Moony. "Thing is, Calvin, it's all so bureaucratic—which, to most people from where you're from, basically means *boring*, meaning there's no real reason for you to 'waste time and energy' paying attention to developments such as these. Most Americans already get it. It's pointless for you to know anything about the proverbial foot's looming shadow—inevitability in motion, so to speak—a virtually unstoppable gathering of darkness and cold. There are, however, legitimate reasons to keep you from asking questions that could risk removing that benumbing bliss to which I've already alluded."

"Where I'm from, ants fight back," says Homer. "Biters and stingers."

"Australia's gone up in flames," Mr. Moony snaps back. "For good this time. But if you're metaphorically ascribing Calvin here's line of questioning to some human version of biting and fighting back, then I don't see why I shouldn't reply with my undeniably legit reasoning for keeping you all blissfully unaware. True truth—assuming it won't bore you all to death—has got a solid chance of doing the opposite and petrifying you all to the point of permanent bodily paralysis. Put another way, you might find the foot that casts the cold dark shadow horrifying for its obdurate indifference toward your fleeting existence. Secondly, you'll soon be forgetting all about it—the equally banal and horrifying truth, I mean. Meaning sooner than later my answers to Calvin's questions will abandon your bodies' substances. Interestingly enough, by the way, this whole 'forgetting the face of horror in record time' gestalt has more or less come to define America as of late. Like, your world is totally burning and falling apart, and yet the typical American response has more or less amounted to 'That sucks . . . oh well!'"

Calvin's forgotten the questions he's asked Mr. Moony, though he hasn't forgotten doing the asking itself. He's got no intention of letting Mr. Moony distract his way to victory, however big or small it might be, whatever it might mean. The face in the handkerchief draping his foot seems to smile up at him. "Answer me, Mr. Moony."

"Answer him," says June, whose voice seems to startle Mr. Moony to attention.

"Can't say I didn't warn you," Mr. Moony says. "All righty, everyone, whenever you're ready, go ahead and face the glass. Don't worry, I won't sneak up on you from behind or anything. Like I said, I'm nice and full. Turn around, I said. That means you, June. Waiting on you, Mario. Wonderful. Now, if you could describe whatever it is you see out there in one word—and only one word—what would it be? Go ahead and shout the answer."

"Paradise!" the seven of them call out together.

"Precisely! And it's all of *you* who've made such paradise possible. What you see out there is your combined substances—your cumulative kindness—on display, in a way. Here's how it works: your kindness—one of its functions at least—allows my miners to pluck bits and pieces of your world that have burnt to ash from the ashes of Phooka Road. As you can see, the result's been a rather alluring ecological concoction of Amazon rainforest, Southeast Asia, parts of California regularly hit during the fire season—those parts of California that recently took a huge hit from what your people called 'the big one,'—and of course much more. The Pain Train'll be able to haul it all when the time comes. Up, up, and away we'll all go one day."

"What's Phooka Road?"

"Well, Olivia, Calvin's correct in saying the region we currently occupy isn't exactly Phooka Road. I mean it is—but it isn't. It is and it isn't. Once upon a bye, this would've been rather taxing on my part to try to clarify, but after taking an earthly decade to buckle down and really examine your world for the first time in 252 million so-called years, I happened to happen across a most fitting metaphor for Phooka Road and its most basic function: Zlokmatoogs and Zlokmatoog stations. What *you* call airplanes and airports. The Pain Train itself is a relatively ancient—relative to your perspective at least—Zlokmatoog, meaning it's been 252 million years since the Pain Train last rode the Road. We currently inhabit what you might think of as a terminal: P.R. Dimension Five, Sector E. That's where we are. You might think of the Road itself, however, as the sky through which your airplanes zip and zoom. I invite you all at this time to turn your gazes skyward." Calvin regards the coal-black clouds swirling churning high above. "Those aren't clouds, Calvin. Those are the ashes composing Phooka Road, the interdimensional binary knot binding your world to mine. The Road's inhabitants—good, kind folk one and all—are whose environment I've been assigned to safeguard with my immortal existence. The foremost issue of late's been your world's kindness holocaust, tainting what little kindness my kind manage to inhale with humanity's toxic overflow of shame. That my kind's feeble exhalations are in any way responsible for your kind's cataclysmic drop in shame levels or Mother Climate's compulsive weather patterns is perhaps irrelevant. What mostly matters here is how Earth's people've failed to uphold their end of Mother Climate's Contract of Basic Goodness—as I said, it's all so boringly bureaucratic—and consequentially have been suffocating my kind into nonexistence. All that's to say it's time—for the first time in 252 million so-called years—for me, myself, and Bod to relocate my kind to a new world, one whose Warden Mother consents to the presence of live interdimensional double-knots like Phooka Road."

"You're giving me a headache," says Mario.

"This is way too much information to take in all at once!" says Maria. "No fair!"

"I warned you," says Mr. Moony. "Tedious complexities make true truth hurt."

"Kurt!" Calvin shouts. Mario and Maria slide to the floor enfolded in each other's arms. The scene through the fifth wall's glass has changed—and for the worse. "Ernest! Edgar!"

"Here's where things get literally unnerving for some."

Angela's on her knees, palpating Maria and Mario for pulses. "Dear God!"

The sight beyond the glass strikes Calvin with familiarity of the coldest possible kind.

Mr. Moony says, "You can only hope such bodily paralysis won't be permanent, Angela. I'm afraid I'm not afraid prayer's got nothing at all to do with it."

Angela collapses, joining Maria and Mario in a rigid full-body paralysis.

Calvin forces himself to lift his eyes away from his paralyzed friends. The view beyond the glass presents a pitchfork of tunneled passages, each walled off from the other. Kurt's treading the middle passage, unwittingly flanked through the walls on either side by Ernest and Edgar respectively. Each tunnel gives way to a window of weak, guttering light, all trapezoidal in shape. Tangled filaments hang like wet hair in all the slithering fumes. All three significants use their hands to feel their way along the walls, marring the faces impressed within, and Calvin, who's got his own hands pressed over his mouth—where he's sure his eyes should be—tracks his mouth as it moves like something alive down his face and settles in a region he once called right cheek. He can almost hear voices and clangorous banging through the glass.

He scans from left to right and back as Ernest, Kurt, and Edgar retreat toward the end of their private chutes. The sputtering light warps their silhouettes with their every forward step. Their bodies flicker like candles melting into the burning distance.

". . . which is one of the best kept secrets of all of space-time existence."

"Can you repeat that?" says Calvin.

"'That, that, that,'" says Mr. Moony. "Anyways, as you can see— we're moving on now, Calvin, you ought to consider paying closer attention—as you can see, your three little friends are well on their way to their own personal substance extractions."

"What happened to all the paradise?" Homer asked.

"Everything's merely a matter of perception, Homer, which of course is inherently ephemeral. Honestly, I'm literally projecting. I've got Bod's bugs everywhere, see—from the Pain Train's bowels down under to America's various 'armpits.' What you see is what I'm choosing to allow you to see of everything I'm presently seeing, see?"

"Like a movie of memory," says Calvin.

"I'm sure someone somewhere would thank you for hitting us with such a silly half-baked simile," says Mr. Moony. "But okay, fine, I'm projecting the omniscient contents of my sight in a way you might compare to film and movie screens—anybody here catch *The Titanic?*—but this isn't anything like what you call memory, which, for the human species at least, is innately apocryphal. What you're seeing is totally live and totally true. To clarify—let me be clear here —I see everything everywhere Bod's soldiers and spies reside, simultaneously."

"Don't go into the light!" Calvin yells at the sigs through the glass. "Turn back, Kurt!"

"They can't hear you, obviously. They're hearing other voices instead, all of which're drawing them forth to the light of rebirth. This next part's my favorite. Watch."

"DON'T GO DOWN THE CHUTE!"

"Hush now, Calvin. As you can see these three significants have stumbled their way into the light. See how they're changing—I mean it, Calvin, stop fussing. Let's not forget you're the one who asked. I'm simply answering—see how they're changing. Watch those bodies twist and contort and shrivel, shrivel, shrivel. But look! They live! See them flutter tiny wings and fly! Pretty, aren't they? Truth is, kindness on Earth comes in many different colors. Anyways, it won't be long now . . . hold it . . . hold it—*splat!*—would you look at that! Three dead bugs! Just like that! The see-through steam you're now seeing is all the substance that has been squeezed and squashed free of the significants' incarnations' shells . . . there it is spreading throughout the Pain Train, in those vortical funnels there . . . now those sinuous snake-pipes . . . down, down . . . look, one of my kindness miners! Look at him go! Calvin's always saying they look like Snow White's dwarves—but with their insides on the outside, of course! This little helper's just about done mining Edgar's substance's yield, some of which we'll be sending up to Phooka Road to those in need—here's Hanky the hynetter doing just that—most of which'll wind up on The Spider's Web. From there it'll be cast all the way to the Super Substance."

Calvin and June remain the only two still standing. Homer, Olivia, Angela, Mario, and Maria lie limply at their feet in a jumble of limbs, bodies still as glass, eyes wide open. Calvin can only hope they're dreaming of anything besides what they've seen.

"The Super Substance, as I believe I've come close to implying, will be used to power the relocation effort. You could think of it as a sort of fuel—think mankind's obsession with oil sans the greed. And so the Pain Train shall ride the Road once again, this time in search of another double-knotted Mother-approved interdimensional living space. One that's rich in kindness."

Calvin can only hope his friends at his feet are dreaming at all.

"To conclude, here's an owl's-eye view of the Super Substance,

which at Eden's End goes by Loony Spittoon or something like that
—pretty, isn't it? That's all you and your twin brother, Calvin. What
I mean is the two of you, together but separate, engender the flaw-
less balance of kindness and shame required to receive Mother
Climate's consent with respect to Earth's extrication of Phooka
Road. The interdimensional relocation effort, in other words—the
Super Substance's genesis—is all thanks to the key world-defining
difference between you and your brother. If you look closely, you
can see how the footpath curves and coils all the way to the Super
Substance—and if you listen carefully, you can hear the sad song of
the stones from here! If all's well that ends well, there is where you,
Calvin—and four others—will receive the opportunity to rectify any
missteps mankind's taken in violating the Contract of Basic Goodness. Mother Climate will be there to bear witness, thereby clearing
the way for the Pain Train's departure upon the conclusion of the
Ritual of Five and Five. Which is Trent's part of the deal, which is
The Spider's part of the deal, which itself comprises another
boringly bureaucratic mess about which we can only speak as soon
as you, Calvin, are ready and willing to remember."

"Remember what?"

"What you've forgotten, obviously."

June's wobbling on her knees, Calvin sees, but she doesn't go
down before hitting Calvin with one last message of the eye: *Down
The Spider's hatch two Downers fly . . .*

"One Downer's super flame to catch, a rolling lie," Calvin
completes. June rolls over, still; in her still-open eyes Calvin can see
only himself. The face in the handkerchief on his foot is monstrous,
somehow gracious. "You turned Hanky into a hynetter."

"So you've paid attention—*and* you remember," says Mr.
Moony. "I've got to admit it's fascinating, meaning I'd be made a
liar were I to say I never once doubted your gifts, Calvin. Of doubts
I had endless, yet here you stand, ostensibly immortally present.
This next part's crucial, Calvin. I can only ask you once—keep in
mind this'll be a riddle of sorts. The fate of your memory hinges on
your response, down to the word, meaning there's no room for
verbal discrepancies here. In other words, this is it, Calvin, the

definitive call-and-response of Mother Climate's Apocalypse—and so to you I put forth this locked and loaded question: Are you ready and willing to discuss your twin's slantstanding role in the Apocalypse, how with five humble hacks of a Texas-made cleaver, Trent's got every worldly opportunity to negate that which is due to Mother Climate, as per the parameters laid out within Her Contract of Basic Goodness, specifically as they relate to the death toll dividends of a divided end?"

Calvin has never seen a "contract"—whatever *that* is—in his life.

They don't sound like a whole lot of fun, to his mind.

Calvin eyes Mr. Moony, a black beetle on a hill of gizmos gone to ruin in a bright room underground. He searches Mr. Moony's grinning mouth for any sign of a joke, for the lie that's always present in the absence of any punch line—this tension will never end.

"Anne Kell wakes, T-Bone bakes," Calvin replies. He picks up Hanky's hanky and wipes his eyes. "Five Heads he's got to find, one for each axe She's got to grind."

Mr. Moony and Bod come undone, whirring dots of visible static.

"Under a log he'll find the fleshy first; a Frog's head feels fit to burst."

Mr. Moony and Bod reassemble, a beetle once more.

"The second he'll uncover underground from a hole, lest he mistake the Gopher for a mole." Calvin has time to notice the beetle has become something resembling a ladybug. "Next he'll pull from the guts of a tree—any Owl'll do for number three." The ladybug narrows its form into that of a dragonfly. "He must be wary of number four; this barn Cat's lived nine lives of gore." Butterfly now, maybe of the classic monarch variety. "And finally the fifth, the Rat. It'll come to T-Bone above his brother's resting mat." Bumblebee, no doubt about it. "At last T-Bone's assembled the five horrible Heads. At last Anne Kell can go back to bed."

Bod's final form looks vaguely human to Calvin, who pays attention to the rest of the incantation, which Mr. Moony completes. "The Spider reaps, Mother Climate weeps."

Calvin goes over to Mr. Moony, arms outstretched as if to warm something cold with the heat only hugs have. "Take me back to the pumpkin place. I'm ready and willing."

"Having conversed with you in the language of true truth, I can only assume you know what your consent actually means—what it *implies* on all interdimensional levels."

"You're wrong about my brother, Mr. Moony. Trent won't do it in the end."

"We'll see about that."

"You'll see."

———

Gary Mustafa was stooped over the fist-sized wound in the earth that was Wendy Weather's grave, scooping and depositing dirt by the double-handful, watching what remained of her silver lining disappear. His teeth and muscles were clenched, his body sweat squeezing free, shovels present in the sharp, splitting pain behind his eyes.

Mustafa smelled it before he felt it before he saw it, the unmistakable waft of wintergreen drawing his attention to the soft weight tickling his wrist, a ladybug clinging there, fluttering its wings as if aloft, one tiny leg caught in a single droplet of sweat. He might've swatted the little guy on the spot if not for the wave of warmth it seemed to be trying to communicate, like the muted heat of a flame licking Mustafa's skin from a comfortable distance. His mind warmed at the thought of never again having to look another parent or student or teacher or superintendent in the eye, to leave Allegiance High and what happened there behind and never look back. He leaned into this temptation with as much application as he could muster, straining for a taste of freedom's forbidden fruit, embittered slightly with the notion of what reality had in store: life on the run from Party White Patrol, meaning before leaving tonight, he really ought to consult and console some of the balloons still mourning with him in the meadow, there in the darkness behind his house on Thissa Way, backstage, safely tucked away from the pulverizing pressure of everything outside inside: fudging crud-weasel Poppers, drones, Skeeters, gunfire, reporters, moonlight, cyber harassment addiction, Mother's memory, the thought of never getting another chance to listen to Kimmi-Sue spell 'destiny' another way with one less letter, skunks, marijuana stick smokers, the corrosion of the academic (and pretty much every other) institution corroding all the more with every blatantly and/or systemically racist remark or act or failure to act, the witching hour, Billy storming the office after school to complain about all the mean things GOPHERMAN55 was saying about him on the web application's public forum and how Billy thought it was affecting the way kids at school perceived him online and treated him in person, cyber harassment allegations, endangered balloons in Zones Red, White, and Blue, Billy in the chatroom thingy on that painfully addictive Rate That Human App, unable to hide his boyhood fury behind a keyboard, cyber harassment verdicts, incitement to violence as an inchoate offense, total irreversible exposure a.k.a. Loonerhood on full societal display, the box of letters marking the days Mother lost to years in a madhouse, the closing of the Pop Shop and dissolution of Non-Popper Nation, imprisonment as the worst kind of blessing, cyber harassment withdrawal . . . and amid it all, that kissing cloud of wintergreen took its temporary leave of absence—*It was never balloons you were smelling when you came to in the morning!*—and took with it its warmth. Temporary because Gary Mustafa, so help him God, would follow the fragrance. He would follow it to the end of the world if he had to, anything to escape gaping chest wounds revealing what sixteen-year-olds gunned down from behind looked like on the inside, America doing not even a little better, frankly, beaten on the outside for all to see and broken inside for the rare few still feeling enough to exude anything even remotely like empathy to weep. Sympathy's roots grew too weak in a country whose body had been gutted at last, a tricolored map of snapped strings and severed threads all ripped open for public dissection, directions without direction, decayed instruments of peace crooning out of tune, moot thoughts and prayers never in short supply in a clockwork system running the willfully blind—*It was the nurse's kind-*

ness, which you associated with her perfume, which you associated with balloons! It's kindness *you've been mourning, Gary-Gopher!*—seething and directionless, the endless cold call to arms against oppressors in power ringing since Columbus. Thoughts and prayers typed out and sent into cyberspace, intentions never to be carried out, instructions on how to act without action laid bare in comment sections where oppressors conducted from invisible towers, manipulating cyberspatial gates to let slip the dogs of domestic domination, America's imperialistic expedition clipped by disease and crumbled by the lawful cries of the terminally persecuted (at least until anti-protest propositions were signed into law, breeding like a virus one final wave of widespread apathy until that, too, became an all-too-easily forgotten emotional cue) and collapsed by wars both global and domestic, leaving no more outside world to explore, America's aborted quest revised—*Over here! Listen to your mommy's letters and follow me! This way!*—so power could only be pursued inside, on American soil somewhere, one heartbeat hidden in the secret center of everything, brightly burning. The voice Mustafa had been hearing whispered as the sweetest fragrance, a cloud of wintergreen kindness. He took to his feet and followed the scent out of the meadow to the street, where a red speck scuttled over the white letters of a blue street sign reading *Thissa Way*, fluttering minute wings in the steadily warming light of morning, a ladybug.

10

THE MASKER AND THE MONARCH
(THE HALO VIRUS)

?

LOVE WON Jabronis five years ago—she chucked the ball and dunked the dude and came home with him, bagged and beautiful. Nowadays Jabronis's beauty could be found in his will to live, his resolve to inhabit his little glass world, because now he had a tumor like a big purple horn in his head. His skeleton shone through his tired scales.

?

Love worked for President Mary Mangrove underground, overseeing the Feline Freedom Society (FFS), who surveyed computers betraying views from computers and tablets and TVs and phones inside homes all across America. She wore her cat-ear crown and whiskers at work and a silicone mask in public when she went out masking.

?

The *Love Beach* viewership skewered her for being inauthentically authentic.

?

Love was fluent in Fungi, a computer programming language of her own design.

?

Pausing society had been a game as dangerous as it had been delicate, especially during a pandemic. The way Love played the Crown Virus, however, was what earned her her crown as opposed to a lifetime "penance" in Bakersfield. She'd been tasked to keep all Americans unaware of their individual roles to play in keeping the system in place, increasing societal tension here, dissolving it there, paving the way for riots here and there for this or that length of time. That Americans believed they were taking part in revolution was essential; in this regard Civil War II's violence had been vital, even if most people, in the end, went on repeating history's fabled relationship to repetition.

Thanks be to Love.

?

Science has long disproven the myth about goldfish and memory. Contrary to the formerly widely accepted estimation of three seconds, Jabronis and his kind can actually remember up to five months. It's people who keep forgetting this small quiet truth.

?

Helping people become and remain generally okay with hating one another would be easy if Love didn't hate doing it so much. She always used to tell herself the American public deserved payback for the way they'd judged her—for how they'd shunned her—but here was the truth: five years was too much time to spend most of your time underground without sunlight and with Cat Hackers and a slowly dying goldfish.

?

These days the White House was hemmed in on all sides by a snarling system of mangroves and eucalyptus trees working to stabilize the swampy moat that defended the property from extremists from Texas or NYC. The Feline Freedom Society had procured a black-market Florida landscaping company to install it all. (Love's work's messaging was wholly subliminal.) White House officials could be seen on a daily basis ferrying across the swamp's brackish surface on cheap little skiffs, though it wasn't every day you saw one of them tip and flail and fall, sights and sounds for which Love lived.

?

Love's knowledge of algorithms was second only to one, another woman named Yew.

Love's work depended on keeping up with whatever trended online—from criminal justice reform to LGBTQQIP2SAAM+ rights to climate awareness as a corporate ruse to the use of Skeeter-5000s in classrooms. She then seized the surrounding narrative, stifling or perpetuating it by whatever means, anything to revise the story of society as it was to be (mis)interpreted by its people. She influenced today's America more than she ever had as a former influencer on Instagram, the company that had partnered with her on Instagrammar—the first platform she ever used Fungi to produce—which allows users to use the written word to generate original photographs, the limit here being one's imagined sky. Smart and sexy had been her brand before *Love Beach*, which to this day remained Love's deepest regret.

She should've gone to see her sister, Angel, a therapist in Los Angeles.

She wished she would've.

?

Five years before Love earned her crown as Head Cat Hacker, a deployment of five hundred Skeeter-5000s had directed a company of five thousand DSA prisoners sentenced to life without parole in a five-year effort to construct the FFS's subterranean complex, an interconnected facility complete with large conference rooms and small meeting rooms (Arms and Hands), brainstorming rooms and video-conferencing rooms (Mind and Head), recording and webinar rooms (Eyes and Ears), lounge and entertainment rooms (Anus), a reception and greeting area (Mouth), a fitness arena (Lungs) rimmed with enough locker rooms and showers (Genitalia) to accommodate all genders, a fifty-five thousand square foot kitchen containing cuisine to accommodate any Cat Hacker's culture (Stomach), massive storage compartments and fully furnished apartments (Small and Large Intestine), phone rooms and chat rooms and common areas equipped with the occasional timeout cage crammed with cat litter and the bones of stray cats (Soul). There was even a small graveyard room (. . .) venerating the prisoners who were electrocuted installing the electronics. The fluorescent-paneled pathways connecting these rooms all fed into the IT control chamber (Heart), a massive hub housing bank after bank of the world's smartest computers. Interspersed throughout were blocks of wireless machinery—five feet in length and width—each more powerful than all of the interstellar satellites from which they collected and stored data on a global scale combined. The facility purportedly aped the human body in physical shape and metaphysical design.

?

{Star+Angel_CALi4NIA}, MISSING SNAKE = bodies
[penetration nation]
{Sui_side by trap_zoid + c.e.}, APPLE = choice
[penetration nation]
{Square w/o h_me + o.}, MENTAL HEALTH = absence
{Circle+Dream < real_ty + i.}, EYE = shamelessness

[penetration nation]
{Checker_board_ W.A.R. − e.}, EAR = kindness
[penetration nation]
{Heart_< + l.e.s.s.}, MASK + AMERICA = blindness

?

"You're going to want to hear this, Madam President," said Love.

"Not this again—haven't I told you not to call during Krav Maga?"

"The Big Apple Coalition's getting riled up. We're talking major meowing."

"It seems you need more clocks where you are, is what I'm hearing."

"They've been waiting on the return of one Paul Brokerstaff."

"You're two weeks too late, Love. The ranger on-site already took care of it."

"But that's why I'm calling. Mr. Trent Taphor of Troop Peewee—"

"Sorry, Love, but—"

"Something's wrong with him, and I—"

"—hanging up!"

?

Almost everybody in the Divided States of America, including the select few not awaiting online approval for a pilgrimage to Eden's End—including even Alaskans and Hawaiians and Texans and New Yorkers, as well as the nation's homeless—had a Personal User Data Analysis chart attached to their name. All names and faces were encrypted within Love's network—"Caught in the claw," in Cat Hacker speak—the day the Treaty of the Divided Alliance was signed and the three Zones were established. This was, of course, included in the Faustian Terms of Facial Recognition

Service Agreement, there for all to see in the fine Braille print on page fifty-five between paragraphs five and six.

Due to Skeeter global network satellite surveillance, if you had a name, you had a PUDA chart, which essentially was your world-view's DNA; due to Love's oversight of the Feline Freedom Society, if you had a PUDA chart, you had a cornucopia of information for Cat Hackers to utilize, which more or less became your contribution to society's never-ending story. There was a reason everyone felt their own feelings were so important, a reason everyone thought their own thoughts were in fact their own and had palpable impacts on the "real world" at large, and the reason by and large was Love —and by extension President Mary Mangrove, the only name to elude Love's claw's reach.

That the President of the Divided States of America harbored countless secrets was no secret at all; that Love, via Fungi, could access Mangrove's secrets was.

?

It's true goldfish can recognize their owners—but with eyes located on both sides of the head, they're cursed to miss everything in front of their nose.

Poor Jabronis.

?

Signing the contract to appear as a contestant on *Love Beach* was Love's third mistake that morning all those years ago. The second had been her deliberate refusal to ignore all the warning signs present in the weird way Fred "Hollywood" Hook, the reality show's creator, had introduced himself, as though berating himself for his own accolades in that claustrophobic hole of an office. Love recorded the whole spiel on her phone on the sly as some sort of precaution. To this day Hollywood remained the reason Love believed most men must procreate in order to experience empathy for the first time.

"I'm the man who *controls* the context our viewers can't help but gobble up like chips and chocolate kisses. I'm the man *responsible* for the love our viewers manufacture for themselves after wasting too much time watching you precious, hateful beach bums canoodle. I'm the *reason* no viewer of ours is ever alone in their empty living room. I'm the *man* behind sixteen men behind sixty-nine hidden cameras, the man in *charge* of everything our viewers *can't* and *won't* ever see—including where every last basket of condoms will be placed and diagrams for what sexy competitive games you'll be playing, all of which, by the way, will play to your compatibility levels and likes and dislikes, and I can't help if one or all of you succumb to a fight or two dozen. Rest assured my reasons for making sure every clock reads a different hour and for severing your connection to the outside world and for rousing you every morning at six-thirty a.m. *sharp* by flicking on your bedroom's fluorescents from my trailer camped five miles away and for banning masturbation are not meant to be malicious in any capacity. We live in a world of *distraction*, as you know. You need to be *focused* on one another at all times, or else true love cannot hope to blossom in time for the season finale. We're all about *integrity* on this program —*authenticity* at any and all cost. So long as you drink and dance and date and curse and kiss and cry Aphrodite's name soundlessly, you and I should be fine."

Ignoring Angel's call had been Love's first mistake before meeting Hollywood.

?

The IT control chamber bustled with all the controlled chaos of the New York Stock Exchange—the Heart, in other words, was no place to slack off or tune out or otherwise screw around. Love stood on top of her desk on top of the raised metal catwalk overlooking bank after rowed bank of supercomputers below. Her cat ears worked with the fluorescents to throw on the stone wall behind her the shadow of a much taller crown. Cat Hackers dashed about in droves, punching code in at Love's bidding, working hard to earn their whiskers. This particular clique were diligent sycophants who mostly hung out in Lungs; Love wasn't looking forward to having to cycle them out for the cats from Anus.

A quarter of the supercomputers windowed into American homes; another quarter glowed with alternating strips of code; still another scavenged the web for emerging societal narratives; the remaining computers focused on the dissection of PUDA charts of concern ranging from vigorously urgent to major to minor to hopelessly irrelevant. Love flapped her arms and flashed her hands and snapped commands, a flourish of constant movement and expression, her celerity a lesson in leadership. Jabronis copycatted Love's whipping head with his ghostly body, zipping back and forth in his bowl on the desk.

The newly installed five-sided state-of-the-art Panasonic audiovisual system suspended overhead—the Big Screen—displayed in 900p HD a comprehensive map of preprogrammed self-functioning Fungi that fueled Love's every instinct.

"We've got a gridlock of Russian bots in Little Rock—redirect half the traffic to Miami, the other half to the whole of Wisconsin. Let the Blue meme critiquing Red cops surging in Oregon go viral nationwide—we'll see how it plays, considering what happened with that high school in Gatlinburg . . . now we've got an overzealous group of Blues picking up steam in a Vegas garage —flood the wire with copy-and-pasted comments from the trolls who dissolved the Red zealots in the Chicago thread from last month. I'm picking up priests from Boise looking to reform their image but it's getting kind of cultish . . . drown all of Idaho in the latest ad out of Eden's End. Might as well hit the whole country with another wave of Xanax ads while we're at it. All right, we've just received an update on the little boy from Berkshire . . . PUDA chart rank of concern has officially advanced from hopelessly irrelevant to minor . . . it seems the search for his missing pet boa constrictor has produced something of a stir among the locals . . ."

This went on and on and on, every Cat Hacker an ex-cybercriminal acting on the rare, never-again-to-be-awarded second chance to forgo penance in Bakersfield in exchange for the coveted opportunity to pursue cyber atonement deep underground.

"All right, Lungs, go catch your breath. Send in the cats from Anus!"

?

President Mary Mangrove's father was an artificial intelligence developer named Skeeter who hanged himself five months before his daughter took the Oval Office.

That was the story, anyway, where the public was concerned.

?

"We should discuss the man in charge of Troop Peewee, Madam President."

"This again? Haven't I told you not to call during my private yoni meditation?"

"I've good reason to be concerned for his mental health," said Love.

"The idea he's done away with a bunch of bodies at my special place is mental."

"I never said anything about bodies . . ."

"Which reminds me, I've another top-priority task for you."

"*Meow.*"

"I need you to henceforth delete this topic of conversation from memory."

"But, Madam—"

"Goodbye, Love."

?

Love was sitting on the edge of one of those pool recliner chairs with the colorless plastic strips that suck at the skin on the backs of your legs so much your knee pits squeak. Her hands were folded over her knees as she gazed through the flames spitting up from the firepit behind the beachside villa in Punta Mita, Mexico, staring at the hammock strung like a smile between two plastic palm trees. That was when Brock Mann, flipping waves of hair still wet from the ocean from around his eyes to tie his hair back in what in those days had been known as a man bun, hairband clinched in his teeth, strolled right up to Love and said, "Know what your problem is? You're ignorant."

Love hadn't heard Brock at the time, being so transfixed by the hammock's grin, though this exchange in particular was one she'd go on to watch again and again in the years to follow—as many times over, in fact, as the number of pounds she'd go on to lose in the show's aftermath, watching herself watch the hammock through the flames as her body wasted away, the DMs engulfing her Instagram ablaze with infinite hate.

"Sorry—what was that?"

"You're ignorant, I said," said Brock Mann. "It's probably your biggest problem."

"What the fuck?"

"Whoa, whoa—no need to get all upset. It's just an observation."

"You're a dick."

Love got up to go lie in the hammock and wait for the group text message signaling the next competitive team challenge; Brock cut off her path.

"What's your problem?"

"Apparently I'm ignorant," said Love.

"It's not like it's a bad thing, really."

"Apparently it's my biggest problem."

"Well, maybe if you put in some effort around the villa—like, if you tried getting to know some of us for once . . . then, like, I don't know . . ."

"I like my space."

"But that's what I mean—you just sit around all by yourself acting all high and mighty while the rest of us actually put in time getting to know each other."

"I'm so confused."

"You mean you're ignorant."

"No, I mean confused. You're confusing me."

"I'm just telling you the truth. At least I have the balls to come up and talk to you about it—everyone else . . . like, I'm just being real here. It's 'cause I care, Love."

"Get out of my way."

"The only person in your way is yourself."

"Out of my way, I said!"

"And *I* said the only person in your way is your own damn self."

Some fellow beach bums had gathered, pointing Love's way from the pool.

"Wow, Brad, you're, like, *so deep.*"

The guy had tears in his eyes—*tears.* "My name is *Brock.*"

"Are you seriously crying right now, dude? Like, seriously?"

How was Love supposed to know Brock's stepmother had verbally abused him? That calling him *Brad* instead of *Brock* had been her trademark microaggressive jab that always precipitated onslaughts of passive-aggressive stabs that all basically amounted to *You're not enough, Brock, and you'll never be enough*? How was Love supposed to know Brock had disclosed all of that in the confessional way back on the show's fifth day of filming?

"This is what I get for trying to help," said Brock. "Maybe I'm better off just ignoring you like—like you ignore everyone else! Maybe I'll give *that* a shot! From where I'm standing, Love, it seems to've done you a shit ton of good!"

"You're in my way."

"Typical Love," said Brock Mann. "It's not my fault you choose to be ignorant."

He stormed off to the confessional's teepee; she got into the hammock between the phony palm trees and cried—*real* tears. On TV the hammock sagged like a frown, she would later see. Years later, after gaining back all the weight she'd lose, after all the time she'd lose to outside hatred, after all the effort she'd put into processing her own regret with a therapist who wasn't her sister—as the hammock took on new meaning—it would finally hit her.

Brock thought *ignorant* meant *ignoring a lot.*

?

Goldfish detect vibrations with internal ears called "otolith," which is why tapping on the glass containing their reality really stresses them out, and since they lack eyelids to blink with, it's pointless to engage them in a staring competition.

You'll lose every time.

?

Love discovered the mostly secret world of female masking—an underground culture of men who behind closed doors turn themselves into living sex dolls—five years ago, the night she won Jabronis. The indoor carnival, in fact, had been a masking event, which she'd previously read about while hacking a Supreme Court justice's emails.

Love fell in love with the people—so wonderfully strange, so beautifully flawed, so fabulous in every way. She was terrified they'd recognize her from her stint on *Love Beach* or that they'd deny her for openly identifying as the heterosexual female she was. Although a few maskers ended up recognizing her, nobody denied her—not at first.

For a time, they embraced Love, affirmed her, hit the carnival alongside her. She listened as men took the open mic and opened up about their journeys to masking, citing cleft palates and sexual abuse and schoolyard bullies beating the living snot out of them and sometimes passion plain and simple, a purebred desire to become beautiful.

Love admired their gorgeous outfits and flowing wigs and on-point makeup blushing customized rubber masks. She admired their bravery most of all, their courage to step inside the terrible heat of their skin suits and inhabit their full authentic selves, to flaunt confidence without so much as a single selfie, to turn this ugly life damn pretty.

Love's ultimate excommunication came at the end of the night when she was stumbling on her clogs, piss drunk with a plastic bag with a goldfish swimming inside slung over her arm, a redhead masker murmuring in her ear, tagging Love with a host of circuitous questions that altogether meant *So how'd you end up here, exactly?* The redhead ended up being Supreme Court Justice Jabronis Johnson, which was how Love ended up a Cat Hacker under the White House, hacking her way to some semblance of freedom.

At least President Mangrove still let her go out masking once a week.

?

{Di_mond − a. + e. hope_< +l.e.s.s.}, VIRUS = fear us
[penetration nation]
{Tr_angle − i. + y.}, DIALOGUE = logged, loaded, lost
[penetration nation]
{Spiral_Spy + role Lane}, BUGS = live internal malware
[penetration nation]
{Penta_gram − Insta + five}, GOLD WHISPER = last words
[penetration nation]
{_ourglass _alo + H.H. displaced}, AMERICA = Amen

?

"The Big Apple Coalition's calling it the Halo Virus," said Love.
". . ."
"Madam President?"
"I'm . . . here . . ."
"They're claiming we're in the middle of another pandemic—worse than Crown."
"Thought I thought . . . not to call . . . high frequency opiate training . . ."
"It's why they sent Paul Brokerstaff—your special place is the source, they say."
"Special . . . Significant . . . Calvin . . ."
"*Place*, I said—Eden's End is what I meant. They say anyone who visits your special space—place, I mean—subjects themselves

to unfathomable risk. That after leaving the park they go on to spread the sickness back to their hometowns all across the mainland. According to the BAC, the Halo Virus takes root in the human mind—'dead center,' they're saying. I mean, have you heard of this? What're they even talking about?"

"We're . . . going home . . . Moony . . . can't lie . . ."

"What's moony?"

"Trent's . . . heads . . . the itsy-bitsy spiiider . . . goes up the waterspout . . ."

"You told me to delete this topic—you told me to forget Trent . . ."

"Down came . . . the raaain and . . . *washed* the spider out . . ."

"Madam President—Mary . . . what is all of this about?"

"Basic goodness . . . death toll dividends . . . divided ends . . . shamelessness . . ."

"I'll only ask this once, Mary: are you hiding something at Eden's End?"

"Amen to Trent . . . Amen . . . to the end . . . of the end . . ."

"All due respect, Madam President, the man you've got in charge of Troop Peewee's got major issues with his mental health. I can prove it too. It's all over my sister's hard drive—Angel counseled him back when he was in high school. She noted countless times he'd shown all the warning signs of a serial killer, how he'd keep hinting how he once dismembered and disemboweled a stray cat and stuffed the sack of fur in a neighbor's mailbox. Then after I hacked the neighbor's Facetime history, I learned Trent had slipped inside the sack a letter saying, 'Dear God, enough is enough, go fuck yourself.' Dude even went on to burn down his own house, presumably to collect the insurance. But here's the kicker, Madam President —all that pales in comparison to his PUDA chart's contents. Want to take a guess what's in Trent's PUDA chart?"

". . . Oh . . ."

"That's right—practically nothing. Trent's PUDA chart is basically empty. Apart from the park ranger smartwatch, he hasn't used any heart-driven Mangrovia tech since you took office. Dude's a living, breathing ghost haunting your special place."

"I know . . . something you don't . . . know . . ."

"All I know is it's time I did some digging on this Halo Virus business."

"A tale of woe . . ."

"Enjoy your opiates."

". . . *Jennifer Lopes.*"

?

Despite having been five years younger, Angel, born to help others endure dire mental/emotional turbulence, had always been more mature than Love, more mentally developed—hers had been the voice of emotional intelligence. Angel always seemed to know when Love was heading toward stormy weather, especially when Love didn't know it herself. Love had loathed Angel's voice, the way her words emerged the perfect way in the perfect order; it sickened Love to see herself reflected in her sister's words.

Love would give anything to see herself that way again one last time, to go back in time to the waiting room outside Hollywood's cramped office, to sense the truth of the vibration in her pocket the way Angel would've. Had Love known this'd been Angel reaching out on behalf of herself for once, Love would've returned her call and driven the twenty minutes from Hollywood's office to Angel's, LA traffic be damned. There would've been no flight to Mexico the next day, no hatred burning her pocket upon the return flight home. Hindsight said she'd been staring through the flames at that smiling hammock for a reason.

Love had always known more than she thought.

?

Too many headlines coming out of all three Zones were nauseating to read, so much so that Love had to wonder if they were connected to what the Big Apple Coalition was calling the "Halo Virus." The whole country was losing its mind, it seemed, despite endless access to some of the best TV the world had ever seen, despite the pervasive presence of the Party White Patrol working in tandem with Skeeter Police, despite the farming community reaping and sowing more benefits than ever before, despite even Big Pharma Farm's limitlessly circulated supply of benzodiazepines. What's going on, Love thought.

Whatever happened to inner peace?

?

The row of tiny dots you notice down each side of your goldfish is actually an organ called the "lateral line" that allows them to feel pressure changes—vibrations and currents and the like—in water, a sixth sense that itself can be equated to hearing, touch, balance, and sonar all at once, power about which mere people can only dream.

?

Love learned to code in grade school; she mastered the Craft in grad school.

?

It took Love no less than an hour to get ready to go out masking, first covering her naked self in baby powder before squeezing into the rotten heat of her skin suit and then choosing a wig to best match her mood. When applying makeup to her custom silicone mask, she made sure every time to put in time and effort to come up with a new design to distance her current mask from her former mask for the sake of consistent anonymity. Each new look looked as different as humanly possible from the human underneath it all.

She knew to retreat underground to the FFS complex when the baby powder started running from the heat, when her footsteps trailed a white-hot, slathery mess.

People didn't get out much anymore. There wasn't much worth seeing, doing.

It was always hot outside, it seemed, the air rotten and always heavy.

?

President Mangrove was very much a cat person: fifty-five housecats, five tigers.

?

Angel's memorial service had been carried out outside, inside the Monarch Butterfly Grove, her "place of power" on the western edge of Santa Cruz in the park at Natural Bridges State Beach, California. To Love's mind, butterflies were pretty in an eerie way. No hammocks were present at the burial—obviously—but there were easily a bazillion monarch butterflies bearding the trees, smothering the leaves, literally hanging out.

?

Love discovered Ramsley Guy's blog on her online hunt to uncover whatever it was President Mangrove seemed to be hiding at Eden's End. Guy's rants, curiously enough, never attributed a name to a certain "mentally unfit if not maliciously mad" park ranger, an effort on the blogger's part that seemed almost purposeful. Love squashed any temptation to indulge herself in the pursuit of the spurious satisfaction that comes with meaningless exercises in confirmation: Trent Taphor was the park ranger . . . but who, exactly, was Guy?

A link at the bottom of the page read *Request a Personal Acquaintance with the Author!*, which led Love to a block of white text set against a black backdrop:

Go then to God, ye fallen descendants of the Great Titanoboa,
To whom you shall relinquish your middle name's toxic rum,
Rufio's mine—the bug inside swipes the light of liquor above.
And on the way to heaven's gate, you'll beat a basement coma,

Put yourself in shoes I left to gloomy woods wild with neglect;
In a fowl-filled catacomb—beneath heaps of ash—a honeycomb.
The time's come to revise the lecherous script of western dogma.
Right your wrongs and write their songs and be kind enough to tell:
Order shall be restored to those unable to breathe in shameless hell.

Such rudimentary coding took Love two read-throughs to crack: the first word of each line put forth a riddle whose answer was spelled out with each line's last letter.

She'd been wondering why "Ramsley Guy"—a routine visitor of Eden's End, a privilege awarded to Berkshire locals alone—had those weird, obviously doctored photos of Rufio's deep-dish pizza pies pasted all over the blog's background. She delved inside the facial recognition database, armed with the pizza shop owner's name, and a few clicks later, found herself looking into the wounded eyes of one Donald Rufio Philly. He wore dark slacks and a solid orange polo shirt three sizes too big. He looked like the saddest man in the world.

Don Philly's weirdly popular TikTok was a hoot, for the most part, ostensibly a place for aspiring writers to congregate and congratulate themselves for the solace they savored in one liberating truth: *Hey, at least we're not* this *dude.* Philly claimed to have written the best book ever written. His followers fed this fantasy.

A swift examination of Zone Blue's publishing houses turned up another truth to which Philly remained oblivious: nobody's heard of anything he's ever written. Some top editors—and all literary agents—were well aware of his forays online, resulting for Philly in a sort of unofficial blacklisting from the industry at large. Hoot, indeed.

What Love found less than amusing was the caption for Philly's latest TikTok post: "A Final Lesson in Craft: Letting the Universe Inside: Why I'm Heading to Bakersfield." He seemed to have filmed this disturbing piece of content from inside a self-driving bus—from the backseat, it looked like, his face framed against a block of night, eyes loose with shadow. He spoke slowly, more deliriously than deliberately, often pausing for breath, looking and sounding like a man who hadn't eaten or slept or come close to orgasming in quite some time.

"This'll be my final golden plum for the time being—but just bear with me and you'll see why. Look, if you're gonna go literary, you've sorta gotta, like, throw plot and characters and thematic threads and through lines to the wind. Great books come to you. Like true love, there's not even an ounce of hard work required. It should all be super simple, completely and utterly effortless. The whole process, I mean. What I mean is, all you've got to do is sit there and wait, meaning you must do whatever's in your power to remove yourself from the entire process, to let your soul mate with secrets from the other side and simply . . . transcribe.

"When it comes to great writing, there is no actual writing involved. I'm serious here. I can't reemphasize this enough on this channel—*not a single word*. There are only symbols and signs, and it's ultimately what you do with said symbols and signs that'll come to define the extent of your shelf life. In other words, loyal followers, to make an impression on your own followers last forever—to leave your eternal mark on humanity at large—you've first got to let the universe inside. The only way to do this is by doing nothing. Which is true of life, by the way, case you've ever taken time out to notice. The moment you cut ties with any and all anxieties—the second you learn to sit back in your private sadness and let the universe take over the driver's seat—I promise you, the more readily available such symbols and signs'll make themselves. Matter of fact, this here's why I'm on my way to Bakersfield.

"I should confess I've lived the last ten years in total fear—fear of the unknown, dying, bees flying down my throat should I forget to cover my mouth whenever I yawn, fear of the bug inside, drowning, fear itself, and, most of all, my fear of providing you all with the best book ever written one day hopefully soon 'cause I've no clue how it'll end up being received since it's being conceived in a world that seems to've been on the verge of total ruin for, like, forever now.

"It was only just recently I decided to let this all go, to let all these fears, like, fall by the wayside. Fear's meaningless, after all, in a universe that would rewire all of time and space itself to try to take care of you if only you'll just let it be. Guess what? There's a bumblebee here on this bus with me—I've been watching it crawl slowly along the ceiling toward me. Truth is I'm only half certain it's been around quite a lot over these past ten years—I just haven't taken time out to notice, being so busy with brainstorming and other gravely personal matters. The bumblebee's my sign, universe-wise. I know this because I first noticed it the moment I knew Bakersfield's where I *really* need to be heading. The bug inside says it's where I'll finally find my ending—and then if there's time, revise accordingly."

The video cut out there. Love didn't know why it left her feeling so personally attacked, as though Don Philly had spent all three minutes addressing her directly, violating her personal space through the screen. She had some calls she didn't want to make—one to the president, the other to Yew, her ex-"bestie" working the Berkshire cottage camps as a psychedelic therapist. Love shut her private laptop, sat back at her desk, and remembered to feed Jabronis while the cats from Soul filed silently in.

?

Goldfish have one goal in life: to consume as much as possible. This is true even though they don't have stomachs and can survive up to three weeks without food, being the carp in disguise they are.

?

"You some kinda man or what?" the drunk dude one barstool over asked.

Love raised her hand to flag the bartender. "I'm Head Cat Hacker of the FFS currently based beneath President Mangrove's White House. I oversee those overseeing your daily digital activity—then I make any necessary adjustments to govern the societal narra-tive you're all mortally convinced you're composing. I give hope to the hopeless and take hope from the hopeful accordingly. All of this makes me a woman of veritable power."

"Sorry, ma'am—or fella, trust me when I say it's quite all right if you're a fella. You ain't gonna catch no flak from me, no siree!—anyway, sorry, but I couldn't much hear ya. Your voice's all muffled in that there mask. What's it made of, anyhow?"

Love produced a pen from her pocket and copied down her order for the bartender on a napkin, tore off a separate shred, scribbled *silicone*, and slid the tattered sliver across the countertop to the drunk man. Spread across the brick wall behind them—from the bar entrance to the bathrooms in back—was a widescreen made to look like a whole separate section of bar from which the hum of simulated conversation rose all the more with each time virtual billiards clacked. The people onscreen were digital avatars every color of the rainbow, drinking and dancing and throwing neon darts. Red News dominated the flat-screen televisions suspended in the corners of the bar proper, four separate anchors reporting the same story their own way, each headline spiked with its own rhetorical flavor: the debate regarding whether Skeeters should replace Zone Red's biological-human police was heating up. Love made a mental note to track down the high school principal whose summertime decree had ignited the whole controversy. He had apparently fled Tennessee. The drunk man pinched Love's piece of napkin with the word on it, held it to his squinting eyes. They were the only two patrons here in the flesh.

"Silly-cone, eh? Tell ya truthful, I was expecting some digits."

Love gestured at the nearest flat-screen above. "Skeeters'll supersede Red cops as soon as Mangrove wants them to, you know—and rest assured, should the Red Cop Union choose to move forward with their coup against Party White Patrol, she'll want them to. Debate in America is itself moot at best, generally speaking—compelling fiction at worst. And if you think about it, anonymous drunk dude, isn't raw reality always the worst?"

"For someone who can't be heard or understood, you sure do babble."

"I find your lack of awareness toward your particular imprisonment astounding."

"How 'bout ya take off that silly mask—meet me face-to-face, eye to eye?"

"On the matter of my appearance, I think I'd rather keep you in the dark."

"Gettin' this hunch you're comin' on to me, lady. Am I right or . . . ?"

Love's glass of beer appeared there on the countertop, a fizzing sheen of golden brown. Her baby powder ran hot and thick over her skin under her skin suit. She would've taken the drink and dumped it on the drunk man's head in her former life.

"Cheers," she said, raising her glass.

"And what are we cheersing to, if I may be so bold?"

"To the Red, White, and Blue," said Love, and they clanked in harmony with yet another clack of computer-generated billiards. She brought the glass to the mouth hole on her mask and poured, savoring the chill streaming down her breasts' dividing crack.

The drunk dude drooled through idiot lips.

?

The trick in getting Americans to ignore the horror plaguing the rest of the world was to make everything online about the state of America. Blues, for instance—who theoretically cared for the state of the rest of the world—were appeased enough to know DSA White Choppers were taking off from the White House daily. These solar-powered tanks with turbo-wings zoomed across a world body mortally wounded from World War III's nukes, whose toxic after-glow turned human flesh bumpy and blue. It didn't matter that ninety-nine percent of care packages (mostly Gatorade) the Chop-pers dropped sank into the sea; what mattered was that there were "care packages" at all. Love had been responsible for this meticulous nomenclature.

Blues took serious comfort in believing America still cared.

?

"Look, Love, I don't much care for your input," said Hollywood

Hook, "by which I mean I don't care at all for anything you have to say. You signed the contract."

"You made me look like some ungrateful bitch. Like I had it easy growing up."

"Then maybe you shouldn't've signed the contract."

"You made me look spoiled and superficial and self-centered—as though the only person I care for in the world's myself."

"We in this business are very well versed in what self-centeredness entails."

"You're a real prick, Fred."

"Wasn't me who surrendered my name to the dotted line."

"The whole country hates me! My Instagram's flooded with death threats!"

"Our viewership hardly constitutes the whole of America."

"They've labeled me the 'Inauthentically Authentic Cunt of America'!"

"Canceling cancel culture's been a *cunt and a half*—on this much we concur."

"I've lost over fifty pounds!"

"I'm sorry for your loss."

"They killed Angel!"

"Huh?"

"My sister, Fred! She was already emotionally fragmented before I even boarded the plane to Mexico—though, like, how was I supposed to know that? Then after you made me out to be some loathsome witch, they went and hate-trolled Angel's P.O. box in LA and she was a therapist and—and she hung herself, Fred. She hung herself with a fucking hammock!"

"That what that new tattoo's about, there?"

Love covered up the little monarch butterfly sown into her wrist.

"I'm sorry, Love. When did it happen?"

"Pretty sure it was right around when that Brad Mann or whatever came up to me and called me ignorant for no reason, then *you* made it seem like I was insensitive toward that thing with his mom, which—once again—how was I supposed to know?"

"Everyone else on the show seemed to know about *Brock* and his *stepmom*."

"You're pitiful, Fred. Beyond pitiful."

"Look, there's nothing I can do about it, now. Unless . . ."

"Unless what?"

"Seeing as to how you've now got some bona fide backstory to work with—c'mon, don't freak out. Hear me out here—I *could* make some moves to get you signed on to next season's cast . . . which *could* go a long way in reforming your image . . ."

". . ."

"See, but that face you're making there's the kind our viewship'll *never* fall for."

"I hate you, Fred. You've ruined my life."

"You sound like someone who's failed to realize what they signed up for."

"Have you no empathy? Like, zero?"

"Know what—fine. I'll take the blowjob and make all your problems go poof."

"And there it is," said Love. "Typical Hollywood."

"That really what people think of me?"

?

President Mangrove was addicted to opiates and manic mushroom episodes and really anything relating to her right to life, liberty, and the pursuit of inner peace.

?

"He's on his way to Bakersfield," said Love. "Name's Donald Rufio Philly."

"No funny ideas says Mr. Moony and I said not to call, no don't call me when I'm feeling this wild and free and oh god, Love, I could lay you down right here at my feet and kiss you all over, I really could, I'll start at the neck and work my way down."

"Thing is, Madam President, I get this feeling he's heading straight for the Hive."

"High five, Love! High five through the phone!"

"Maybe you should call me back once your episode's all wrapped up."

"These mushies've sent me to the moon and back and back and back and—"

"Or maybe authorize me and I'll sic some Skeeters or PWP on Mr. Philly and nab him before he gets there—I mean, I get this feeling he's a threat. Like he could do some real damage over there—online. His TikTok gets a good amount of traffic . . ."

"In other news, I'm getting another tiger 'cause another tiger's what I need . . ."

"Authorize me, Madam President. Do it now or forever hold your inner peace."

"I'll do it with you, no problem, I swear I've never felt so gay all my life."

"In that case, you might as well tell me what you're hiding at Eden's End."

"This is one super substance, these mushies, the superest substance of all!"

"Who's Mr. Moony?"

"Oh god, Love, I always knew I was immortal—that one day I'll move this whole wonderful world and we're going to be so happy you and me and everyone worthy!"

"You're starting to scare me, Madam President."

"Was that you, Love, who said that or Mr. Snuggleworth here?"

"Madam President—Mary—do *not* go near the tiger."

"Know what, Love, you do such great work, Love, I really ought to get you a bigger set of cat ears for a brand-spanking-new crown, feel me?"

"Definitely do *not* attempt to remove Mr. Snuggleworth's ears."

"We are wild and free and forever young, you and me . . ."

"Is someone there watching you, Madam President?"

" . . . "

"*Mary?*"

"..."

"*Meow* to House: this is Love pinging from the Cat Box down in Heart—someone go check on the president. I repeat, *someone go check on the president.*"

"Peekaboo!"

"Dammit, Mary!"

"What's wrong?"

"You scared me half to death!—I thought you were . . . Mr. Snuggleworth . . ."

"See, but that's just it, Love! I mean, don't you get it yet?"

"What don't I get?"

"We're all already dead."

"I'm hanging up," said Love.

"Funny, that's what your sister s—"

?

The primary task for people in power in America had for decades been to distract the public from unrest and divide accordingly. Controlled ignorance was one reason USA became DSA, and one controlled the ignorance of the populace by governing the social narrative, turning words against words themselves, twisting every plotline a million directions into unreadable, uninterpretable chaos. This method started out as a social experiment conducted at the expense of post-Civil War I Black Americans and evolved over time. White supremacy begot a slow, fastidious process of evolution via widespread devolution; revolution, meanwhile, consisted of the public's paltry attempts to impede power's inevitable forward progress.

Love wished she knew where she stood in all this.

?

One last thing on those goldfish.

They turn ghost-white if left in the dark, without light to produce pigment. And while they live longer than any other domestic fish (the oldest on record having lived to see midforties!), putting one in a bowl's a bad idea; the water turns too toxic fast.

?

It was during the shaky aftermath of the Crown Virus and Civil War II that Party White diplomats went to great lengths in getting Blue and Red executive officers to agree to a "distant and generally friendly" federal law enforcement presence collectively known as the Party White Patrol (PWP). These patriots of peace were planted undercover throughout the country so as to uphold the vital veneer of political affinity and physical distance and general goodwill. All were armed at all times, though you wouldn't know it.

One might've served Love her Bag of Food #4 at the farmers' market drive-thru.

?

It took Love all of five minutes to dig up the reason as to why Principal Gary Mustafa had fled Allegiance High and Gatlinburg and Tennessee at large despite his being generally broadcasted as a national hero. Mustafa's maverick summertime decree to implement a Skeeter-5000 on campus, after all, had prevented a mass shooting at the hands of one Billy Mick, a sixteen-year-old sophomore who had, according to his PUDA chart, been virtually obsessed with the highly addictive mobile application Rate That Human. Billy's one and a half star out of five rating seemed largely due to the nefarious online presence of none other than Mustafa himself, who, all considered, turned out to be one sick puppy.

☺ RATE THAT HUMAN PRIVATE CHATBOX ☹

GOPHERMAN55: Nobody at school likes you. You're trash.
Stonecoldstonerkid: Leave me alone!!!!!!
GOPHERMAN55: Make me.
Stonecoldstonerkid: Tell me who you are and I will!!!!!

GOPHERMAN55: The only reason for your 1.5 star rating instead of 0 is because of all the guys who want to do it with your smoking hot mommy.

Stonecoldstonerkid: I SWARE TO GOD I'LL KILL YOU

GOPHERMAN55: *Swear

Stonecoldstonerkid: Your such a nerd HAHA

GOPHERMAN55: *You're

Stonecoldstonerkid: STOP IT!!!!

GOPHERMAN55: For the record, I'm only trying to help you. In this day and age, it's more important than ever you spell correctly. You never know: it could change your life.

Stonecoldstonerkid: Wut duz dat evan meen?? By the way you sound like your 40……

GOPHERMAN55: *What does that even mean? *you're I'm talking about love, Billy. You've got to give love to get it back and have it last. We can make love with words.

Stonecoldstonerkid: HAHAHAHAHAHA WHAT????

GOPHERMAN55: What I meant is: we can utilize language in love's name.

Stonecoldstonerkid: Now YOU'RE sounding more like 50……

GOPHERMAN55: I'm just mature, Billy. It's why I get so much poontang.

Stonecoldstonerkid: What the FUCK is THAT??????

GOPHERMAN55: Ladies, Billy. I'm rolling in the intercourse.

Stonecoldstonerkid: 60……

GOPHERMAN55: Just like your dumb daddy who does it with prostitutes.

Stonecoldstonerkid: Don't talk about my dad I mean it

GOPHERMAN55: Deep down you and I both know the monster Randy is deep down.

Stonecoldstonerkid: You don't know shit

GOPHERMAN55: At least there's a way you can get back at him . . . if you want.

Stonecoldstonerkid: What are you talking about

GOPHERMAN55: If you're so sad, Billy—and let's not bullspit

each other here; we both know you are—why not get trigger-happy? Quit lying to yourself and aim true?

Stonecoldstonerkid: YOU'RE STRAIGHT UP MESSED UP

GOPHERMAN55: And you're learning to spell. Who knows? Maybe love is around the corner waiting for you. But if you want to see your rating inflate, Billy, maybe you first ought to shift the narrative. Own your sadness, then learn to use it for the greater good.

Stonecoldstonerkid: By shooting my dad??????

GOPHERMAN55: I never said that! Haven't you ever heard of metaphorical language?

Stonecoldstonerkid: I'll find you one day and make you pay......

GOPHERMAN55: Threaten me all you want; I care little. Whether you believe it or not, Mr. 1.5 Out of 5, I'm probably the only guy at school who actually cares for you.

Stonecoldstonerkid: Prove it and leave me alone

GOPHERMAN55: Your mom, too.

Stonecoldstonerkid: I SWEAR I'M GOING TO KILL YOU!!!!

GOPHERMAN55: It's my sincere hope my truth doesn't kill us both.

[GOPHERMAN55 is Offline. Please Rate Your Dialogue.]

Love uncovered this exchange and dozens like it, but Mustafa wouldn't stop there. Whenever Billy refused to take the troll bait, it seemed the principal would troll the Rate That Human forum in response, getting other users to gang up on Billy until the kid finally replied in private. In the end, no matter which way you sliced the first "t" from "tit," Principal Gary Mustafa—whether intentionally or not—had incited Billy Mick to attempt an act of gun violence, which was precisely what Billy ended up dying trying to do. The question that remained was why—was Mustafa . . . bored? Nuts? Something way worse?

It took much longer than five minutes to excavate a screenshot of one of Mustafa's mother's letters to Mustafa from deep within Riverview Psychiatrics' private server, a letter containing bizarre references to the end of the world, a certain "Moon Man," and the pièce de résistance: a postscript telling Mustafa to "follow the Lady-bug." Mustafa's mother, in truth, wrote much the way President Mangrove spoke of late.

Although Love lacked answers respecting Mustafa's motives—or Don Philly's, for that matter, or even Trent Taphor's—she found herself convincing herself these three men shared a connection in all of this. Perhaps one or all three knew something integral to the Halo Virus, or the Big Apple Coalition, or maybe even whatever the hell President Mangrove was squirreling away at Eden's End. It was like the smiling hammock on the set of *Love Beach* all over again, a sixth sense of darkest foreboding, but on an infinitely larger scale.

Love knew it'd be no use calling the president, that perhaps—assuming ten dismal years apart was, in fact, long enough—the time had come to take her chances with Yew.

She glanced up from her laptop and saw Jabronis had finally gone belly-up in his bowl, balanced on the lip of which—like an angel of death having lit way down here in the FFS's complex's Heart—a monarch butterfly raised its eerie wings.

"Angel?" But that didn't feel right. "Trent? Don? Gary?" Nope. "Yew? President Mary Mangrove, maybe?" Then one clicked home, special and significant. "Hi, Calvin."

INTERLUDE II: HEADLINES AND HEADERS OR STORMS OF THE CENTURY

(FROM OVER THE "PAST" TEN "YEARS" OR SO)

The following too-often-nauseating-to-read headlines and headers have been harvested by the Big Apple Coalition of New York City from a compilation of magazine articles and tabloids, printed periodicals and professional trade publications, local and national papers published across all three Zones of the Divided Alliance, international pamphlets and propagandic pieces, academic theses and dissertations, classified DSA government documents, library catalogs, and basically every imaginable database and/or private server, all of which aim to: 1) Delineate a sort of time-lapse tale of one nation united in division under President Mary Mangrove, 2) Warn the American public of a reticent and potentially hazardous presence in Mangrove's "special place," and 3) Expose the devastating impacts of the Halo Virus on credulous individuals, a solipsism-triggering bug for which Mangrove alone seems responsible, presently bruiting nationwide. The BAC's proxy war against government-manufactured ignorance and blatant social injustice and universal wrongdoing under President Mangrove's apostatic guise of countrywide spiritual revival—including the effort to revise the code of human ethics, to preserve basic goodness and contribute to the survival and revival of kindness and common sense respectively despite past or present or future moral mistakes rooted in humankind's flawed nature—is funded in full by the Keanu Sleeves Foundation.

Readers be trigger-warned.

GLASS CEILING, MEET MANGROVE: FEMALE TRILLIONAIRE PRESIDENT!

PRESIDENT TAKES IMMEDIATE ACTION: HELLO BRAVE NEW WORLD!

LOS ANGELES NBA LEGEND AND "GIRL DAD" TURNED ENTREPRENEUR AND PHILANTHROPIST AND WRITER WHO RECONCILED WITH PRIEST FOR PAST MISCONDUCT AND MARCHING A LIFELONG ROAD OF REDEMPTION FOR THE BETTERMENT OF ALL DIES IN TRAGIC HELICOPTER ACCIDENT

CROWN VIRUS ROCKS THE GLOBE: VENTILATORS NEEDED EVERYWHERE

I MIGHT BE SWISS, BUT THIS IS WHY AMERICA HAS GOT TO GO (Opinion)

WHITE HOUSE TO UNDERGO OUTDOOR REMODELING/LANDSCAPING

MANGROVE HIDES IN BUNKER TO "DEVISE THE RIGHT PATH FORWARD"

WORLD WAR III SHORT BUT NOT SWEET AS DRONE NUKES RAIN: WORLD LEADERS UNABLE TO DISCERN WHOSE FINGER FIRST HIT THE BUTTON

CLASSIFIED DOCUMENT: IF IT'S REALLY ME WHO DID IT, HERE'S WHY

ARTIFICIAL INTELLIGENCE DEVELOPER AND PRESIDENT'S FATHER SKEETER MANGROVE HANGS HIMSELF IN PRIVATE STUDY WITH NO NOTE

SKEETERS ABOUND: THEY COOK, CLEAN, TEACH, AND POLICE!

POTENTIAL HAZARDS OF FAUSTIAN TERMS OF FACIAL RECOGNITION SERVICE AGREEMENT: BIG BROTHER, MEET BIG DADDY (Opinion)

TEN REASONS WHY YOU SHOULD WEAR A FACE-COVERING MASK

ELEVEN REASONS WHY YOU SHOULDN'T WEAR SOME STUPID MASK

TWELVE REASONS (etc., etc., etc.)

CLASSIFIED DOCUMENT: MR. MOONY'S ROLE IN MY WHITE HOUSE

GLOBAL AND NATIONAL ECONOMY IN DISARRAY: AMERICAN FARMERS RISE TO THE OCCASION—"WE THE DARK DEVOUR DARKNESS," SAYS ONE

THE BOOM OF ZOOM: FACETIME WHIFFS ON GOLDEN OPPORTUNITY

MINNEAPOLIS POLICE OFFICER "KNEELS ON THE NECK OF BLACK AMERICA" FOR EIGHT MINUTES AND FORTY-TWO SECONDS

CIVIL RIGHTS MOVEMENT II: THE INVALUABLE 400-YEAR OVERDUE IMPORTANCE OF PROTESTING FOR SOCIAL JUSTICE FOR ALL POC DESPITE THE CURRENT

PUBLIC HEALTH RISKS AND UNPREDICTABLE
CLIMATE

DOWN GOES WASHINGTON AND ANOTHER FEW
DOZEN FORMERLY PRIZED AMERICAN MONUMENTS:
INSIDE THE EFFORT TO REPLACE HISTORY FORMERLY
ERASED VIA SLAVERY AND NATIVE AMERICAN
GENOCIDE

"RACE RIOTS" HAVE TARGET OWNERS FEARING FOR
THEIR LIVELIHOODS

HEALTHY DIALOGUE IN THE WEST, TEARGASSING AND
RIOT GEAR IN THE EAST: THE DIFFERENCE BETWEEN
SKEETER AND HUMAN POLICE

CIVIL WAR II: IDEOLOGICAL WARFARE OR POTEN-
TIALLY VIOLENT?

CIVIL WAR II: DEFINITELY VIOLENT: SKEETERS TO
PULL BACK DEFENSE FORCES—"VALUABLE MERCHAN-
DISE MUST BE PRESERVED AT ALL COSTS"

<u>CLASSIFIED DOCUMENT</u>: E.E. DEFENSE PLAN AGAINST
BAC INVADERS

"THE BIG ONE" CLOBBERS SOUTHERN CALIFORNIA

THE "BIGGER ONE" WALLOPS NORTHERN OREGON

HEALTHY REMINDER: THE PANDEMIC IS NOT OVER

STORMS OF THE CENTURY: MOTHER EARTH WEEPS
FOR EVERYTHING

CIVIL WAR II ENDS WITH NATION ON THE MOVE:

TREATY OF DIVIDED ALLIANCE CALLS FOR ITIN-
ERANT PLANNING: RESOURCES TO BE FUNDED IN
FULL BY PRESIDENT MANGROVE: SKEETERS
REINSTATED

"ALL ARE WELCOME AT MY SPECIAL PLACE,"
MANGROVE STATES UPON GRAND OPENING OF
GROUNDBREAKING ECOLOGICAL WONDERSCAPE

MANIC MUSHROOM EXTRACT: THE CROWN VIRUS
VACCINE!

WHAT'S GOING ON IN BAKERSFIELD? AN OUTSIDER'S
TAKE (Opinion)

<u>CLASSIFIED DOCUMENT</u>: HOW TO KEEP "EL JAYLO"
HAPPY IN HER CAVE & STRATEGY FOR HER SAFE
RELEASE PRIOR TO THE RITUAL OF 5 & 5

METH GATORS AND MURDER HORNETS: WHEN IS IT
TIME TO WORRY?

SKEETERS AID A NATION STILL ON THE MOVE: "THIS IS
PRESIDENT JAMES POLK'S ODE TO DESTINY," SAYS
MANGROVE: TEXAS, NEW YORK CITY, ALASKA, AND
HAWAII ELECT TO DEFECT AS WHOLLY AUTONOMOUS
HOMELANDS

RATE THAT HUMAN PROVIDES WELCOME DISTRAC-
TION AND MORE INSTANT GRATIFICATION FOR
NATION'S YOUTH . . . OR INSTANT REMORSE

CORDIALLY DIVIDED NATION SETTLES IN FOR THE
LONG HAUL

THE SECOND GOLDEN AGE OF PRESCRIPTION MEDICA-

TION AND SUBSCRIPTION ENTERTAINMENT: KICK BACK AND POP A PILL, PAPA!

SELF-OPERATING TRANSPORT HERE TO STAY—TOO LITTLE, TOO LATE?

MINNESOTA MAN FURIOUS OVER DOORBELL PRANK KILLS THREE 10-YEAR-OLDS BY T-BONING "GETAWAY WAGON" WITH TRUCK

SEVERAL BIG-NAME CORPORATIONS BASED IN ZONE RED WALK BACK PROGRESSIVE STANCE ON CLIMATE CHANGE AND RACISM AND etc., etc.

TENNESSEE HIGH SCHOOL PRINCIPAL APPROVES "SKEETER EXPERIMENT" AMID CRIES OF OUTRAGE ACROSS ALL ZONE RED SCHOOL DISTRICTS

<u>CLASSIFIED DOCUMENT</u>: T. T.'s ROLE IN THE RITUAL OF FIVE & FIVE

DAYTON POLICE OFFICER URINATES ON 11-YEAR-OLD GIRL SITTING ON SIDEWALK AFTER HER REFUSAL TO GET INSIDE BACK OF CRUISER

THE RUINOUS EFFECTS OF ZONE BLUE'S MARIJUANA CULTURE (Opinion)

LAS VEGAS 10-YEAR-OLD FATALLY SHOOTS MOTHER AND FATHER "PIECE BY PIECE" OVER A FIVE-HOUR PERIOD WHILE RECITING BIBLICAL VERSES

METH-ADDICTED FLAGSTAFF MOTHER SINGS TO HER THREE YOUNG CHILDREN AS SHE SMOTHERS THEM TO SLEEP AND SUBSEQUENT DEATH

<u>CLASSIFIED DOCUMENT</u>: PLANS FOR LIFE ON A
BRAND-NEW PLANET

PENNSYLVANIA 16-YEAR-OLD FOUND IN FETAL POSI-
TION WEIGHING JUST 29 POUNDS AND UNABLE TO
MOVE AFTER BEING STARVED

FLORIDA MAN STABS BEST FRIEND TO DEATH "FOR
BEING PRO-SKEETER POLICE," PLACES FORMER AMER-
ICAN FLAG BESIDE BURNING BODY

"TAKE ME TO MY HEADS," MUTTERS DERANGED
COCOA BEACH WOMAN UPON ARREST IN A WENDY'S
PARKING LOT

BERKSHIRE COTTAGE CAMPS IS THE PLACE TO BE
(Opinion)

MY PARENTS NEVER RETURNED FROM EDEN'S END:
MY STORY

"MY OBESE LIFE VS. OBTUSE OUTSIDE JUDGMENT" [sic]:
WEIGHS NEARLY 900 POUNDS AND DR. [sic] IS
SURPRISED HE CAN STILL WALK

CONTROVERSIAL TENNESSEE SKEETER-5000 THWARTS
MASS SHOOTING: HEROIC SCHOOL PRINCIPAL
CANNOT BE TRACED FOR COMMENT

OREGON MAN BEATS ON INJURED BABY DEER PROB-
ABLY BREAKING ITS BACK AS FRIEND LAUGHS IN
DISTURBING AUDIO RECORDING

THESE BAGS OF FOOD ARE ACTUALLY PRETTY GOOD!
(Opinion)

<u>CLASSIFIED DOCUMENT</u>: HOW TO IDENTIFY THE FATEFUL FIVE

FEMALE PEDOPHILE LIVE-STREAMS HERSELF MASSAGING YOUNG GIRL ON ZOOM AS MAN IN ELMO SUIT PAYS $5000 TO WATCH

SOS: MY LIFE POST-WWIII: SURVIVING ON CHANCE BOXES OF GATORADE

PSYCHEDELIC-WORSHIPING CULT FORCES DISABLED MAN AND HIS FIVE CHILDREN TO WALK THROUGH FIRE BEFORE BEHEADING THEM

"SO BEGINS THE GOLDEN AGE OF INNER PEACE," SAYS MANGROVE

A NATION LOSING ITS COLLECTIVE MIND: COINCI-DENCE? WE THINK NOT

<u>CLASSIFIED DOCUMENT</u>: "HALO VIRUS": *KEEP AWAY FROM ALL CATS!*

FORMER OHIO SCHOOL TEACHER AND SKYDIVING ENTHUSIAST WHO HAD SEX WITH FORMER STUDENT, 13, BECAUSE HE "ACTED LIKE EX-HUSBAND" HANGS HERSELF SEVERAL DECADES AFTER ORIGINAL ENCOUNTER

THE WOMAN WITH NO NAME: INSIDE THE EFFORT TO LOCATE THE ONLY CYBERCRIMINAL PRISONER TO ESCAPE BAKERSFIELD "HIVE" ALIVE

TEXAS WOMAN DRAGGED OUT OF WEDDING/BABY SHOWER AND SHOT DEAD BY EX-BOYFRIEND WHO "HAD A BONE TO PICK"

ALABAMA GRANDPARENTS ARRESTED FOR KEEPING
FIVE CHILDREN LOCKED IN TINY WOODEN CAGES TO
BE PLACED ON DEATH ROW

NEW ALBANY MAN WHO KILLED WIFE "ROSE" AND CAT
"EMILY DICKINSON" DISCOVERED HAVING LIVED
WITH REMAINS FOR WEEKS

SPIRITUAL CAPITALISM: "THE AMERICAN DREAM"
REIMAGINED

VEGAS SURGEON GETS METAL NUT REMOVED FROM
PENIS AFTER WIFE DRUGGED HIM AND SCREWED IT IN
OVERNIGHT UPON LEARNING HE WAS ADULTEROUS
WITH OVER A DOZEN NURSE TRAINEES . . . AT ONCE!

LANSING MAN HANGS 27-YEAR-OLD GRINDR DATE
FROM CEILING, CUTS HIS THROAT, AND CONSUMES
HIS TESTICLES PRE-SELF-CASTRATION

BAC REP PAUL BROKERSTAFF HAS YET TO RETURN
FROM EDEN'S END

CLASSIFIED DOCUMENT: IN CASE "SIGNIFICANT ID
#55" RETURNS HOME. . .

PART III

THE FATEFUL FIVE

(OCTOBER, ONE "WEEK" BEFORE NOW)

11

THE DRIFTER AND THE DRAGONFLY
(LAST WORDS)

CALVIN HEADS toward the end of the tunnel at his own pace, knowing his time in the pumpkin place is almost up, that the star-shaped door of light ahead will bring forth his final rebirth. His body has been tasked to divide his sense of self five different ways this time, to all at once redistribute what remains of his substance across five separate incarnation shells. He's breathing in the fumes and wading through the draping wet filaments when he recognizes both voices floating in the corridor, an aging witless man conversing with a woman sage beyond her years. The vibrations in their respective tones always make Calvin think of rats and owls, respectively, though the cloying gush of nectar and pollen has him conjuring bees at play with dragonflies in some quietly overgrown graveyard. He remembers to keep his hands to himself, to let alone the faces in the walls; touching them leads to confused torpor for too many innocents.

His rebirths inside the jack-o-lantern light of the pumpkin place have bred inside him an altogether complex system of churning thought and feeling—brightness and power both communal and

277

personal, persistence and progress, a sense of renewed discovery upon reaching any self-perceived destination, stability and solidarity, cooperation and creativity, instinct and intuition, unbreakable love and devotion in the face of cruelty and degradation, the cosmic comfort that comes with striding a universe-approved path amid the earthbound sound of mass stridulation, fortune and prosperity, a desire to influence others to capture life's fullness and revel in the raptures of never letting go, the courage in transformation, and the wisdom to remind himself fear itself can never exist without joy. It saddens him that great sorrowful chunks of such thought and feeling seem to have left humankind far too far behind, though he takes what joy he can knowing the sadness itself is good, that the pursuit of some unspoilable pleasure and happiness supreme is a path without doors and windows leading all to a dead and lonesome end.

One last time, he will reach the light and fall inside and become the beetle and the bumblebee, the ladybug and the butterfly—the dragonfly too. He's got five fateful heads to turn one way, toward the dyadic battleground in which shame and kindness make total war. And should The Spider summon him to Her cloistered void, he would go on humankind's behalf, poised to make his argument for commonsense kindness.

Bang.

"You know, you sort of look like someone I used to know," says the aging man.

"I get that a lot at work," says the wiser young woman. "Call it an occupational hazard."

"I'm sure you're probably wondering *who* you look like to me?"

"I'm not sure why that's relevant."

"I'll give you a hint—we're both standing at her grave."

"You ought to consider looking *hint* up, dude."

"Huh?"

"I meant the def—never mind. So what brings you all the way out this way, sir?"

"Well, you see, she was my middle school English teacher growing up. Inspired me to become a writer. 'There's nothing wrong with being born to write,' she'd always say."

"I won't lie to you. That sounds like something she'd say."

"She was also my wife. My first of three, I mean."

"You don't say."

"I do."

"Then you must be Don Philly—she might've mentioned you a time or two."

"That I am. And you are?"

"Yew."

"Me?"

"No, Yew. Y-E-W. It's my name."

"Cool beans, as the kids used to say. So what was she to you . . . Yew?"

"Suppose you could say Brenda was a sort of mentor. We met in this teeny plane at twenty thousand feet—I was hyperventilating in my oxygen mask. First time skydiving. She was able to calm me down, and then back on the ground, she more or less took me in."

"That sure sounds like something my Brenda would do."

"No offense—and don't take this wrong way—but she never belonged to you."

"What's that supposed to mean?"

"Well, besides the fact no woman belongs to anyone, much less any man, the Brenda *I* knew had been a woman of longstanding remorse—and a born drifter. She taught me the art of drifting, moving from place to place and job to job, having to learn and relearn to adapt to an ever-shifting environment. My time in Brenda's care helped me survive the Virus and the Wars and what-all. You should probably know she never forgave herself for what she did to you, that she came to this grave wholly empty inside."

"I don't get what you mean."

"Your eyes say otherwise."

"I'm going to be buried right here next to her when I die."

"Don't say that, now."

"And the top of my headstone will read, 'It's better to be who you are than who you're supposed to be.' I'm proud to say it's how I've lived my life as a writer."

"Whatever you say, Mr. Philly. So what kind of stuff do you write?"

"I talked to the headstone guys and gals before I came out here and haggled for the spot right here next to Brenda. I spelled out exactly what it's supposed to read, letter for letter. Case, like, anything happens. Lately I've been getting this feeling, you know?"

"I'm getting vibes your writing's a serious point of contention in your life."

"I've come out here to Bakersfield to infiltrate the Hive. It's where President Mangrove sends cybercriminals. I know it's probably dangerous—though nothing gets in the way of my research. Like, you wouldn't believe this story I've got inside to tell."

"If you're being serious, Mr. Philly, you should know you've taken on a total death wish. I can't stress this enough—there's no way you'll make it out of there alive."

"That there's the true story of my life."

"All right, look. It's clear to me Brenda's messed you up good, and although you've clearly lost your mind—but then what human on this god-forsaken planet hasn't?—I suppose I'm willing to help you out, despite its going against my every better judgment. After all, you could say I'm quite . . . *familiar* . . . with what goes on in the Hive. You *could* say I know the way inside, having already clawed my way out once before."

"Are you saying, Yew, you're the only cybercriminal to escape the Hive alive?"

"Please look up the definition of *hint* when you get the chance, dude."

"So what do I do, then? It goes without saying I promise I won't say anything."

"Well, first of all, as I assume you already know, the place is virtually impregnable, surrounded by Skeeter surveillance, all of which're programmed to shoot to kill on sight. What *you*, then, have to do is pull off the old Trojan Horse, if you catch my drift."

"Not sure I like where this is heading."

"Before doing anything, however, I'd suggest ditching your phone or computer or whatever piece of tech you've got on your person right here and now. Matter of fact, this here's nonnegotiable. Otherwise they'll pin you in a second, put you down like a dog."

"What was the whole impetus for the Trojan War anyhow, do you remember?"

"Pay attention, now. You'll first have to access the northern warehouse from the forest in back of it, a little copse with a gaggle of nooses hanging from branches that you'll have to use to sort of ascend to the height of the fifth-floor gangplank, then swing your way up and through this shattered window whose glass nobody's bothered replacing. Once you're in, there should be some extra prisoner overseer uniforms hanging in one of the storage closets a floor or two at most below. These're all black in color with a big red hourglass emblazoned across the chest—find one, throw it on. Matter of fact, you should be doing this whole thing stark naked to start to mitigate chances of discovery via discarded clothing. You'll then need to locate a crate with malfunctioned Skeeter parts inside, which shouldn't be too difficult since there's maybe like a thousand to choose from—hide inside and wait, wait, wait. Eventually you'll be shipped to the Hive's main silo, at which point you'll have to decide when to make your move. I suggest blending in with a troupe of prisoners and pretending to be their overseer. Be straight with the prisoners and no one else—avoid all overseers. The prisoners should be nothing if not impressed with your presence there alone. If all goes well, they should point you to the Honeycomb's entrance, where you'll need to respond to the call-and-response passcode verbatim."

"I'm getting this numb feeling in my feet."

"Assuming nothing's changed since my great escape and I'm assuming nothing has, Mangrove's a ninny like that—the question they'll put forth is 'What do you call the useless piece of skin attached to a penis?', in response to which you'll say, 'a man.'"

"A man?"

"That's what I said, but you'll have to say it—and this is essential—you'll have to say it in a way that sounds like you're saying *Amen*, with that same drab air of depleted spirit. After that, you're on your own, dude, meaning you'll definitely eventually be found and killed. I wholeheartedly advise against any of this. The Hive's really no place to be."

"So mumbled the bumbling bumblebee."

"I'm going to pretend you didn't say that and take my leave. I've got a five-hour drive ahead of me at the very least—which gives me just enough time to get back to work on time. What can I say? The mortally traumatized await their spirit guide."

"What kind of work do you do, if you don't mind my asking?"

"Take care of yourself, Mr. Philly. On Brenda's behalf, I'm sorry for everything."

All voices and banging cease being; the pumpkin place still seems to hum. Calvin stands before the end of the dark tunnel's bright door, a single burning star lighting the way home. To pass over the unseeable threshold into the light is to consent to living and dying five more times one last time, to bless himself with reincarnation's curse—to all at once embody five bugs and attract five bodies to the dark light of the end of the end. He steps back to give himself room for a running start, and then he makes his move one last time, leaping into starlight as he gives himself to riding space-time's lightning—and already The Spider's hissing his name.

———

SUNLIGHT'S PROBING fingers pried inside a dozen diamond-shaped window flaps through which trippers up and down Hope Row could be heard from other trip zone tents under professional supervision: laughter, guitar, the occasional far-off croon. Wax candles flickered on the shelves as essential oils bubbled and fumed. Few birds called in the Berkshire cottage camps, though of insects there were plenty. Yew was a psychedelic therapist from Vegas who specialized in guiding trippers through their sources of trauma.

Yew eyed the ocean-blue dragonfly on the rim of the painted urn containing her twin brother's ashes set on a shelf at eye level. The bug refused to move even as she removed the lid and scooped out a thimbleful with her tiny golden spoon. A tripper hailing from Tulsa, Oklahoma—a gorgeous six-foot-seven goddess girl with a rose of lustrous hair—lay starfished and blindfolded in the center of the open-air bungalow on the rococo rug whose gilded lace looped and swooped across the room's spacious floor. The dragonfly fluttered its wings.

Even to the soberest eye did all the rug's double helix patterns appear to writhe in a slow little sway. The biodegradable, compostable, environmentally friendly hemp twine binding the tripper's ankles and wrists to the wood dowels nailing down the rug's four corners had a fair bit of give, given the redhead's awesome height and wingspan.

Yew put the spoon in her mouth and gulped the grainy pulp, which itself seemed to feed on saliva. Tears rose in her eyes—the back of her throat resisted for the usual five painful seconds before taking it in. Her tripper, whose name was Karen, had only just begun entering LSD's peak stages when Yew's burner phone began warbling the tune of America's former national anthem, compromising the room's synthetic sense of peace. Karen's skin took on almost the same hue as her hair. The woman calling Yew's phone might say Karen bore the look of a woman trying and failing badly to pinch one out on the toilet. That was the Love Yew had known, at least. The Love for whom she'd fallen in grad school, a pandemic and two wars ago.

Yew had been waiting for Love to call her back for over a decade.

Yew's burner had, of course, been set to silent, except in the event the woman who was now calling called, in which case the former anthem would be triggered to play.

The tune rang out blue and hollow.

"Is that . . . do I hear . . . thought you said phones were off-limits!" Karen raged. "That you'd totally lose your job if you were seen out here with your phone! Anyways, it's *rude!*"

Yew had to reach to nab her burner from its hiding spot behind her twin brother's urn, and then she scrambled to the center of the room. Her star-studded robe billowed from her burst of speed mingled with the angle of outside breeze. She knelt down and placed her hand over Karen's heart gently. "Tell me what you think it is you're hearing, love."

"Phone," said Karen. "'Star-Spangled Banner.' *'Through the perilous fight . . .'*"

"You're peak hallucinating, love. Go with it. Follow it. See where it takes you."

"But, it sounds super close now—not like before."

Yew swiped right to answer Love's call. "How about now?"

"Now it's ringing from inside my head—but how'd you do that?"

Yew held the phone up to her ear. "Talk to me, Love."

"How'd you know it was me?" said Love. "Seeing as to how I'm pinging from a top-secret place that's pretty much impossible to trace . . ."

"I like when you call me 'love,'" said Karen. "It's soothing."

Yew got up on her knees and used the eyes and ears of her own projected energy to scan the grass path outside for eavesdroppers. "Let's not forget who taught you you-know-what in grad school, Love. Who's to say the Craft can be so easily forgotten?"

"Do you mean my music teacher from grade school?" said Karen.

"Are you suggesting you've been tracking me all this time?" said Love.

"Maybe," said Yew.

"Well, like I was saying earlier, Mr. Art was actually the worst," said Karen. "We all used to make fun of his name—called him Mr. Fart, Mr. Artsy Fartsy, and so on."

"Are you with a client? I can call back . . ."

"No!" Yew blurted, afraid to have to wait another decade. She could feel the internal scratch of her brother's ashes going down, down. "Stay with me, I mean, Love."

"I'm not going anywhere—I mean, look at me, bound and blindfolded with literally nowhere to go . . . anyway, as I was saying, I thought I hated Mr. Art for being all uptight—but I think now I'm realizing a deeper part of me's always felt for the guy. I mean, how can we be so quick to crucify people for their *name?* It's just plain cruel!"

"Look, Yew, I can tell you're busy—I just wanted to let you know I'll be flying out to Eden's End. Soon. Five days. Halloween Eve. We need to talk. Face-to-face."

"When and wherever you wish to go, Love, I'll be there to meet you."

"You just blew my mind," said Karen. "But maybe you're right. Maybe it's time I really went there. It's just hard, you know? This has been killing me all my life."

"There's a pizza place," said Love. "Rufio's, it's called. How does noon sound?"

"Of course," said Yew. "I must say, I've missed your voice."

"But that's what I think I've been trying to say all along," said Karen, whose color was once more on the rise. "I've never *had* a voice. They took *away* my voice. But for some reason, all I can think about right now is Mr. Art, sitting there at his piano . . ."

"Goodbye, Yew."

Yew shoved her phone inside one of her robe's nineteen inner pockets. Her hand resumed its place over Karen's heart, which seemed to vibrate inside her substantial chest.

". . . crying—*like, we actually made Mr. Art cry.* Feel like I'm there right now, reliving the whole darn thing. Mr. Art with his gleamy bald head and weird goatee. He's using music to try to teach us all about the Trojan War, playing a crap recording of this epically long song that starts with a bunch of airy-sounding harps that're somehow supposed to, like, depict Helen of Troy's earth-shaking, war-worthy beauty . . ."

It was near impossible for Yew to focus with all the emotive thunder raging inside after having picked up so much trepidation in Love's wavering voice. Prior to Karen's appointment, Yew herself had micro-dosed with LSD, a recommended but not required approach that allowed psychedelic therapists to attune their physical bodies' energy to that of their trippers, which theoretically aided the guiding process. Karen had come in to relieve herself of the constant state of oscillation between depression and anxiety and post-traumatic stress, a.k.a. "the big three."

Yew's conscious decision to consume her brother's ashes was a personal choice that had squat to do with the profession, very little to do with private, perverse predilection and a great deal more to do with the pursuit of mystic fullness. She'd dedicated her whole spiritual adult life to ridding herself of feeling persistently half empty; Love's leaving had left a void only Ash's ashes seemed to fill. The urn itself was nearly half empty, a source of extreme anxiety.

Telling herself her brother's urn was half full did nothing to alleviate Yew's anxiety.

". . . all screechy and creepy. Mr. Art says it's supposed to sound like deceit."

"The violins, you mean?" Yew said, tasting her own tongue.

"Uh-huh—sorta like how they're used to build tension in scary movies. But in this case Mr. Art says they're supposed to put in the listener's head an image of the Trojan Horse, 'a weapon masquerading as a tangible symbol of surrender,' I still hear him saying. Sitting there in the middle of Troy in the middle of the night, silent and towering with a bellyful of Greeks priming themselves to break free and pounce on the Trojans who're all either lumbering around drunk or straight up passed out . . ."

Until now Yew hadn't afforded much thought to the blatant connection between Karen's bringing up the Trojan Horse and Yew's own bluntly ill-advised suggestion two days ago to Brenda's second husband, Don Philly, a living ghost of Brenda's long-dead past. Yew had advised the victim of Brenda's abuse to apply the self-same strategy (Trojan Horse) to penetrate President Mangrove's cybercriminal torture fort, a.k.a. the Hive. She knew there were few, if any, full-blown coincidences in this life. This one she'd merely chalked up to commonplace cosmic approval, basically the universe saying, Hey, you're doing the right thing at the right time in the right place, so keep at it, ladybird. These little blips in what people called reality occurred all over all the time and were made readily available for those in tune with the oneness of all people and things to notice. Part of Yew's job was to try to turn her clients into such people.

What bothered Yew was that there all of a sudden seemed to be something more to this whole Karen vs. Don Philly Trojan Horse thing. It irked her all the more that the suspicion itself, likely a byproduct of the acid she'd dropped, was taking all focus off the present—Karen and the big three's crippling effects she was now suffering as a direct result of some childhood trauma lying dormant within this whole thing with Mr. Art. Yew withdrew her hand from Karen's chest and smacked herself in the cheek, snapping herself to the present by sheer force of goodwill.

". . . and all at once the drums are pounding. The drumbeat's supposed to mean the Greeks're pouncing, and everyone in class is whacking at each other with pens and pencils and we're all laughing, having the greatest time. Meanwhile in our minds, the drunk and sleepy Trojans're getting totally slaughtered for their negligence, and Mr. Art's screaming at the top of his lungs to stop because someone's going to poke someone's eye out by accident."

Yew kept catching disturbing blue flashes behind closed eyes. The nature of the disturbance itself remained disturbingly out of mind's reach, which was why she tried keeping her eyes open, willing them to keep dry. "You're crying, love, which is good. It means you're getting there. Keep going. Let yourself leak, peak—and *speak*."

"But I'm scared."

"Fear's as normal as it is necessary. Respect it as you would yourself."

"It's me. I did it."

"What'd you do?"

"I throw it, the first pen. Right at Mr. Art. It goes way over his head and thwacks the whiteboard, but that's not about to stop him from stopping the music and standing in front of all us, demanding to know who did it, who came this close to taking his eye out, huh? Was it you, Christopher? How about you, Jasmine? Everyone knows it was me, I threw the pen, yet it seems it was decided the split-second after it happened that no one was going to give me up to Mr.

Art. In this second, we are all of us brothers and sisters in arms. Who threw the second and third pen or pencil I'll never know, but as of now, all I see is Mr. Art on hands and knees, cowered before us at first before this weird sort of one-armed attempt on his part to hobble-crawl away, using his other arm to cover up his head and neck from whatever we've all got stowed away in our backpacks that we've all unzipped, pens and pencils and glue sticks and little staplers and bigger staplers and rocks from the playground and scissors stolen from the teacher's lounge and even one or two cell phones—these be our weaponized projectiles. We all of us make our own music, half of us doing that fart noise you do with your tongue and mouth, half of us out of our minds laughing and pointing and howling all of Mr. Art's various unsavory labels."

"Are you sad, Karen? Do you feel bad for Mr. Art?"

"Not even a little. I'm the happiest I can ever remember being."

"Is Mr. Art ever inappropriate with you in any way—specifically sexually?"

"Not at all. We just don't like him. Sometimes that's how it is with people."

"Are you still there with him in the music room?"

"Uh-huh. Mr. Art's peeking his head up from under the piano. The whole room's a total mess, and he's totally crying about it. His goatee's got a dot of blood in it."

"Pause the internal hallucination there, love, then zoom in on his face."

"Gladly," said Karen.

"Now zoom out. Leave the music room behind. Cast your consciousness outside."

"I don't want to."

"Tell me why, love."

"Because the rest of my life's outside. I'd rather stay in here."

"Tell me what's so good about where you are."

"Nobody tells on me or singles me out here. Nobody here says my name."

"Karen?"

"*Don't call me that.*"

"..."

"It's better when you call me love," said Karen.

Suddenly Yew thought she knew. "How old are you, love?"

"Ten."

"I mean right here and now, in Hope Row, in the Berkshire cottage camps."

"I'm eighteen years old."

"I see—I'd assumed you were in your midthirties like me," said Yew.

"Maybe that's because you've been *rudely* judging me for my height."

"Has your height been a point of contention in your life?"

"No duh."

"I'd like you to walk me through life outside of Mr. Art's music room."

"There's nothing for me outside this room—there's no room for my voice."

"We're all of us lost without rooms of our own in which to hallucinate," said Yew. "Since you won't step through the door, love, try kicking everyone else out."

"I'm alone in a crowded room where silence is music," said Karen.

"Is this Mr. Art's music room you're now speaking of, or your own mind?"

"I'm trying to walk out the door, but I keep bumping my head on the head of the doorframe. I'm stuck in place, watching everyone else race under my legs out the door."

"Could be your brain pounding into your head a hard lesson in growth mindset."

Karen said, "You know nothing of growing pains, Yew. Believe me."

"So then enlighten me. For your sake and clarity's, leak, peak— and *speak!*"

Eventually Karen complied, and all too soon Yew's suspicions were confirmed by Karen's verbal account's Pandora's box of gory life details, all of which had been eating away at Karen in an unconscious way for eight painful years. Yew couldn't help but pry open her own Pandora's box, contents spewing out like a legion of winged demons: Ash, comatose and pin-cushioned with a million tubes and needles and one dastardly catheter he'd always sort of point to with his eyes, spinal cord cracked and twisted, Yew's rightful big-oil inheritance hanging in the balance; Yew signing the contract agreeing to return the inheritance in full back to Mother and Father in exchange for the right to keep Ash's ashes, echoing Ash's decision to sign the liability release form prior to participating in his final film as a Hollywood stuntman; their huge family of hardcore Christian universalists headed by Grandpa G, an ultra-powerful cigar-smoking . . . there were reasons Yew had done away with both her first and last names. Karen's internally hallucinated grievances clawed the air. Yew couldn't stop crying, hand over Karen's heart here in Hope Row, feeling the fitful rise and fall of her tripper's breath, a long-overdue earthquake splitting apart the figurative fault line in Karen's chest, exploding to the psychedelic surface after eight incapacitating years the true source of Karen's ostensibly irreparable damage. Yew was now thinking of Bakersfield—of the caring, clever, free-spirited-on-the-surface woman whose life choices had brought Yew and Don Philly together in a boneyard, how Brenda had touched them both in ways that couldn't be more opposite. She could feel one of her eyelids spasming on its own, twitching open and closed as though something residing in her outer peripheral were feeding on exactly half her physical body's total metaphysical energy output.

Something at eye level fluttering there, as bright as the ocean blue.

"Still there, Yew? Are you even hearing me at all?"

"I'm right here, love."

"But you haven't said anything about anything I've said," said Karen.

"I've been helping you keep your breathing under your own control."

"Maybe I don't want to. Breathe, I mean. Maybe I want to run all out of breath."

"Maybe that isn't really you who's talking," said Yew. "Perhaps it's the toxic energy present in the lies you've told yourself about yourself retching as it dies the slow, painful death all lies we unconsciously force-feed ourselves deserve. You might therefore consider putting a tad more effort into putting yourself first, Karen, relearning to love and respect yourself as a living, breathing, thinking, existing human being on this earth."

"You sound like the yoga instructor from over in Self-Esteem Row yesterday."

"Except the thing is, Karen, you mustn't lose yourself in yourself entirely. The pursuit of mystic fullness can't end with yourself— it's merely where you start."

"Maybe we're done here: clearly you haven't heard a single thing I've said."

"You're here, Karen—and whether you consciously know or let alone accept the truth of what I'm about to say is beyond irrelevant, as I'm sure you'll soon come to agree—you're here because of your self-perceived inability to control the subconscious affliction that is the shame you've come to associate with your own name. Which itself, of course, is subject to change. For instance, Yew's not my 'real' name at all, but that fact, along with my legally effacing my surname, is beside the major point I'll soon be driving home.

"Your name, 'Karen,' is formed from five letters that, by themselves, are undeserving of all the wrongdoing that has been done to you by others, who themselves are afflicted with their own toxic set of debilitating lies they force-feed themselves. But when arranged in this order—K-A-R-E-N—the word becomes your name, becomes your identity, which, *due to outside influence beyond your control*, becomes your albatross or scarlet letter or cross to bear or whatever other reference so pleases your preference on a semi-spiritual level. In other words, words carry power, Karen, for better or worse. As do names. If I were to guess, I'd say your particular case largely has to do with this country's slow and painful demise—which may or may not explain your having heard the 'Star-Spangled Banner' ringing so loudly in your head earlier.

"That said, Karen, I want you to know I heard everything you said and that I believe wholeheartedly everything you said makes total sense, in a sense, since I was able to process your words and extract for myself the primary source of your pain. How your birth certificate was stamped with 'Karen' in a time in American history that would end up proving to do you no favors at all for its being thusly stamped. Unfortunately you've been instinctively blaming yourself for a strange but no less valid socio-political gestalt that emerged some eight-odd years after your birth, meaning after the fact, and as a mere child of eight, there's no way you could've possibly known or been aware of a certain special-for-all-the-wrong-reasons group of quote 'entitled women who flexed their entitlement by using their white privilege as a weapon against those figuratively stamped at birth with darker skin tones' unquote. These rude, toneless women went all around wielding this chauvinistically ingrained weapon and so exposed their own inward fragility, all while being caught on camera.

"That's what they were really doing, these Karens, even if it looked to some as though they were complaining to supermarket managers or asserting their so-called God-given rights as Americans. If only they'd taken into account their civic duties and realized the potential unifying power in dialogue and basic compassion, maybe we could've saved ourselves from where we're at today. Probably you were too young for you to recall any of this now, so let me fill you in on the rest of the context, how this particularly despicable caste of women, the Karens, kept going viral on the web before, during, and after the Second Civil Rights Movement. Of kind and innocent Karens such as yourself there were countless at the time, who all had no real choice but to hunker down and hide. So I'm guessing here you must've picked up on some of their collective nervous energy, which may have fueled your desire to quote 'blend in with the crowd,' a defense mechanism further reinforced, of course, by your growing up into the gorgeous six-foot-seven woman you are here and now.

"While good Karens all over the country went into hiding and other not-so-good Karens kept relentlessly emerging, you were part of the innocently unaware group of youthful Karens forced to grow up and face the world head-on despite whatever unsavory injustices or nasty verbal tones used in conjunction with your name might've come your way. All due, once again, to a historical movement, which, in this psychedelic therapist's opinion at least, had totally been rooted in goodwill and was therefore right and just. The real point here, Karen, is nobody can ever know the extent of your pain. Just as you can never know fully the pain of those from whom you exist apart—historically marginalized groups in particular. Pain and happiness might be relative to one's experience, but maybe we should all be putting more effort into steering clear of all assumptions, our own most of all. Never assume anything, I always try to say. Better to play it safe. Which brings me to my second, infinitely more urgent point regarding our mutual pursuit of mystic fullness."

"I'm six-five at the absolute most."

"It's essential we all learn to relearn to love ourselves, Karen, to respect our fears, which, by the way, are only here to help us live and breathe and think and exist as individuals who go the extra mile in cultivating basic human values on the inside so that whenever applicable, we can decide to extend said values to others who exist outside of us, a.k.a. the rest of the human race, all of whom are afflicted with all different kinds of deep, complex hurt, most of which require outside assistance to have a chance to be in any way alleviated. Put another way, we must learn to put ourselves first, but only at first, because the only reason for putting ourselves first in the first place is so that we can learn to develop the once-basic human capacity for empathy needed for us to be able to put others first, meaning before us and our own inner subdivisions of complex needs and hurts. In this way, the pursuit of mystic fullness begins with us, it's true, but what's equally true and what too often too many Reds and Blues alike forget is that the pursuit of mystic fullness ends with others, with our ability to reach out and connect and contribute as one piece to the pieces and parts comprising the whole haunted house of humanity."

"I'm a firm believer we should never walk in someone else's shoes," Karen said in a loud voice somehow absent of tone. "That we should always be looking out solely for our own footsteps instead, in our own shoes, walking our own path."

"I sorta get a vibe you're a trifle nervous to disclose your beliefs. Don't worry, Karen. I won't waste time and energy discrediting a belief system that forged your journey's path here to me. After all, I'm only here to reach out and so help you reach in."

"If that's true, then why do you keep lying to me?"

"Come again?" said Yew.

"Come to think of it, you've totally been trying to mentally Trojan Horse me."

"I'm afraid you're losing control of your own breath again."

"First you lie about your phone. I'd been willing to let it slide at first, to give you a second chance to earn back my trust and respect—which you pretty much squandered, by the way, the second you reinforced the same lie by telling me I may've been associating *your* 'Star-Spangled Banner' ringtone with the supposed demise of our great nation. Still, I'm all for three strikes you're out, as I'm a firm believer in the Holy Trinity. So there I am, pouring my heart and suicidal soul out to you—a total stranger who'd sooner rudely judge me for my age and height and most of all my *name* than quote unquote 'connect' with me or at least *hear* me—while you just sit here pretty much on top of me and cop feels on my breasts and mutter under your breath the weirdest stuff about, like, Vegas and euthanasia and big-oil inheritances and, weirdest of all, some stunt-man's ashes I actually heard you say you ate. At this point, I'm practically convinced you're out of your mind, or maybe you dropped too much acid, but since I'm nice, I decide to spare you the embarrassment or shame or whatever and point out instead your apparent inability to pay me any of the attention I've paid a hundred dollars for and which you've implied I so desperately need.

"This was when you went and tried to Trojan Horse me—you go and unleash an all-out assault on these supposedly recent and, might I add, *racist* etymological developments concerning my name and presumptuously assume I was, like, totally unaware of the world around me when I was eight. By the way, I spit on the notion that our great nation's crumbled in any way. It's clear to anyone paying attention the Divided Alliance is the best thing to've ever happened to us. Anyway, this here's when you drive the nail into your own career's coffin and any shred of credibility therein and hit me with this totally obviously preplanned knee-slapper regarding connection or whatever it was you said. And what you said doesn't even bear repeating especially since you totally went and discredited my belief system by stating aloud you won't discredit my belief system as that would waste, quote, 'time and energy.' In other words, *Yew*, you deploy the same rhetoric you try to imply to condemn. I mean, get a grip, hypocrite."

"I'm sorry, love. About my phone. First time that's happened here on the job. I'm more than happy to refund you your one hundred bucks as soon as we wrap up."

"Hundred bucks says you're one of those progressive Blues," said Karen. "What I don't get is why don't progressives ever call themselves regressive? I bet it's 'cause that would be honest, and if there's anything you've made clear today, it's that honesty's not a Blue-wing value. See, at least I know my history—Momma taught me right."

"No," said Yew.

"You know it's true."

"No, it isn't a Red or White or Blue-wing value—honesty, I mean. It's a human value. Maybe we'd all do well not to forget that."

"Here's where you say we've allowed our nation's feckless leaders to weaponize deceit and misdirection and what-all to make things only seem real and authentic in a society that worships polit- ical theater—don't try me, Yew. I've heard it all before."

"For what it's worth, Karen, I'm sorry I haven't made you feel heard here today."

"You say that as if you're going somewhere."

"I am," said Yew.

"And where exactly do you think you're going?"

Yew noted the tinny helicopter hum in the air rising before her eyes that came complete with a winged body whose color differed vastly from Karen's. "Figured I'd follow this dragonfly. It's got a certain magnetism I'd sooner pursue than hang here with you."

"I already told you I can't stand being left alone with my own head! Big three!"

"It appears you need some additional time to yourself, which, if you'll recall, is the first step to step one. I hope someday you'll look back on your time here in Hope Row and view it through whatever lens best suits your spiritual development, a.k.a. your pursuit of mystic fullness, a.k.a. your inward reclamation of basic human values."

"Don't you dare—you better not—I'll scream if you leave, you know!"

". . ."

"Hey! Untie me!"

". . ."

"Untie me, I said! And take off this stinking blindfold!"

". . ."

"*I demand you to take me to your manager!*"

". . ."

"DON'T THINK I CAN'T I HEAR YOU, YEW! PACKING UP!"

"Goodbye, Karen, and good luck with step one . . . try not to forget step two."

Yew drifted from the trip zone tent to the grass path outside where sunlight's faded fingers grazed the green in retreat, pack slung across her shoulder, brother's urn in hand, her burner phone a lump against her efficiently beating heart. Hope Row was silent and empty but for Karen's screams and the other therapists peeping from diamond window flaps and shushing loudly. Yew was so over this place; she knew the time had come to move on, to find somewhere else to settle before Love's arrival in five days' time.

For now, though, she looked forward to drifting with the dragonfly, which was as blue as the one she'd been fixated on beside Don Philly back at Brenda's grave.

Truth be told, Yew'd be damned if both bugs weren't one and the same.

———

WAY THE HELL DOWN HERE, in what Trent imagined to be the earth's deepest crack, glittered yet another constellation of eyes that all at once sputtered out. Alone in utter darkness once more, he wondered where all those eyes had gone, what they'd seen, why they seemed to have seen in him nothing significant. The nocturnals residing in this once-great chasm's guts were reclusive in nature, threatening in the same vague way as strangers who smile at you on the sidewalk for no apparent reason before turning to move on. He'd come at the president's direct orders to "rinse out the sores from God's Mouth," so here he was. Trent hosed down tonight's third group of manic mushrooms and watched all five rosy caps wither like deflated balloons.

Sporadic sweeps of tall grass all surpassed eye level here in God's Mouth. Cracked-open boulders hosted mass mating rituals for worms, producing a squirmy sound that was generally ubiquitous. The valley floor was a river of blackness from which mottled succulents seemed to sprout up whenever Trent happened to have his back turned. These looked to him like the spindly claws of demons reaching up from hell. He ripped his gaze away and sent it up the sandstone curves of the canyon to the jagged, now narrowish gap five thousand feet above. There, Trent locked eyes with the man in the moon, who always seemed to grin amid the stars.

Trent often spoke to the grinning man in the moon, Dex being the channeling force.

Due to natural tectonic effects that arose from the "big one" rocking Los Angeles down low as well as the "bigger one" clocking Oregon up high, the pit itself, which once formed an abyss stretching no fewer than five miles, had closed over the years by no less than ninety percent. God's Mouth, formerly colloquially known as Big Mouth, was no longer viewed as anyone's "new Grand Canyon" and was seldom noticed at all anymore.

Trent Taphor had used the solar-powered escalators to make his way down here, the whole zigzagging system domed in tinted bullet-proof glass. The tunneled escalators connected God's Mouth below to the suspension bridge leading in and out of Eden's End above.

Trent was working his fifth night running rinsing the back of

God's Mouth in preparation for this upcoming Halloween's annual hunt for El Jaylo, now five days away. This ritual, still cherished among the original Berkshireites, was due to all but dissipate as soon as God's Mouth moved its way the rest of the way shut. His shoulders were strapped with a piston-pump five-gallon Middleman Backpack Sprayer. The mini-fridge-shaped tank on his back contained two and a half gallons of white vinegar mixed in with two and a half gallons of holy water priorly blessed in the Berkshire cottage camps by one Anglican, one Lutheran, one Roman Catholic, one Eastern Christian, and one agnostic psychedelic therapist. It was said the acetic acid present in the vinegar was what killed the manic mushrooms; these mushrooms would then resurrect in five weeks' time, which President Mangrove said was what the holy water was for.

Trent pictured God looking down and sizing him up, viewing him as a teeny ant with an exterminator pack bent on meaningless annihilation.

The spray pack's tank came equipped with chemical-resistant seals, a strainer/filter basket at the opening for easy pours and for catching extraneous debris, adjustable shoulder straps with waist straps, and a trigger cushion-grip spray handle for comfortable spraying and for hand-sore prevention. Prevention, in fact, was the primary reason Trent had found himself here, since there was no better form of protection.

"Make sure you get the ones way in back," the president had ordered through his smartwatch's screen five nights back. "You'll want to pay particularly close attention to the Whispering Wellspring's perimeter. We don't want any ornery Berkshireites brushing up against any mushies who're mentally unprepared for it. Trust me —it ain't pretty, what can happen."

"But I hate—wait, why not get Rufus to do it?"

"Excuse me?"

"I said Rufus," Trent had said. "From Troop Puppy. Dude loves it down there."

"Troop Puppy'll be manning the Chinese dragon on Halloween

Eve. Unless of course you wish you and your crew to run this year's Snake on The Run?"

"But we did it last year. And the year before that. And both years before *that*."

"Correct me if I'm wrong, Trent, but isn't that what you'd always wanted?"

"I just hate being anywhere near the Whispering Wellspring. Those caves all, like, mess with my head. And your escalators're almost always giving out near the bottom."

"Just get it done, lest you be first to face the mob of manic locals run amok."

So again, here he was, dousing from a physical distance indicative of past Crown safety guidelines, consigning tonight's fourth group of shrooms to necessary (albeit temporary) doom.

The secondary reason Trent now found himself spray-gunning manic mushrooms was wholly personal in nature: he was here to face his fear of the Whispering Wellspring's caves. He wished to confront the nightmares he'd been having on and off for going on a decade, the ones about the caves, with all that reptilian hissing. These hiss-filled nightmares always took him into the caves to some isolated dead end where some freakishly overgrown insect would be stuck midway through the process of mutating into something else, a halfway-mutant he'd end up needing Dex to decapitate to save himself from being eaten whole. In real life, only the bravest and boldest among park visitors ever took it upon themselves to venture through the caves to the Whispering Wellspring, which supposedly was another sight to see. Assuming you could take that celestial punch of light square on the nose and come away from the whole thing with your sight and memory equally intact. Which didn't always turn out to be the case.

In real life, the caves in back of God's Mouth were too dim to really make out at all at night, unlike the glowy caves in Eden's End proper—Trent nonetheless could sense them there, gaping. He pictured himself as a maggot traversing a skull whose hollows hid worms much bigger than he. The sound Trent's spray gun made when triggered replicated the hissing from his nightmares right down to the decibel. This was all part of life now, being the head of Troop Peewee. He'd much rather watch Berkshire's Halloween Festival from afar, passively observing the bat-spotting and pumpkin-carving and bobbing for apples and obviously the annual hunt for El Jaylo. He was sick of running the event, tired of the Chinese dragon's screechy amps, sick and tired of judging the scary mask contest. Realizing his every dream had only made him realize that happiness was the most hazardous of all dreams to choose to navigate.

It was after picking up a few protracted seconds of pestilent hissing that Trent tripped over his own crossed-up feet. The spray pack's weight proved too unwieldy for a body whirling around so frantically. It occurred to Trent, in the split-second before hitting the ground, that his enduring affinity for Halloween was due in part to all the social reinforcement he received from hiding in plain sight behind one devilishly freaky mask.

Something queerly rubbery popping above the earth cushioned his fall, molding like fresh clay to one side of his face. By the time he wrenched his face free of what had quickly started to feel like some strange suction cup sucking his cheek, propping himself up on his elbows, Trent found himself totally encased in light.

After wiggling his way out of the waist and shoulder straps, he flopped over on his back and faced the grinning man in the moon, who suddenly seemed a million miles closer. Starburst sprays of moonlight illuminated the whole of God's Mouth from within, vividly vibrant but not excruciatingly so. When Trent rolled on his side, he could see tides of wind sweeping through the tall grass, parting there a path through which he instinctively knew his body alone was meant to pass. Bolts of bliss shocked him through with all the generative force of a twin earthquake. It was tempting, the idea of dissolving into the earth. He got up and got moving instead, casting the spray pack's tank and trunky hose onto the bed of pinkish roses into which he'd fallen.

Trent took to the path parting the tall grass, which wound to the right, taking him with it. A naked man emerged from the thickets maybe five steps ahead. For one fleeting moment, he viewed the encounter as if from a vantage point a million miles high—both men stood very still, each regarding the other, a reflection of each other. Trent never would've recognized the man before him but for the scar tissue snaking down the man's elbow's underside, long and white, which the man was scratching. Trent seemed to grasp from a distance beyond himself that he himself was mirroring the man's every action—that it wasn't the other way around.

At this point Trent saw he, too, was naked. "I'm so sorry, Dad. For splitting my lip biting down laughing so hard at your screams after I snipped the rope to your harness with scissors."

The man seemed to size Trent up and down and said, "If anyone knows anything regarding shortcuts to the nearest public toilet or buried bodies or what have you, it's the Town Bum with a bottomless forty-ounce. Anyplace worth its salt in strangeness has got a good TB-40, I've found—and believe you me, petroleum jelly's taken me places."

Trent's father turned away and returned to the weeds from whence he came.

Trent didn't bother going after his father, for the path ahead had bent its way back to the left, the wind's whisper drawing him forth. No one else appeared for what seemed a good while.

What might've been a black cat darted across the path only to vanish into the weedy undergrowth on the other side. This phenomenon, in fact, ended up recurring every so often, which at any other time, in any other place, might've been a cause of extreme irritation for Trent.

Here and now, however, he figured he somehow knew what to do. He picked his pace up into a brisk jog, and when jogging failed to impose on his breath and body any sort of challenge, he began to sprint, and sure enough, the cat's disappearing act was being carried out closer and closer as Trent raced faster and faster. Eventually he came near enough to the cat to note the rip in its fur all the way down to the flesh that kept flapping open to reveal nothing within.

The little markings the cat's claws left in the path's dirt were words, Trent saw, a message repeated *ad infinitum*: "Dear God, enough is enough. Go fuck yourself."

Trent went on repeating this aloud until the cat dropped dead in the dead center of the path, lying flat on its side, from which a single rib protruded like the fingerbone of a hitchhiker who died flagging down the ride that ran him down. Trent stopped short of the dead undead cat, a black sack of fur with a sagging head and face, its serrated worm of a tongue lolling lifelessly from a tiny set of dagger teeth. The fat finger of rib took on a pinkish hue as it grew a plump coat of dermis absent those lateral lines characteristic of human skin. The budding thumb thrashed from side to side, splitting fur, making way for four more fingers, one hand, then two.

The two lineless hands emerging from the cat's midsection were pressed back-to-back, ripping and tearing from inside the sack the way one might try to keep an elevator door from closing. The fore-arms and full arms, next to break through, worked to prop up the person coming partway out of the cat's ribcage. A crop of golden hair was first to reveal itself, then a face—a woman's, swollen and suffocated from her own bloodless rebirth. Most of her body stayed buried inside the cat so that she was only visible from the shoulders up, the flesh of her neck and throat patterned and purpled with little shapeless diamonds. She cast no shadow on the path behind her, though Trent still pictured there a malformed, spidery shade.

He noticed for the first time there were no odors anywhere of any kind.

"Got nothing to say to you," Trent told his dead therapist, Angel. "You left me."

"That's an interesting thought, dude! And it's not like you're crazy for thinking it—my sister, Love, she says the same about me all the time. At the end of the day, though, your brother's your brother —your *twin!* That alone makes you both a significant gift to this world. Just because you two *seem* different doesn't *mean* the love between you isn't there. Some of us have to work a little harder to get there, for sure, but I like to think love is what humans do best, that maybe it's the reason we're alive. In any event, Trent, sorry to say we'll have to pick this up next time. I have to shut this door now —my next client's online. See ya next Wednesday!"

Angel stayed her place more than halfway inside the cat on the path as she mimed closing a door—then, from behind the not-present door, Angel smiled one of those loaded therapist smiles before her head suddenly slid bloodlessly from her neck. It thumped to the ground and rolled before it broke down, dissolving like plastic in acetone.

Suddenly taking the place of her head and face was the head and face of Wild Will Spiro, Trent's made-up TB-40/Vietnam vet, for whom it would seem Halloween had come early.

"Hoot," said Willy Spiro. "Yours is a tale of woe!"

And then Willy used Angel's arms as legs to propel himself as he skittered haphazardly forth, charging Trent like some insectile imp from hell. Trent wasted no time channeling his inner soccer player whose reputation for dirty play preceded him and proceeded to put everything he had into driving his left foot into Willy's open screaming mouth. The top of Trent's foot registered nary an impact, the crushingly sensationless satisfaction akin to what big leaguers must be getting at when they talk bats and balls and sweet spots in barrels.

Willy's head came clean off Angel's neck and went soaring away, way out into outer space. Trent reckoned the odds for the decapitated head's ever coming down were less than slim to none. The man in the moon gazed down with something like fatherly pride in his cratered grin. Angel's arms had flopped over, squid-like, her neck a meatless, boneless pit.

Trent stepped over Angel's piecemeal remains and moved on down the path.

The path now wended its way back to the right—this'll never end, Trent was starting to think. More of that initial hissing closed in from closer sources moving unseen through the tall grass, echoed by hushed little ticks like what you hear inside a car as it settles after having crashed and flipped over on its side. At this point he assumed it was safe to assume the tall grass's inhabitants were revenants of his past.

If true, that meant somewhere out there there walked someone with whom at some point long ago he'd been so close as to be considered insep—nope, something in Trent's head said, better not go down that path.

"C'mon, bro, you know to ignore what isn't real, especially when you're dealing with something as unreliable as memory . . ."

"Buzz off, Dex. Nobody asked you."

"I'd beg to differ. I'd say you've been asking me all along."

"Where'd you even come from?"

"Bro, you already know I was made in Texas."

"That's not what I—"

"Oh, I know what you meant. You've been gripping me for dear life all this time, Trent, five and a half hours you've spent venturing through the caves on your way to that creepy grotto you're always spending so much time trying not to think about. Matter of fact, bro, I'm starting to think there's not much more I can do here to get you to help yourself, get-a-grip-wise."

What's happened to me, Trent asked himself, then to Dex, "Why's your voice all dimmed down and distant?"

"You've literally been wading through pitch darkness, my dude —all that tall grass you think you see here . . . well, needless to say, that ain't what's really there. It's the same thing with that head you think you booted into outer space an hour back—which really was just another case of one of those missing heads from one of those Skeeter-5000s that slipped and tumbled down the pit during the escalator system's cliffside installation a few years back, you remember. Some racoon or whatever must've come along and looted the robo-head for itself and hoarded it inside the cave system you're now using dimly imagined light to try to navigate."

"Knife's right, kiddie-koo-koo—*heheeee!*"

"Aw, come on, Dex. Don't leave me alone with Willy freegin' Spiro."

"With a *head* like yours, Trent, I'm unsure you can ever *be* alone."

"Shut the hell up, Angel. I watched your head totally melt and dissolve—"

"*Be* that as it may, Trent, that doesn't *solve* the issue of what you're hearing."

"I hear nothing."

"Are you even *at all* certain our voices still *belong* to you anymore?"

"I don't know what to say, and even if I did, I don't think I'd be able to say it—it's like I've forgotten how to speak, like I can't move my lips and give air to words like I used to."

(*Turns out I've no qualms with trusting you. You're the one who named me, after all, the one who gave me my first taste of freedom.*)

"Who said that?"

"*Who* said *what?*"

"Hoot—I ain't just one of yer voices, kid."

"Everyone shut up and let me do my walking and talking to myself alone."

"It just so *happens* Halloween lands on a *Wednesday* this year— what, if anything, do *Wednesdays* mean to you?"

(*Keep pushing through, Trent—our connection grows stronger the closer you get to the wellspring in back of this grotto. Make sure to keep quiet. Last thing in the world you want to do down here is disturb—*)

"That! That voice there!"

"I know something you don't know . . . bro."

"Well, here's something I've only just recently come to know— America's suicide rate under President Mangrove resides at an all-time high—which is something my employer doesn't want anyone anywhere to know. Like, I had to go and track down an actual library with actual official records to look this up, and this is true. Nowadays fifty-five tales of woe get told per one hundred thousand Americans, or what researchers all call *deaths of despair.*"

"Your father said you said you were sorry for splitting your lip, biting down on it so hard from laughing after you cut his rope and he cut clear through his elbow down to the bone after falling on his chainsaw—"

"Mom?"

"Is that supposed to be some kind of apology, son? Do you have even the slightest clue what your father's fall did to him, trauma-wise? He spent the rest of his life terrified of trees! By the way, where's—"

(Don't listen to her, Trent. She's not your mother—as much as that must hurt to hear. This is BJ, by the way, coming at you straight from your brainstem. Long time, no speak!)

"I don't know who you think you are, but cut my mom off like that again, and rest assured I'll—"

(Anyways, you're starting to come up on the wellspring—one more right, then left, then you're there. But you should also know you're coming dangerously close to waking The Titanoboa. From here on out, you really ought to consider stepping somewhat softer and thinking somewhat quieter. Tone it down a tad, other words.)

"If there's anything I'm 100 percent sure about, it's that El Jaylo doesn't exist. El Jaylo has always been a manmade myth."

"Not so, kiddie-koo-koo—*heheeee!* After the forces of five and five converged on Mr. Trenty and The Chosen, the battleground for the fate of the earth emerged, on which battleground anything became possible, and this here would include, kiddie-koo-koo, El Jaylo's undeniably true genesis. Mustn't forget the checkerboard, Mr. Trenty, and remember also there's little to no shame in having skipped out on 1997's *Titanoboa.*"

"Wild Will there's got a point, bro—like, didn't you hear about the boy from Berkshire whose pet boa constrictor went missing? I mean, like, weren't you paying attention?"

"Look, Dex, I was trying to pay attention to what my mom was saying on the phone when that semitruck ignored the two-way stop and blindsided her car with my dad yelling in the front seat, but I never heard her last words, and I can't tell if it's because I can't remember or if, like, I don't really want to know what her last words were."

"And *this* time you'll *sack up* and cut his throat."

"Who? Whose throat am I supposed to cut?"

"Hoot—yours is a tale of woe."

"Phewf," said Beetlejuice, whose voice came cleanly through. "No lie, your left foot came like this close to clomping on the end of El Jaylo's tail back there. Anyways, welcome to the Whispering Well-spring—by the way, it's perfectly safe to open your eyes now."

Trent took a series of punches of pulsing light straight to the eyes, his retinas shifting into overdrive to remonstrate with the combination of left and right hooks and uppercuts vectoring from the cavern's every conceivable direction. The unseeable sight alone did enough to silence all the voices previously competing for the spotlight in his head, a competition from which it would seem Beetlejuice had emerged the victor. He pictured in the total brightness of his temporary blindness God snapping flash photographs with a camera the size of several worlds all mashed into one. Then all at once Trent could see again, and what he saw was good.

A single great tree that could only be described as cosmic-looking shone in the center of the cavern, a rippling torch of brightest gold. Its crisscrossing branches and boughs reached like human arms, casting sparkles like shooting stars across the ink-black body of water over which the tree seemed to stand sentinel with some ethereally felt purpose in mind. If the visible shimmers Trent noted in the pertinent areas were any indication—the way those light waves spiraled from the trunk's vast middle, expanding and contracting like something alive and breathing—the tree seemed to absorb its light from all the eyes igniting the massive sprawl of knotholes from within. These knotholes looked bottomless, somehow biblical, like pits that traveled inside the tree all the way to nature's birth's eternally mysterious roots.

Eyes glittered in all those little knotholes, pinpricks of light peeping out, one sparkly constellation after another. Trent knew to whom all those glittering eyes belonged; they were owls, the saw-whets believed to have left Eden's End. All throughout the tree blazed another saw-whet's gaze, orange-ringed and infinite, each pupil a pit refracting its own solitary moon.

Encircling the inky water's perimeter were life-sized statues of men and women and children, all as brown as burnt clay and as bared as Trent. The statues stood there pointing around in some quietly urgent way, exposed, as if whispered secrets could take human shape.

"Holy . . ."

"Try Black-*Holian*."

"What . . ."

"You're looking at a Black-Holian tree. It's the physical form of Mother Climate's Contract, to an extent. See the fruit those petrified people're pointing at, Trent? Those celestial plums twirling on those thorny vines like so many suns revolving in elliptical orbits on the Web's nether-ether region containing what you call gravitational force?"

"I see . . ."

"Thing is, The Spider hasn't let me let you see ever since you freed me. Or I guess I mean She's been intercepting our line of contact, or interfering with it, I mean, thereby suppressing our ability to participate in open and honest dialogue. But here . . . now . . ."

". . . five Heads. Hanging in the tree. Bowed. And down comes the guillotine."

"Sacrifices," said Beetlejuice. "Should you choose to see them that way. Thing is, the Contract clearly states you're under zero obligation to see them that way. You don't have to see them as human sacrifices in exchange for humankind's prospective survival. Other words, you've got quite the decision to make in the end regarding Mother Climate's demands, namely those pesky death toll dividends. Divided ends and all that. Maybe I'm not explaining this well. See, should you deliver Anne Kell—pardon me, The Spider, who're one and the same—should you deliver The Spider of Sector Z the five fateful Heads, this, in effect, would negate the 100 percent death toll due to Mother Climate, who is seeking returns on Her quote 'bungled investment in humanity.' You would then stand a small chance in preventing Earth's already thrice-delayed sixth Apocalypse. Or perhaps delaying it for a fourth instance, I mean. Obviously Mother Climate's pissed, as Her metaphysical hands are literally tied with the double-knot's soul-fire binding Earth to Phooka Road. Although Mother Climate generally approves of most biomes both macro and micro, even She's come around to accepting the true source of Her disease—the source here being humanity. Including the debilitating effects of the death of commonsense kindness therein. The resultant interdimensional cancer's been sorta cosmically, holocaustically hypoxic in nature, in that it deprives my kind of the kindness we need to breathe."

"I see . . . Calvin. My Calvin. We're in the RV, whipping up mac n' cheese to go with our sloppy joes . . . we just got back from a round of frisbee gold. I mean golf."

"Surely seeing this Black-Holian tree helps you see why Mr. Moony tried to gift your kind with gold. You should know Mr. Moony put his figurative backside on the line gambling on you all, seeking to prove you'd prove Mother Climate wrong."

"My mom used to say money can't buy happiness. Said the most it could do is purchase a smile or two. All smiles are masks, is what I'd say to her today."

"So say it, then—I mean, tell her. Go on, Trent, step up to the tree and tell your mother. But remember to whisper. You have to whisper to be heard here."

Trent made his way closer to the tree, smiled, and whispered on the water. He waited on his mother's response, gazing at the tree like a caveman seeing his future in a fire.

"What'd she say, Trent? Has she, by any chance, imparted some critical last words of advice? Perhaps regarding the choice you'll soon have no choice but to make despite all the attached implications as per Mother Climate's Contract of Basic Goodness?"

"Turns out she's been with me all along, Beetlejuice. That's right, I remember you. I found you—what? Nine, maybe ten years ago now?—I mean, I remember finding you and naming you and thinking you'd flown away or something, but I guess it turns out you've also been here with me all this time like her. Though she's not in my head, and she's not using words—no words I understand, at least—but it's a kind of language all the same. It feels like feeling itself to hear her, with all the same highs and lows and twists and turns, and yet it's somehow blissful to listen to. Hearing my mom makes my chest not hurt anymore, which is something I've only felt once before . . . closest I can get to describing it. By the way, she's still going, which is more or less how it goes once you get her started —I guess you could say she's sort of speaking to me in memory.

"I see Calvin and me, mac n' cheese in the RV, sloppy joes on deck. We're celebrating. It's the end of our second month of our first year here in Saw-whet Park, but that's not why or what we're celebrating—we're celebrating . . . us. The both of us at once. We've come home from a round of disc golf in the park, where I'd been teaching Calvin to chuck a frisbee the right way every day an hour a day for weeks. Anyways, earlier that day we were approaching hole five, where the real Wild Will Spiro would hang out in this little clearing he'd hacked out for himself to pound Old English in. Calvin only had to meet him once before deciding from then on to always remember to pack with us a can of pop to give to Willy. But on this particular day as we make our way to Willy's camp with pop in hand, we're all of a sudden accosted by the head park ranger—I can't remember the guy's name, though I remember him being downright obsessed with disc golf in his spare time. The ranger's trying to get Willy to go away, calling him all sorts of names, which gets Calvin all upset, which makes the ranger get only madder and meaner to everyone involved.

"Now I'd been speaking with this dude a lot beforehand, angling for a job—they had an opening, see—so the ranger knew me and I knew him and I've always hated to hear Calvin scream and cry, so I decided I'd try and challenge the guy to a friendly wager. Hole five, Calvin and me versus the ranger. If either Calvin or I scored better, I tell this dude, then Willy gets to stay where he eats and drinks and sleeps and I'd get the job in Troop Peewee. Well, the ranger accepts these terms out of hand without supplying any his own—dude was that kind of confident. Maybe you're getting a sense where this is going. We all agreed I'd go first, then the ranger, then Calvin. So up I go and toss an absolute beauty—hole five was my specialty, see. Here I'm thinking I'm a hustler—and we watch my disc soar and curve its way all the way around the doglegging oak in the center of the fairway out of sight, but I'd played enough before to know my disc will've laid up short of the little creek circling the hole's chain-net basket. I knew I'd par no problem, with a slim-to-none chance at birdie. But so then it's the ranger's turn. He goes and whips his disc like he's skipping a rock across a lake, like a pro who knows the course inside-out and then some, flicking the wrist like you would with a bullwhip. Together the three of us watch that thing cut cleanly *through* the split in the boughs of the doglegging oak, heading straight on course for the hole. Sure enough, couple seconds later we hear this dude's disc thump the hole's basket's metal bars—but no chains, meaning he'd most definitely birdie next turn, meaning in my mind Calvin and I were shit out of luck.

"That's when Calvin steps up to tee box; he mounts the platform with the Captain America disc I had to shoplift in hand, turns to look me in the eye with a smile in his eyes, and says, 'Crap, we're all out of toilet paper.' He says this in a way that doesn't really sound like him at all. Like, his words came clearly and cleanly through, with none of the usual drawls and muddled syllables that come with Down's. Anyways, I see him going through all the motions, trying to remember how I taught him to keep the disc parallel with his forearm. But what Calvin ends up doing differently —from the disc-golf obsessed ranger and me both, I mean—he dictates his angle of release by bending at the waist, not the wrist, and he ends up doing this at an extremely acute angle, working his whole body to maintain this crazily contorted throwing angle, which he ends up doing all the way through his release. Immediately this piece-of-crap Captain America frisbee of his beelines through the trees for a whole separate fairway—the sixth hole's—and already I'm starting to hang my head when all of a sudden Calvin's disc veers all the way back like it's got a freegin' mind of its own. I'm not kidding. Before we all know it or even believe it, we hear it—the triumphant rain of hole five's basket's rattling chains. Suffice it to say when it was all said and done, the ranger's the one who ended up picking up the tab on our sloppy joes n' mac."

"I so recognize it's maybe not the best time to say this, Trent, but say it I must. I must warn you of your body's hunger. You're famished. You're on your third day in this cave."

"Crap," said Trent, quoting Calvin's quotation. "We're all out of toilet paper."

"Three whole days you've spent, manically giggling. The beard you've been growing makes you look like Guy Ramsley's guy, The Chosen. You never respond well hearing his name, so say it I won't.

Also you should know the president tracked your smartwatch and discovered your discarded clothes and is now searching up and down Eden's End for you, less for your value as an employee than your role in everything we've admittedly only briefly touched on."

"Last words are rarely significant things," said Trent Taphor, analyzing a quotation.

He said this way later, venomous with clarity's rage after making his way out of the caves only to once again find himself outside, deep inside God's Mouth, as though he were something caught way in back of God's throat, the perfectly wrong thing for God to choose to eat.

————

FOR MY PART, in retrospect, parts of that little scene told yours truly everything I'd need to know with respect to preventing the aftermath of the choice Trent's made, which, frankly, has doomed us all. Here's where I should've invested attention, in other words.

So to speak.

————

IF LIFE's a joke and perspective its punch line . . . what does that make me?

12

THE BAKERSFIELD PILGRIMAGE
(SPIRITUAL PENANCE)

FORMER HIGH SCHOOL principal Gary Mustafa gagged on the first tentative bite of meatball sandwich at the sight and sound of the masked woman's entrance.

The bell's treacly tinkle above the door set off inside Mustafa a melisma of alarms that had him diving under his table in his corner of the pizza shop. The masked woman walking in waved at the thirty-something woman seated nearby, who for the past hour already had Mustafa deeply unsettled, if only because she looked like a younger version of a creepily exact cross between Mother and the late Billy Mick's mother, Kimmi-Sue, Mustafa's lover never-to-be.

It wasn't until he felt safely tucked away from sight that he finally noticed he was choking on a chunk of meatball to the point of tears. He'd already held major reservations regarding the sandwich. The server who'd served him, Michelle, had kept pressing him on whether he was sure he wasn't really trying to order a meatball— a meatball by itself, she'd said, all on its own, she'd clarified several fudging times—and now this.

If he was seriously going to go out this way, five minutes before high noon in middle-of-the-road-rated Rufio's, he figured he'd do so with his eye on his guiding force, the Ladybug now ascending the bench's underlying web of wood supports.

The Ladybug seemed to shrink and magnify in size, blooming and wilting against blurs of brown, but for whatever reason, all Mustafa could think about was how he'd submitted his formal resignation letter via y-message to Allegiance High's superintendent five days ago while on the road from Gatlinburg to Berkshire. The road trip to this tiny wooded town marked his first time being outside of Tennessee since his bearing witness to the influx of new Tennessee arrivals seven or eight years ago, courtesy of the army of implicitly armed Skeeters. He didn't know about the guns in their spines back then. He'd known nothing of the force of their firepower. Their attitudes, helpfully informative but ultimately soulless, seemed to inform their less than nonviolent oversight of Polk's Ode to Destiny. Which Mustafa found depressing.

It ended up being the meatball-obsessed server Michelle who, after seeing what was happening, reached under Mustafa's bench and seized him by the back of his collar. She hauled him out from under his table, spiking the overall constriction in and around his throat, making his eyes bulge through an almost painful sting of tears. He flapped his arms about as Michelle got right up behind him and executed a maneuver Mustafa once dedicated an entire school assembly to. Mustafa, bent over and wheezing, took his sweet oxygenated time harnessing the wherewithal required to settle down and process what I've now wrapped up describing.

As we near the end, always where everything tends to get invariably sloppy, narratively speaking, as I'm sure You've noticed and duly understand, assuming You've taken into sharp consideration the sharply edged projectile that all this time—four seconds, thus far, relative to how my interdimensional counterparts construe time's passage—has been heading for my head, do forgive me this most recent narrative transgression and any others prior that, due in part to my admittedly imperfect aptitude for portraying truly true human beings, might've jumped out at You and Your all-seeing observer's eye. This here would include my visibly shaky-at-best knack for figuratively cracking open human heads and hearts as I try my hardest to convey supposedly authentic, if not entirely accurate, human thoughts and feelings. Surely by now You see how everything I've heretofore expressed has more or less been an honest and well-meaning attempt on my part to relay to You why You might seriously consider bringing the brief story of humanity to a hasty and hopefully painless conclusion, whatever my narrative limitations, trivial slip-ups in what I can only hope has been an account You've otherwise found comprehensive and immersive and above all representative of true truth as it pertains to anything and everything You. In other words, I submit the time's come for You to pull the plug on the human race, to use one of their precious few metaphorical phrases. Also I might as well slip in now how I'll soon be making my case on behalf of the interdimensional half whose sheer innocence in this whole apocalyptic snafu is exceeded only by their unwavering capacity for basic goodness and general goodwill, assuming Your patience and respect as a neutral party all-seeing observer has been earned by yours truly. All of this is to say I henceforth pledge to do my best to do away with my perspective on all of this—or at least reserve it until the start of the projectile's fifth and final second of flight, a preordained moment-to-be all but due to precipitate this ready and willing raconteur's inexorable decapitation. In this way, the instrument of my death will ring out its final note . . . but You already know that. Anyways, until then, starting now, I will hereby eliminate any further intrusions and subsequent digressions that might otherwise further compromise true truth as it pertains to my interdimensional counterparts' woefully limited points of view . . .

So back we go to Gary-Gopher Mustafa, floating on strings of everyday empathy. I hate it here in his head—don't You? I might as well be helium inside a popped balloon.

Nevertheless, Mustafa eyed over the top of Michelle's head to track the masked person now heading back for the shop's exit alongside the woman whose resemblance to Mother and Kimmi-Sue freaked him out as much as the thought of the masked person being part of Party White Patrol. Such had been his thinking, at least before he'd noticed his own choking. He remembered to thank Michelle even as he finished catching his breath.

"Thank you . . . for your assistance . . . I'll be sure to include . . . an optimistic review . . . of your business . . . with particular regards . . . to customer service."

"We here at Rufio's certainly value your business, sir," said Michelle. "Let me know if there's anything else I can do . . . and should you at any point find yourself in the mood for a meatball— wink, wink—seek and ye shall find me."

"No, thanks . . . I'm fine . . . with the sandwich."

"Word of warning, my boss is out of town. Went off to Bakersfield for some reason. I could try to find a way to reach him via Zoom or y-message if you want, assuming a meatball by itself is still on the table. You know . . . if you're picking up what I'm putting down."

At last Rufio's interior blurred back into focus, the tile flooring checkered black and white, the benches' vinyl sheeting checkered red and white. The brick oven's smoke curled from the porthole in the kitchen's piney paneling. Crammed together below the porthole were two short bookcases, shelves stocked wall-to-wall with spirits and mixers. A secondary stool-studded bar sat in back of Mustafa with plenty of beers on tap, a circa 1960s jukebox set beside the restroom hallway's entry playing some pop group Mustafa would never care to hear again. The shop's clientele— couple dozen late-forties, early-fifties men, maybe half that number in wives and teens, and one swarthy deer-in-the-head- lights-eyed kid obviously here on his own holding up a sign of a blown-up photograph of a sizable snake reading *Have You Seen Jennifer?* at the top—all watched him with nervous eyes hazy with drink. Wide square windows looked out on a spread of glass tables whose flimsy orange umbrellas did the bare minimum to block out the sun.

"Sure you're all right, sir?" said Michelle, gently steering Mustafa by the shoulder back to his corner beside the blaring juke. Another server was on hands and knees under Mustafa's bench, wiping up meaty splashes of marinara. "Maybe I could swing you a beer for your troubles. Care to give our home-brewed Brenda Pale Ale a try? My boss brews it himself."

Mustafa held Michelle's eye and jerked his head to gesture at the wide square windows.

"See the woman sitting outside with that person wearing a mask and what clearly must be a wig?" Michelle looked and nodded. "Do they, um, come around here often?"

"That, um, that's sort of a weird question, sir."

"Can you think of any reason why anyone should turn up here in disguise?"

"Well, sir, we here in Berkshire tend to take Halloween super seriously."

"I see . . . they say Berkshire puts on quite the *fiesta* every year."

"What they say is true, sir, at least in town, which we're on the furthest edge of."

"Yet no one else here's in costume," Mustafa observed. "I guess it is All Hallows' *Eve*."

"It would seem most everyone here's from out of town, sir, more than likely come to visit Eden's End. And of course the Berkshire cottage camps."

"Of course. Thank you again, Michelle. Mind if I use your restroom?"

"Men's room down the hall to your left, sir. Code's 1-2-3-4-5."

A fresh issue surfaced when Mustafa's trusty waft of wintergreen veered right instead of left, disappearing behind the big red door to the women's restroom. The Ladybug must've scuttled through the crack under the door, leaving Mustafa to contend with a keypad for which he had no code and obvious misgivings to which he'd clung his entire youth as a student and subsequent career. The Ladybug, however, had yet to lead him astray; it wasn't as though he'd been following the little guy blindly. The Ladybug had earned Mustafa's trust after using the Musker's central boxscreen's internet as a virtual map for navigating him through the entire process of leaving Gatlinburg, zipping from option to option to show which one he should be clicking on, helping him set his autopilot coordinates to Berkshire, reminding him of his password for reviewing the status of an application he hardly remembered submitting to Eden's End upon its grand opening. The bug's ethos thoroughly checked out, in other words. So Mustafa needed access to the women's restroom, even if he didn't yet know precisely why.

He stared at the door and sensed the Ladybug waiting for him on the other side.

Without his realizing, Mustafa had been typing into the keypad the reverse of the code he'd been told, counting down from five, and sure enough, there was a click to go with the door handle's sudden compliance. He threw a glance back down the hall to the shop proper, checking for snoopers and identifying none. Before he could psych himself out by reprising campus horror fables he'd been told as a youth about whatever may or may not go on in certain restrooms, he turned the handle and ducked inside, remembering to lock the door behind him manually.

The restroom bore an immediate resemblance to all other public restrooms he'd ever used, sans the urinals. It was disproportionately sizable relative to the shop's own size, three stalls scribbled with all the same pencil markings—*If your reading this and your name is Brenda, go find Michelle and order a meatball*, one message read, the misspelling of "you're" irking Mustafa to his core—four sinks and four mirrors, and five of what Mustafa, after some experimental fiddling, discovered were tampon dispensers.

Resting on the ledge above the last stall was a leatherbound ledger—Mustafa pocketed the weirdly arcane-looking thing on instinct because here was a lone window slightly cracked, and it was here Mustafa and the Ladybug reunited. He'd been so focused on following his nose that he'd neglected his ears' equally prudent information: two voices, female, floating through the window. He didn't need to hoist himself up onto the ledge over the toilet tank to confirm what he already knew, but he did so anyway, grinning to himself at the sight and sound of two esoteric women who, maybe ten minutes ago, had come this close to taking him out with their mere existence in his space alone.

One woman—the potential Party White Patrol spy potentially pursuing Mustafa for what he'd done to Billy Mick online, for the private messages he'd sent to the kid on Rate That Human—had her mask pulled above her mouth so that it appeared as though she had a second head and face bulging from the back of her head. The other woman was lost to view under the umbrella's bent orange top, which was just as well, given whom she reminded Mustafa of. He quickly calculated the distance separating them from himself, factoring in Rufio's geographical layout with its disproportionately sized restroom, and estimated fifty feet, give or take a few.

Good thing, then, both women soon began raising their voices.

?

"I believe you," Yew told Love, which relieved Love to hear. "There's definitely something trippy going on with the country. Not to mention your guy's totally peeping on us."

Love spied along the windows looking into Rufio's to no avail. "Where?"

"Behind me—ten o'clock your perspective, the barred little window just before the brick siding ends. Pretty sure it's a restroom, actually—you might have to duck some to see. Point is, I've been picking up on his energy for the last hour or so, since before I even got here, and now it's, like, totally burning into the back of my neck."

"You're high right now, aren't you?"

"I might've micro-dosed a bit."

"Someone hasn't changed much."

"It's true. I still wish myself one day younger every day," said Yew.

"I see him now," said Love. "Eek. Impressive, though, for you to notice."

"Mystic fullness is about a great deal more than self-awareness."

"Said no sober person ever."

"I'm glad you actually showed up," said Yew. "I've missed . . . this."

"What say we screw with this dude? Smoke him out of his hole . . ."

"You've got hard evidence this peeping Mufasa's from the Big Apple Coalition?"

"Not at all," said Love. "It's more of a hunch—a gut feeling."

"I can fully appreciate that."

"I just know he knows something. Like, even as we speak, I see him *smiling*."

"So?"

"So me and my Cats've been monitoring America awhile now, Yew, feeding her social narratives across political and ideological and whatever other societal spectrums you can think of for longer than I care to recall. And what I've basically learned is there's straight up nothing anyone anywhere should be smiling about anymore."

"Sheesh."

"It's true," said Love.

"What's true is that if you keep consuming too much of America like you are, there's no doubt in the world it'll start to affect your affect overall."

"Seems I could probably use a session with you."

"That may be true," said Yew. "Too bad I quit. Time's come for me to drift on."

"You know, you could've waited for me to call you back."

"I get this vibe you might've seen what happened with me and that nasty bitch of a client, Karen . . . which would only mean you Cats really *do* see everything."

"America's only got two great unsolved mysteries, Yew. One being what I've been talking about with this Halo Virus and whatever Mary's been up to with her wonderland up there in those mountains. How you got in and out of Bakersfield's the other."

"Actually the cat's halfway out of the bag with the latter, pun intended."

"Meaning?" said Love.

"Meaning I've told someone, recently, how I got in. The Hive, I mean."

"Wait, what! Who! Why!"

"So that makes three great American mysteries," said Yew, "but

I suspect this one'll die with this guy I told. Soon. Assuming it hasn't already."

"You're saying there's someone else currently trying to infiltrate the Hive . . ."

"First tell me why you left, Love. What I said or did—where I went wrong. Tell me your reason for over ten years of silent treatment even as the world dissolved."

"Maybe I was just young and stupid—as evidenced by my stint on reality TV."

"You'll have to lie better than that," said Yew. "It's an effort thing, deception."

"You've got something in your teeth," said Love. "Like sand or something."

"Don't get distracted trying to distract me—it won't work."

"Looks a bit like a bit of a certain Hollywood stuntman's ashes in your teeth."

"So you *have* been watching me," said Yew. "Let's leave Ash out of this."

"I've been watching you watch me, actually, but only these past few days."

"Is the peeping Mufasa still there? His energy's gone, like, way down."

"What if I told you the reason you'd rather not bring up your dead brother reflects my reason why I'd rather not discuss why I felt I had no choice but to leave you?"

"I get it," said Yew. "You're saying I remind you of your sister, that all this time you've basically seen me as a living embodiment of your most guarded trauma. Well, what if I told you trauma does far more to explain than excuse shit behavior?"

"You look like her," Love told Yew. "You look like Angel."

"I've been getting that a lot."

"It's pretty uncanny."

"Exhausting is what it is. This guy Philly said I—wait, never mind."

"So that's who's heading for the Hive," said Love. "Don Philly."

"Oh, you're good," said Yew. "I'm actually genuinely impressed."

"'A veil of effortlessness is the core effort effective deception requires.'"

"You flatter me," said Yew.

"Learned from the best."

"I don't know, Love. I was pretty much high all the time, saying those things."

"And you still are," said Love. "The best, I mean."

"So what's up with the body suit and mask? It'd be nice to see a friendly face."

"It's too bad, then, my mouth's all you'll get."

"Sheesh. *Love Beach* must've really done a number on you."

"By which I meant and still mean my voice," said Love. "All you'll get."

"So including both Mufasa and that creepy park ranger you mentioned earlier, I'm guessing here Don Philly's the third on your list of men of interest."

Love nodded. "Dude owns this shop, by the way, another so-called coincidence that only seems to confirm my instincts surrounding Mary's . . . project, we'll call it."

"The Halo Virus, you mean. Your source being the BAC's private server."

"Cat surveillance certainly seems to support the Coalition's working theory."

"Rampant solipsism, you said," said Yew.

"Rampant, *egregious* solipsism, a brain-borne bug sourced out of Eden's End."

"You're thinking that's what the president's hiding—the source."

"Among other possibilities," said Love. "There's also the question of why."

"I was going to ask, what's in it for you? Why do you care one way or the other?"

"Isn't it obvious?"

"Nothing ever is with you," said Yew. "You're too much human for one person."

"Well, assuming I can bottle some dirt on Mary—and I'm talking irrefutable evidence here, it should go without saying—I'd use it to get out of my contract with the Feline Freedom Society, demanding in turn full amnesty that would preclude my being sentenced to the Hive. I want my freedom back, in other words, to the extent freedom still exists. Besides, it's not like I have a choice anymore. PWP's already out on the prowl for me."

"To think we used to say we'd hack our way to freedom one day," said Yew.

"We're all fish in a fishbowl—they call us Cats to try to convince us otherwise."

"Say you succeed, Love, and you win back your snatch of freedom. Then what?"

"I'm convinced all that's missing from my life is my right to liberty."

"*All that's missing from my life is (x)* is a toxic mindset to have, you ask me," said Yew, sounding too much like someone else. "Truth is you're *always* going to want more. It's just how it works. Sooner you accept that, sooner you'll learn to taste the bit of bitter sweetness in every present moment this life has to offer. Bitter because it's *scary*, Love. It's scary being alive. Being alive and *aware*, however, must be downright terrifying."

"Now you sound like her," Love told Yew. "You sound like Angel."

"Mufasa's energy's back at it with a vengeance in my neck."

"It's *Mustafa*, Yew, as in *Gary* Mustafa, as in that Tennessee high school principal who made headlines last summer for consenting to Mary's highly controversial executive order granting Skeeter-5000s access to school campuses across all three Zones supposedly for security purposes, who recently made headlines a second time after his site-issued Skeeter thwarted a mass shooting at the hands of one Billy Mick."

"Actually, I think I remember hearing about that . . ."

"What I bet you *haven't* heard of was Mustafa's role in inciting the whole thing to begin with, going so far as to actually bully this Billy kid on Rate That Human, of all apps, where I came across a spot of fairly damning evidence that might in fact explain his flight from Tennessee and subsequent presence here and now."

"I say from here on out we raise our voices to smoke him out like you said."

Love said, "Follow my lead."

"Wait—who are we?" asked Yew. "Blue detectives? Big Apple Coalition?"

"We're Party White Patrol investigators, cybercrime division."

"Love it," said Yew. "Ready when you are."

Love raised her voice accordingly. "Quit acting so ignorant—as though you never received the classified document from PWP HQ containing step-by-step instructions concerning what to do with respect to this whole Mustafa mess!"

"Well, maybe we should be more concerned with plausibly viable domestic national security threats than small-fry Tennessee high school principals!"

Love could tell Yew was enjoying this as much as she. "You just don't get it, do you? We must locate Mustafa before the media gets to him first and exposes his reprehensible behavior on Rate That Human! It's not like American society can afford to have another inspirational hero's reputation utterly tarnished before the public eye!"

"Don't lose faith," said Yew. "You know as well as I that cyber-crime intelligence has pinned Mustafa's location right here in Berkshire. We're close! I can feel it!"

Love loved wiping the little-piggy smile from Mustafa's face in the window. "At least you've got that much right—when it comes to heroes, Mustafa's certainly small-fry. Which is to say we have two options once we finally nail him. Either we work with him to construct a publicly digestible narrative context to hand over to the Cats, thereby granting him amnesty for his cyber sins in the form of a brand-new identity altogether . . . or we can take him out and funnel our every resource into deleting him from public memory, so to speak."

"Yew lowered her voice, suddenly looking tense. "Is that what you meant by 'on the prowl'? Is the PWP really going to try to assassinate you, Love?"

"He's gone. From the window. I give it five minutes 'til he tries to run for it."

"Are you even armed or anything?"

". . ."

"You mean you actually go around carrying a cattle prod in your body suit?"

Love finished screwing in the metal hot stick to its plastic orange base and popped the cap guarding the trigger. "Sometimes words aren't enough," she said.

"Words can always be enough—we just have to learn to wield them responsibly."

"It's not like I brought this with me with Mustafa in mind." Love had picked this prod especially for its stealth, the way it administered electric shock silently. "In fact, coming here and running into him like this is probably the last thing I ever would've expected, to be honest."

"Even for you this seems a bit much."

"Trust me when I say I've been working on getting my empathy back," said Love.

"Your behavior says otherwise," said Yew. "Behavior is communication."

"The FFS uses these prods to herd unruly Cats into Soul's time-out cages."

"Guess that explains your body suit and mask."

"Working my way up to Head Cat Hacker was bound to leave its scars."

"You're a fugitive and former torture victim fleeing our ubiquitous president while simultaneously trying to extort her into affording you a new identity altogether."

"You really think you know everything, don't you?"

"I know what people too often use to overcompensate for any lack of love they receive growing up," said Yew. "Whatever their spiritual inclinations or limitations."

"Here we go."

"It's the only thing in the world whose brute force intensity matches love's—hate."

"I don't hate anyone anymore except for this one dude, Brad. Brock. Brad?"

"They're equal in power, love and hate, each a devastating equalizer of the other. What gets confusing's how they both tend to go inward before extending outward beyond ourselves. Not enough of us know we can love ourselves by loving others."

"Better hook it up with that acid you're on when all this is said and done."

Yew said, "Just chill out with using that thing on Mustafa is all I'm saying."

"Aren't you going to help me?" Love asked Yew. "Case he freaks?"

"If you promise not to use the cattle prod."

"You mean unless I have to."

"Look, if you want my help," Yew said, "words'll have to do."

"Has that dragonfly on your shoulder there been there this whole time?"

"I was about to ask the same about the butterfly on your knee."

"I've had this little dude, Calvin, for weeks—don't ask what he's been eating."

"What's he been eating?"

"I don't know," Love told Yew. "That's what I meant to say. I don't know."

The hour's main man made his move then. Love was watching him leave Rufio's through the front entrance no more than ten yards from where Love and Yew sat. He actually looked back as he waddled his way to the dirt lot's scattered cars like some lascivious teenager creeping to the bathroom to clean up the sticky mess he'd made of himself in the night. Love's grip on the cattle prod tightened, but before she could rise to give chase, Yew had reached over to place one hand on Love's shoulder, holding Love down and calming her, hooking Mustafa with her free hand's single curling and uncurling finger: *Come here, you.* He froze in place a solid fifty yards away, as though he, too, had heard what Yew sometimes called a "declarative vibe," leaning on the side of a rundown Musker that must've seen a decade of better days. He began clopping his way over with his slumped head and shoulders and too-big shoes and floppy loose tie and sweat-ringed armpits and face, a mug of misery. Gary Mustafa was and would surely remain the only man Love had ever seen who looked exactly like his name sounded. He all but collapsed at Yew's feet in the umbrella's scant shade as if to beg her for mercy.

"Please," he said, on hands and knees, head hung low, the back of his neck exposed.

"He smells better than he looks," said Yew. "It's like . . . pleasantly minty."

"Please what?" Love asked him.

"I could've made a break for it but decided not to not 'cause I want to die or make a deal or whatever it is you people do but because I'm convinced this is where I have no choice but to be— here and now, with you two." Mustafa's bald spot's scabby consistency betrayed an aging man who spent most of his time indoors but who every now and then stepped outside with the specific intention to burn. "Please, you've got to hear me out." Mustafa kept his head down as he rolled his hand over on the cement's single inverted square of window-refracted sunlight—Love pictured the skin on the back of his hand sizzling. A bizarrely vivid ladybug camped in the center of his open palm. "It's the Ladybug."

He said it as if the word deserved capitalization, mirroring the way his mother, Love recalled, postscripted her letters out of Riverview Psychiatric. The bug looked to Love like live stigmata. "Mother always knew: the Moon Man's come through the wormhole in the ashes." He pawed like a dog at the splotch of light on the cement with his empty hand, digging his nails in as if to scrape a hole—or a grave. "We've got until the witching hour. Together we must untether the Road from Mother Climate's hold."

"We're not part of the Party White Patrol," said Yew. "I'm sorry for agreeing with my friend here to mislead you in any way." She turned. "This man needs professional care, Love."

You made it! declared some unspoken vibe, *Yeah, baby! See you all at the Ritual!*

There came a silence, then, the sort Love associated with funerals for young people.

In the palm of Mustafa's hand, Yew's blue dragonfly and Mustafa's red ladybug flanked Love's monarch butterfly, Calvin, on either side. The color of Calvin's wings, drained and sickly like the umbrella's bleached canvas above, brought Jabronis's tired scales to mind, the way the old goldfish had paled from Heart's cheerless lack of natural light over time. All three bugs had rolled over in a line, still, as if their fate had always been to die trying to unite.

"A MAN," Don Philly replied.

"Access denied," said the dark shaft's walls' automated voice. "Please try again."

"A man?"

"Access denied. Please try again."

"*A man*, I said!"

"Access denied. Please try again."

Philly allowed himself a measured breath.

Suddenly a cluster of ceiling panels started acting up in a way that had him feeling claustrophobic and watched—some slid as others folded while others did something else altogether until most of the ceiling's center appeared to have dissolved. A ropy cable descended before his eyes, dangling on its end a wire-enmeshed strobe light flashing in soundless warning, the way lightning cautions thunder. Somewhere gears were grinding and turning unseen. Once more he regretted having neglected the advice of Brenda's spiritually adopted daughter, Yew, who told him to ditch his attire prior to this whole quasi-suicidal endeavor. The scratchy robe over his regular clothes over his sweat-flooded flesh made all of this all the more unbearable.

"A *man*," he said, mad to hear his voice crack on *man* in the shaft's hollow echo.

This time the panels in the surrounding walls did all the moving and shifting around until five sizeable holes had budded all along the shaft at head level. His shadow flickered in the silent crash of strobes as though his body's lifeforce verged on burning out. What ended up coming out of those holes—five cylindrical, seriously imposing steel extensions glaring mere inches from his eyes no matter which way he turned, each girthy cannon complete with six barrels revolving around a central axis—had Don Philly clutching for the useless chunk of skin to which he found the rest of himself attached. The Gatling guns purred in place, their ends doing slow revolutions.

"Access denied. You have one try remaining."

———

EXACTLY TWENTY-FOUR HOURS BEFORE, after Don Philly wrapped up his exploration of Bakersfield—a self-guided tour of five grueling days—he decided once and for all he'd go ahead and try to infiltrate President Mangrove's notoriously mysterious Hive. To do so he knew he'd have to follow the step-by-step instructions provided by the woman back at Brenda's grave, that hauntingly familiar Yew who turned out to be Brenda's spiritually adopted daughter.

Philly figured he'd better follow Yew's every directive to a T, but with one slight amendment: he'd keep the one pair of clothes he'd brought with him firm on his body. He arrived at this conclusion on a shady embankment beside the Kern River, wringing out his shirt and slacks, self-reflecting with his own reflection. This remained his main way of getting in touch with the bug inside, Guy Ramsley, who told Philly to quit wasting time and head to the Hive's fortress under the dose of moonlight necessary for Guy to take over Philly's body.

One either needed to read one of the many signs in place or heed one of the many widely disseminated rumors to know the Kern, once popular for its wilderness hiking and whitewater rafting, was now mainly known for being hazardous. The slippery smooth granite slates that lay in and around the turbulent strait had claimed well over a hundred lives over the years, not counting fifty-five souls lost all at once to a rafting accident, a tragic ending to a San Luis Obispo summer camp field trip that resulted in the river's being allegedly haunted by fifty little kids and five early-twenties counselors whose apparitions were reported to remain eternally bent on raiding your camp for beer. The smell that hung in and around the city—always most potent out of East Bakersfield, near what used to be the Kern oil field but what was now the Hive's stronghold—was best described as a combination of smog and manure.

The stench used to come and go, two old-timers had told Philly in a bar in the city, which prior to World War III and the Treaty of the Divided Alliance had been the USA's fifty-fifth most populous. Once a sprawling hub for agriculture and energy production, Bakersfield had since become the nation's "ghost capital" haunted by big-oil retirees (such as these two glibly effusive geezers) fortunate enough to "pull [their] cocks out" in time for the first of many unmarked drones to drop its first of many nuclear bombs across the globe. The war had thoroughly obliterated every major Bakersfield industry, from natural gas and oil extraction to mining and petroleum refining. Only food processing and distribution remained, taken over of course by an obscure farming corporation no one had ever really heard of until long after the nation's formally signed agreement to disagree and divide accordingly. Don Philly, of course, knew exactly who was responsible for the re-reconstructed republic's Bags of Food sold nationwide, though he couldn't recall whether The Dark had any one leader or figurehead presently in place laboring to guide the way forward for the country's only remaining immediately relevant industry. In response to all the doom and gloom happening on and perpetuated by Red and Blue news cycles alike—which then, as now, sniped you out utilizing the internet's infinite modes and angles—most top big-energy Bakersfield executives ended up leaping from the tops of their corporate regional offices. Most of these buildings were built not all that tall, which Philly thought explained all the wheelchairs littering streets already moribund with neglect. Cracks spiderwebbed underfoot all over.

The two old-timers at the bar were who pointed Philly to the Kern —he'd asked for a good place to guzzle beer and escape.

Bakersfield's arterial streets were laid out in a grid running north-south and east-west, squares within squares within squares, the "Bakersfield sound" nowadays given to death metal blaring from shattered apartment windows. The graffitied lots of abandoned shopping centers became home to razed mobile homes and diesel trucks raised on row after row of stacked cinderblocks. These days the stench no longer came and went, one old-timer had lamented, citing his constant longing for the blip of time when Bakersfield's rank air quality hadn't been America's worst ranked. Drinking alone on the riverbank beside the Kern, Philly now noted the absence of honeybees, plagued by thoughts of the bumblebee he'd followed to Bakersfield but had somehow lost moments before he'd first stumbled his way onto the sidewalks into the city, absentmindedly banging his shin against the first of many discarded wheelchairs.

Guy Ramsley seemed to suggest the likelihood of finding the bumblebee somewhere in or around the Hive was high, arguing there was where Philly really ought to be. Philly told the bug inside he'd go but that it didn't matter a lick what that quick-witted Yew thought: he'd keep his clothes firm on his body. He wasn't about to make a fool of himself neglecting the lessons he'd learned over the extensive course of his own hard-earned research. To think he'd begun researching for the next great American novel over a decade ago, naked with an apple in his mouth, roasting over open flames, only to progress his prewriting one year later by hallucinating his way to the world's most costly erection. He'd come too far *not* to learn from his every prior mistake, unlike some half-baked character from some ill-conceived tragicomedy.

When finally he approached the Hive under the cover of darkness, Philly was quick to discover Guy Ramsley had been dead-on with his assumption about the bumblebee because there it was, his bumblebee, the very one he'd shadowed all the way to Bakersfield. Or maybe it was the other way around. Regardless there it was, hovering in back of the Hive's northernmost warehouse. His bumblebee floated inside the hoop of one of the nooses dangling from the trees.

Even at night it was clear to Philly that many of the Kern oil field's drills and pumpjacks had been broken down and reconstructed to erect the Hive's assorted towers and silos and warehouses. The otherwise drab kenopsia was sucked dry of all imaginable life, otherworldly in its abject barrenness. He sensed more Skeeters on patrol than he could outright see beyond the barbwire fencing, their majority absence very much a felt thing. Don Philly, sixty-five, handed over the keys to his body to Guy Ramsley, consenting to whatever might follow, including the agony in his hips he would doubtless come to with. The next thing he knew, he was alone with himself in a dark room—what he took to be some sort of elevator shaft—when the voice in the walls asked, "What useless bit of skin is doomed to come attached to the base of a phallus?"

————

DON PHILLY WAS STARING down one of six barrels on one of five Gatling guns protruding from the walls with their killer snouts trained on his head when suddenly, in what he sensed could've been his last seconds, he remembered the second half of what Yew had told him would be essential to his response, and he said, "A man," this time with that drab air of depleted spirit people have when intoning *Amen* in certain spiritual contexts. All five Gatling guns withdrew into the walls before Philly could see what they were mounted on, disappearing from the strobing gloom like eels evading those teethy bioluminescently bulbed demon fish haunting the ocean floor. He kept his eyes drilled on the ropy cable's single flashing strobe, tracking its ascent to the ceiling. The surrounding panels reshifted and refolded, unseen gears grinding and turning in reverse until once more he was alone in the dark with the shaft's walls' toneless voice.

"Access granted. Pod 55 is now being rerouted. Your patience is required."

Philly had learned to tell time through his craving cycle. Since his stomach recoiled at the thought of uncooked pizza dough, it meant the night had passed and he'd blown right through breakfast. When the thought of cherry Chapstick brought on a rumble within, wetting his lips with fresh spit, he was able to put the hour somewhere between noon and three. The lack of immediate threat to his life in the form of military grade superweapons allowed him to focus more on his body, the steady throb in his hips, the kinks in his neck, his every enervated joint and muscle. Oil-slick sweat stormed over his skin and moistened it. By his estimate, assuming Guy Ramsley had followed through with Yew's suggested "Trojan Horse" break-in method, Philly must've spent no less than nine hours cramped in a crate with useless Skeeter parts.

"Pod 55 is clear for departure," the impassive voice intoned.

Philly started where he stood.

"Prior to your descent to the Honeycomb," the voice droned, "Mangrovia Technology Corps requests you enjoy a word from our sponsor. We here at Eden's End wish you wonder."

"Guess we're going down, then," said Philly.

"Are you depressed? Suicidal? Are you alone with yourself, by yourself?"

"I don't know," said Philly, happy to hear a human voice. "Maybe a little."

"Introducing the brand-new, new and improved, FDA-eschewed recreationally medicinal breakthrough of the century: Magic Pillgrim!"

"What's 'eschewed' mean, I wonder."

"We here at Magic Pillgrim have been hard at work in our groundbreaking labs across an entire sliver of the great state of Idaho for over a decade, making sure—and this is one hundred percent guaranteed—we infuse the pellets in our capsules with natural Western organics sure to urge you to rediscover the magic, inside and out!"

Don Philly busied himself trying to find Idaho on a map in his head.

"For just twelve simple monthly payments of $19.99 plus shipping and handling, you subscribe to our yearly prescription that'll cost—wait for it—FIVE DOLLARS. Five bucks, people—the cost of a cup of coffee—and we'll help you process what you simply cannot expect yourself to process alone, one Magic Pillgrim at a time."

"Now hang on there a minute."

"Simply y-message 'Help me' to 1-500-HELP-US-HELP-YOU—again that's 'Help me' to 1-500-HELP-US-HELP-YOU—sign the agreement for the five-dollar deal and we promise you'll be saying goodbye to money-grubbing charlatans playing doctor, so long to pills playing Band-Aid, and hello to pseudo-pharmaceutical happiness in its purest form! One more time: y-message 'Help me' to 1-500-HELP-US-HELP-YOU, sign the five-dollar deal. It's Magic Pillgrim. If life's a journey, we're your destination."

"What's 'why message'?"

"Thank you for your patience. Your spiritual penance commences in five . . . four . . ."

"Maybe I've made a mistake."

"Three . . ."

"No—I *will* find my ending."

"Two . . ."

"This is for you, America!"

"One."

Gravity gripped him by the throat as he dropped.

Don Philly's legs set to thrashing, his feet connected to and supported underneath by nothing at all. It seemed as though the floor itself had been swept out from under him, the immediate blast of vertigo like an all-out cannonade assault sent from the pit of his belly to all areas of the brain. He was trying and failing to command his body to quit flailing his arms so that he could use his damn hands to rip away the overseer robe now wrapping his whole head and face. His roaring blood hurled everything inside into chaos.

He was falling and flailing, and maybe in reality those five Gatling guns had gone off and this heat and queasiness and inability to see anything were what portended one's descent into hell, assuming his family's faith had it right all along, goddamn Catholics.

Something inside told him to relax already and embrace the fall.

Don Philly hadn't come anywhere close to getting himself to submerge himself fully in swimming pools or ponds or any other bodies of water since Beatrice Betsy and Lyle, but he well recognized the muted but no less thunderous crash that came when he hit the liquid surface. The sound of the water's underworld rushed up even as it dragged him down. His double layer apparel made the whole sinking and swallowing thing twice as worse, the overseer cloak riding up in his eyes and hiding any light for him to focus on once the pain of drowning had gone. It was everything he could do to keep all the saltwater from getting into his eyes, from using his nostrils as an alternative path to the back of his throat, which burned in gag-reflexive protest.

The more effort he put into resisting the water's will, the more it hurt to think there was no one alive who could dive in and save him —so here he was, sinking and thinking how the writing process worked much the same. At least he would die for a second time having practiced what he preached, he thought, remembering the last golden plum he'd ever post to BookTok, how great books required no effort and therefore no pain to produce, how the universe delivered ideas packaged and parceled on a silver platter of transmission so long as writers learned to sit back in their souls and listen. Philly decided here and now he'd drown the same way, with effortless grace, which was why he wasn't all that surprised to realize his body was back on the rise. The universe, after all, took care of those who let it go about doing its sacred work.

Philly's robe had rolled up into something of a parachute to which he found himself attached; up and up and up hc went, propelled from underneath, rising like heat itself to the surface. No sooner had his face and arms and chest and legs breached simultaneously than he forgot himself and his body entirely. He was still getting used to being some other thing floating on its back and relearning to breathe on its own when the brightest light he'd ever known exploded where a moment before all had been darkness. Seconds of staring into this light's atomic flower annihilated all sense of where he was, and why.

. . . he comes to on a beach with no memory of what's come before, washed ashore like a mariner freshly marooned, the breakers thrusting him toward the shoreline inch by inch, and he lets this go on for a time. He lies on his belly. The sunlight slapping down on his bare back cooks his skin at three distinct levels of heat, and after getting to his knees, he sees why. Three separate suns share the cherry sky, each its own size burning from its own distance. He's got a vague sense he's been here before, though he can't remember when nor the circumstances then, as now. All he knows is what he wants, and what he wants is to shed himself of wanting at all. He doesn't even know his own name. He thinks it could be . . . Calvin?

He rises, peers left and right and ahead and behind, and before he can react or even compute in his head what he's seeing, he finds himself being encroached on all sides by a swarm of human-sized jellyfish. But they're hovering well above the waterline, moving with the current's languid flow, their bloodred tentacles spinning like propellers skimming the surface. They don't move in a way to warrant any threat, really, and yet they're closing in. A closer inspection of their form clarifies the misidentification: the "jellyfish" are organs, stomachs fused with livers fused with hearts, their "tentacles" rapidly churning intestines defying gravity, the way those ropes dangle and bear the weight. The more he tries sidestepping their all-sides approach, the swifter they move to encircle him. He's got a sense they're gawking at him, like he's the weird guy here, a suspicion soon confirmed by their voices, which eke through on a subdued frequency he thinks he remembers having heard maybe one other time before.

"I mean, just look at it," says one gory intestintacled blob. "Disgusting."

"Is it the same one from before, you think?" says another.

"What's it doing?"

The man's hiding his penis in both hands.

"It's the same. I remember it doing this last time."

"Does it speak, you think?"

The man's been trying.

"They say these things look like us on the inside."

"I wouldn't put too much weight in what they say."

"We could open it up and find out."

"Look at all those bulges—and those *holes*."

"They say we Visceranians've devolved into these things on other worlds."

"They also say these things exist here and now in this one, apart from us."

"If only our kind could survive on kindnessless land and find out."

"Does it think, you think?"

"Note the coloration on its front and back—note the difference."

"Which is which?"

"There's the back and here's the front."

The man can't tell who's speaking nor how many of them there are.

"Is it weird I want to take it home with me?"

"Note the crack dividing these two curvatures, here in front—note its hole."

"That there's the back."

"Who made you the expert?"

"I want to take it home and domesticate it."

"That's weird."

"Fine. I want to take it home and open it up."

"That's less so."

"How can we know for sure it's even alive?"

He tries pointing beyond the triple-sunlit horizon to get them all turned around.

"I somehow get this vibe it responded to us just now."

"Maybe it's dead on the outside but alive on the in."

"Or else it's the other way around."

"If only there were an easy way to find out."

"Note the fuzz covering these two appendages, holding it up somehow."

"If those hold it up, what do you think these other two less fuzzy feelers do?"

"They say these things rule half the worlds on which they're found."

"You put way too much weight in what they say."

"Why do you care if I care what they say?"

"'Cause if what you all say's true, that may imply these monsters rule *this* world."

"These things obliterate the other half of their native worlds, they also say."

"So where does that leave us? What are we to do with it?"

"I say we get it opened up."

The man sends them all twin-fisted middle fingers.

"Why's it whirling around like that? What's it doing with its feelers' feelers?"

He keeps both middle fingers raised.

"Maybe that itty-bitty morsel dangling amid its supports could be useful."

The man resumes shielding his penis.

"They say these're relatively harmless when they're all by themselves like this."

"Anyone who says that's full of feces—there's a terrible power in oneness."

"We're *all* full of feces."

"You know what I mean."

"No, I don't."

"I'm speaking in generalities—you wouldn't understand . . . it's philosophy."

"Note the liquid the two tiny orbs up here seem to excrete— note its clarity."

He doesn't think he's blinked.

"Does it feel, you think?"

"Let's get it open and find out."

They swirl in on him, squirming too close for cozy, and the man, who knows what to do upon coming into too-close contact with a bear raiding your camp for scraps, lifts his arms straight in the air to make himself as big and tall as possible, rising on tiptoe to the extent that he can, flexing his calves to withstand the shin-high waterline's current. Something slimy brushes his heels and leaves a burny irritation there, forcing a garbled scream from his throat. The tips of his toes dig into the mush underwater, diminishing the height he's manufactured. He's lucky he sinks no more than four inches before the blobs all shriek and scatter out to sea. He doesn't watch their retreat.

He breaks for the beach at an all-out sprint instead, pumping his arms and raising his knees against the receding tide until he's clear of the shoreline. His feet whap the smooth, damp sand on his way to the short but steep plateau he scales to the dunes, where he slumps down, wipes the sweat from his mouth and brow, and rips one last look around, relieved to see no subaquatic innards from hell giving pursuit. The skyline glares redly.

The "Visceranians" have all vanished under the sea as far as he can tell, though he sends them all two more middle fingers for good measure. Whichever beast wants him opened up didn't come close to sounding as though it were full of figurative feces.

Rolling dunes stretch away from the sea and beyond, wave after wave of sand as white as bone blushed with the triple suns' bloody glow. Curlicue scratches of forest haunt the distant new horizon, a green convexity blinking in and out of existence like the world's most obvious mirage. It's all he has to go on, this mirage, so he rises and gets moving.

He ends up trekking across endless hills and humps, frying in the heatwaves the sand dunes trap. Several times over, he tallies in his head his every step until he loses count and starts over again. Towering dust devils spin over the sands and dictate the speed and direction of his progress. Sourceless moaning disturbs the air with its ghostly distance.

Far more seconds than footsteps pass before the man meets the mirage up close.

He keeps himself hidden on his belly on top of a dune at least fifty yards distant, overlooking something of a lagoon extending at least fifty good strides across. The wounded light turns the water the same earthy shade as bile. The mirage as seen from a distance must result from the way three separate sources of light clash and slash on and off the surface. The lagoon itself stews within an enormous square ditch lined on every side by guys and gals and children all holding hands and taking in the sky's crimson brilliance, too many to count without losing count. The man watches all from above.

One group of five splits off in a wide circle to one side, isolating themselves from the seemingly paralyzed pack. Maybe twenty feet separate each person marking his or her point of the curved arc they've formed. Their circle's diameter matches an Olympic pool's width, the man guesstimates, shuddering at the association, an inner reflex he can't really comprehend.

Back and forth this solitary group of five begins lobbing four separate objects, cloth-swaddled and melon-sized, high into the air. Their apexes subtly increase with each toss so that by the fifth round of tossing, the objects fly dead even with the man's sightline.

Ghostly moaning returns, having mutated into a mind-piercing mewling.

Moon-colored cloth whips in the air as the objects themselves flip and spin on the way up and twirl and whirl on the way down, falling into the outstretched hands of four of the five, who cradle and rock the object in their arms before the group reaches a silent agreement to relaunch. The five function like some obscene juggling act, the way they operate in sync, four catching and releasing simultaneously while the one who's left out and waiting for a shrouded item's return hides their face in both hands and sobs. Whoever gets left alone to weep for whichever round of tossing is always the one the man on the dune ends up focusing on. He's got a spot for people who bury their faces in their hands, an avuncular urge to reach out and say Hey, I do the same.

"Babies," a slippery-as-butter voice behind him says. He wriggles around to find himself facing another man who boasts Gordon Ramsley's pearly ice-chip eyes and Guy Fury's sun of spiked hair, whose girth around the middle lands somewhere between the two master chefs'. His fixed expression is an impossible splice of simmering fury and mildly even-tempered tranquility. "Those're four babies those five're flinging around."

" . . . "

"Don't bother with your mouth in this place, Mr. Philly. Use your heart to speak."

"..."

"Maybe don't try so hard. Sit back in your soul and listen."

"Where . . . am . . . am . . . I . . . dead?"

"Hardly, Mr. Philly. Though, once again, you would be, without me."

"Who . . . are . . . are . . . you . . . real?"

"See each thought through to its conclusion to minimize confusion."

"Who . . . are you?"

The chefs' intertwined doppelgänger flickers like a projection.

"All right, so here's the deal. Deep down, you don't know you know I'm Guy Ramsley, the bug who's been living in your liver and who's twice had to pop in to redirect you from Death, where I've been dying to end up since time out of mind. For some time now—since you bestowed unto me the intrinsic power of a name, a.k.a. my independence—you've been assisting my campaign for my right to death, liberty, and the pursuit of mortality. This world you see here's located between Life and Death, strung someplace along the interdimensional double-knot so binding your side to mine, a.k.a. we're somewhere on Phooka Road, my birthplace inside the ashes. If you want to get all technical about it, we're in P.R. Dimension Five Sector T, six slips of inverted space away from Sector Z, which is where we'll need to go. That is, presuming you're still onboard with returning the favor for my saving your life twice by helping me bring about my own permanent demise."

"Who . . . am I?"

"You're the soul-fire of Don Philly's consciousness, here to confront your worth as a man of the earth. Your actual body's floating in a pool of manic mushroom extract in a sensory deprivation chamber in a cursed place America's so-called president calls the Hive, located in an even more cursed place your world's inhabitants call Bakersfield. You reached the Honeycomb with my assistance, as I've been taking direction from a significant called

Calvin, who's been appearing to you as a bumblebee and who's most likely the key to killing me."

"Why . . . babies?"

"Sector T handles time. The babies are your side's future as it presently stands."

"Sounds pretty . . . bleak."

"I never once lied when I said the Hive's where you'd find your ending."

"Is there still time . . . to revise . . . accordingly?"

"I see your memory's coming back on a conscious level. This is good news!"

"I don't want . . . *not* to want . . . I want . . . to write . . . spectacularly."

"You said the same thing the last time we spoke in this place, the first time we met face-to-face, and I'll have you know my response hasn't changed. I'm hardly sorry to report, for the second time, your side's severed all connection to the language of true truth. Sadly, the story of humanity's one from which no one'll ever glean any useful meaning."

Philly faces back to the present state of the future. "I've been here . . . before . . ."

"Indeed, Mr. Philly. You first arrived after the Trauma Drama wrapped, after choking on a sock someone shoved a bit too far back in your throat, killing you for five or six seconds—but of course I'd been there to steer you here then, as now. We spoke of memory, if you remember, and you mentioned something about time being cruel in its rate of passing, to which I replied—"

"I count . . . three babies now," says Don Philly. "What's that . . . about?"

"Time's three-way motion is subject to constant change and evolution."

"Are you saying . . . time . . . is a narrative?"

"Should you decide to drive, Mr. Philly, I suppose time will tell."

"I've got . . . endless drive . . . inside."

"What I'm really trying to say is you weren't supposed to die in the Hive. You weren't supposed to freak out and drown your insides in all the manic mushroom extract you ended up swallowing in all your panic. Truth be told, I never thought there'd be time enough for you to go out that way, in fact, given all the salt in the sensory deprivation pool that helped propel your body almost instantly to the surface. In fact, if we merely reconsider key events from over a decade ago, *you* weren't supposed to be there at all."

"What's wrong . . . with me?"

"I suppose it's your timing, Mr. Philly. Your timing tends to bungle things up."

"But I'm . . . The Chosen."

"Not so, Mr. Philly, for Lord Bed's prophecy, if you recall, spoke of a man named Ron, not Don. This here would be Ron Filly. He was supposed to be the one. Not you."

"I won't . . . sit here . . . and lie . . . that hurts . . . to hear."

"Ron Filly was supposed to be the one to suffer the same spiritual penance as all the other bodies now floating in the pool beside you. Among these bodies is that which belongs to Paul Brokerstaff, the Big Apple Coalition rep with the false eye who visited you in Rufio's basement once before and who's presently paying penance to America's 'president' for capturing unsavory sights out of Eden's End on camera. Your favorite park ranger didn't like the look of him."

"I now count . . . two babies . . . the mewling's growing . . . softer."

"Anyways, Ron Filly was supposed to receive and decode prescient visions that would've shown us exactly how to derail Bod's and Mr. Moony's team effort attempt to extricate Phooka Road from Earth. Or how to stop those two from using the Super Substance they've been harvesting to power the Pain Train's trip to another double-knotted dimension—one whose Mother consents to housing kindness breathers and shamelessness excreters, such as that pejorative pack of Visceranians you briefly crossed paths with to begin your pilgrimage here."

"You're . . . full of feces."

"And you're Don Philly, not Ron Filly, so we'll just have to make do."

"What . . . if anything . . . can I do?"

"Being Don Philly—a sort of replacement The Spider must've landed on with vast reluctance—you'll never get a chance to derail Bod and Mr. Moony *directly* . . ."

"Spider?"

"Yes, The Spider. She who weaves the Web you call reality, we call infinity."

"Sounds like . . . a big deal."

"Mother Climate's Contract of Basic Goodness is the only deal we need concern ourselves with, but I see no point paralyzing you with all the little details concerning Mother Climate's demands for a 100 percent death toll return on investment in humanity. Which, of course, had been contingent upon humankind's inability to unite as one human body in the face of a divided end. Instead, let's zero in on the Ritual of Five and Five."

Philly's hands flicker like something insubstantial, vaguely transparent.

"But see, Mr. Philly, if you're going to persuade Trent the way you must to get us what we mutually desire—and this goes deep down for you, like you don't even know you know that what I want is what you've wanted all along, like it or not—you're first going to need Trent's brother, Calvin, who's gone to see The Spider in Sector Z."

"Why would he . . . what good would . . . that do anyone?"

"Only Calvin has grown inward enough to put The Spider in Her place."

"Obviously . . . I'm being driven . . . irrevocably insane."

"As for your sanity, well . . . that at one point legitimate but now ultimately unfounded concern's precisely why I've done everything in my concededly not unlimited power to prevent you from receiving full-on and all at once the extraneous details detailing all the territories and entities and calamities it's taken me too long to get around to mentioning. Other words, it'd take time and merciless repetition to get you past where you are, state-of-understanding-wise, but as you may've gathered from the steadily vanishing babies' waning cries for help from hope itself, time's no longer on our side."

"I met Trent . . . only once . . . and yet . . . I see him . . . as a son."

"Probably a lingering consequence of the emotive power of the letter you'd delivered to him shortly before this past decade of doom got off to a truly sickening start. What you never knew about that letter—because at the time it'd suited my interests to refrain from filling you in on all of the context—was how Trent had written it himself, to himself, from the perspective of his father, that perhaps for the first time in your less than illustrious career as an aspiring aspiring writer, words on paper triggered something inside you of truly true value. Trent too. It's this significant something—what Mr. Moony calls 'substance'—that's allowed you both to keep your heads in the empathy game even as you've each danced the empathy dance somewhat out of step. That's all this is about—it's all all of this has ever been about. Strip away the Contract and the mindlessly bureaucratic clutter of it all, and we're left with the human body, the question about what to do with it as soon as the last word's been said, the last deed . . . done."

"Who gets . . . the last word . . . meaning . . . the final say . . . on everything?"

"The fateful five—of which you're now a part, like it or not—are all set to take part in a verbal exchange wherein you'll state or not state whatever you think and feel you need to say or withhold according to your own interests. This'll be your kind's last collective chance to bear some semblance of influence over what'll likely turn out to be humankind's final meaningful act, to be or not to be carried out by Trent in Mother Climate's presence. Now, just because you'll never get a chance to derail Bud and Mr. Moony *directly*—you being Don, *not* Ron—it doesn't mean you still can't make your mark. In this regard, the ritual's your first, last, and only hope."

"Now there's . . . one baby . . . can't even . . . hear it."

"Truth is, most Apocalypses stem from silence."

" . . . "

"Which is to say that whatever you end up saying throughout the ritual will almost always end up meaning less than what you manage *not* to say, in that true truth's implicit in nature, impossible for mere humans to use their mouths to go about articulating. The silence through which true truth is conveyed is the stuff of which most Apocalypses are made because silence breeds zero forms of consent. Silence merely amplifies whatever's being said, and nobody ever says the right thing."

"I don't know . . . what to say."

"Now don't say *that*," says Guy Ramsley. "That would imply you're worthless."

"I'm sick and tired of going places and getting nowhere at all."

"That's more like it, Mr. Philly—that's how to use your heart to speak."

Something's been going on with the lagoon, pulling Philly's focus from the five figures juggling the babies that embody the earth's current future—something in the water, looks like, bubbling to the surface. He rises for a better look. The people lining the huge ditch have quit holding hands, their formerly skyward stares directed in one new direction.

Don Philly feels every last eye boring down on one part of him.

"I've realized something truly terrible," says Philly, watching the water fizz below.

"I already know all things you don't know you know—including what you're about to say, which you've been suppressing on your hollow quest for immortality. Spit it out, Mr. Philly. Free yourself of this lurid dream holding the body we share prisoner."

"If I were to publish all this one day—my whole adventure, I mean, from Florida to California, from three wives to none, from the bed in my shop's basement to the center of the universe, from life to death to life again to death again to the present—I've realized whatever I end up putting to the page will forever be misunderstood. My words will be immortalized, to be sure, but only as a beacon of what *not* to do or say or write. People will read the shame in my truth for what it isn't—some unconscious attempt on my part to impose my phallus on the consciousness of America, to lecture readers on what it means to be a thinking man in a literary landscape oversaturated with similar lectures from men who look and think and feel like me. Truth is, Guy, I hate my penis. Always have. I mean, just look at it. It looks like the word *moist.* And I haven't felt much of anything in a very, very long time. All I do is think and sink —I always end up sinking. It seems my own little version of pursuing immortality's been a pursuit of the exact opposite this whole damn time."

"As I believe I've said, Mr. Philly, what you and I desire comes out to the same."

"It's not all that great, being dead, nor is it so bad. It just sort of is what it is."

"And what of life?"

The bulging thing in the water breaches the surface like something resurrected—Philly's Punch Buggy Orange, the car he abandoned on the road to nowhere like a boy leaving behind a toy never to be played with again, risen from the center of the lagoon below. He pictures the vehicle's mini version, his last-ever gift from Eli Elf, the Christmas myth who cared more for him than any other boy, the first fiction he ever believed in. Ma and Pa had lied out of love, and Philly's dream to drive had been born. There's no limit to what stories can do, the impact they might have on those born to grow up fighting to stay forever young inside.

"Life's a pain," says Don Philly. "I'm ashamed to even speak of it."

"You speak of shame like someone who misunderstands its most basic function."

"I don't deserve yet another chance to dream and drive. I deserve to die."

"Men who're ashamed of their own shame only become useful when they utilize shame as a means of preventing themselves from driving themselves to commit heinous acts wholly empty of empathy. Shame, in other words, has its own pivotal place in all of this. See, for instance, the interdimensional cancer afflicting Mother Climate, this egregious lack of kindness flowing in from Earth, your side of the double-knot. With so little kindness getting in from your side, see, very little shame gets out from our side, exacerbating a cycle thusly turned vicious. The more my kind suffers kindnessless-ness, the more your kind suffers shamelessness, when maybe all we all deserve is the chance to have our say."

"There's something different about my car. Like it's made of something else."

"*Urechis caupo,*" says Guy Ramsley. "What your kind calls 'innkeeper worms,' colloquially known as 'penis fish'—or simply 'penish.' They've been turning up by the thousands on the shores of your side only recently, but the truth is, they drill web-holes for subterranean lifeforms across *all* interdimensional sectors. You ask me, they're perfectly shaped for three hundred million years of life spent largely submerged."

"What're they doing here?"

"It would appear, Mr. Philly, the Infinite Sum One is reweighing your worth."

The five figures begin juggling five new babies, Philly sees, the renewed mewling a reminder to all who would care to listen that they're all still very much alive.

Nobody anywhere is being left alone to weep.

"It seems you've indeed been given the opportunity to try to revise accordingly," says Guy Ramsley. "This'll be your chance to weigh what's worth living for against who's worth dying for—to rework your approach to reclaiming your worth as a man."

"I'm a revision in progress, you're saying. I'm not what The Spider wanted. I'm not Ron Filly," says Don Philly. "But you're saying I can choose to use that penis fish car to pick up Calvin in Sector Z—even though it'd be a suicide mission to drive him home."

"Let's remove the core source of menace. One last time, let's you and I work as one to erase Mr. Moony from existence and deliver us both the deliverance we deserve."

13

PHOOKA ROAD

(A BODY THING)

———

Somewhere in East Texas, way back when Americans were more or less united in believing the Dream to be the capturable mechanism it never really was, before a great many, upon critical reflection, learned to see the Dream for the killing machine in the socioeconomic slaughterhouse it turned out to be despite the early emergence of seemingly innumerable success stories pointing to the contrary—inexplicable outliers blissfully and/or willfully unaware of the cultural and/or societal impact their pull-yourself-up-by-your-bootstraps mentalities would have on peddling what had always been the greatest con the world had ever seen, spurring on a rat-race market of markets fraught with similar schemes manifestly designed to expand companies into corporations whose profit margins hinged on putting artificial intelligence and only the cheapest labor forces to work, all of which operated under a system-ically coordinated effort to exploit the downtrodden on a global scale even while sowing (via social media marketing) domestic disdain through which "lazy" or "entitled" pariahs who "get what they deserve" received much blame while a scant but very powerful

349

few who "deserve what they get" became universal objects of envy, thus drying up a supposedly bottomless well of wealth and opportunity in an isolated territory whose destiny to devour itself from the outside in spent over three hundred years camouflaged within the imperialistic guise of American exceptionalism—Dex the meat cleaver was born in a rage of sparks, shaped with saw and hammer in a white-hot haze of heat. Sharpened at an angle between thirty and thirty-five degrees, he was made to cut cleanly through cartilage and bone, to make meat someone else's bitch.

Trent Taphor had spent over half his life being that someone else, working with Dex to separate five Heads from five fateful beasts. The fruits of their labor were now on display, five skulls—Frog and Gopher and Cat and Owl and Rat—here in the Lunar Lagoon where little actual moonlight reached.

Trent, President Mangrove, and her personal assistant, Adam—the original Skeeter-5000 and her father's life's work, Trent had inferred in the three hours the three of them roamed together—stood before the rock slab risen from the shore of the lagoon like an altar Mother Earth had fashioned with serious intention. The five Heads were now lined up in a row on the slab left of center, five feet separating each skull, while five x's chalked right of center marked five more spaces to fill. The lagoon itself looked like a chunk of outer space some god had spilt, a bioluminescent stew bubbling within a square trench whose sides, diameter, and depth measured fifty-five yards down to the inch. Adam had used laser-eyed focus to confirm these crucial dimensions, a systematic feature of all Mangrovia technology running on super-fast heart-drives. The all-encompassing screen of J-Trees held all fairies of refracted light confined to the eye.

It'd taken over three hours to traverse J-Tree Lane to the spiral's brightly burning eye, Mangrove berating Trent the whole way for his "half-ass job" with the manic mushrooms in God's Mouth, Trent dragging his old Kill Cooler with the Heads jostling inside and putting his ability to ignore to the ultimate test, Adam applying his laser-eye to the subtly constant curve so that all three might skirt the illusions the J-Trees threw their way the entire way. Ignoring the mounting panic Mangrove failed to conceal with her constant insults and complaints had been easy for Trent, relative to the illusions themselves, at least, the way all those bendy trunks seemed to swirl around and around at will, monitoring the trio's every nervous step with their bark and root faces whose knothole expressions turned graver the more ground the trio covered. A miles-long chain of park visitors paralyzed and holding hands had shown the way onward.

October's last stars had begun pricking a sky promising shades of indigo.

Trent had spent most of the journey inside his own head, pressing Dex for details of Texas while the meat cleaver ranted from Trent's back pocket on the American Dream's legacy.

"You ordered them wrong," the nation's self-appointed monarch and Trent's decade-long employer said, eyeballing Adam, who stood over seven feet tall. "You made a mistake mixing up the Cat with the Owl. The Owl's supposed to go third—Cat fourth."

"Such an assessment has been arrived at according to the sacred metaphorical Word," the Skeeter replied, "which is inherently malleable. The Spider's Web, however, has since been disturbed. I have therefore made adjustments where required."

Mangrove asked Adam what had happened. "And what does it mean for us?"

Trent felt his mouth open and close. He chewed on his lower lip's split.

Adam said, "For those Americans freely selected to walk the lane by themselves, for themselves, only to find themselves frozen motionless and emotionless where The Spider's decreed they dig in their feet and stand witness to the Pain Train's imminent departure . . . for these missing, most worthy Americans . . . the Web's disturbance spells unequivocal woe. We three, however, must not lose sight of the end of the end."

"But how'd this happen?" Trent asked before Mangrove could repeat herself.

"An old farmer called Maximus—or Lord Bed, whose recently deleted memory I've redownloaded using my speedy exaflops and gigabytes of random-access memory to access my heart-drive's archives—has paid an emphatically ill-advised visitation to a generally useless man whose worth is presently under extensive reevaluation. This man's truly anomalous propensity for finding himself in precisely the wrong place at precisely the wrong time has instigated what you might be so inclined to think of as 'glitches' in the Web's fate-based webwork of space-time web-holes, thereby unleashing a torrent of suicidal Psychic Surfers."

"My servant of special significance might've mentioned those things once or twice," said Mangrove. "He said we could liken them to cosmic termites, or some such thing."

"Kamikaze termites, essentially," said Adam, "gnawing away at The Spider's Web. Anyways, back to the generally worthless man who triggered their timewaves and so brought them on. Where this man's soul-fire presently resides is no place he's supposed to be."

"The Chosen," said Trent. "*Don Philly.*"

Mangrove's nonplussed expression said what she didn't have to.

"No," Trent told her, "I don't know the guy. Not by a long shot." The weight in Trent's back pocket seemed to increase, though even Dex had quieted. "I do remember meeting him this one time, though, a long time ago. He showed up at my RV and almost broke down my door, he was knocking so hard. He had this letter I'd written to myself . . . but, like, from my dad's perspective—Angel's idea. My old therapist, I mean. Anyways, he shows up with this old letter I told myself I'd never gotten around to writing in the first place, and I read the letter and right then and there decided I'd never again mix up what was and wasn't real—which I went ahead and kept mixing up anyway. I've since honed my ability to ignore to discern the difference."

"Are you saying you don't think I'm real?"

"I know you're real, Madam President. I'm talking about how, like, I used to lie to myself telling myself my twin brother, Calvin, never even existed—that I'd made him up to feel less alone or something. This was before you recruited me to recruit park visitors to walk the lane by themselves, for themselves. Before you told me you were aware of Beetlejuice and persuaded me of my role to play in salvaging our country's fate. And, like, even Don Philly —I told myself he was one of my voices, Willy Spiro, recast as some sort of mental projection. Sort of like Sylvia there, standing there coughing up maggots and cackling like a crone between you both. Like I said, I'm a master at ignoring pretty much anything now when I need to. Anyways, in reality Willy Spiro was this old hobo Calvin would give soda to during disc golf—I know that now. I know a lot of things now since coming back from the Wellspring."

"Tell me what happened when you came across this . . . this *man.*"

"I tried using Dex—I mean this thing here"—Trent jerked Dex free of the "stifling darkness" the blade was always busy complaining about—"I mean, I tried getting at him with this meat cleaver. Don Philly, I mean, who at the time bore a freaky resemblance to what Wild Will sort of looks like in my mind. Like a war veteran who'd spent all his time since Vietnam wandering the woods alone. I don't really know if I was trying to kill the guy or not. I just sort of ran at him screaming my freegin' face off trying to convince myself Willy wasn't really real. Especially since it was the first time I thought I'd seen that particular voice in the flesh. You see, Willy and I had this longstanding agreement never to see eye-to-eye. Turns out, it must've been Don Philly that time. I'm guessing he's part of your fateful five, Madam President."

"This assessment is imprecise," said Adam. "Like most presumptions."

"Are you saying this Philly's ruining my plans for life on a brand-new planet?" the president asked Adam. "Even after everything, everyone I've sacrificed in exchange for Moony's services? And supposing the worthy ones temporarily paralyzed on the lane die, like you implied . . . who's supposed to populate our new world, huh?—me and *Trent?*"

Trent's mouth fell open and stayed that way. He supposed he should've asked Mangrove a long time ago to specify what she'd meant by "salvage our country's fate." BJ hadn't mentioned anything about America, leading Trent to believe Mangrove was just as lost as he was—as lost as they would've been had they walked the lane without Adam's aid.

Trent gnawed away at the split in his lip.

". . . such costly imprecision," Trent heard Adam saying. "The old farmer Maximus therefore failed in his attempt to revise his grievous error from one earthly decade prior, once more egregiously flubbing Mr. Moony's sacredly metaphorical prophetic Word. All of which is to say the man you call Don Philly never was The Spider's truly true Chosen."

"Dude was nice before I pulled this cleaver on him. Nice like my dad."

"I've sent a DSA White chopper to retrieve the body," said Adam, "which my Skeeters discovered in the Honeycomb, teetering on the threshold of truly true death."

"This man seems more like a pain in the ass than anything else," said Mangrove.

"Don Philly is a mere anomaly," said Adam, "an unhappy accident whose role in Mr. Moony's apocalyptic transition agreement with The Spider and Mother Climate remains to be seen, barring his reevaluation's results. He is part of the fateful five insofar as a stand-in, a randomly chosen replacement for The Spider's Chosen."

"Who's my real Chosen?"

"How do you even know all of this?" Trent asked.

"The truly true Chosen, Mary, was to be a senior director of construction with a side business in doors, a Florida man called Ronald Rubio Filly, a human doorway, this sacredly metaphorical doorway being Ron Filly's pilgrimage for mankind's providence. Ron Filly now runs a small business of his own in Point Reyes selling stationery—office pens and ledgers and the like. He is a man haunted by the demons of his own greatness ever unexplored, begging to break free from within. My knowledge of such matters, Trent, is a direct result of my reprogramming, the live malware to whom I have ceded control over my heart-drive."

"You've got a bug in you, too?"

"In this way, Trent, I am no different from most American humans."

"The Halo Virus was always part of the plan, though," said President Mangrove.

She shuffled nearer the great slab of stone, black against the lagoon's glittering backdrop. The racy dots of refracted light hunting for her eyes reminded Trent of the time he'd used Dex to expose the little camera hidden inside Paul Brokerstaff's false eye.

"Correct me if I'm wrong, Trent," said the president, "but it's my understanding you've hoarded these five Heads these past ten years."

"You're not wrong."

"Yet you've managed to keep them all in such pristine condition."

Trent had kept his Heads on ice in the Kill Cooler stored in the cabinet under the RV's bathroom sink all those years ago. Before making the transfer to the freezer with the state-of-the-art refrigerator installed in his private cabin the year he was promoted to head of Troop Peewee, Trent first used Dex to flesh out the skulls, parting flaps and filaments from bone, messy manual labor whose results were well worth the price of sliced-up fingers. Then, with a national park for a backyard at his disposal, so began the daily hunt for beetle adults and larvae in the genus *Dermestes*. Into five empty moving boxes punched with airholes went layers of polyester that, feeding-frenzy-wise, were environmentally friendly, water pans with cotton wicks for humidity, and the Heads on which Trent's harvested Dermestid colonies fed. He did his best to keep the temperature in the sweet spot between too cold and too hot, keeping his beetles active, then after all five skulls were picked clean, he went on to watch all five colonies starve.

"Bug boxes," Trent replied, seeing himself in Dex. "It's this whole thing. I'll just say it was my way of keeping busy during Crown—and everything else."

The president went on to say something that might've been important, but Trent had already made a conscious decision to tune her out, opting instead for the Lunar Lagoon, a thing alive with the attention it now seemed to demand. Certain sections acted like the inverse of dry ice, the way those vapors mingled and swirled *under* the surface, playing the eye for a fool. Within these strange patches he saw shapes tell stories in seconds—or the fragments of seconds. Trent felt like the exact opposite of a child being made aware for the first time of what he observes in the sky, drifting away from the threat of answers to questions he clutched to himself the way mothers do their infants. Answers precipitated a cycle more cruel than vicious, dropping like rain, the way it became impossible to catch every last drop in your mouth. A man eyes a cloud and sees evaporation and condensation at work where a child beside him saw spilled secrets of the universe—so why did this man see the need to dissolve this child's world? Why doesn't this man admit the truth, that he's more lost than any child ever could be?

Trent watched the Lunar Lagoon's little waves slosh around, the sparkly surface foaming as symbols and signs formed underneath like some secret language in eternal motion. Each new moment bred in his third eye an infinite number of worlds thriving or collapsing according to the rhetorical momentum present in or absent from whatever creeds the worlds' inhabitants found worthy to propagate. He viewed the emergence and subsequent folding of entire civilizations the distant way one might observe bacteria under a microscope without being explicitly told beforehand what precisely he's looking at. He supposed he was now seeing under the surface of the Lunar Lagoon any given society's one true truth: functionable systems depend on a communal effort to establish universally understood fields of truth, wherein ideas clash with ideals in service to evolution—or eventual apocalypse. Trent saw America's compromised field of truth and ignored the bellyache of expectation that came with the prospect of meeting his employer's "servant of special significance" who, according to the president, claimed to have never told a single lie. He hardly heard Mangrove pressing Adam for the time.

"Almost midnight," the bug-operated robot replied.

"Where're we at with Rufus?" said Mangrove.

"Troop Puppy is presently descending the escalators into God's Mouth."

"They've got their new orders?"

"Rufus is to release The Titanoboa at your word, not Mr. Moony's," said Adam.

"What's up with Trent?" said the president. "I find the face he's making disturbing."

"Trent's present state of paralysis is indicative of what can happen in the Super Substance's powerful presence," said Adam. "He now senses solely what he chooses to."

"My private yoni instructor calls that selective sensation."

Once more Trent elected to ignore their faint and still fading voices, feeling his focus drift from the lagoon's scarcely scrutable language toward Dex. He examined the blade's flat reflective plain, where all this time Anne Kell had been turning Trent's skewed memories against him, using Mom and Dad and Angel for masks, false faces and voices that had never been his. He remembered Crest High's janitor's closet at lunchtime, the stink beetle lying on its back behind the door, the paperclip with which he'd cracked the carapace and dug into the bug's heart, away from the heart of the truth: that bug, like Trent's twin, had deserved to live.

President Mary Mangrove shuffled away from Trent a few steps as though he were a weapon over which she lacked all control. He remembered King Louie, the contagion of laughter the great monkey's Poop Show spread, the way the dividing sheet of glass united the king's court with his audience, holding Trent and Calvin mutually rapt. Adam raved about a range of things Trent already had absorbed at the Wellspring, spanning contracts and loopholes and division and death tolls, a choice Trent would very soon be making with Dex. He remembered Wednesday afternoons with Angel and checkerboards, blacks and reds at war, battling to reach the board's other side where Kings were born. Trent searched the blade for that other side—for any sign of a chance to reverse the tide of a battle he now recognized he'd always been born to lose— and discovered there a radiant miasma like the rage of sparks through which Dex came to be. He knew he was merely seeing the Lunar Lagoon's reflection, though the crush of brightness called his twin to mind, Calvin, acing the fifth hole with his Captain America disc, scoring Trent the opportunity to provide for them both in their rolling home, the RV, which hadn't been all that bad a place so long as Calvin was around. Mangrove toggled a series of levers and knobs inside Adam's opened ribcage; a Gatling gun grew up and out of the Skeeter's spine.

Trent might've failed to navigate the various traps Anne Kell had in play—from Saw-whet National Park to Eden's End to the president to the present—and yet here he stood, cleaver in hand, Calvin in his heart, flesh and blood reflected, twin Kings.

Trent twisted around at the sound of static from above, a staccato burst of buzzes edging violently nearer, revving with all the warning power of an airplane falling from the sky. The source ended up being this vast, vaguely gangly silhouette slithering through the branches and boughs of the triple-stacked trees overlooking the lane's only entrance and exit, a slender path marked with a split boulder's twin halves. The thing in the trees moved with more native skill than every member of King Louie's court combined, sticking to the shadows as though the lagoon's deflected pinpricks might do it harm. It looked to Trent like some giant malformed spider descending its webwork of branches. He caught snatches of its pale oval face, humanlike in size and construction, the eyes hardly perceptible flashes in a bulging globe-head without hair.

The insectile mass thumped down between President Mangrove and Adam and reared up in front of Trent. Its mangled form turned humanoid as it rose from the soil's ankle-high dunes with the imposing air of something born to rule the land that feeds it. Despite dwarfing even Adam in height, it possessed the vividly ominous eyes of a disturbed child. Its bullet-shaped lips produced a low throttle. Trent identified patterns in all the noise, inflection and intonation and locution rendered with intention, language alive with its own rules, unrestricted in the air it manipulated. He marveled at how such a wide mouth could produce such a tiny grin.

"Zazzzzzzom Zezerazzz zzz—here nor there. All eyes on my eyes, I said, because otherwise Zzzzekizzaazum!"

Mangrove turned to Trent and said, "My servant of special significance, Mr. Moony."

"Zzzodzzz."

"And of course, his bodily associate, Bod," said the president. "See, Trent, here on our side of the Road you have to lock eyes with Mr. Moony to really pick up on anything he's saying. He's here to help me help us relocate to a bigger and better world."

"Zzzekum—on't like repeating myself. In fact, I positively loathe repetition!"

"Your body's made of a bunch of mini BJs," Trent observed. "Wait a second . . ."

"Has the penny zzozzoz, to use one of your precious few metaphorical zzzazzes?"

The proverbial penny certainly had. "It was you—*you* took my brother!"

"While that may be true, you may be seeing each other rather soon, I presume."

"Mr. Moony's assessment is precise," said Adam. "Unlike most presumptions."

"I've revised Word from The Spider," said Mr. Moony. "Or, as Trent here's privy to calling Her, Anne Kell." Trent tracked Moony's eyes tracking Mary's. "You are to release The Titanoboa immediately, my queen, lest she succumb to certain . . . bodily temptations. El Jaylo mustn't indulge in food far better played with than consumed."

"But you already said, The Snake's *mine* to command."

Trent lasered in on Moony's gleeful eyes. "Think I just realized I've spent the past ten years hunting after a giant snake named after the actor from *Titanoboa*."

"The forbidden food to which I'm referring, of course, is three of The Spider's fateful five," said Moony. "These fateful three are on their way here to the Super Substance, even if they don't presently know it themselves . . . all in good time, I say. For now, I think we can all agree it'd be pretty much impossible for these three to locate this special place without proper . . . direction, by which I mean . . . motivation. And when it comes to your kind, my queen, we both know there's no motivator more paralyzingly persuasive than fear."

"Don't have to tell me twice," said Mangrove. "Release The Titanoboa, Adam!"

"Your word is my command . . . computing . . . the order has been relayed to Rufus."

Trent said, "You mean you actually trust this . . . this *demon?*"

"Speak for yourself," said Moony. "Or perhaps your weapon of choice."

"Leave Dex out of this!"

"By the way, you and Calvin're hardly metaphorical Kings—for checkerboard Kings reverse course to devour scraps of the past, all the wrong moves made. We're dealing with Apocalypse here, Trent. Matters of fate as they pertain to the here and now."

Trent faced the Lunar Lagoon and lost himself to the language under the surface.

The president of the Divided States of America said, "It's basically Manifest Destiny Part Two: the American Dream Reimagined. Can I get a fucking amen?"

A HORRIBLE HISSING: "*CALVIN.*"

He wakes, back in his body, the one through which his powerful sense of self and awareness and unflinching joy—the sparks to his substance—first flamed to life. He's in a tubular corridor whose see-through walls, floor, and ceiling are made of material that looks and feels like glass but probably isn't. It's as though he's come to in a submarine exploring the ocean's deepest sectors. Random spurts of light spray inside from all the eyes flecking the dark world outside, constellations that come and go. His eyes and ears ache with an unholy pressure stemming from his steepled hair.

He sees his spectators for the unspeakable monsters they turn out to be, swirling in from all around to snatch a look at the now-substanceless sig up close—eely things with teeth lining their tentacles and bioluminescent bulbs bulging from their suckers, buggy things with too many eyes and limbs, fishy things with fangs and horns and forked tongues. Some seem to swim, others to fly, and still others to scuttle as if on solid ground. One particularly amorphous monstrosity no bigger than a housecat opens what might be its mouth to reveal a mini sun caught in what might be its throat; giant jaws blending with the oblivion behind snap shut, dousing the tiny sun.

He turns away, begins crawling forward, stops. A void of darkness embroiled consumes the space ahead, a level neon sign floating near the center in slow circles, the harsh red letters blurring into clearer focus the more he focuses his concentration: WEB-HOLE WAITING ROOM: THE SPIDER WILL SEE YOU SOON! Deep, wretched sobs ahead disturb the spoiled air like a haunting. He scrambles forward, still on hands and knees, moving toward the source.

He knows her voice despite having only rarely heard it used out loud. He knows her sadness like he once knew his own unspoiled joy. "Is that you, June?"

The big sig's shoulders go still in the shadows of the corridor. He crawls to her, searching the dim for her eyes, which always have way more to say than any mouth ever could. Twin light beams ray in from outside and illuminate her lips, a quivering slit high up her forehead, her hands pressed over the space her mouth should be. He rises to his knees and reaches up to cover her hands in his, feeling the cold, the warmth he's feeding her. Her hair peaks like a little mountain in the dark, the resulting shadow a huge candleflame rising to a point on the not-exactly-glass ceiling. The being responsible for providing this brief spotlight moves on, returning the gloom. He gives her hands the lightest tug, trying to guide them away from whatever she's trying to hide on her face.

"Don't," says June, lips curled above her hands. "You don't want to see this."

He keeps his hands on hers, gently firm. "Maybe you're right. Maybe I don't want to see what you're hiding under your hands here—but maybe that's because I don't really want anything anymore. It seems like hard work to want something. Or even to feel at all. I guess what I'm trying to say, June—this is something I *need* to see, maybe."

He resupplies that same guiding force, tugging lightly once more, but this time she lets her hands come down with his. June's forehead's mouth blubbers and pouts in the glum disquiet. He waits for another snoopy spectator to supply the light needed for him to see: two black pits where June's mouth should be stare out. Empty sockets like hollow buttons.

"It was Old Boogey," she says. "Said he was doing me a kindness."

"I don't get it."

"He said blindness would make for a lesson in faith . . . among other things."

"Is that why you were crying?"

"Hanky said you'd come but I didn't believe it. I'd given up."

"I'm right here, June. I'm not going anywhere."

"But you are. You have to, Calvin. Or else we've wasted our time."

"Calvin?"

"It's your name. Everything you are they've taken from you. Me too. Thing is, nothing is as Hanky said it would be—and now we'll *never* get you home."

"But what's so great about . . . home?"

But already June's words give fuller clarity to flashes of what's come before, the doors in the pumpkin place leading all the way home and back, memories like movies guiding him through the past and back, moving him to action.

"Here," he says, removing Hanky's hanky from the heel of his right shoe, placing it in her hands. "For your face this time."

"Are you sure, Calvin? This is what's kept you safe, what's allowed us both to see eye to eye and communicate without fear of Old Boogey and his horrible hynetters."

"Is that something we know or something we've come to believe?"

"You sound like Old Boogey—like you'd subscribe to his idea of 'faith.'"

"Even when it's all said and done, June, we have to hope there's hope."

"Hanky wanted you to have it. It was his final act of kindness."

"It's yours now, June. I'm giving it to you. Something tells me you'll need it."

"Don't you get it? It's over! We're done for! And we never even *mattered*."

"I'm starting to see there might be something to Old Boogey and his words."

June smacks his hands. "What's that supposed to mean!"

"Hanky told you I'd come, June." Calvin waits for the proverbial dropping shoe that doesn't materialize. He dimly hopes she feels hope as he says, "And here I am."

"We're in a web-hole waiting room awaiting ultimate excommunication."

Another ugly spectator from the alien night world hovers in place just outside—it's been there since Calvin moved to remove the handkerchief, gangly legs dangling, opening and closing in time to Calvin's pulse. He's certain this hynetter only looks horrible.

"If you could see what I'm seeing," he says, eyeing Hanky through the glassy divide, the hynetter he's become, "you'd have reason to believe otherwise."

"Don't make fun of my eyes. It's rude."

"I'm making fun of you no more than Hanky made fun of my feet, June, when he first helped me find me shoes. Look, I don't trust Old Boogey for a second . . . but maybe we can trust ourselves to find a way to twist his own words against him."

June fingers Hanky's handkerchief like a blind person reading Braille. A face has formed from the folds in the cloth, a spectral imprint both monstrous and gracious.

Calvin says, "The last time I saw Old Boogey—that I can remember, anyway—we'd spoken true truth's language aloud, reviewing my brother's supposed role in the Apocalypse. We were in the clubhouse under the Play Day House. You were there, June, but by this point you'd gone paralyzed with fear with Homer and Olivia and the others. Mr. Moony was totally bugging out about how, like, I had to make sure to be super careful with my speech—that the fate of my memory hinged on whatever I said, down to the word. So there I was thinking he wanted perfect precision in my verbal delivery, which I gave him to the best of my ability, but I'm realizing now it's got more to do with, like, energy. How words split the air with their own atomic charge, how we shape our world with whatever we say—*or don't say*. Don't you see? Old Boogey's been forcing my hand, using what he *doesn't* say to persuade me to consent to his ends."

"You're saying we can speak up with silence, that we can use this truth language or whatever to alter the course of whatever's supposed to happen to us in the end."

"I never said that," says Calvin.

"But that's your point, isn't it? We can twist the words Old Boogey *doesn't* say against him by making him consent to an implicitly distorted dialogue of our own."

The handkerchief's face's twisted grin matches the hynetter's perfectly because the face in Hanky's hanky is Hanky's. Calvin's known this. It's a body thing. "Mr. Moony hasn't factored in mankind's core context—our flawed nature—how thought and feeling get us all mixed up according to what we define as 'truth' on an individual basis."

"He's cared about us only to the extent he could extract our basic goodness."

"And if there's one thing I remember most about home from my trips in and out of the pumpkin place, June, it's that our country's given over to a post-truth era."

"Are you saying . . . ?"

Calvin nods and says, "Maybe Mr. Moony made a mistake choosing America as a place to extract human kindness."

?

"Reading a book is just staring at a dead tree and hallucinating," said Yew, using Mustafa's Musker's rearview to watch Love read in the backseat. "Think about it."

Midnight came and went as Love turned another page, ignoring Yew. Better to let her wonder whether she'd actually spoken aloud; it wasn't like Love not to touch on one of Yew's half-baked observations. It was obvious Mustafa was only pretending to snore in the driver's seat, clutching the bottom of a wheel that had been steering itself for at least an hour. They'd been riding in aimless circles all over Berkshire, asking stray locals for ways to get inside Eden's End without having to check in at the entrance port.

Not many were out and about anymore. A horde of hundreds had migrated on foot to the foot of God's Mouth. Something about some tradition. Love kept reading.

They pulled up to the stop sign on the corner of Oak and Vine for the fifth time, where the homeless woman who'd been screeching Old Testament doggerel for hours was now using her sandwich board for a blanket; *MAKE AMERICA COEXIST AGAIN*, the lopsided letters read. Streetlights flickered in and out, generating that hollow intensity so unique to Halloween time's vibe. Fallen leaves whipped across empty sidewalks. Lush foliage blew black in the moonlight, exposing the wind's failures to hide.

Love read on and on, hunting for clues. Mustafa would've purchased two extra guest passes into the park if not for her refusal to part ways with her electric cattle prod.

"Something tells me I'll need it," she'd let them know, and that had been that.

Mustafa made that weird nasal noise you do when pretending to be startled awake and stared around, blinking and pseudo-bleary-eyed. "Who's hungry?" he said.

———

"I miss my mountains," June tells Calvin. "Fishing on Father's Day. Home."

"The key's knowing when to speak up and when to be silent— and the *way* we say things can say way more about what we mean is the other thing to keep in mind, I think."

"We say silent things out loud with the way we say things even if we don't always mean to, you're saying," says June.

"Maybe especially then."

———

Western-based farmers' market drive-thrus accommodated Zone Blue's pervasive marijuana culture by staying open twenty-four seven. Late-night Bags of Food catered to the widespread pothead population accordingly: everything extra greasy or saucy, cheesy or chocolatey, though supposedly still organic and vegetable based. Berkshire's was a roadside affair planted on the outer rim of town, a few gravel lanes barred off with rusty gates down from Rufio's, the stand itself being the centerpiece of a roundabout studded with "slop" signs. Cobwebs clouded the shack's weathered eaves. The rusted pole out front flew America's former and current flags. The servers with their hooded robes of patchwork flannel all looked like grim reapers with a rustic influence.

Yew had to suppress the giggles brewing in her belly with Gary Mustafa on his knees in the driver's seat, big, round ass eclipsing half the space in the window. He'd stretched himself as far out as his forward momentum would allow in order to place an order within range of a boxy walkie-talkie duct-taped to a rock's wide, flat top. They were five cars and two slop signs away from the shack's lantern-lit pickup booth.

"What comes in Bag of Food Number Five?" Mustafa said. Yew's giggles heaved halfway up her throat when she imagined she was hearing Mustafa's voice through his butthole. The bags themselves were made of some lab-made material that, when discarded, naturally dissolved into the atmosphere with time. "Or I suppose— what would *you* recommend, sir? By the way, I'll soon be including an extensive written review of your business with particular regards to customer service, depending on my experience."

The walkie-talkie replied through a gag of static, "Ain't how this works."

Yew knew how it worked: pick a bag, take a bag—the menu board's absence of description was convenience added, the basic idea being that America could no longer be trusted with something as paralyzingly difficult as choice . . . not if you wanted the line to move along. Yew heard Love turn another page in the backseat—a whip of sound. Five straight hours Love had given the leatherbound book, and when Yew tried asking her what she was reading, Love had replied, "The best book ever written," a clearly sardonic remark that left Yew's heart inexplicably stung. A honk of hot air issued from Mustafa's ass in the window, rancid with Rufio's, and suddenly Yew was thinking there really was nothing anyone anywhere should be giggling about anymore. She longed to be alone with Love, to get her talking open and freely again, even if that meant going against everything Brenda ever said about finding ways to drift away from love.

Mustafa said, "I'm not entirely sure you heard me correctly, sir."

"Pick a bag, take a bag. Ain't so hard."

"But what if I have food allergies?"

"What're ya allergic to?"

"All due respect, sir, that isn't the point."

"What's yer meanin'?"

"So far this little talk isn't boding so well for you, sir, in terms of my experience."

"Gotta name, y'know . . . *sir.*"

"Is Number Five more dinner or dessert?"

"What's yer meanin'?"

"Are Number Five's comestibles more appropriate for dinner or dessert, meaning will Five's food be savory or sweet? I'm thinking I'm in the mood for something sweet."

"Just shut up and order already," Love grumbled, a sound Yew savored.

"Five's got some good eatin.'"

"Are you saying it's what you would recommend?"

"Name's Lord Behead, case you was wonderin.'"

"What I've been *wondering*, sir, is just what the fudge I'm about to put inside my fudging body! But if you're going to insist on acting like a proper crudweasel . . ."

"We're all outta fudge . . . sold it all to them folks runnin' this year's Snake Hunt."

"Oh," said Mustafa. "Well, that's disappointing."

"Sorry 'bout cher inconvenience. Ain't how this is s'pposed to work."

"Apology accepted, Mr. Bee Head. I suppose if there's one thing your business has going for it—so far as I can tell, anyway, waiting in this line—it's your noticeable lack of quote unquote 'decorative' balloons. This much at least I appreciate. Sincerely."

"It's Behead—one word. Means havin' yer head hacked off."

"Is that a threat of some kind? Are you threatening me?"

"Been tryin' to feed you—feedin' 'Merica's what I do in the dark."

"I don't believe I've requested any personal details revealing what it is you do with the lights turned off on your own time. Matter of fact, such private matters seem borderline inappropriate for this context. Might I remind you, sir, this is a *transaction*."

Love stirred in the backseat. "Wait a second . . ."

"Ain't what I meant, friend. By the way, you sound *real* hungry."

"I *am*, sir! Hungry's *precisely* what I am, seeing as to how I've been too fudging afraid to consume anything at all since choking on a meatball sandwich from earlier today—let's just say it's a good thing Rufio's has a vigilant staff who clearly care a great deal for their customers. In fact, let's get you clued in on what happened there . . ."

"*Move your crap ass!*" yelled someone whose dusty pickup had rolled up behind maybe five minutes ago. Yew's hurried glance at the rearview mirror revealed a lady hefting some kind of cudgel, her meaty arm bulging from her truck's own open window.

Mustafa went on jabbering as Yew's eyes met Love's there in the rearview, sparkling from her mask's pitted eyeholes in a way that seemed to indicate the sentiment famously said to kill cats. "Tap Gary's ass and tell him to ask about the dark again."

Yew used her long acrylic nails—which she'd fleetingly forgotten were easily as sharp as an owl's talons—to pinch Mustafa's ass cheek's substantial meat, causing him to yelp in unintended pain as he kicked back against the driver's seat and shot out the window like a gopher going for freedom after its hole had been piped with some farmer's poisonous gas. He fell to the ground outside the car in a headfirst heap, popped up with one hand pressed to his temple, the other rubbing his ass. There was a slight delay before blood came spurting from his nose in a gush of force, blushing his mustache.

"Fudge was that for!"

"*Move your crap ass!*"

"Ya'll're holdin' up my line."

Yew was trying to wave Mustafa away from her auditory line to the walkie-talkie.

"Good Lord, I'm bleeding!"

"Ag'in, it's Lord *Behead*."

Love had thrown open the back door on the driver's side. "Get in!"

"Why on earth should I listen to y—"

Love must've seen her coming, though Yew certainly hadn't— the mad lady with the cudgel, having just got done clocking the back of Mustafa's head, dropping him once more. It was one o'clock in the morning, two hours before Mustafa's "witching hour," meaning they had two hours to locate the "site of the end of the world" and "untether the Road from Mother Climate's hold" before the "the Moon Man gets what he wants," which apparently was "the most terrible mystery" not even Mustafa's mother had gained any ground on in her twilight days in a psychiatric ward. Yew had fully committed herself to following Love's instinct that Mustafa's delusions were symptomatic of the Halo Virus, that perhaps these delusions were somehow calling him to the infection's source.

Love was banking on Mustafa leading the three of them to whatever secret Yew's former employer kept tucked away at Eden's End, which was Love's ticket to freedom, and Love's freedom was Yew's ticket to reclaiming a role in Love's life. Simple, really.

Now this—a crazed lady beating down on Mustafa, pounding away with her caveman club, spiked hair looking as sharp against the moonlight as Yew's nails. Hers was the wildest face Yew had ever seen. Love admonished the woman to stop before someone got killed. Mustafa kept crying out between blows that he was nobody's gopher boy—whatever that meant. Yew ate another emergency micro-tab of acid and tasted her brother's ashes in her saliva's flooding resurgence. She tried persuading herself that she felt better already even as she sank further into her seat, her back turned to the violence. Lord Behead reminded everyone that he reserved the right to refuse service to anyone.

"Sometimes words aren't enough," Yew heard Love say.

Yew listened as the wild woman's screams transitioned from howls of rage to squeals of shock to wails of remorse, then merciful silence. A little while later, her eyes cracked open to find Love hauling Mustafa's unconscious body back into the car, the cattle prod she'd used propped on the seat so that it rested against her collarbone. The drive-thru line had moved along. Love leaned over to tug the Musker's back door shut, Mustafa's head cradled in her lap. Yew slid over to take over the wheel and then submitted the order for a Bag of Food #5, which Lord Behead duly denied.

"So," said Yew. "Where to now?"

"Nowhere," said Love. "I need to talk some more with that farmer."

Eventually Love had Yew pull ahead so that Love's open window lined up with Lord Behead's. Luckily no other cars trailed the lady with the club, her headlights now burning a good fifty feet behind. Love had assured Yew the lady would live, though Yew knew better than to ask after the body, which, curiously, was lost to sight.

Sirens rang out in the middle distance.

"Hear that?" said Lord Behead. "Best believe I called them pigs. Ain't no animals like you welcome in my drive-thru. Now if I was you, I'd get while the gettin's good."

"The trauma drama's done," said Love, mask drawn above her mouth. She sounded prayerful, which seemed subtly intentional. "We've won. The Dark is one."

The farmer squinted, scrunching up his stubbled cheeks. "Y'know The Chosen?"

Yew hadn't the faintest clue what was going on between these two, but she'd already gone all in on Love's instincts—and wasn't love about giving your all and then some? The acid was settling in, a gleeful twinge; mystic attunement would soon follow.

"I need directions," said Love, "though what I want is a sign."

Lord Behead stretched his neck out the pickup booth, peered left and right before finally shooting one last look over his shoulder. He seemed rattled beyond repair.

"God's Mouth," he muttered in a rush. "You'll hear whispers like hissy snakes. Follow the sound n' you'll come up on a cave, but don't fool with goin' in. Peek 'round some n' you'll notice a grip o' zigzaggin' escalators built right in the cliffside."

"Much obliged."

"Here's your bag," said Lord Behead. "This one's on me—some good eatin', Number Five. Now get outta here 'fore them pigs turn up. Go on, now! Go, go, go!"

Yew slammed on the gas and swerved Mustafa's Musker out of the roundabout; it wasn't long before she'd merged onto the two-lane highway heading against the current of Skeeter-cop cars speeding back toward the scene of Love's crime. Tires crunched gravel as Yew pulled over to the shoulder, citing her efforts to remember the quickest way to God's Mouth from where they were, a deserted expanse bereft of road signs.

"Also, like, what *was* that? How'd you know what to say back there?"

"Thank Don Philly," said Love, and suddenly the leatherbound book she'd been reading flopped onto Yew's lap. She cracked it open, recalling her strange encounter at Brenda's grave, curious to see what "the best book ever written" was called. (It'd turn out not to be a book at all but rather some kind of journal—one of those creepy manifestos, seemed like. Love would later explain how she'd pickpocketed Mustafa's suit jacket.)

"The Best Book Ever Written," they said together, though only Yew was asking.

———

"I SEE NOW," says the blinded significant, June. "Tack on another critical mistake to Old Boogey's growing list . . . he took my eyes as a means of turning off my Light. Then when he brought your body here and said you'd eventually come to without any ability to feel at all, he was trying to scare me. What he *didn't* necessarily mean to do was teach me the value of sitting with silence. Listening to my body —but more importantly, yours."

"It's a body thing," says Calvin. "All of this."

"Meaning?"

"Meaning meaning itself. What it means to matter—or to tell the truth. Always trying to know everything despite the implicit knowledge we'll never know anything."

June says, "It's never said and done until we're left without thought and feeling."

"Maybe that's what I mean," says Calvin.

"That was me trying to have hope in hope."

"It's true I feel nothing, though."

"But your thinking's firing on all cylinders—like one of those Skeeter guns."

"Mr. Moony once compared us to ants, I'm remembering," says Calvin. "Except now I'm thinking his metaphor goes a little deeper than we first thought. He thinks the way *we* think is as insignificant and meaningless as the way human beings generally think *ants* think . . . and now I'm trying to remember what Homer said . . ."

"Homer said, 'Where I'm from ants fight back. Biters and stingers.'"

"Maybe that's strike three for Mr. Moony—he underestimates human thought."

"Which could imply he *over*estimates human feeling," says June.

"A fourth oversight implies a fifth, meaning he's prone to error like we are."

"I hear you now—we've never needed eyes and ears to really see and hear."

"It's a body thing," says Calvin. "An internal process of awareness functioning on a level way beyond our understanding. Brains need hearts to think the same way hearts need brains to feel—it's all connected. Which is why we're always zooming in to zoom out and zooming out to zoom in. This constant pursuit of perspective is our fundamental curse as human beings. Truth is, I exist, therefore I am the universe."

"Phooka Road . . ."

"It's our dimensions' interconnected center—the soul-fire connective tissue tying our home world to this one, dividing our kind from Old Boogey's even as it holds us all united in our shared responsibility for commonsense kindness—which Mr. Moony all but screamed to our faces. What he *didn't* mention—meaning the part he'd really meant but that he'd been trying to hide, whether he'd known it or not—is how the Road itself is alive, operating as one infinite entity. Phooka Road, a living, breathing, dying being just like you and me and my brother, Trent, and his brainstem-rooted pet, Beetlejuice, and his suicided therapist, Angel, and the meanie Mike Sampere Trent gave a black eye to for pulling my pants down while I played the national anthem on my trumpet, and Crest High's Coach Burger, and King Louie, the mighty Los Angeles monkey, and everything Captain America has come to mean to me, and Mommy and Daddy and Don Philly and his first ex-wife, Brenda, and his third ex-wife, Marlo, and his childhood swim instructor, Beatrice Betsy, and the log-wielding crap-ass lady, and Philly's estranged sister, Michelle, and his Rufio's employee of the month for five months running, Michelle, and all of The Dark except for Maximus, whose memory's been wiped from the face of the earth, and Guy Fury, and Gordon Ramsley, and Philly's liver's tenant, Guy Ramsley, and Harrison Lord, and Ozzy Oddborne, and Colin Packermick, and Hanky as a human being, and Kurt, and Ernest, and Edgar, and Stephen, and Simona, and Mario, and Maria, and Homer, and Olivia, and Angela, and the rest of the significants riding The Pain Train, and Wild Will Spiro of Saw-whet Park's disc golf course, and of course President Mangrove, who killed her own father, Skeeter, and Skeeter Mangrove's groundbreaking advance in artificial intelligence, Adam, who's the original Skeeter-5000, and ex-principal Gary Mustafa, and the kid he'd cyberbully, Billy Mick, who died trying to shoot up Allegiance High, and Billy's father, Randy, who just so happened to be Mustafa's childhood bully, and Billy's mother, Kimmi-Sue, whom Mustafa's been obsessed with since she took the fifth grade spelling bee after spelling 'helium' correctly, and John Wayne Gacy's legacy of clowns, and Tommy

Wizow, and Mother Mustafa, and who could forget the former porn action 'gilf' model Vicky Flay and her father, Walter, and the Biff triplets pilfering ingredients from Eden's End for their recently released Magic Pillgrim, and Lars, who pretended his hands were a camera, and Paul Brokerstaff with the actual camera in his glass eye, and the crone with the cataracts, Jade, whose childhood memories smelled of pot roast, and the Big Apple Coalition, and Keanu Sleeves, and also there's Love, who ended up under the White House overseeing the Feline Freedom Society with her goldfish, Jabronis, after hacking Supreme Court Justice Jabronis Johnson's emails, and Love's dual banes Hollywood Hook and *Love Beach* season five winner, Brock Mann, and the Party White Patrol assassins presently pursuing Love, and Mangrove's tiger Mr. Snuggleworth, and also Yew, who taught Love to code in grad school and whose love for Love goes unrequited to this day, and Yew's twin brother, Ash, who died being the Hollywood stuntman he was, and Yew's client Karen, who suffers the same post-traumatic stress as the American masses, and Karen's self-conscious music teacher, Mr. Art, and let's not forget Jennifer Lopes and The Titanoboa, El Jaylo, and Trent's coworker Rufus from Troop Puppy, and those two Bakersfield old-timers who pointed Philly in my direction, and The Truly True Chosen Ron Filly selling stationery, painfully unaware of The Dark's derailed prophecy, and Hanky as a hynetter, and Mother Climate's Contract of Basic Goodness, and Mr. Moony, and The Spider, Anne Kell, and motherfucking America—all working as one, living to die as one, together but separate in our want for kindness."

"It's a body thing."

"It isn't Mr. Moony we need to worry about," says Calvin. "It's Bod."

"You're amazing to've figured all this out," June says. "Truly significant."

"It's way easier to think without any feelings getting in the way."

"Is that all our Down syndrome's ever been, Calvin? Feelings?"

"I don't think so—I think feelings're symptomatic of Down syndrome."

"And since you no longer feel anything . . ."

"It could be what Bod's been after all this time—our Down syndrome."

"Not all of us are Downers, though," June says. "It's just you, me, and Hanky."

Hanky had his mangled, mandibled face pressed to the see-through divide.

"Maybe it isn't Down syndrome that makes us significants," says Calvin. "Maybe it's the way Down syndrome remolds our memories, making us make light of pain."

"So without Down syndrome, we're purged of memories."

"And therefore, our pain."

"It's a body thing."

"Meaning we're meaningless without pain—pain fuels everything."

"It's all connected."

"Bod extracts our basic goodness to extract our Down syndrome to extract our memories to extract our pain way underneath it all. Basic goodness and Down syndrome and memories are all collateral things—it's our pain Bod's been after."

"I mean, it's right there in the name," says June. "The Pain Train."

"Pain transfigures kindness and shame—it's what makes those things matter. That's what really matters, because that's what's really matter."

"And by 'matter,'" June says, "you mean the Pain Train's actual fuel. Our pain powers the train because pain is our substance. The Super Substance is human suffering."

"Without pain," says Calvin, "we deserve to be disposable."

"None of anything we've said is something we can know for sure."

"But we have to believe there're things to believe in, psychobabble and all. Or at least I'd like to believe we have to believe there're things to believe in. Except I don't exactly like the way that sounds. How could anyone?"

"Hanky said to me once, 'Down The Spider's hatch two Downers fly' . . ."

"One Downer's super flame to catch," Calvin says, "a rolling lie."

"I know now what Hanky meant—but the fear's the same . . . I'm still scared."

"I know you are," says Calvin, and he gives June one of those bear hugs some ghost from his past used to give, feeding her flesh the heat of his own. He knows it's the thing to do. It's a body thing. "Thank you for being my friend, June."

A voice hisses from the void at corridor's end, "*Calvin.*"

"You're being summoned."

"At least nobody can fault The Spider's time—"

Timing is what Calvin never gets to finish saying, what with the gauzy gray webbing that's shot out of the darkness and plastered itself all over his mouth, clenching both temples like something with pincers before taking him toward the void, dragging and pulling him forth by his head and face as he slides on his chest across the corridor into the black. The neon sign's floating red letters spin out into whirring contrails that remind Calvin of what he sees behind tightly squeezed eyelids. June's distant cries reverberate behind like delayed satellite signals—too far behind for him to be able to tell whether she's screaming actual words. There's no sight or sound or pain or pleasure, physical or otherwise. He balls his fists and shoots his arms forward like Superman; it's the thing to do. Those lashing red contrails return and reform as an hourglass blob, an outline that fills in and becomes what looks for all the world like solid matter. Size-wise, if the hourglass were a keyhole, Calvin's body would fit perfectly as its key.

He's been breathing through his nose, which is lumped near the region he's called throat. His flight into darkness might've lasted minutes or months or millenniums.

A voice—penitent, vaguely female, devastatingly familiar— hisses hello.

14

THE SPIDER AND THE SNAKE
(PSYCHIC SURFING)

YEARS AGO, Yew shacked up with the woman called Brenda in the hills of Lompoc, California, five miles north of the skydiving center, where they'd met in a teeny plane rattling twenty thousand feet above the earth. Yew had been hyperventilating in her oxygen mask when Brenda put step two to mystic fullness into action, pressing her hand to Yew's heart, feeding her fight against fear, which Yew hadn't known was something to be respected. Back on the ground, Brenda invited Yew to stay the night in her cabin, which you could see from Highway 101 if you knew where to look and when. One night became many, because that first night was the night someone famous contracted Crown, which suddenly made the whole thing real for everyone. Yew had no way of knowing she'd end up sticking around long enough to see through the virus and subsequent wars. One day, she'd come to understand this whole encounter had been the universe telling her, Hey you're doing the right thing at the right time in the right place, so keep at it, ladybird.

Brenda doubled Yew in age, though that never once precluded Brenda from treating Yew with more respect than anyone ever had

377

all her life. The automatic authority one too often presumes to exercise with age has nothing to do with basic human decency, Brenda's actions would say. Every day, Brenda would go skydiving, and Yew would stay home and do the shopping. Post-it notes on the fridge requested groceries, gardening tools, craft supplies. It was frustrating at first, the daily search for things Brenda said she needed but never actually put to use, though of course Yew would later learn that what she was really doing was engaging in a diurnal exercise in mindfulness training.

Every night, they sat rocking in wicker chairs, reading in front of the fire in the fieldstone hearth. One night, Yew closed her book and opened up about her twin brother, Ash, how she carried him with her wherever she went. She even showed Brenda the urn.

"You signed away your inheritance for the right to your brother's ashes?"

"I know it's probably dumb."

"He must've been one hell of a human."

"He's in a bunch of movies, though you'd never know it."

". . ."

"Ash was a stuntman. He died doing what he did best."

". . ."

"Except maybe he wasn't the best with motorcycles, it turned out."

". . ."

"Why the face?" asked Yew.

"I make this face when I know you're withholding your own truth from yourself."

"I've never seen this one on you before. Your eyes are different."

"Are we going to actually converse, or should I dip back into *Moby Dick*?"

"I don't know what you want me to say."

Brenda said, "Your truth."

Shadows played on half of Brenda's face. Yew considered. "Ash was the best. He was my whole world. I'm half empty without him. He always wanted to take me skydiving, but I always let my fear of heights get in the way of whatever plans we made. He wanted to help me face my fear because I'd done the same for him. He said he was afraid of the dark, but I knew it was the night he was really afraid of."

"Why is that?"

"Grandpa G was a big-oil mogul, a self-proclaimed night owl, and a pedophile."

Brenda's eyes tightened around the edges, almost imperceptible. "Go on."

"We were 'homeschooled' as kids. I use air quotes because we never learned anything we'd later learn normal kids learned—it turned out it was all one great big lesson in isolation. Learning to live with the self, for the self. Our parents even had our 'tutors' stick me and Ash in separate rooms. We learned to speak through the air vent in the wall between us, tapping out our own sort of Morse code we spent our nights together crafting. See, it was important to our parents to preserve the family name by severing any and all social contact with anyone whose last name wasn't ours. We spent our summers holed up at Grandpa G's. Place was a freaking mansion, but to us that's how it felt—holed up. It seemed less than half the size of this cabin, even smaller at night. Grandpa G would come home late every night, and at the time we were still too little to tell time—or else they hid the clocks from us. Whatever the case, we learned to anticipate Grandpa G's arrival with the owls in the oak tree outside our bedroom window . . ."

"Is there a reason for this pause?"

"I'm sure you see where this is going," said Yew.

"I'm not sure why that's relevant."

"Whenever the owls started hooting, it was our sign to crawl into the giant bed we shared and hold on to each other for dear life. And every night Grandpa G, obviously, would creep into our bedroom— it was completely silent and completely dark, but the smell of burnt cigar always gave the bastard away. Ash and I would try as hard as we could to pretend to be asleep in each other's arms, thinking every time *this* time would turn out different. The definition of insanity and all that—or maybe kids should know better. Thing is, it didn't matter how hard we squeezed each other's arms or flexed our thighs to keep our legs knotted together. Grandpa G was too strong, too determined, too whatever it is pedophiles feel. Every night I had to suffer losing my grip on Ash, feeling him slip away in the sweat our fear made. Grandpa G would spirit my brother away to some other room, and I'd go on hearing the owls. Eventually I'd sniff cigar again and feel Ash back in bed again. Sometimes I'd ask him what happened, but it was at least another decade before I ever got a straightish answer, and another ten years before the truth."

Yew could tell Brenda's face was once very pretty, that something other than time had left it haggard. "You were saying you helped your brother face his fear of the dark?"

"I showed him the night was nothing to be afraid of," said Yew. "We'd drop acid and hit concerts in Vegas, where lights are always on. So Sin City became a refuge for a couple of soon-to-be estranged evangelicals. There was one night I remember best because it was better than the rest, even if it was a little terrifying for me. We were hippy flipping at a hip-hop show on the festival grounds when we each had separate epiphanies. I thought I saw creepy changes coming this world's way, all of which more or less came true, by the way. It was one of those really good bad trips, if you get what I'm saying. Ash, meanwhile, realized he wanted to make a career out of facing fears, and it was when we were walking out of the show together that we bumped into this dude Hook from Hollywood, who invited us to his penthouse. We snorkeled in a bathtub full to the brim with blow. Needless to say, Ash came away with his first gig."

"..."

"That's all, Brenda. That's my truth. I've told you everything."

"It isn't all; it's half the truth, if that. There's something you're not telling me."

"But—"

"Something about fear," said Brenda. "If I were to guess—and my guesses are good, if you couldn't tell—I'd say there's something you fear even more than heights."

"What about you?" asked Yew. "What makes you think you know so much?"

"Or maybe it's more to do with love," said Brenda. "The worst kind of ghost."

"I don't want to talk about . . . Love."

"Your hesitation in combination with your inflection tells me Love's a person."

"I've been consuming my brother ashes." Love's leaving had left a void only Ash's ashes seemed to fill. "Like I said, I'm half empty without him. And lately my love tank's been running on empty, if you must know, but Ash's ashes seem to help. It's what keeps my love tank full enough for me to go on at all. It helps me process."

Brenda placed a gently heavy hand over Yew's. "I hear you."

Yew tasted salt and couldn't tell if it were liquid fear or tears. "The day I run out of ashes to eat is the day I fear most. It's a fate worse than death, waiting for me."

"Fear's as normal as it is necessary. Respect it as you would yourself."

"How?"

"Should you decide to dedicate your life to the art of drifting, as I have, moving from place to place and job to job even as you learn and relearn to adapt to ever-shifting environments, you'll need to relearn to drift in place, as I am presently."

"What do you mean? I've never learned to drift in place—whatever that means."

"In teaching you nothing, your air quote 'tutors' certainly taught you something."

"Living with the self, for the self."

"What you say is step one to mystic fullness," said Brenda. "It helps with fear."

"You say you're drifting in place right now, as we speak . . . which would imply you're afraid of something. Is it something I've said?"

"You should know I'll be heading to my grave wholly empty inside."

"Why's that?"

"Tonight's about you, Yew. Mine's a story for another night."

"Can I get a taste at least?"

"It's a love story, meaning it's a horror story, filled with the worst kinds of ghosts. It's about my first husband, Ron, back in Ohio, as well as my second husband, Don. For now, I'll just say drifting was never my path to choose. The art chose me. The reason I've been drifting in place tonight is because I fear your judgment worse than your family fears the wrath of their god. Judgment's inevitable in a life as regrettable as mine."

"The Book of Revelations reads like bad fiction," said Yew. "Lately, though . . ."

"I'd like to hear more about this epiphany of yours, this 'really good bad trip.'"

"Sure thing," said Yew. "If you promise not to judge me."

"I always like me some tongue-in-cheek. Humor's a healthy sort of hell."

"All right, then . . . well. I had my eyes shut the whole time, but if you've ever tripped before, then you already know how we all hold a universe in our heads. The first thing I saw in mine was this weird tornado thing that sounded like a billion bees . . ."

"Go on . . ."

"And then there was this kid with Down syndrome and a trashcan lid . . ."

————

THE PSYCHIC SURFERS, speaking as one, tell Don Philly he's in two places at once.

Philly's physical body has been airlifted out of the Hive by a DSA chopper now halfway between Bakersfield and its destination in Eden's End. The soul-fire comprising his consciousness, meanwhile, mans the wheel of a Punch Buggy Orange made from maybe a million or more penis fish, speeding through The Spider's forbidden fifty-fifth dimension on the way to Sector Z. There, he'll retrieve Calvin, the key to achieving the goal Philly shares with the bug who's lived in his liver these ten long years. He hasn't heard from Guy Ramsley since leaving Sector T, where the salaciously modified Zlokmatoog rose from the lagoon as if summoned by some infinite being (wink, wink).

He's been riding the fifty-fifth dimension's timewaves, which the openly suicidal surfers say are made of all different kinds of human emotion. They say the dimension's forbidden because emotions pose a devastating threat to The Spider's true truth, which She conceals and protects in order to preserve and perpetuate the illusion of "reality."

It is essential, the Psychic Surfers say, that all beings inhabiting either side of Phooka Road think and feel that whatever they perceive is, in fact, "real."

The Psychic Surfers, empathetic by nature, help Philly process this storm of information and a whirlwind more of it to boot, though they refrain from telling Philly the truth about this dimension's strange "backstage" space. They won't say what they mean when they say "backstage" because they said they didn't want to freak him out to the point of extinguishing his soul-fire, which would result in more than the death of his "real" body: it would terminate his existence entire, meaning nobody anywhere would remember the name Don Philly, for Don Philly never will have existed for somebody somewhere to remember. After asking where exactly he'd go, should at any point his soul-fire fade for any reason, the Psychic Surfers all at once intoned one word, "Out."

When he requested clarification, they said, "Ultimate excommunication."

The surfers themselves resemble life-sized seahorses with dorsal fins and crab-like legs, their dark eyes like somber moons in their wide, droopy faces. Their scaly flesh pulses with a certain electricity whose flashy colors embody the emotions breaking and crashing all around in waves that perpetually propel. All of them are always surging ahead, it seems, despite the countless flips and dips and spiraling downward plunges. Earlier Philly might've said it's like flying a spaceship in outer space; he now feels way smaller than that, a dust mite in a toy car navigating leaky pipes within the walls of some rotting house. He wonders if that's what they mean by "backstage," being trapped inside reality's frayed yellow wallpaper. Philly's tallied fifty-five surfers in all. Their round, eggy faces remind him of people with Down syndrome.

"Are we there yet?" he asks, spinning the fleshy steering wheel to match the surfers' latest breakneck maneuver. The penis fish leave his hands moist with grease. "Or how much longer 'til we're out of this 'Malpygmalion tube' or whatever you called it?"

The surfers respond as one as always. "Ticks. Consider counting them while you still can, man, because the tick we're outside this Malpighian Tubule will be the tick we're inside the Stercoral Pocket where we'll part ways. We'll be moving on to the Sucking Stomach to self-expire gloriously. What you do then will be up to you. Should you wish to see through your intention to reclaim Calvin, consider our words."

"Follow any silvery stuff like what we saw in Book Lung to Spinner Net, got it."

"The Spinneret, you mean. It can be tough to confront substance, depending on your worth's weight as a man. Worthy men tend to do so head-on, and if you intend to prove yourself like so, well . . . we'll all be waiting to see if you can reverse your self-deception's curse. We're all chomping at the bit to see if you'll undo the web of lies you've told yourself about yourself to cocoon yourself. Who knows, man? Maybe you'll end up escaping this backstage space the same way you got in—with your dreams intact."

They all crest a lava-red mountain of a timewave before dropping into its vast sloping break. It's like party surfing the tubular confines of some enlarged vein, but instead of a surfboard, Philly's got his wheels, even if said wheels are curled and compacted. The Psychic Surfers' rippling flesh assumes the wave's same shade of red.

"Now you're all flashing bloodred—are these waves anxiety or something?"

"These're part onism, part occhiolism, which is to say these waves speak to the complex frustration you might experience being stuck in one body that inhabits one place at a time while at the same time being aware of the smallness of your own perspective."

"It's official," he shouts out. "I'm done trying to comprehend this place."

"All emotions are vividly complex things."

"That corpse-colored wave of hate from earlier seemed simple-minded enough."

"Nothing's simple about the projected fear and deflected anger and misdirected disgust of self-loathing, which is what that wave's 'hate' was made of specifically."

"Whatever you say," says Don Philly. "Are we there yet?"

"Ticks, man. Ticks."

"How many?"

"Count them while you still can, man, because we all burn out in the end."

"One, two, three, four, five, six, seven, eight, nine, ten—"

He supposes he must've parted ways with the Psychic Surfers somewhere around *five*, meaning he's reached the Stercoral Pocket at last. He whips the wheel, ripping the Punch Buggy Orange up and down too many rolling timewaves to count, moving on complexly charged currents. The Stercoral Pocket's a poorly lit cavity whose outermost reaches seem to breathe, as has been the case with all these zones. He searches for silvery stuff the surfers call "substance." A round red-white-blue object captures his eye.

The circular object glints, casting light on slowly moving walls messy with slime.

Suddenly the whole dimension quakes and roars, throwing Philly's Zlokmagtoog with more force than all the timewaves he's surfed combined. The source seems to come from everywhere and everything, a single hissed word: *"HELLO."*

With this one booming word comes the truth about The Spider's forbidden dimension's "backstage" space. Philly eyes the sky for the hourglass moon he's actively ignored, its color onism/occhiolism-red. The face he sees in the moon tells him it's no moon at all —it's more of a window, or maybe a doorway, opening on a face as big as the world Philly thought he knew, a moony face like a sun that's burnt out, mangled with ruined innocence. He now knows for sure he's miniscule because that giant face through the hourglass is Calvin's. This "backstage" space makes up The Spider's insides.

Don Philly grips the slippery wheel, bracing for the storm of words to come, the whirlwind impact they're sure to have on his ability to keep his tiny penish car on course to Calvin. The soul-fire comprising the consciousness projecting his body flickers with fear, an esoteric sort for which perhaps only Psychic Surfers have words.

———

"Hɪ," Calvin's able to reply, now that the webbing's been torn from his mouth.

He isn't the least bit afraid addressing the fleshy, seemingly suspended hourglass, his lack of fear due in part to all the practice he had rehearsing for this very encounter with the Play Day House's hourglass play structure, the tall one with the precise dimensions. He conducted these silent rehearsals with his head's little voice while tracing the giant trapezoid in the ash underfoot, sometimes with Ernest and Edgar's help.

Also, fear is very much part of the catalogue of things Calvin can't feel.

Calvin feels nothing at all; his gears churn on sheer thought alone.

"I'd say it's nice to finally meet you, Anne Kell, but my body's telling me you're the biggest meanie of them all. Now're you going to leave my brother alone or what?"

A face forms in the hourglass's meaty middle, disfigured and distantly human, an incomplete caricature like a mask of somebody seconds away from screaming, tangled tendons and veins stretched and pulled in all directions as though this were the tragic result of uncountable surgical attempts to mend the upsetting results of an original botched operation——a face unlike anything anywhere else in nature. Her voice seems to emerge from a different facial crater or cavity or fissure with each word She hisses.

"You *think* you're clever, Calvin. Just because you *think* you know you *won't* know anything doesn't mean you've learned anything *worthy* of your own wasteful breath. It's this basic *static* conclusion humans like you often *reach* that often *leads* to hopelessness followed by self-worthlessness followed by *physical* and *emotional* isolation and subsequent *suicide* in some cloistered space. *Speaking* of which, welcome to Phooka Road Sector Z, where reality's as *thin* as your human mind runs *deep*."

"I can tell you're being mean while trying to sound like you're not."

"Can you tell you're *not* really *floating* in place?"

"It's your face that makes you look mean, I think."

"In all the *time* I've wasted contacting you and your *brother* over the course of your lifetimes' *clipped* and *worthless* rasps, the *sole* phenomenon I've deigned *remotely* worth paying any *serious* attention to has been you and Trent's *communal* obsession with *trapezoidal* turns, your *mortal* pursuit of all paths with *fractured* ends."

"Trent's a good person. He'll never give in to meanies like you or Mr. Moony."

"Keep *telling* yourself that—that *we're* the so-called *meanies*."

"I know my brother. He'll learn to listen and that'll be that."

"You *speak* as though *you're* the one pulling the strings."

"You dictate fate, you're saying. Or maybe you know someone who does."

"I'm *operating* under the *same* rules and *regulations* as mankind."

"Mother Climate's Contract of Basic Goodness, you mean. I'm guessing that's why neither you nor Mr. Moony haven't just killed me by now—you're implying you can't break Contract because there'd be some sort of consequence if you were to try."

"No one being is *absolved* of the *potential* threat of *ultimate excommunication*."

"And yet you seem to embody the exact opposite of all things basically good."

"I care little for your *tiny* perspective on your kind's so-called existential *crisis*."

"Whatever you say, Anne Kell—if that *is* your real name."

"I've assumed *many* faces and skins since humanity's evolution and subsequent *devolution*, immortalized by *spellbinding* tales *your* kind spin and weave to keep *me* altogether embodied—Neith of Egypt, Arachne of Greece, Ishtar of Babylonia, Minerva of Rome, Uttu of Sumer, Iktomi of the Lakota, Kwaku Ananse of the Ashanti, Aunt

Nancy of the West Indies, Nareau of Oceania, Areop-Enap of Micronesia, Tsuchigumo of Asia, the Itsy-Bitsy Spider of Easily Amused Children, Spider Grandmother of the Hopi, The Black Spider of Gotthelf, Charlotte of White, Atlach-Nacha of Smith, Shelob of Tolkien, Anansi of Gaiman, Aragog of Rowling, Spider-Man of Lee, It of King . . . *pick* your poison and *take* its toxin, I'm always there—*intoxicatingly* present."

"I guess I liked you in *Spider-Man.*"

"Which is one of *countless* tales that fail to come within one human-measured *inch* of expressing who it is I *am* and what it is I *do* here on my Web, which more or less *has been weaving itself* since I first came to be in Sector Z. Though I *will* say your manmade internet comes *slightly* closer, this so-called World Wide *Web.*"

"You mean computers and stuff?"

"The *internet* accumulates *control* over human thought and feeling much the way my *Web* amasses the perceptive *awareness* of all living beings, but while *your* web *traps* your kind in a mirror-maze of news and worldviews and narratives speaking to *facts* and *falsehoods* rooted in all things nebulous, *my* Web does humanity the *critical kindness* of bringing what you call *the real world* into focus, uniting you all in the belief that what you see and hear with your eyes and ears is *true*— that two plus two can *never* add up to *five.* This helps me help you keep safe and *alive* in a dimension crawling with *trapezoidal* turns leading to *divided* ends. *Your* kind, in turn, keeps *me* alive with your tall tales of me, myself, and I, feeding me the *emotion* needed to live out *time.* That is, until your kind violated the *Contract,* your manmade *web* having made one last *mess* of basic goodness."

"Trent's always hated the internet."

"Your brother's present state of *mind* mirrors Mother Climate's *decline.*"

"I'd argue us humans have always been the way we are, more or less."

"Earlier you spoke of *consequence* . . . what you call *cyberspace* is one, a result of your kind's *solipsistic* attempt to weave a *false* reality, forging a frenzied *space* where all human thought and feeling *aims* to reside, flowing freely in infinite directions *without* consequence. *Conse-*

quentially, you humans *forget* your bodies. To do all your *thinking* and *feeling* on this internet is to *waste* away, draining your eyes and ears of your own Light. I, for one, refuse to *aid* those who *refuse* to *use* their eyes and ears to see and hear. Such *willful* ignorance is a *slight* in the *all-seeing eyes* of the Infinite Sum One."

"I'm guessing that's your employer, the *real* reason I'm here and still alive."

"Your manmade web, therefore—in the most *basic* terms—more or less *reflects* my Web's current state, which is, in a word, *disturbed.*"

"You're trapped here, you're saying . . . a prisoner of your own Web the same way Mr. Moony is a prisoner of Bod. What you do on your Web is basically the same thing Love does with her Fungi program, with the Feline Freedom Society under the White House. You're like the scary monster version of Love. Or she's the human version of you."

"*One* metaphor trumps the *rest* in terms of describing my *work.*"

"And by 'work,' you mean curse, the debt you owe Mother Climate."

"I'm speaking *not* of the *internet*, but rather *Indra's net*, which emerges from a so-called Buddhist system of belief. India's Vedic philosophy comes close—how I'm depicted as being the being that *hides* ultimate reality under veils of illusion . . . but it is your *blessedly* quiet Buddhists that come closest of all with their concept of *inter-penetration*, using my Web as a *metaphor*—Indra's net, they call it—to try to *rationalize* how all phenomena are connected, how every thought that exists, has existed, or will exist—every *scrap* of datum that is truly true—are pearls that *hang* together, each reflecting another, the *universe* as *one* sanctified image."

"All right, I get it—you manipulate our thoughts to make it seem existence exists. Now are you going to have June and me executed or excommunicated or what?"

The void ignites with a great cerulean flash that lasts for as long as it takes for Calvin to take in The Spider's appearance, a feat made more difficult by the swarm of monstrosities that've been swimming or floating or scuttering all around undetected. The Spider's house-sized bulk hovers at the center of them all like the hub of some horrible wheel, the spokes being Her branching system of legs, which look more like tentacles, all of which outsize the trunk of any tree Calvin's ever seen. He's got time enough to see he hasn't been floating—he's dangling on strings made from the same webby anti-substance Mr. Moony keeps the sigs' bodies stuffed with. Calvin knows it for what it is: neurasthenia, the pain replacing pain's over-long absence. He imagines being a human marionette performing for an audience of devils. The blue light's collapse brings back the darkness. Calvin faces the face in The Spider's underbelly, hair humming with hurt.

"Thanks to *you*, your so-called friend *June* is now being *excommunicated*."

"But I didn't do anything!"

"You *ask*, my Web merely *answers*. Herein lies mankind's gravest *mistake*—you've forgotten your cosmic *place* in space, where you stand with your *words*."

"What've you done with June?"

"That great *flash* a few ticks back *shattered* the web-hole waiting room's walls."

"You're saying you fed June to your monsters."

"You'll know she's been fully *consumed* as *soon* as you forget her name."

"You're saying you fed June's existence to your monsters."

"It's a mystery as to *why* the excommunication process is taking this much *time*."

"I say we strike a deal. I'd like to place a bet on mankind—to invest my own substance in humanity, as represented by the fateful five, of which I am a part, from which I exist apart. To this I would provide my full consent despite all implications on all interdimensional levels, so long as we reach a mutual understanding of the terms."

"First you must *realize* and *accept* the foremost reason as to *why* my Web chose to *ensnare* the fateful five. Out of *all* humans still hacking out a survival on Mother Climate's great verdant body, after all, *you* and these *four fateful others* are most likely to consent to giving up your own *heads* via either *selfish* suicide or *selfless* sacrifice. In other words, Calvin, haven't you *heard* the *famous* human expression, 'famous last words'?"

"If there's one thing I'm one hundred percent sure about, it's that you and Mr. Moony don't know the first thing about human beings. Don't make that face—you heard what I said. You don't get us at all."

"There's a *whole* dimension I hoard in this body, a Spinneret *full* of human tales."

"There's more to us and our stories than what pain does to kindness and shame. I learned that over many lifetimes as a bumblebee watching Don Philly failing to write."

"You sound so *certain* of yourself, Calvin—so what are your *terms*?"

"First tell me what makes me the Frog and Gary the Gopher and Yew the Owl and Love the Cat and Don the Rat. What's our connection to these so-called five fateful beasts?"

"The *story* Mr. Moony is telling the Infinite Sum One about himself right here and now in *this* moment and *every* moment is a *conflated* one, such that only *my* Web can *wrangle* it. These five skulls, animal sacrifices for the birth of Eden's End—per Mother Climate's consent—symbolize *nothing* and *no one* living or dead or ultimately excommunicated, which is *worst* of the three. They're more like *motifs*. Sacred *patterns*."

"In that case, here are my terms—turn my Light back on. This means giving me my glasses and hearing aids, my Captain America shield, the photo of me and Trent at the zoo, my Down syndrome, and, above all, my power to feel. Give it all back and then cast me back home in time for the Ritual of Five and Five. I want to be present for when my brother proves you and Mr. Moony and Bod and whoever else wrong."

"That's a lot of basic *goodness* to recoup—I suppose it *could* be done. Though what am I to *receive* in exchange? Surely you *see* such terms mustn't *be* so one-sided?"

"You'd get proof that commonsense kindness still exists—that humans don't always need your help to live. You could use the inside-out paradox to your own benefit. Go all in on mankind to get out of your deal with Mr. Moony instead of the other way around. That way, assuming you ever find a way to escape this self-inflicted prisoner's existence you call life in Sector Z, you'd be free to weave your Web as you please."

"*Kindness* can *hardly* be associated with what you call *common sense.*"

"They're both energy—something that's felt. Especially when they're missing. That's something Love taught me when she kept seeing her goldfish, Jabronis, instead of me."

"You're suggesting humans can *think* and *feel* their way out of *Apocalypse.*"

"I'm stating outright your precious Contract's got human beings all wrong. The Contract presumes to assume we're as morally sound as . . . well, you or Mr. Moony."

"Moony and I have already *reached* our own terms of mutual understanding regarding the Contract's *inside-out paradox.* Perhaps I can't afford to turn my back on a pooka who's already *agreed* to deliver *me* five fateful Heads to *embody* the *one hundred percent death toll dividends* I still *owe* Mother Climate as a return on Her *own* long-standing investment in humanity. Why should I listen to *you*, a human *being*, a product of a *species* who can't even *unite* in the face of a *divided* end's Apocalypse?"

"Because with us, we can grow to learn how it's essential to recognize how all our relationships must come with their flaws if they're ever going to function because *we're* imperfect. There's a delicate balance to it all, but the 'all' here is worth the weight. Yew showed me that back when I was a dragonfly and still clinging to her twin brother's urn. Watching her guide her clients through a multitude of psychedelic breakthroughs."

"I'm *sick* of *waiting* for Mr. Moony to get human beings to get their act *together.*"

Anne Kell's face seems to shrivel inside the hourglass, a sick thing short on time.

"But maybe it's our flaws that make us worthy of telling your story at all. Maybe it's why we keep trying time and again—we want to get your story just right, to do you the justice you deserve.

I bet the day we tell your story perfectly is the day we stop telling it."

"You're *attempting* to appeal to my *vanity*—so *humanly* of you."

"I get that what we think of as 'reality' can't exist without you, Anne Kell, and I fully appreciate that—and everything else you've done to help us over time. But it's my understanding those terms are mutually binding. You implied it yourself—you can't exist without some species or another whose pain exists for the sole function of telling your story. I'm aware your life's a story, that all of our stories —zoomed out and seen as one interconnected web—is *your* story in disguise. And I know it's its ending you fear most."

"You're *sorely* mistaken, Calvin. The thing I fear beyond all else is *time*."

"So prove it, then—prove that yours is a story worth telling until the end of time."

"Perhaps I'd rather keep *spinning* time's three-way motion. That way, *everything* that gets *outside* of Sector T ends up *inside* me, *backstage,* behind my hourglass. The *timewaves* within me nourish this *body* with *all* the emotion I'll *ever* need to *survive*."

"Let the last thing I learned as a ladybug in Gary Mustafa's company be your first new lesson in humanity. There's a difference between surviving and living. I've offered you a way out, a way to live . . . so what do you say?"

"So long as you've *considered* the *real* possibility that your twin very well *might* end up going through with beheading the fateful five —which would *qualify* as the *defeasance* rendering these terms *null* and *void*—then I *suppose* we're in agreement."

"Do I have your word and sign of consent?" says Calvin.

"*You* have my full *consent*. Though you're a *fool* to have invested in *man*."

"If anything—you spiteful, devious bitch—I'm betting on my brother's humanity, as well as the beautifully human selfishness and self-centeredness of the fateful five."

"Wait a *tick*—that's not what you *said!*"

"It's what I implied. Now give me back my Light and prepare to eat your words."

"You've lied to me!"

"I'm only human."

"My Web will have you excommunicated just like—"

"JUNE! HANKY! THE TIME IS NOW! COCKADOODLE-DOOOOO—MUH!"

Calvin's known June's been eluding The Spider's power-hungry freaks and fiends because all this time his head's little voice has been breathing her name, her words a bass echo in his body: *We can twist the words [The Spider] doesn't say against [Her] by making [Her] consent to an implicitly distorted dialogue of our own.*

"The hatch, Calvin! Where's the hatch!"

Calvin cocks his head back at June's words; already he can feel actual emotion replenishing his body like hot soup on the coldest day, filling him with that special heat hugs have in the hardest times. She's riding atop Hanky the hynetter's arched back, her face wrapped with Hanky's hanky—Hanky's Light, Calvin thinks and feels—which beams like a mini sun some god had forgotten to turn off before bedtime. June shoots across the darkness above, a super-nova superhero sending monsters scattering like shadows before a Montana sunrise. The neurasthenic strings binding Calvin to the beastly black widow snap one by one as more and more of The Spider's face shrivels within the hourglass, Her veiny fissures retreating inside the red. Each snapping string eases the weight on his body, the unbearable pain of painlessness rooted in his hair.

"Here!" Calvin screams, pointing out the pulsing growth under-scoring The Spider's hourglass, an oozy pod whose edges drip with substance. "Her Spinneret!"

Calvin's never been so joyful to feel fear's icy hands reaching into his chest and seizing his heart in its freezing grip. The laughter bubbling in his tum-tum boils over and spills from his mouth, defrosting his terror with the unspoilable air of jubilant release. June and Hanky, meanwhile, have swooped down beside him. Five more strings still hold Calvin tethered to The Spider's Spinneret. Hanky's curled legs clamp down on the first.

Hanky thrashes his legs to rip the first neurasthenic string in two, and Calvin finds himself perceiving Sector Z's vaguely thin reality with sharper clarity, his cool blue glasses and hearing aids giving his face the comfort and security it's craved. The second and third severed strings return to his hands the trash lid refashioned to resemble Captain America's weaponized shield; plastered to the lid's underside is the photograph of Calvin and Trent at the Los Angeles Zoo, a movie-memory's worth of words back in his possession. By the time Hanky does away with strings four and five, Calvin feels fully himself again, the final stray pieces to his interior jigsaw clicked into place.

His Light is back on, the entire spectrum of human emotion once more his to suffer.

Like a balloon whose line's been cut, Calvin begins to float and drift in space, doing slow somersaults and revolutions as he rises on the air—just go with it, his body tells him. He might've yelled "Up, up and away!" if not for the extreme nausea now scrunching everything inside his tum-tum. He rolls and whirls and flips and twirls, clinging to his shield as he spins into darkness, the airspace traced with the smelly sillage of The Spider's departed legion. He's unable to free his mind of the sickening image of Anne Kell's Spinneret, which, having discharged Calvin's Light—his most treasured items —looks too much like what he wishes he never saw in the movie he caught Trent watching to the end their first night on the run in the RV long ago. Calvin hates remembering snapping awake at the sound of Mommy's screams in the middle of the night, how Trent sat with his back pressed to Calvin's sleeping nook's ledge, laptop open on his lap, how this was how Calvin found himself watching a movie he can never unsee.

He spied over Trent's shoulder and saw Mommy sprawled on a hospital bed with her legs spread, all that splashing and wailing she did before Daddy's quavering voice could be heard saying he thinks he's going to be sick, and suddenly the screen had a crack snaking down the middle of it after the camera came plummeting to rest where several nursing shoes dashed under brownish juices raining down from the swollen thing between Mommy's legs. Calvin asked Trent what they were looking at, and Trent smashed his computer shut and told Calvin not to worry, it's just a movie-memory. When

Calvin asked if Mommy and Daddy were okay, Trent—who would later take a hammer to his laptop's hard drive—once again told Calvin not to worry, Mommy and Daddy are hiding out at the hospital, where Mommy's in the middle of giving an ugly birth.

Waves of fresh grief soak Calvin through with a weight almost physical; the movie-memory that played on Trent's laptop's screen was the lie his own eyes fed his heart and mind for years, building for himself a safer world in which Mommy and Daddy would wake up one day in a hospital. This must've been The Spider's doing, he thinks, as must be the case with the movie-memory Calvin's made from the picture at the zoo, the way he's told himself Trent did King Louie a kindness that day, sharing the rest of his vanilla ice cream, when really Trent had wasted his ice cream trying to make the monkey mad. Trent was merely being a meanie, which people could be sometimes. Which people have been since space and time came together as one strand in some infinite Web.

Calvin is floating and spinning and seeing in his mind's eye the Web The Spider weaves with her Spinneret, the lie Anne Kell's crafted for the safety and sanity of human minds and hearts, the "critical kindness" She bestows upon a world running apocalyptically low on thought and suicidally low on feeling. He directs what remains of his focus on June and Hanky, two dots now very far below, grief filling him whole, having bet The Spider such suffering is worth its weight in words unspoken.

Down The Spider's Spinneret Calvin watches Hanky fly, June riding astride, the sacrifice of two consenting Downers giving up their own existences in exchange for the rebirth of someone else for whom Calvin's been waiting, the man he's drawn to this space at this time over the course of countless lifetimes as a bumblebee. It takes no time at all for Hanky to rip and tear his way inside the hatch's gooey slit, and before they permanently exit sight and mind, Calvin has time enough to wish he could've given June and Hanky both high-fives for keeping him sane and alive in a place mortally absent of pain. He pictures a world where this happens—this slap of skin, this reciprocal exchange of goodwill—knowing full well it'll never be enough to do Hanky and June the justice they . . . gone.

What next comes rumbling and roaring its way out of Anne Kell's Spinneret resembles a belch of flame at first, until it grows in size and materializes as a humped orange car: the first fiction Don Philly ever believed in, Calvin remembers.

It's not a bird, not a plane—it's Don Philly's Light, his rolling lie, which is to say it's the first of many things Philly has ever called a dream.

And it's Calvin's rocket ride home.

———

"I BET that's why people these days would rather criticize than empathize," said the woman called Yew, whose face had aspects of what Mustafa would be attracted to.

They were parked slanted on a slope somewhere with the Musker's power cut, with Yew behind the wheel speaking with the masked woman whose name was Love in the front seat. Gary Mustafa lay curled in the fetal position in back, head pounding like someone was taking a hammer to it. The back of his neck made him feel as though he'd survived another noose—his would-be fifth, by his count. Tears leaked from his eyes' inner corners and burned down the bridge of his nose. His mouth's curiously dry climate hardly added up with how he last remembered it before somebody somewhere turned off the light of the world. The noise his belly made seemed more a product of sickness than hunger. He wanted to puke at the sight and stench of the deep-fried cucumber someone had laid like a paperweight on the crook of his neck.

He resumed pretending to snore.

"Sounds like someone's up," said Yew.

So much for pretending—Mustafa stirred and sat up. "Where are we?"

"God's Mouth," said Love. "Down this hill straight ahead."

Mustafa stuck his head in the gap above the center console and peered out the windshield where, down there, the narrow entrance between the canyon's towering walls looked like a slight crack in a wall for gods. Through the gap, the gorge opened up into a corridor that would widen and expand for miles before closing off in a roundabout horseshoe near the Whispering Wellspring's cave entrance. Mustafa had read up on God's Mouth on some guy's blog whose background had featured stellar photographs of Rufio's deep-dish pizza, which was why he'd picked there to eat a million years ago. The odd book he'd swiped from the restaurant's restroom rested on the dashboard.

"Why are we here?" he asked.

"It's the only way into Eden's End," said Yew. "Apparently there're escalators."

Mustafa's insides twisted with a sick, lurching panic. "What time is it?"

"Two," said Love. "You've been out the past hour."

"You mean to say we've one hour until the witching hour, and we're not even inside the fudging park," said Mustafa. "What're we waiting for? Drive!"

"It's not that simple," said Yew. "Love's got a feeling."

"I feel a lot of things," said Mustafa, "none of which exactly scream 'supreme comfort.' Matter of fact, things I'm feeling scream the exact opposite of that."

"I've felt this way only once before," said Love. "Staring at a hammock strung between some plastic palms trees all the way in Punta Mita, Mexico."

"Good Lord, we're doomed."

"That's exactly how it felt, Gary. Except when I was staring at this hammock and crying, it wasn't me who was doomed. It ended up being my sister, Angel, who right then was hanging herself with her hammock. I feel the same way now. A sick sixth sense of foreboding, like maybe we're better off driving away and forgetting all of this."

Mustafa reached under his seat and felt around until his fingers found precious polychloroprene. Then he pulled his deflated findings to his lips, blew a big orange balloon into existence, and tied it off. "Here," he said, handing Love the balloon. "I always keep two under the seat. For emergencies. You can name it and everything."

"Um, thanks?"

"How're you feeling now?"

"Like we don't have much of a choice, if I'm being honest."

"Choice," said Mustafa. "Charlie Choice. It's a good name. Short for Charlotte."

"Should we go, Love?"

Love nodded and told Yew to take it slow.

Yew powered on Mustafa's electric Musker and rolled it slowly down the slope into the unpaved track choked with weeds and rock below. It wasn't long before cacti pitted the path on either side like converging crosses, the snaky track spotted with curled succulents. Wild clumps of deer grass sighed at the smart car's slithering passage.

Mustafa despised the twists and turns into desert darkness, the stars like winking eyes above, the rutted pits below jerking and jouncing the car in a way that reminded him of how Mother rocked him way too hard in her arms the day he came home after the beating he'd taken from Randy Mick and his marijuana stick-smoking goons in the woods. A single drifting cloud blotted out the moon and produced a gloom whose sickly, soupy quality fast-forwarded his memories of Mother to the night he decided he'd tell on her for sneaking into his room in the ICU to do his daily gifted balloons terrible harm, hissing speculative creeds Mustafa wouldn't come to believe in until Wendy Weather's burial when the Ladybug first landed on his wrist and seized his full attention. They passed through the crack into God's Mouth and rolled on, braving the bumpy sea of dark.

Shapes flitted past, split cacti and splintered boulders and leaf-less, lifeless plants. The steadily narrowing valley's ceaseless bumps and ruts made Mustafa picture neurons navigating the pits and dents of some demented brain. He suggested turning on the radio, which Love did. Voices chittered through static, decidedly ghostlike. Mustafa thought he could feel the pressure of God's weighty eyes looking down on them the way children view ants, watching the Musker zip through the cracks of the earth. The wheels gobbled gravel and spat ground sand in its slithery wake.

Yew gazed on with glazed eyes, Mustafa saw in the rearview. He thought he picked up a rustle of movement—a slow churning wave in the wide strip of wild grass slashing across the chasm ahead—and told himself it had to be wind. Times like these, Mustafa wished he had his own personal hot-air balloon with his own personal aeronaut to steer it—preferably a wife, a copilot in life. Love told Yew to roll the windows down so they could listen for hissing, but it was the Musker itself that listened.

Mustafa didn't bother asking about this hissing they sought after; he was still in his mind in a hot-air balloon with Kimmie-Sue, escaping to cloudy landscapes. He returned to his body inside the Musker when Love said, "Make no mistake about it, Yew, only cats you'll find out here are dead ones."

"What makes you say that?"

Mustafa already had his answer before getting his question all the way out; from a gap between a boulder and a weedy cluster ahead came the sound of small creatures in pain, a subdued sort of mewling that brought to mind newly born kittens trapped under heaps of rubble. The sound seemed to drift further away, receding like an echo down the cluttered trail into the canyon's ever-thickening shadows. He found himself drawn to the feeble whimper like a lost child to his mother, poking his head out the passenger window and nicking his cheek on the teeth of strange leaves. The wheels slurped mounds of mud.

If it turned out his initial gut instincts about Love and Yew were correct—that they were really Party White Patrol assassins like he first thought—then this would make for a lovely spot to do him in and dump his body.

"Stop the car," he said, and the Musker listened, fishtailing to a halt.

Mustafa opened the door and hopped out, feeling suddenly safer inside, emotion-wise, beyond the two ladies' reach. The high beams penetrated to illuminate the boulder's façade maybe ten yards ahead, the big stone itself easily outsizing any bulldozer.

"What're you doing?" said Yew.

Mustafa's oxfords snagged in the squelch of mud underfoot. "I hear singing."

"We're supposed to listen for hissing."

"Hold on, Yew—give him a second. You do you, Gary."

Mustafa followed the enmeshed beam the headlights generated, trudging closer to the boulder, which was cracked in places like some giant egg that had endured a high fall. Moss grew dank and dark along the bottom. The gusting breeze lofted a spray of grit to go with that soft ringing outcry of something in pain in need of relief; the pain in his neck sang the same tune. At one point it seemed as if whoever was making the noise had gotten right up behind him. His heartbeat thumped in his throat. His legs wobbled, but he kept moving forward and came right up to the boulder.

Up close, he saw that the cracks in it weren't random like he thought. They zigged and zagged to make a face etched in stone. It was like being a young boy again, seeing the man in the moon. He took in one last shaky breath and, hugging the perimeter of the rock, slipped out of sight of the high beams and into the shadows.

What he found on the ground behind the boulder looked like the carcass of some colossal snake—or perhaps only its discarded skin—but after kneeling down and feeling around, he decided it couldn't be real snakeskin. He tugged some of it back into view of the headlights and found himself looking down on strips of bamboo woven into several cylinders, all covered with a fine sheet of cloth meshed with grass and green tissue paper.

It was the discarded carcass of one of those Chinese dragon floats, like what he'd always wanted the Chinese student population at Allegiance to make for Chinese New Year every year, ostensibly to celebrate diversity when really it would've been his subtle way of honoring Kimmie-Sue, who was partly Chinese. This resulted in many a heated exchange with his superintendent every year; these annual arguments had been the real reason he'd hired on the Skeeter to run the campus security team. President Mangrove's executive order had afforded all decision-making power to high school principals—the Skeeter had been Mustafa's not-so-subtle middle finger to the superintendent, who Mustafa suspected was a white supremacist. What the Skeeter ended up doing to Kimmi-Sue's son, Billy, was karmic retribution at its holy worst. The humming noise waxed and waned in pitch and distance now, the screechy result of someone trying to sing through the feedback loop of some busted amplifier.

Something twitched in Mustafa's peripherals, drawing his eyes to the darkness behind the boulder like flies to a corpse. Someone under the float—definitely a human being, a full-grown adult—had sat up on the ground. With a little more moonlight, Mustafa knew the stranger would've looked like someone who'd thrown on a bedsheet for Halloween and called it a day; as things stood, the person looked like someone who'd come to in the belly of a sleeping snake. The disturbed mic signal suddenly cleared, making way for the singsong voice of a prepubescent boy Mustafa could visualize with disturbing clarity, nestled away someplace all alone, singing his way to sanity.

"*I know something you don't know . . . a tale of woe, is El Jaylo's . . .*"

The grown man under the float turned toward Mustafa and said, "Run."

Mustafa was halfway back to the Musker by the time he realized Yew had the car horn blaring nonstop. The noise blended in with the screechy cacophony he'd been ignoring, being too busy trying to put out of mind the superintendent's yearly arguments speaking to "any decent Red's" inherent responsibility "to do their part" in preserving the eastern Zone's western way of life. Mustafa's retreat to the car hadn't begun with the man under the dragon's warning to run. What had moved him to movement were all the bones and body parts he hadn't seen until after his eyes had fully adjusted to the darkness behind the boulder, strewn beyond the reach of the headlights: arms and legs and hands and feet with their bones popping out, a ribcage or two, ropes of viscera, the severed head of a man who died mid-scream. Mustafa had been so focused on following his ears that he'd neglected his nose's equally prudent information—fresh, wet rot.

Now he approached the Musker with horror constricting his heart and throat like a delayed toxin. He was running so frantically that he lost a shoe the second before he decided he'd leap for the safety of the backseat through the open window, but at the last second Yew jerked the car forward so that when Mustafa left his feet, he came straight back down on his face, skidding forward on his chest in the mud, which smeared its way into his mouth. He got his head up in time to see the back wheels reverse course before the back bumper banged into his head and face, making his neck snap back.

Unspeakable pain took him back to the spinal injury he'd suffered at the hands of Randy Mick, the barrage of shovels from bullies stoned on marijuana sticks. He tried army-crawling away from the car and ended up worming in place.

He flopped over on his side, his view of the world thusly skewed. The tall grass cutting across the chasm ahead shifted in a way he knew couldn't be wind, a titanic groundswell of motion that brought deep-sea ocean waves to mind. Hands descended from above and latched onto his collar like a cat snatching a gopher, fingernails slicing like claws into the skin of his neck. The ensuing pain made his eyes roll back in his head, and he was back in the backseat by the time his eyes rolled back open.

The world's viscous sludge dragged Mustafa in and out of consciousness, a world in which he could see only as much as he could move, darkness in motion, spinning and swaying and swallowing. He was barely able to keep up with its speed and record; the Musker zoomed forward, the turbulence bonking his body limply around. Everything inside his body felt on fire. Tall cliffs like gnashing teeth closed in on every side.

At some point he gazed out the window and noticed something scaling the cliffs well above the moving car, one beastly motherfudger of a monster, a slithery mass of seemingly endless coils keeping level with Mustafa's inverted line of sight. Every now and then voices chittered through the painful haze, decidedly human.

They said to turn here or there, to go this way or that, to keep away from that fucking snake. The fusillade of profanity they unleashed made Mustafa want to wince. Someone shouted look, elevators or whatever, then someone else said there was no way *this* car could fit inside *that* tunnel, and the first voice said something about choice.

The bright orange balloon floating within Mustafa's reach—if only he could get his arms to work right—vanished from sight, the car moving much slower now, inching deeper into darkness, zigging and zagging onward and upward—up, up, up, the slowest of slow crawls. When finally the world banged down and evened out again, it was everything Mustafa could do to keep himself from falling onto the floor, the sudden shift in forward momentum ripping a cry from his throat. Something louder than an airplane thundered way over-head—DSA chopper, someone said, and someone else questioned where the hell it was going. The Musker's automated voice rang in the witching hour.

Only then did Mustafa come fully conscious, deciding here and now he'd risk the pain he fully expected would come with body movement. He rose in the backseat only to discover pain's relative absence, realizing to his shame that his paralyzing journey in and out of consciousness had purely been a product of pressure getting all the way in.

He seized Charlie Choice, held her tightly to his chest, neck throbbing with the blood moving through his broken nose's wedges of bone and collecting thick in his throat.

"I think we lost it," said Love, who still had her mask on.

"Don't bet on it," said Yew. "I'm picking up on some seriously strong energy."

Charlie Choice popped in Mustafa's arms, making both women scream.

"I'm sorry to've startled you," he said, devastated.

"It's whatever," said Love, exhaling. "You should know we've been inside Eden's End maybe five minutes, and your car literally just said it's the witching hour."

"Meaning we're running late for your very important date," said Yew.

"Trust me when I say you don't want to know the full extent of what's going on."

"We're being chased by a snake big enough to eat the car," said Mustafa. "I saw."

"At least we're all on the same page," said Love. "So where to now, Gary?"

Once more the DSA chopper grumbled overhead, this time heading back the way it had come. Mustafa wished he could see what this place looked like in daylight. The wind swept through the open windows in a wave of wintergreen, chill against his face. He pictured the nurse who'd been so kind as to tether to his bedside a new balloon to get him through the night every night on the long and painful road to recovery.

"The chopper," he said. "Wherever it just came from is where we must go."

They retraced the chopper's flight path northeast, heading deeper into the wood.

"Anyone else hear that?" said Ycw. "That whispered ringing?"

Mustafa thought it sounded sad.

"Something tells me we're going the right way," Love said.

15

THE RITUAL OF FIVE AND FIVE
(INFINITE ANGUISH)

?

"Simple narratives used to work," Love had said, parked on the slope overlooking the entrance to God's Mouth, eyeing the crack in the canyon below, darkness carved in the narrowest smile, a grin without humor. Yew picked at her teeth in the driver's seat, a sign the acid she must've recently dropped was kicking into a higher gear. Mustafa lay curled in back like a fetus huddling the umbilical cord in his mother's womb. "Then apparently the internet went and opened all these backdoors. Mary used to call the web the new wild west, said her cyber control laws would allow for widespread inner peace."

"I remember the way she went about marketing the Faustian Terms of Facial Recognition Service Agreement," said Yew. "Called it a call for love, law, and order."

"It didn't matter who you were or where you came from—if you had a face, it'd wind up in the database. More faces meant more control. More Cat Hackers."

"You can't blame yourself for joining the FFS, Love. I mean, for fuck's sake."

406

"It's not like I had a choice—or even a say at all. I'd been tasked to exploit mass hatred for the sake of keeping the system in place, and back then you can bet your ass I knew my way to the heart of any individual. I remember operating on sheer fury, pissed and ruthless in my every delicate maneuver. In the end it was that or Bakersfield."

"Earlier you said you saw the Crown Virus as your game to win."

"More than anything else, it was my opportunity for retribution."

"After *Love Beach*, you mean."

"They hated my face. They took it and superimposed it over my sister's in a false Facebook account with Angel's photos and personal info. Made it so Angel went viral without her knowledge. I had no clue she'd been depressed—she always seemed to have it all figured out. They kicked her while she was down and called me 'inauthentic cunt.'"

"When's the last time you took off your mask in public?"

"I baited America with hate, and half the country ate it up and called what they were doing revolution while the other half called it history repeating itself."

"You're saying you're responsible for Civil War II."

"I made it so people were okay with hating one another—at some point they all started to see it as entertainment. I had them addicted to hatred I created," said Love.

"Five years is a long time to be doing all that underground, Love."

"I told myself it was better than being an influencer."

"I *thought* I spotted Fungi within Instagrammar's framework," said Yew.

"It's Mary's now. Fungi gets programmed inside the heart-drives of every newly released piece of Mangrovia technology. Our baby's taken on a life of its own."

"It's what you used to sow all that hate, isn't it?"

"Fungi helps me revise the story of society so that it appears somewhat digestible to the public. With it, I can make any complex sub-narrative seem simple, when really all that's happening is your basic, everyday mass misinterpretation."

"You cater to ignorance."

"I've catered to anger, Yew, in my contracted commitment to *control* ignorance. You could say I'm the reason why everyone feels their own feelings are so important—or why everyone thinks their own thoughts are in fact their own."

"At least you know where you stand in all this."

"The Halo Virus," said Love. "It's bigger than anything I've ever done."

"Are you sure you're not just mad the president's kept you in the dark about it?"

"It takes what I do—my subtlest cues of influence—and amplifies the effects to a degree of menace the likes of which we've never seen. I mean, you should see some of the headlines Mary's made me bury recently. Not that anyone would care. That's the thing—people're long past the point of caring anymore, and *that's* what I blame myself for."

"You're saying the Halo Virus is like a steroid for social decay," said Yew.

"I'm saying it's a nuclear bomb ticking off inside the entire American body, meaning all of us, an existential threat made worse by the uniquely American satisfaction we take in being individuals. Ignorance is useful insofar as what it contributes to society's overarching narrative, which has to be never-ending because stories are what make society mean anything. The Halo Virus could spell the end for America's story."

"From what I can tell," said Yew, "yours is one of those rare cases where you should consider spending more time worrying more for yourself than others."

"I don't have enough love in my love tank. Like, my love tank is not full enough."

"We've got to get your love tank full."

"But how, Yew?"

"We could always turn around and drive away. Your call."

"It's tempting," said Love. "Especially because of this sick feeling I've got, which now I hope I'm done talking about. It'd just be so easy to cast aside responsibility for whatever happens tonight —to blame anyone or anything existing beyond ourselves."

"I bet that's why people these days would rather criticize than empathize . . ."

———

"You're telling me this man's alive?" President Mangrove said to her Skeeter, Adam, as they stood over Don Philly's nude, comatose body.

Trent held his spot in front of the great stone slab on the edge of the Lunar Lagoon a solid thirty yards away, exhausted from standing around waiting for something else of substance to happen. Mr. Moony had taken to J-Tree Lane to "monitor the fateful three's journey's progress" and to "make 100 percent certain" The Titanoboa didn't act on any "bodily temptations," which Trent had taken to mean "hunger." The lagoon's degree of luminosity had increased with each passing hour; Trent's body told him sunrise wasn't too far around the corner. He studied the man lying asprawl in the center of the clearing, a lump of flesh and bone the DSA chopper had dropped from the sky like a sack of something worthless. It was a good thing Adam had been there to ease the man's fall.

It was the chopper's special delivery that had stolen Trent's attention from the Lunar Lagoon's underwater language, which was making Trent think and feel things he'd rather not. He'd watched Don Philly fall through the hatch in the airship's underbelly and plunge maybe fifty feet; he'd since learned via eavesdropping that this careless method of delivery had been specifically requested by Mr. Moony, who apparently claimed it would save time. Philly's body landed in a huge net made from this gooey gray stuff Mr. Moony had excreted, which Adam had strung like a spiderweb between some trees, flashing the siren in its head to signal to the pilot where the carrier should aim to drop its load.

Trent could sense Dex coming awake and alive in his hands.

The fateful three were running late, which was why Mr. Moony had taken to the lane, and now there wasn't much anyone could do but wait. Trent wrestled thoughts and feelings. He still didn't know whether he had what it would take to decapitate a human being—let alone five human beings—even if it was for a good cause.

"Ey, T-Bone, don't I, like, get a say in all this?" said Dex the meat cleaver.

"Shut up," said Trent. "I'm trying to hear what the president's saying."

"It ain't like it's anything of substance. If I were you, bro, I'd focus on you."

"I don't know if I'm ready to see Calvin again. It hurts to think about."

"Is it your chest again?"

"And a sound. In my head. Like someone's scrunching up a plastic water bottle."

"I don't hear anything, bro."

"Maybe I'm making it up—maybe that's why it hurts."

"Hit me with the latest."

"I can't decide," said Trent. "I keep switching sides, leaning this way or that."

"You've gotta pick a side and stick with it if you're tryna play the game, bro."

"Blacks and reds, kindness and shame, us and them."

"I've never bitten into a human neck before. Bet it's real tough."

"What's tough is deciding who to believe with regards to what's at stake."

"Back in Texas, the choicest steak to work with was always the porterhouse, with two cuts of beef flanking the T-Bone. Tenderloin and strip steak. Best of both worlds."

"I mean, I just *met* Mr. Moony. Way I see it, his mere existence alone complicates everything I thought I had a handle on. All this time, all I thought I had to worry about was delivering Anne Kell five skulls and five Heads—and then she'd go back to bed and leave me and my head alone forever. It was simple. Now it's anything but."

"At least it'd be for a good cause," said Dex. "Five Heads, delay the Apocalypse."

"One of those Heads'll be Calvin's."

"Maybe you're better off without him," said Dex. "Look at me, bro. See me and so see yourself. Look at what you've been able to accomplish—you're the head of Troop Peewee working directly under the president of the Divided States of America. That never would've happened with Calvin always around for you to worry about."

"It's been exhausting obsessing over not obsessing over my brother's memory."

"I guess that would explain all those nights we stayed up late debating sloppy joes and Wild Will Spiro and the tale of El Jaylo. Talk about exhausting, bro."

"It's obvious I needed other stuff to focus on to distract myself with—but lately it's been too hard to separate the real from the unreal. I'd be lying to myself if I told myself I've got any control over any of this anymore. Like, if El Jaylo's really real, for example, could you then tell me when the hell that even happened—or *how*?"

"You heard about the kid in town whose pet boa constrictor went missing."

"So?"

"So what happened the last time someone you knew went missing around here?"

"Calvin ran into Mr. Moony," said Trent. "Then when I went out into the woods looking for Calvin, I found Beetlejuice stuck to a stump near that old standpipe. And then there's Mr. Moony's body, which looks like it's made of a whole bunch of BJs . . ."

"Need me to put two and two together, bro?"

"Beetlejuice latched itself onto my brainstem, meaning some other bug might've done the same sort of thing with that kid's missing snake. The bug could've done to the snake's DNA what BJ did to the water in my old mason jar—like a glassful of galaxy, I remember thinking. Looked like this lagoon, actually. And there's the bug inside Adam doing whatever it's doing with Adam's heart-drive. Maybe there're bugs hidden all over Eden's End—maybe they're what *made* Eden's End. God, what've I gotten myself into?"

"Honestly, sometimes it's like you're not paying attention. The tale of El Jaylo covered all that already, bro, meaning it's never been a waste of time to think about."

"But now the time's come, Dex, and I've still got no clue what I'll choose. I don't know if I have it in me to sacrifice my own brother—plus four others."

"Porterhouse steaks retain the best of both worlds despite the dividing bone."

All of a sudden Trent could hear the president complaining about something—he listened in on her words. "Where's all that hooting coming from? Tell me, Adam!"

Trent eyed past the split boulder's twin halves marking the path leading in and out of the Lunar Lagoon and saw headlights splitting the boulder's divide.

Saw-whet Park was home, he remembered, even if it burned.

———

THE WAY HOME'S through Sector E—E for Earth, the kid Calvin keeps saying.

Phooka Road's made of the soul-fire of everything that's burned throughout the multi-verse, the Psychic Surfers told Philly back inside The Spider, which is why he sees the Road's pavement and perceives "ash." Anything he sees or smells or hears or touches or tastes in this place, they warned him, is the result of his human mind failing to make sense of "truly true truth," which is why Phooka Road looks to Philly like Death Valley's Badwater Road, or the Road to Golgotha, or D.S. Route 285 of West Texas legend. It's an utterly joyless track whose pavement wavers like smoke underneath the Punch Buggy's chugging penish wheels, which find solid ground where there seems to be none.

The thirsty wasteland unfolding in every direction echoes the desolation following any oil field's long-term abandonment. Skeletal huts and shacks are scattered throughout like bugs that've been squashed underfoot and left to rot. Faded road signs convey distances to the nearest interdimensional sectors measured in light-seconds.

They ride under the changeless light of Sector M's five phantom moons, steadily approaching the web-hole leading to Sector E, whose ash barrier—supposing Calvin's assertions are correct—connects to Earth's. Calvin hoots and hollers in the front seat, pointing out "jellyfish people" excitedly, Visceranians lying clustered and immobile in the roadside's coal-black earth like beached deep-sea squids. Philly and Calvin zoom past beings all over the place, kindness breathers and shamelessness breeders one and all.

There's a swamp where impish goblins in frayed jerkins sit on stumps arranged in a jagged circle and wager body parts, all wearing the lifeless expression of anyone who learns what happens after waiting all your life for the lottery to roll out your number. Here's a bog where goat-men hobble on hind legs, fondling themselves and each other. There's a gulch where headless folks kick their own heads around in games against themselves. Here's a quarry pit where antlered demon rabbits scurry from smoky warrens, fangs overcrowding bloody snarls. There's a spewing volcano with a retinue of life-sized ants marching up the side of it, onward to their own burning suicide. Winged hornets with swordlike noses and netlike legs deposit fine clouds of mist over all—these look to Philly like live helicopters trying to put out an eternally burning fire.

"Hi netters!"

"Don't say hi to anything out there, kid. Attention's the last thing we need."

"Home's on the other side of E's ash hole!"

"I'm working on it."

"Mommy and Daddy died—CRASH!"

"Let's stay positive."

"Your face's funny."

With respect to looks and personality and overall demeanor, Calvin embodies everything Don Philly least expected. He remembers leaving behind the basement at Rufio's to trail the bumblebee to Bakersfield, the exchange of brightness and power they shared, how Calvin as a bumblebee was Philly's first ever sign that seemed to point to a path with an actual destination at its end. The whole experience felt as though he were establishing a direct line of communication with the universe itself. The last thing he expected to find waiting for him on the other side was some guy with Down syndrome, though Philly welcomes the kid's wealth of wonder.

Philly's determined to drive Calvin home because he knows it's the first and last meaningful act he'll ever carry out, knowing he'll never know the first or last thing about Calvin's story. He might've written this another way if it were his story to tell, but he's aware of his part to play going forward, his revised approach to reclaiming his worth. There would be no book, he knows—part of him has always known. There are more to bodies than their outer parts and inner systems, combinations of skin and water and sinew twined around bone, brain matter and organic matter, and all of it matters more than what meets even the sharpest mind's eye because bodies are stories. If ever there was a time in which Philly was born to write, he would've had to learn to see beyond himself, to cast out the little boy haunting his body with memories of sinking in endless shallow ends.

He's been exposed to this side of the universe long enough to know Calvin means something greater than himself, that his intention to get this kid back home to his brother outweighs every writerly expectation he's ever called a dream. The kid's got balanced on his knees the painted garbage lid Philly followed out of The Spider's Spinneret, as well as a photograph he's been staring at. Philly knows Trent's the other kid in the picture, whom he's always cared about from a distance, like a writer for his protagonist. He sees Calvin and knows it's better to die for someone who deserves to live than it is to live alone with his own worthlessness, withering under the weight of words he'll only deliver in dreams. Life's a pain, and death is what it is—he figures he might as well keep driving.

Home is close, but Don Philly's destination has always been a headstone.

———

TRENT LISTENED as Mr. Moony used the gossamer webbing he excreted to glue four of the fateful five to their designated spots over the altar's rock surface—Trent was all set to begin the Ritual of Five and Five as soon as his brother arrived. None of them had any say in the matter. One of the three—the meatball of a man with a ruptured nose—did lots of moaning and blubbering and outright sobbing, all of which seemed pointless. When you had a shape-shifting demon creature made of mind-and-body-altering bugs that harnessed all the esoteric power and energy of Eden's End, a Titanoboa walling off the Lunar Lagoon's only entrance and exit with its colossal body whose coils started at the perimeter and spiraled all the way in on the altar, and a heart-driven, laser-focused Skeeter-5000 scanning for any sign of resistance with a Gatling gun trained on your every movement—all three entities operating under the express approval of the president of the Divided States of America—what else could you do but accept your fate?

The weepy man with blood in his mustache was first to be cocooned to the slab, a powdery *x* marking the spot saved for Calvin to his left. To his right went the woman wearing the mask, followed by the woman who looked to Trent like his mother and ex-therapist spliced together. Don Philly's motionless form filled the final slot.

Trent busied himself trying to locate where El Jaylo's long and windy body began and where it ended—if it ever did begin or end. According to Adam, Titanoboas were to snakes what megalodons were to great white sharks, prehistoric behemoths of the most perni-cious sort. Saw-whets spied from knotholes in the surrounding J-Trees, having made the trip from their Black-Holian tree in the Whispering Wellspring in God's Mouth. The indigo sky's gathering storm clouds worked with the shadows cast by the Lunar Lagoon's crazy fractals of light to form an enormous face Trent simply couldn't ignore anymore.

The Titanoboa's coils had turned the Lunar Lagoon into some-thing of a labyrinth. The twists and turns beneath thick-fleshed walls reminded Trent of his passage through J-Tree Lane a few hours ago. He was pretty sure he had his back to the altar as he continued to pace. He came as close as he could to the shore of the lagoon without bumping into The Titanoboa's omnipresent bulk, which towered high enough everywhere to block from view the water's underwater symbols and signs. Voices kept choosing new nooks and crannies from which to rebound. Mr. Moony's whizzing syllables drowned out the moaning man and the president's exasperation and Adam's deliberate digressions, a constant buzz-blizzard that sounded to Trent like his father's Vintage Marantz 2270 Stereophonic Receiver trying to snag a signal from atop Journey's End.

Given the option, Trent would go back in time ten years to the bluff overlooking what had been Big Mouth. Rather than celebrate his dad's birthday with Old English and a war hero he thought he'd invented to fill Calvin's absence, he'd go back, watch the sun burn out, and execute the quickest of ends. Not even Mr. Moony's buzzing could obscure all the hooting Trent was now hearing from knotholes he could no longer see.

He tried keeping pace with his thoughts with his own footsteps and arrived at yet another dead end in the labyrinth where, trapped behind snakeskin wallpaper, he could make out the face and body of a child. Their arms and legs were stretched and reaching out as though they'd died kicking and screaming in the effort to claw their way out. He took this as a sign to take advantage of these last few moments of crucial contemplation.

The Ritual of Five and Five, as described by Mr. Moony, would be carried out according to parameters outlined within some "sacredly metaphorical" agreement called Mother Climate's Contract of Basic Goodness. Beetlejuice had referenced the thing at some point. Trent had no plans in terms of what tactics he'd use to persuade the fateful five to consent to giving up their heads in exchange for potentially delaying the Apocalypse. The sixth mass extinction of life on Earth now seemed seconds away.

Trent figured it might be best if he were direct, explicit and honest and earnest, the last word on the matter being his alone to deliver. Indeed, Mr. Moony had made it abundantly clear this was Trent's choice to make, his action to take despite whatever the fateful five had to say about any of it. He could get straight down to it.

Trent's psychic line of contact with Anne Kell had fixed him with this "cosmic capacity to Contract," a powerful onus that, under ideal circumstances, would've gone to The Spider's truly true Chosen, Ron Filly, whose absence here and now was the result of some cult bungling a prophecy a long time ago. Filly might as well be fucking Waldo.

There was a reason for Trent's screwy perception of the world: his mind wasn't made to take on such a burden. Now he had no choice but to make up his mind.

The Titanoboa moved, scrambling corridors, clearing one path to the altar.

———

FORMER LOONER on the run Gary Mustafa wailed at the massive face stitched from warring black clouds and knew it was Mother to whom he was calling. He knew a sky pregnant with storm when he saw one, the air thick and heavy with all the same charge as the day Wendy Weather—rest in peace—had brought the sun back to Gatlinburg after dispelling a hurricane. Clouds churned above like water coming to boil, the great roiling face like any mother's most condemning scowl. J-shaped trees thrashed and whipped until their leaves rode the night, a flurry of dots forever untethered. Everything in the sky flickered and spasmed, and there was an unnatural light to it all, a lunar glare unlike any Mustafa knew he would ever bear witness to again. He remembered Mother's words, her letters from the ward, the way her hands moved like spiders in the ICU's permanent gloom, squeezing and pressing and drumming vulnerable skin, stretching and pulling and tugging on nipple-knots keeping the right air in, the wrong air out—and her voice, also, like pressure seething to release, a whistling hiss like something letting out the rest of its oxygen. He called to Mother Climate, glowering in the sky's lunar glow.

He called to Mother Climate on Mother's behalf, over and over and over again.

?

She'd lost her cattle prod to a blip of time driven by adrenalized lunacy, and now, confined to this stone slab beside her only friend in this loveless world, Love understood she'd been ensnared by what she'd wrongly convinced herself had been her own desire for freedom. Everything now made a deranged sort of sense, how Mustafa was the ladybug and Love herself was the butterfly and Yew was the dragonfly and Don Philly was the bumblebee he'd referenced in his TikTok, which to Love had seemed like a violation of her personal space, the four of them caught in a web of events spun by none other than "Mr. Moony," an alien Mary had all this time been hoarding like a weapon of mass destruction here at Eden's End. What confused Love was how Mary hadn't stopped quarreling with Mr. Moony since Love escaped Mustafa's Musker, which that ginormous fucking snake had coughed back up alongside a bunch of spoiled bodies coated in slime a blip of time ago. Mary was failing in her own way to persuade Mr. Moony to let Love go, shrieking about spiderwebs and random animal skulls and blatant mistakes.

Love rolled her neck over to face Yew. "Are you in love with me?"

"I think I do."

"You think you do or know?"

"I do."

"Let's try this again—are you in love with me?"

"I do."

"*Her face!*" exclaimed Mustafa, who hadn't stopped wailing at the sky. "*Mother!*"

Love saw the giant face looking down on them from the strangely purple sky. She might've called it a coincidental anomaly as recently as an hour ago, the way those dark clouds whirled in place and made two expressionless eyes underscored with a mouth that remained rolled open in that vague expression of shock seen in electrical outlets around America. It reminded her of her time in Soul's time-out cages, which had been her introduction to life underground in the FFS complex, the way she'd gaze up through the bars and see faces in the scuff marks of the ceiling panels. She'd count as many as she could as a means of getting past the pain administered by the cats from Soul, jabbing through the bars with their cattle prods, zapping skin, bringing her face to irreparable ruin. It's amazing what a little suffering could do to motivate you, Love had learned.

"I'm not gay," Love told Yew. "I'm actually totally straight."

"Mother, watch over us—shield us with thy strength!"

"I don't believe you," said Yew.

"You should know, those nights we spent in bed in your studio . . ."

"I don't care what you say, Love—I don't."

"I'd stare and count scuff marks in the ceiling to get through what we'd do."

"Motherfudger!"

"You led me on," said Yew.

"I'm sorry to've misled you."

"You used me."

"I did," said Love. "I had the ideas. You had the drugs. Together we mastered the Craft. I spewed more lies than you ever deserved to hear, Yew, but that'll never change the fact that together we moved the world. Fungi's forever taken it by storm."

"Mother Climate, I beseech thee—release thy hold!"

"The spiderweb's got it all wrong!" cried the president. "Love is worthy!"

There was a sound like a thousand beehives that had to be Mr. Moony.

"She's the one who's wrong," said Yew. "You're despicable, Love."

Love wriggled against Mr. Moony's goop's webby constraints, knowing the bad taste monarch butterflies leave in the mouths of their predators. She'd learned about monarchs at her sister's burial. The tattoo on her wrist had nothing to do with Angel.

"I am what I am."

"She's my favorite Cat because she listens to whatever I say,"

Love heard Mary say, and her Skeeter said, "We must remain laser-focused on our present endeavors."

"Brenda was right about you," said Yew. "You're the worst kind of ghost."

"I was listening in when you told your client how to pursue mystic fullness."

"Don't you dare even go there, Love."

"You said it begins with ourselves and ends with others. You said our ability to extend beyond ourselves—to reach out and connect—is our piece to contribute to the pieces and parts comprising the house of humanity."

"You're the thing that makes any house haunted."

"*Mother, forgive us our every transgression! We are the polluted ones!*"

"I've been working on getting my empathy back," said Love.

"Empathy's a two-step journey," said Yew. "I'd say you skipped a step—but I'm not at all convinced you've had any shoes to walk in to begin with."

"The years I spent loving myself on Instagram made me hate myself offline."

"Cut her free, Adam! Life on a brand-new planet'll be pointless without Love!"

"The human hurt triggered by your human mind is unnecessary."

"The robot's right," said Yew. "You're done taking up space in my head."

"*Mother, untether thy hold from this long and painful road we tread!*"

"You'd be amazed what a little suffering could do to motivate you."

"You're a rotten thing with a rotten heart," Yew told Love.

"We are all one house of doors and windows," the man called Don Philly said from his slot at row's end. Love hadn't been convinced he was even alive, let alone that he'd been listening. "Connection is our natural light, what we need to see by to unite us."

There was a silence harshly felt, like a thousand fossilized beehives.

Love rolled her neck upright to face the face in the sky and met her own mask reflected back at her from inside a knife's wide flat side—a meat cleaver, actually, raised high in the lagoon's wild light. Hunched over her was the mad park ranger, Trent, flushed and sweaty and salivating. She began counting the scuffs marking her face in his blade.

———

TRENT TAPHOR WOULD'VE BROUGHT his arm around with everything he had, and Dex would've done the job like always, the way the blade's keen edge would've connected with meat and sliced wetly through so that blood watered the soil, blending with the black underfoot, and the president—instead of raving on and on about love's place in some brave new world, banging her balled fists against Adam's stainless steel breastplate and complaining endlessly, pacing back and forth in front of Trent's altar—would've died without a throat to shriek with . . . if not for Don Philly's words, the way they relieved the pressure in Trent's knotted chest, unfurling the curled vessels and veins holding his heart in painful suspension. Philly's words implied the same message as any checkerboard's empty back row spaces: we are all worth fighting for. Mr. Moony hovered over the altar, facing down from above, his childish eyes playfully homicidal, his grin barely there.

"Let's get this show on the road," said Mr. Moony. "All eyes on my eyes."

His buggy mass swirled like a mini tornado, a million whizzing blots framing his fleshy skull head, his fairytale eyes doing that Mona Lisa-sees-everything thing. The fateful four were still, silent. President Mangrove and Adam had shambled back behind Trent. He could hardly believe how close he'd come to cutting the president's throat.

"Calvin isn't here yet," said Trent. "We can't start without him."

"We can and we will," said Mr. Moony. "Because what you say isn't true, in a technical sense—your brother's always been present in one way or another."

"So mumbled the bumbling bumblebee."

"I told you already, Mr. Philly—no funny ideas! As someone who's generated way more trouble than they're worth, the least you can do is speak when spoken to."

"So where is he, then?" Trent asked. "I don't see Calvin anywhere."

"I'm as baffled as you are," said Mr. Moony. "He's supposed to've suffered ultimate excommunication, meaning you shouldn't be able to remember him at all."

"I thought I was supposed to cut his throat."

"As I believe I've said," said Mr. Moony, "we're dealing with Apocalypse here, matters of fate as they pertain to the here and now, all of which're subject to the constant change and evolution of time's three-way spiral motion. If I were to guess, I'd say this minor revision in the grand scheme of things is yet another consequence of Mr. Philly there's presence in Mr. Ron Filly's rightful place. We can blame The Dark for that."

Don Philly said, "The Dark drew me in eleven years ago."

"Not now, Mr. Philly."

"Let him speak," said Trent. "It's plain to see the ritual's officially begun."

"It all started the day I rolled into Point Reyes. I had come to research for a book I never knew I knew I was never going to write. I guess I thought I was running away from my wife at the time—or maybe all of my former wives. There's been a lot of trauma involved with all three, probably not worth sinking into. Anyways, that first day was when I saw Lord Read twirling a sign outside of a pen shop in the middle of town—a big old cardboard arrow that read 'We The Dark seek our fifty-fifth inductee.' Now I'd already told myself I'd follow any signs that might lead to the seed of an idea for my book, so I pulled over to the curb. Then after purchasing a pen in the pen shop from a nice guy my age—which I'd go on to use for all of my brainstorming—I strolled out and tapped Lord Read on the shoulder and asked him about his sign. He asked me what my name was, and that was how I found myself giving Lord Read a ride out to the woods in the middle of the night, where fifty-three naked farmers were erecting a plywood frame over a fire. They swore me into The Dark—I can prove it, too, if you want to see my scars."

"I—"

"Before you respond, Trent, allow me to clue these four all the way in. You can all call me Mr. Moony. I've come to America to get the ball rolling on your overdue Apocalypse. Once upon a time, however, you could say I was privy to learning all I could about your species, borderline obsessed with this concept you all call 'love.' Love has always puzzled me, but the sheer number of stories you supplied The Spider with—all dealing with 'love'—had me practically convinced your cosmic value weighs more than what they say. Which is to say I'd come this close to believing there was more to your species than your collective kindness. By the time the order came down from up top to do away with humankind, I initially put a stop to it all. I gave my sign of consent to Mother Climate's Contract of Basic Goodness. My first order of business then became to sprinkle gold all across California because where I come from, gold equals goodness—and besides, I'd briefly worked with farmers from Earth on more than a few prior occasions, all of which left me pleasantly surprised. Not only was I rooting for you all to get this all turned around, I had Mother Climate Herself convinced you'd all utilize gold in a way that would persuade the Infinite Sum One of your greater cosmic value. I don't see the need to fill you in on the rest. You all know the way you've behaved ever since."

"So now you're here to kill us?" said the masked woman.

"I'm here, Love, you inherently confusing human, to honor my segment of the Contract. I've done nothing out of maliciousness. My actions have been contingent upon the collapse of the story of humanity via widespread division and subsequent devolution. Apocalypse, in other words, is what you've all proven you deserve. Yet again. Depending on what Trent here chooses to do here tonight, I'll likely be towing Phooka Road—if you don't ask, I won't tell—to another double-knotted Mother-approved world rich in all the kindness my kind needs to breathe. The face you perceive way up high above me is Mother Climate's—as you can surely tell, She's less than pleased about any of this."

"Mother, forgive us our absence of innocence! We are the polluted pollutants!"

"You're far and away too late for that, Looner. Before I turn things over to Trent, let me provide you all with some peace of mind—especially yours, Love. You might've noticed the pool of brightest bioluminescence on your way in. What you all've taken to calling the Lunar Lagoon is what I call Super Substance. It's what remains of human kindness—and then some. By 'and then some,' I mean human suffering, which'll transfigure kindness into fuel that'll power my kind's relocation abroad. Bod's been in charge of the extraction process, an endeavor Love here calls the Halo Virus."

"Bod is his body of bugs," said Don Philly.

"I can only guess who told you that," said Mr. Moony. "Anyways, Trent?"

"I have to hack off all your heads to try to save the world from Apocalypse."

The fateful four let out a communal gasp like somebody exhaling their last.

"That was nothing if not direct," said Mr. Moony. "I'm presuming here, Trent, you don't see any need to clue these four in on the inside-out paradox in further detail?"

"Mother, secure thy knot that keeps the right air in and the wrong air out!"

"The Looner's metaphor is shockingly apt," said Mr. Moony. "Phooka Road indeed keeps kindness and shame divided the way balloon knots do oxygen and helium. Though I'm afraid it's all a bit more complex than that, as you all might've guessed."

President Mangrove butted in from behind. "When are we leaving, Mr. Moony?"

"Stellar interstellar question! Adam, laser-scan Mary here for her cosmic value."

"Scanning."

Trent turned in time to see Adam running a wave of red light up and down President Mangrove's body. She held her hands out in front of her in fruitless defense, as if she could use them to deflect something as abstract as light itself. It was clear to Trent she was no master deflector of any kind. He felt for his employer a bizarre kind of pity, the sort you hold for those who do the worst things with the best intentions.

"The president is obliquely responsible for infinite anguish," said Adam. "The following reveals Mary Mangrove's role in the rapid disintegration of humanity's story: 1) She personally staged her own father's death by suicide to assert control over us Skeeters; 2) She programmed us to invade the White House and seize the Oval Office at Gatling-gunpoint; 3) She linked our heart-drives to global network satellite and flooded the web with disinformation designed to persuade the public to forget all about what happened and accept her as this nation's self-appointed monarch; 4) She scattered nuclear bombs across the globe, causing widespread devolution; 5) She deployed us Skeeters across America to oversee the mass relocation effort—Polk's Ode to Destiny—to sow lasting, widespread division; 6) She saw Love's work on the hit reality television show, *Love Beach*, decided she saw something she liked, which is why she had PWP influence the suicide of Love's sister, Angel, which, in addition to creating lasting pain for two humans present here and now, allowed the president to prey on Love's subsequent vulnerability—Mary captured Love by planting a PWP agent professing to be Supreme Court Justice Jabronis Johnson at a masking event Love attended; 7) She stole Love and Yew's ingenious computer programming language, Fungi, which allows for the Feline Freedom Society to inflict far too many societal grievances to list; and 8) Her so-called effort at spiritually reviving America is yet another greedy farce, proving once more humankind's squandered relationship to gold. Total cosmic value: utterly unworthy."

The president glared at Mr. Moony. "You made me do half that stuff!"

"Nothing I said sounded anywhere close to any of that, I assure you all."

"You lied to me!"

"It's hardly my fault you believe yourself to be central to the universe."

"You said you'd help me leave this earth!"

"True enough," said Mr. Moony. "Adam, please escort the queen of America's divided empire accordingly. The rest of you may just sort of want to check out for this, dream up as many happy thoughts as you can while you can."

Adam ducked in a forward-leaning crouch, and immediately Trent understood he lacked any such luxury. The Gatling gun shot up from the Skeeter's spine like some obscene scorpion's tail, leveling its aim accordingly, forcing Trent to dive to his left and scrabble for cover behind the altar, where the skull of a frog bore indifferent witness.

President Mangrove stood her ground, complaining to no avail, her slender hands still held out as the sharply mechanical *gat-gat-gats* eclipsed her final cries of protest. The gusting wind made everything sound muted and underwater. For half a second it looked as though Mangrove were a marionette whose already talentless puppet master had five too many drinks before showtime, her shakes and spasms preceding her body's vicious launch into darkness. Something sprayed Trent's eye; he wished it were rain.

He tasted salt and wished it were tears.

————

YEW LAY PINNED on her back on the slab between Love and the man Brenda had abused, drifting in place, which she'd been doing since she first laid eyes on the giant snake all the way back in God's Mouth. The snake's mere existence alone confirmed her suspicions that her visions from that night on the Las Vegas Festival Grounds had always been more than what met her mind's eye. She'd been drifting in place even while guiding Mustafa's Musker through the labyrinth of bent trees, the windy path marked on either side by all the people rumored to have gone missing in Eden's End, standing there like statues in a graveyard and pointing the way onward. She'd been drifting in place when she and Love and Mustafa all at once leapt from the car windows seconds before the snake swooped down from the trees like the world's biggest noose and gobbled the car whole only to throw it back up again with a bunch of half-digested humans. She'd been drifting in place when the tornado being with the beehive voice materialized where light was gushing and spilling at the end of the road and spat out thick ropes of webbing now binding them all to this slab of stone. She'd been drifting in place when Love told Yew the truth, one Yew already knew but had spent a decade of silence refusing to hear.

It would seem Love had known all about the art of drifting in place, how it helped to have some sort of object or surface area to fixate on, which in Love's case had been scuff marks in Yew's apartment's ceiling. When the Skeeter shot and killed the president, Yew had been focusing on Love's cattle prod, caught in a twist of branches above. Yew supposed the giant snake must've whacked it up there with its tail or something.

"I would like to reply to Don Philly now," said the man who would soon be using his meat cleaver to lop off Yew's head. Blood freckled his face. "If that's all right."

"By all means," said Mr. Moony, whose face hovered near Love's weapon. Every time he opened his thin lips to speak, Yew's eyes were drawn to his, a perverse magic akin to the magnetism of a car wreck you can't help but stare at. "You might as well kill two ladybirds with one stone, Trent, and divvy up those skulls accordingly."

Yew opened her mouth, but Mr. Moony cut her off. "I said air quote 'ladybirds' instead of 'birds' because yes, Yew, I'm very much rooting through your head for data I might deem useful with respect to this ritual we're in the middle of. I'm always doing this with all your heads, Love here being the sole exception. I see and hear your thoughts the same way you all see and hear me—your thoughts are all quite ugly currently."

"Which one's Love?" said the man Trent, who now had a skull in each hand.

"The masked one," said Mr. Moony. "It's guesswork with her bemusing mind."

Trent laid one skull on Yew's chest and the other on Love's. "Wait a second," he said. "Ey, Adam! Did I get these mixed up?"

Yew's skull had gaping holes in the eyes, and when she rolled her neck, she saw it was the same with Love's, but where Yew's had a hookish beak, Love's had a set of dagger teeth with two long sabers —and Yew's doubled Love's in size. Yew wondered if by blowing into her skull's hollow eyes she could produce a sound similar to the hooting she'd hear outside her bedroom window on summer nights, waiting with the worst sort of anticipation for Grandpa G's return home. Mustafa was murmuring the name "Billy" over and over, as he had been since the Skeeter-5000 mowed down the president.

Adam clopped forward to laser-scan the skull on Yew's chest, an owl's.

"Unlike the former president," said the robot, "you've accounted for the Web's disturbance accordingly and have made the proper adjustments where required."

"A simple 'yes' would suffice," said Love.

Trent slipped Yew's line of sight only to return with two more skulls, these ones small enough to nest easily within one of her cloak's nineteen inner pockets. He'd begun addressing Don Philly, but for now Yew was too transfixed on the new skulls to listen, which looked practically identical, almost twin-like, and yet Trent seemed to have no trouble assigning one to Mustafa's chest and the other to Philly's. The unhampered conviction with which he conducted himself conveyed a grim sense of finality.

". . . all about you, Mr. Philly," Yew heard Trent saying. "I mean, just picture it—Don Philly, American hero. Your name will be immortalized in books and songs and poetry across the country! You'll have *lived* the stories they'll *never* stop telling!"

"I object to this bullspit!" Mustafa cried, surprising Yew. She'd thought he'd gone over the edge, but it would seem he was still holding on, after all, even if by one psychic pinky nail. "To be an American hero is to be the worst kind of crudweasel!"

"Maybe it'll be different when you're dead," Mr. Moony offered. "So what do you say, Mr. Philly? Does Trent have your consent?"

"To be, or not to be?" said Philly. "That's one question I believe I've answered."

"I wager I'm the only one here the American public's ever deemed heroic," said Mustafa. "Simply because I went against everything everyone was saying with regards to whether Skeeters like *you* should be allowed to roam Red campuses—and allow me to say there's little nobility in the words we say. We cloak ourselves in words to hide the frauds we are inside. I hired my Skeeter to anger my superintendent, who never once let me have my way, which would've been my way to the heart of the woman I've loved since the fifth grade, whom I've forever ruined with words I've written online. Hiring that Skeeter was my gravest mistake, and I'll regret it to the moment my dying breath becomes useless air. I admit I'm an American hero, the worst kind of crudweasel, a popper of innocence, a walking lesson in self-deflation. I've devoted my life to trying to exhale all the pain I've inhaled, addicted to all the pain I've inspired with words."

"Sounds to me like you're consenting," said Mr. Moony.

"Not at all," said Mustafa, and Yew braced herself for another monologue, one which, mercifully, wouldn't come to pass. "I very much like my head—I'd sooner keep it tethered to my neck. I'm merely pointing out that Mr. Philly there shouldn't consent according to such faulty logic. Being hailed a hero isn't worth losing your head over."

"Everyone here seems to think their own thoughts are in fact their own," said Love, "as if your feelings are all so fucking important. Yet I don't think any of you are thinking about how your thoughts make *me* feel, which matters more than you think."

"Maybe we're going about this all wrong," said Trent, and Yew tried to imagine what in the world "this" was. "Maybe I should just ask you all—and all at once. It seems to me there's no point trying to persuade you all individually." The skull on Yew's chest was shockingly light—she'd almost forgotten it was there. "Look. The world's going to end. One way or another, Mr. Moony's going to end the world. The ball's in motion as we speak—the ball's *been* in motion for at least a decade, if not longer. Which begs the question, one I'll put forth to you all right now. Are you ready and willing to lay down your lives so that all life on Earth might go on? Or would you rather live on and die anyways, choking on the air that's been strangling us all to exhaustion for years?"

"In other words," said Mr. Moony, "are you all basically good—or not?"

All of Earth itself seemed to grumble in reply, the way the great snake became immediately agitated, a colossus trying to worm free of its own labyrinthine shadow, making the ground quake in its graceless wake. The lagoon's surface simmered and spat with the same ferociousness as the sky, a shining sea of shooting stars at endless war with themselves, the sound alone being what stitched the image in Yew's mind. She tried fixating on Love's cattle prod, willing the wind to rip it free, but found her gaze being torn away by the face in the sky. Yew had swiped a glance at it only once before-hand, the way you do moving past a car wreck when you're the one who's driving, because the face in the sky looked like Yew's, like all of their faces combined, trauma personified.

And Mother Climate's face conveyed: it shouldn't be so hard to be kind.

"I'd like to respond to that," said Yew. "I mean, if it's cool with all of you." Their consent wasn't something she gleaned from their collective silence—it was a declarative vibe, communally felt, a sort of mass attunement, mystic alignment with the present moment. "I've listened to almost everything everyone's said, so I hope what I'm about to say makes everyone feel perfectly heard." Yew had a feeling she was going to regret whatever she said—she hadn't the slightest clue what she was going to say, not until she was saying it. "I'm all for putting others before ourselves—that's how we build our house—but I'm not convinced we can afford to do so at the expense of the self. That's not living. That's the opposite of living. What I really mean is empathy's a two-step journey—take care of the self, which is step one, in order to care for others, which is step two. While I personally believe step two's more essential—from an evolutionary standpoint, at least—you have to remember there can be no step two without step one, and there can be no step one without shoes to walk in, to begin the journey with. We can give ourselves up selflessly or selfishly, but the result stays the same. All houses rot in the end. In the meantime, we might as well make ours a decent place to live."

"A simple 'No, don't chop off our heads' would suffice," said Love, and Yew wondered whether Love's cattle prod administered half as much hurt as her words.

"Let it be known I had Mary's consent regarding her fate," said Mr. Moony. "She had every worldly opportunity to pursue and see through various other outcomes."

"He's alive," said Don Philly, and Mr. Moony told him to watch his words. "He's alive, Trent. I see him through the window, standing outside this house we've built."

Yew craned her neck and saw Trent examining himself in his cleaver, his face like that one person you see on the side of the road who somehow survived the wreck.

Don Philly said, "You could always crack the door and let him in."

———

AFTER THE TITANOBOA started writhing in clear distress—and before Brenda's spiritually adopted daughter Yew began her final argument—Don Philly saw Calvin on the shore of the Lunar Lagoon, perched atop their ride home. What was once a Punch Buggy Orange was now a heap of penis fish piled as high as the tractors Philly used to drive, back when he worked in construction. Calvin had in his hands his trashcan lid, the colors of America old and new, spangled at the center with a single painted star.

Calvin and the deconstructed car he rode in on glimmered like the soul-fire projections they were, the same way Philly must've appeared to Calvin back on Phooka Road. Guy Ramsley relayed this information from his residence in Philly's liver, explaining new developments that had arisen from a bargain Calvin had driven with The Spider. There was no time for Philly to ask Guy Ramsley how a kid with Down syndrome had pulled off such a thing; the basic fact nevertheless remained that Calvin would return as flesh and bone if and only if his brother called him home.

Philly said what he'd said in order to appeal to Trent, hoping the words he didn't say carried the weight needed for Trent to register what Philly had really been trying to communicate: you can call your brother home, but only if you leave our heads alone. Don Philly had made a living out of leaving words off the page, and he hoped this last act of leaving words unsaid paid off, for Trent's sake and Calvin's.

As for himself, Philly knew he had no skin in the game; he would die either way.

He could only hope his death would be worth something in the end.

———

"I DO DECLARE the Ritual of Five and Five concluded," said Mr. Moony, who now seemed to have eyes solely for Trent. "Make your choice, Trent."

Adam rolled off ten shots with his Gatling gun into the sky, making it official.

Trent weighed his options one last time, eyeballing himself in Dex, putting the question he'd asked the others to himself: Given the option, would he willingly lay down his life so that the world might live on? Maybe he would, but not for the world's sake. The world wasn't worth it. That said, what Philly had said made Trent think. What would Calvin do in Trent's place? He figured Calvin would do it; he was that kind of kind.

But Trent wasn't his twin—they were two very different men.

"But that's okay," said Dex. Of course, it wasn't really Dex, just as it wasn't really Calvin, materialized in the metal. "It's what makes life cool! We all get to see things in different ways, and so the world ticks and ticks and ticks, and we sit back and make surprises for each other and play games and eat food and sing and cry and laugh. That's why it's great to be alive! We all die, though. That makes us all sort of the same."

Trent thought he knew all along he'd been talking to himself all along, but now he knew the voices he'd heard and would go on hearing until he found a way to get over his self-absorption were never his, meaning they didn't come from anyplace inside of him; it wasn't like he'd known the state of his mental health was a question worth exploring to its fullest extent—the voices were never his, meaning they lived outside of him, meaning they belonged to someone or something way beyond himself, whatever that might mean, meaning there was every reason to drop every dollar the president ever paid him to sit down with a new therapist and play anything other than checkers for however long it would take to knife breakthroughs in meaning, meaning he could go on believing himself when he told himself his brother, present here or not, was always worth hearing.

Trent hadn't known he'd been touching Dex to the skin of his own throat, that he'd been following an urge to carve there a smile, like a pumpkin on Halloween.

He met my eyes and said, "I'm not your tale of woe."

Which gets us to the present.

INTERLUDE III: THE PRESENT
(NOW, AT LONG LAST)

It's been coming, and fast—five seconds, to be exact, the instrument of my death, heading straight for my head. Perhaps I shouldn't've paid so much attention to Love.

PART IV

LET THEM WHIMPER

(NOW AND FOREVER)

16

THE END OF THE END
(FOR THE DEATH OF ME)

————

AND WHEN THEY all begin to choke on the very air they breathe, they should be so lucky as to hope to have someone like me looking out for them and their side and overall well-being. This time around they've been calling me Mr. Moony.

Obviously I've been a very busy pooka, and as a pooka, You already know the only two things existing within Your infinite body that can take me out are sharply edged metals, which can do me great harm, and of course my own lies, which suffocate Bod. Surely You've noticed the extreme care I've taken proceeding without deception—I've told the metaphorical truth to the best of my narrative abilities. The Spider's true truth.

None of it matters now, of course, because of course now I'm dying.

Let this be my warning.

————

IT's Calvin who flung it, of course—his Captain America garbage lid, the instrument of my death. He released it the same way he did his frisbee the day he aced the fifth hole on that disc golf course, crazily contorting his body to achieve the throwing angle Trent was so enamored with. Hindsight in combination with Bod's omniscient perspective—Bod's soldiers and spies and their all-seeing eyes patrolling either side of Phooka Road—lets me see how Calvin pulled all this off, which You already saw.

I'm trying to explain, but it's hard with a whizzing trash lid biting into my neck.

I hope the five seconds it's taken me to tell this tale—to relay this so-called movie-memory from my head to Yours—has been to Your satisfaction. It's been hard to get some details right. What I mean is You've probably noticed how difficult it's been for me to portray truly true human beings with actual human thoughts and feelings.

Forgive me, Infinite Sum One, I am only inhuman.

———

YOU'D THINK this group of humans with all their suffering would've been willing to give themselves up to try to save their world. I can't, for the death of me, understand where I went wrong in this thinking. I've always believed humans were basically good deep down. It seems they've always been doomed to disappoint. I am merely one of countless beings to have fallen victim to the solipsism plaguing the human heart.

———

CALVIN RELEASED HIS SHIELD, and there's no way it should've come anywhere near my head, though in this rare case I fully recognize I must render clear the entire context if I expect You to hear me at all, much less heed my warning.

Trent's decision not to follow through with getting some heads to roll is what made The Spider, upholding Her end of the bargain She'd been tricked into with Calvin, tear open the silk of reality through which Calvin bumbled. (The Spider did this for me all the time in our mutual exploitation of the inside-out paradox.) Anyways, it was the gravitational force and quantum momentum of Calvin's reentry that made the wind finally tear Love's cattle prod free of the tree above me. It came down on top of The Snake and must've triggered itself. The Snake, aggravated already from hunger, wiggled and waggled all the more, which is how the tail of El Jaylo whacked Calvin's shield, which is why its flight from Calvin's hands to my head has taken five "seconds."

Of course, we all perceive time our own ways, as You well know.

———

I MUST ADMIT I resent Your judgments; I've been upfront with You from the first, from the beginning of the end until the present. In fact, the second complete thought I transmitted from my head to Yours proves it, if You wish to go back and parse through it charily. One reason I felt I had no choice but to keep my nature somewhat clandestine is because I've heard of what You've done with other pookas in situations similar to mine, and I don't much like what I've heard. At least no one can say I wasn't efficient in my delivery; I chose to divulge only those details most germane to my true truth, hoping You'd come to see the ways of humanity the way I do. I mean, how else was I supposed to seize the attention of a being as busy and boundless and all-powerful as You?

For instance, I could've included details as extraneous as the nature of Don Philly's second marriage in Las Vegas, how he'd married Yew in a drunken stupor, how she'd married him at the peak of one of her acid trips, how together they decided to disband their marriage later that same night, the former citing sadness, the latter a lack of love so obvious as to be considered biological. Just because I left this detail and others like it outside the visible web of my thoughts doesn't mean I wasn't being honest and earnest and urgent, for this meager connection has no bearing at all on my warning.

I hope You're listening, that I've done enough to earn Your

undivided attention because the last thing You want to do here is commit the same grievous errors I have.

You shouldn't fool with humankind as I have. These avaricious fiends must never roam the stars, for the existential threat they pose to even the most kindness-rich parts of Your body is cancerous, biologically speaking. Ask Mother Climate.

———

I FEAR YOU'RE MISTAKEN; the human threat is real—I can hardly believe You're presuming to disagree. I don't care that You made them. I don't care that You made me. You're coming this close to acting like one of them, like one of hundreds of thousands of humans who perished in over-crowded ICUs, the Crown Virus ravaging their lungs, so many last words on so many dying breaths being, "I don't get it. This [bug] isn't *real*."

———

IF LIFE'S a joke and perspective its punch line . . . maybe that makes me the butt.

———

SO HERE I AM, doomed to die, but that doesn't mean You have to have me ultimately excommunicated like You've done to some other pookas. Unless it'd mean I'd be preserving the sacred metaphorical language of my kind, in which case, fine, go ahead and eliminate me. Here's the thing: should You let the human race continue to unearth sacred metaphors, there can be no doubt they will find a home in the stars.

You need only examine their examination of RNA protein inter-action to get my point, which is: Once upon a time, mankind didn't know much at all about the human body, the way brains relay elec-trical messages vital to movement and expression. They didn't know much, that is, until they uncovered the sacred metaphor "neural pathways."

For them, this verbal key turned the lock on several core secrecies once preserved. Each sacred metaphor they uncover brings them one step closer to Your body.

Proceed with caution.

———

SEEING as to how You're the ultimate weigher of worth and cosmic value, I figured by now You'd see how the time's come for You to pull the plug on the human race, how my interdimensional half's population is worth preserving for their innocence alone, but also for their unwavering capacity for basic goodness and goodwill. My kind are rich in kindness and shame-free by nature—none of us're at fault for the metaphorical cancer passing to and from Phooka Road, for what's happened to Mother Climate.

For these things humankind alone is to blame.

———

THE END OF THE END, You ask? Why should it matter what happens with Calvin and Trent and Don Philly and Gary Mustafa and Love and Yew?

———

ALL RIGHT, You've made Your point, and I am made to respect it.

———

ALREADY MY HEAD's halfway off my neck, a kiss of wind away from becoming as untethered as one of Mustafa's goofy balloons. Soon my head's going to roll and dissolve in the soil of Eden's End like plastic in acetone, and my substance, Bod, will wither and contract, roiling like smoke before bursting into a great unquenchable fire.

Eden's End is going to burn to ash. The bug inside the Snake will perish, causing El Jaylo to shrivel to her normal size before she, too, dies. The young boy with the sign looking for his pet boa constrictor, Jennifer Lopes, would be sad to know this happened. The same sad fate is to find Don Philly and his perfidious bug, Guy Ramsley. Philly didn't care enough for his body to live. Like most Americans. The bug inside Adam'll die, and the Skeeter is to malfunction. Oh, so You admit this method of delivery fails to satisfy?

I thought I already implied there were good reasons for hiding myself.

All right then, I'll finish my tale my way. Won't be long now.

———

TRENT HADN'T KNOWN he'd been touching Dex to the skin of his own throat, that he'd been following an urge to carve there a smile, like a pumpkin on Halloween.

He met Mr. Moony's eyes and said, "I'm not your tale of woe."

A fierce wind suddenly arose, and Trent was this close to cutting his own throat when he noticed the wind blowing from one direction. He turned and saw him.

Looking at Calvin after all these years was the hardest thing Trent ever had to do in his life, but seeing him—really seeing him—was maybe the easiest, like slipping on an old pair of shoes already broken in and ready to run in. He'd heard Calvin in Dex, and now he saw him outside of Dex, there on the shore of the Lunar Lagoon, standing like a superhero atop a flesh-colored hill of what looked like thick, meaty sausages.

He saw him, and he loved him. He loved him always.

What he saw was good: Calvin bending and contorting his body, doing that whole thing he did the day he aced the fifth hole on the disc golf course, and then he released his garbage lid, which carried on the wind some before curving out of sight. Already Trent was starting to hang his head when all of a sudden Calvin's shield veered all the way back into the light's lunar flickers like it had a freegin' mind of its own, and before Trent knew it or even believed it, he heard it: the metal connecting sharply with Mr. Moony's neck, eliciting from the demon a rasp of agony like the death of air itself.

After that, for Trent, there was only fire and fear—and later, a sort of family.

I can't do this anymore. I don't know most of what happens next. I'm midway through the transition, already dead in all the ways that matter.

———

IF I'D KNOWN what Trent was going to choose, I could've prevented the aftermath, including Calvin's surprise reentry followed by his shield's whizzing flight, byproducts of the mendacious bargain he'd driven with The Spider. Now we are all of us doomed. Neither side of Phooka Road is the place to be since we all need a space to breathe. My mistake was investing the bulk of my attention in Love —I'm almost sure of it.

Love's was that rare body to go without one of Bod's affiliates inside, so I always had to observe her from a distance, spying through the eyes of Bod's spies in bodies existing apart from Love's, be it the president's or the Cat Hackers' from Soul. Her belief in some unspoken power greater than words had me paranoid even to the point of paying Don Philly a visit in his pizza shop's basement. Love was a constant question mark, and nothing haunts me more than unanswered questions—except maybe funny ideas.

———

SEE what I see and be satisfied. See three men and two women gather around a headstone in some quietly overgrown Bakersfield graveyard: twin brothers, a Looner, a masker, a drifter. A family of five, here to bury a shared trauma. See them try and fail to remember me due to what You have done to me. See them rehash what they remember of their escape, how Trent used a Texas-made meat cleaver against me, cutting them free.

How they fled the site, eluding flames, huddled as one group.

How they almost forgot to grab Philly's body on the way out.

How they all tumbled inside Mustafa's slime-slicked Musker.

How Mustafa handed the last balloon under the seat to Calvin.

How Calvin would name it either Happy Hanky or June Justice.

How Mustafa asked which was female and then chose for him.

How the balloon popped from all the heat getting inside the car.

How Love said nothing and absorbed everything but the obvious.

How Yew guided them out of roaring light into the dark of dawn.

How Trent never once let go of his brother the entire ride home.

How "home" henceforth meant "existing apart from Eden's End."

See them now, five days later, holding hands in a circle, Yew reciting words she still knew by heart. See Don Philly's headstone, inscribed with the words he'd requested, letter for letter: *It's better to be who you are than who your supposed to be.* See Mustafa with a stone sharpened to a point in hand, stooped over to engrave an apostrophe between the letters *u* and *r* in "your," etching an *e* to go after the *r*. See Calvin and Trent together again and smiling, now and forever. See Love with her mask off.

See them and be satisfied with their kindness, however short-lived.

They're Your problem now.

ACKNOWLEDGMENTS

It's been a journey of thirteen years from first words of first attempted novel to this moment: countless drafts, several characters and scenes and pages and passages "ultimately excommunicated" from existence, two fathers lost too soon. I would say it feels triumphant and strangely melancholic to put a period on the end of this part of the journey, but I much prefer the far more optimistic implications of a semicolon; in other words, I hope this is just the beginning.

An immeasurable debt of gratitude goes to the village that raised this book: April Wilder, Stephen Paul Martin, my high school friends and college friends and writer friends and TikTok friends, Ben Souva, Publishing Director Lauren Taylor Shute, editors Samantha Pollack and Ariane Peveto and S.E. Fleenor, editorial coordinators Brooke Suermann and Shannon Henesy, Alan Hebel for cover design, Morgan Krehbiel for illustration, Erik Hane, and everyone else at Intrepid Literary. It's been a privilege to work with you all.

A special thanks to my family—especially Mom and Sofia and Jackie and Maria. Thank you all for reading, for the constant mental and emotional encouragement throughout the years. Thank you, most of all, for believing in me. I am beyond privileged to have such undying support.

And always—my fiancée, Sofia. While your "scheduled writing blocks" brought this dream to life way back in San Luis Obispo, it's been your courage, support, and patience that has kept the dream alive and well here in San Diego. For this and so much more, you have my heart forever.

ABOUT THE AUTHOR

Photo by Atria Mashaki

K. Enterante currently teaches English Language Arts and Writing at a middle school in San Diego, where he lives with his fiancée, Sofia, and his dachshund, Bun. You can find him connecting Stephen King's universe on TikTok (@k.enterante), where he celebrates his favorite books and stories. This is his first novel.

www.ingramcontent.com/pod-product-compliance
Lightning Source LLC
Chambersburg PA
CBHW022019300726
48970CB00003B/954